The Lies I Tell Myself

Tati Vogt

D1496146

DEDALO
PUBLISHING
GROUP

An imprint of Dedalo Publishing Group

Los Angeles, CA

Text Copyright © 2021 Tati Vogt

Cover Photography © 2021 Dedalo Publishing Group

ISBN: 978-0-578-93137-1

Hey, let me introduce myself. My name's Cassie, I'm 15 years old, and I think I'm living a nightmare. Please-please, let it all be a nightmare. I should have known where it all leads, but no, I wanted to have some stupid drama in my life. I thought I'd love the drama, where I'm the main character. Until today, at the Homecoming Dance, when it all blew up in my face.

If you asked me at the beginning of the school year, what's my most prized possession? I would have told you — my lies. Yes, my lies. And I know what you're thinking right now. Lies? Who prizes their lies? I'd gotten used to the idea that no one would want to spend any time getting to know who I am, or what I want. I felt like most people enjoy the idea of me, but not the real me. Every time I'd lie, people seemed to like me more. Of course, because I'd tell everyone what they wanted to hear. Everyone wants a fairy tale. That's why I kept lying. No one wanted the truth. Everything real, every secret thought I'd keep inside me. I truly believed my lies would set me free.

With each step along the way, I built my house of lies. One stacked on top of the next. Lies to my friends, family, Elliot, and Jake, one lie right after another. I built it up so much that before I knew it, everything was totally out of control! I thought I could hide forever. My fake reality wasn't focused on friendship or worrying about love. I didn't feel like I was missing out on anything. I didn't have to live in constant fear of being a good friend. My lies protected me.

The problem with lying is that it's hard to stop once you've started. I have to be honest with myself and stop the cycle of madness now. I have to start telling the truth, and it doesn't matter how difficult this situation is. Can I even do that, not to lie all the time? Is it even humanly possible? Everybody lies, but it's usually something small. Not like me... Nobody lies like me. Yeah-yeah, I know there is a difference between meaningless lying and the type of lying when you lose everyone close to you. Truth is definitely a new skill for me.

I've been thinking about where to start — my family or myself. I guess with my family because it's so easy to fall in love with them, not with me. But I'm not trying to get any sympathy. They're absolutely incredible — no doubt about that. So here's my first day of high school before my lies all came crashing down.

Chapter 1
The Worst Day Ever

My mom and dad met each other in high school, and... yeah, it's exactly what you think. They have been together ever since, happily together. But, unfortunately, the only skeleton in their closet is me.

I'm an only child, which means one thing — I'm surrounded by love and support 24/7. My mom owns a little bakery in the neighborhood, which would be so awesome if I liked sweets and baked goodies. My dad works at the bank, doing things really I don't want to understand. They met at the beginning of high school and started dating a couple of months later. There were some problems with my grandparents not getting along. My mom's parents didn't love her dating a white guy, and my dad's parents weren't thrilled about him being with a black girl. But my parents stayed strong together, and no matter how much other people may have judged or belittled them, they never let go of each other. That's pretty much the story of their life.

Therefore, my #1 goal is not to meet a guy during my first year of high school, so I don't just like them. I can see how some people dream of being more like my parents. I'm just not one of those people, I think it can be great, marrying your first love in high school, but it's just crazy in most cases. I can tell you first hand. It's not as endearing as they'd like you to believe.

My parents are amazing people. They give so much to the community. They have amazing friends, and most of them are from the good old days. They're very giving, which attracts a lot of people. Sometimes those people try to take advantage of them. I genuinely believe that's why I had to go through so many "friends." People kind of come and go. I've learned not to get too attached. Give them what they want, and try to have fun for as long as it lasts. If I told that to my parents, they would disapprove of my opinion. I bet they'd say something like, "Cassie, be yourself, and people will accept you for who you are."

I don't think that advice works well for me. I think if someone asks me,

"Why are you so upset with your parents? They sound so wonderful?" The reason I'm irritated at them is that I made a huge mistake this summer, and it's kind of their fault.

Well, what has happened this summer? To make a long story short, I went to summer camp, where I met Jake. We started hanging out, but I wouldn't say we were dating because we were never... on the same page. I don't know what got into me because I told him that I loved him. That behavior isn't me — so not me. I don't reveal my feelings to boys. It's embarrassing, and the entire situation with Jake is the worst ever. I can still see his face when I said it. He mainly was confused and freaked out. *Did he say anything? Umm... about that — yes, he did say, "Cool." It says it all. Who says "Cool" in response to "I love you"?*

Wait a second, I forgot to add that we immediately broke up right after that happened. I did break it off. It wasn't the same after Jake didn't say, "I love you" back. Waiting for him to change his mind was a terrible idea, a recipe for disaster on both sides. Someone will get hurt even more. The way I handled this was classier and quicker. At least, that's what I choose to believe. *And come on? Who doesn't say "I love you" back? I'll answer this one — a person who doesn't love you and will never love you. There is no reason to waste your time.*

The only question I can't quite answer is why I even asked him. I guess it was just the spur of the moment. What would you do? Imagine a perfect sunset by the lake in the forest. I was aware that it wasn't the right thing to do. Yet, it didn't stop me from taking a leap of faith. I was doing what my parents always suggested. *Okay-okay, it was a fantastic setting, just like in the movies. I'm not a movie geek, but even I couldn't resist such perfection. Who knew even that couldn't make Jake say, "I love you" — I leaped into saying the sacred words, even though it was way too early.*

Circling back to Jake, I think the only thing you need to know about Jake is that he's a quarterback. I'm sure that summarizes everything you could possibly need to know about him. And he's probably dating another girl already. We went to the same middle school, but he didn't even know that I existed. Now we're going to the same high school. I'm a freshman, and Jake is a senior. So yeah, after our breakup, we haven't talked, so I'm aware it will be awkward. However, I hope it's not going to be a big deal. It's not a big deal to me at all. Plus, he's a senior. Likely, we won't even run into each other.

Well, today is the first day of school, and I have to admit it's not what I expected it to be. My parents and I are standing in the middle of the living room. Dad's currently looking around for the car keys, which are in the bowl by the door. He does it every time. Mom is dealing with flowers. Please don't ask me why. I don't know. This is my first day of high school, and I know one thing — I don't want or need flowers. In no universe, there should be so many! Unless I want to be "that" girl with flowers in school. Nope-nope-nope. This isn't happening to me.

"Dad, keys are in the bowl," I say, pointing and glancing over to the kitchen. "Mom, we really should be going."

I remember a car commercial I saw once. A perfect girl is about to go to high school on her first day, she gets a brand new car! Giant, perfect goddamn bow on top! Her excitement in slow motion. Oh, you don't even know how much I'd like to be that girl right now. To be fair, I'd totally settle for an old car, any car. I can't wait to get my driver's license. Just to avoid this embarrassment.

"Oh no, honey, I think we're ready to take pictures of our little pumpkin," mom says, grabbing a million balloons from the other room. *Mom is totally going to post these pictures, and everyone will see them. I try to tell myself, "I can handle this," but nobody's reputation can take this.* I frown and grimace. Mom glances at dad, a little confused and a little concerned. I know what that look means.

"Oh, no… do you hate it?" she says, turning to my dad. "Jay, I think she hates it!"

Yeah, this is officially the worst day. Mom is about to start freaking out. I thought this day was supposed to be about me… I guess not. I'm shaking my head and trying a new smile. The only difference between the Queen and me is I'm not waving. Well, there are thousands of differences, but I wonder if waving might help.

"You don't hate it?" my mom's eyes light up. I nod.

"You do?" she says, so I start shaking my head instead. "You don't?"

Lies. You see, it's so much easier to lie than it is to tell the truth, coded in protecting somebody's feelings. I just can't even. Literally can't even.

"I don't like them, mom," I say with dead eyes, "I love them!" The look I give people when I'm obviously lying. I'm clearly polite, but people never want to understand that. The only thing they care about is you're doing what they tell you to do. Nobody wants to know the truth because truth hurts. That's why I usually cozy up with a blanket of lies. It's soft and warm, and it always finds a way to cheer me up.

"Really?" mom asks, staring at me with those puppy dog eyes.

"Really! Of course, I love it. Thank you, guys!" I look down and take the balloons from my mom. "Let's go outside, and make this memorable moment stick forever."

We need to get it over with this embarrassment. I can't believe I'm doing this. The faster we start, the faster we'll be done. Just breathe, Cassie. I open the front door, ignoring the fact that their faces light up like a Christmas tree from my lies. This is why I'm an expert in lying.

"So what exactly did you guys have in mind? Should we..." I can't even finish the sentence because my mom takes my hand and moves me in front of the door.

"I was thinking about…" my mom says, running towards the car. She opens the trunk. *Uh-oh… thinking? I wonder what humiliation she has in store.*

Mom comes right back, holding a sign "Happy First Day of High School." *Yep, this is about right. These pictures are going to haunt me forever.*

Mom gives me a sparkling look. I can't believe how close it is to her "half bottle of wine" look. *I just need to think more positively. On the bright side, it's just a picture. I can do this!*

I say, "Love it! So you want me to hold the balloons, flowers, and the sign, right?"

"Well, I can hold the flowers, honey," dad comes to my rescue. "I don't think you have enough hands for everything."

"Great, so I'm gonna hold the sign and the balloons. Right?" I clarify.

"Is that okay?" mom asks.

"Of course! I love it," I say and pose for my parents as they start taking pictures — a lot of pictures. At least, they do look pleased.

"Do you wanna check if you like it?" mom asks me after taking about a million photos. I'm not even exaggerating.

"No, I'm good."

"Are you sure?"

I nod. *Am I sure? I've never been so sure about anything in my life. Am I sure that I never want to go through this again? Yeah... I'm sure.*

"Yes, mom. I just don't want to be late," I explain, trying to keep my smile. "It's my first day, you know."

Both of my parents nod in response. I hope it's been enough awkward interactions for one day. I'm looking forward to getting out of here. Hopefully, it's going to be more normal at school. I look around, which is obviously a signal to my parents — *hey, guys, I don't know what to do with these balloons, but I'm not taking them with me.*

"Where should I put these?"

My parents look at each other. *Oh no, guys, this is NOT happening. I'm not showing up to my first day of high school with enough balloons to form my own Macy's Thanksgiving Day Parade! Please, pretty please. It's time to use my puppy dog eyes.*

"Well," mom says, and my heart is about to break into a million pieces. "Let me take them."

"Thanks."

Full of relief, I pass the enormous amount of balloons to mom as she goes inside. Dad is trying hard to catch my eye to talk, but I'm pretty good at avoiding him. So instead, I walk up to the trunk and open it up. I quietly put the sign down when I realize dad has been standing and staring at me the whole time.

"What's up?" I ask, pretending I don't know what it's all about.

"It's a pretty big day… Huh?"

"Yeah, it's a pretty big day for me."

"Well, for all of us."

There it is. I turn around and look at my dad. His eyes are brimming with tears… Why does everything have to be "us"? Why can't something be just about me? Just me. The one who is actually having to go to school and do the work. Do all parents make their child's every step about them?

"Can't wait for graduation. It's gonna be an even bigger day… for all of us," I say in response. *I should have checked my surroundings because mom just came up behind us. The second, she heard me saying that she makes that sad, choking noise. It reminds me of the noise little puppies make when they're left alone. It's something between a crying puppy and an old squeaky chair, impossible to ignore. Nope, nope, I can't deal with this right now.*

"It's not gonna happen tomorrow, mom. Don't worry," I say. As I glance at the car, I add, "So should we get going?"

"Oh yeah, we don't want you to be late on your first day as well," mom says, nodding and still choke-sobbing — my dad hugs mom.

"Great," I say, closing the trunk. "Guys, please, stop staring at me."

"How do you know that we are? You aren't even looking at us," dad says.

"Because I don't need to look at you two to know," I reply. We all get in the car without saying anything. Dad starts the engine, and we're driving away. *Finally.*

The first day at school is the most important one. Of course, it's still school, but I'm thrilled to start a new chapter in my life. You can be a new you at high school and meet new people you have never seen before. To be fair, many people from my middle school are about to say "Hi" to each other today. But I'm not losing hope about meeting a few cool, new people. I don't feel too much pressure because if it doesn't happen, it won't be the end of the world.

However, the odds aren't on my side. Especially when my dad pulls up in front of the school, I can only imagine how my parents start crying while they're hugging me. I've had enough embarrassment for today. *So, the goal here is to get out of the car as fast as I humanly can. Hopefully, before my parents get out and make another scene. Nobody likes a mommy/daddy's baby girl.* I unbuckle quickly and lean forward.

"Okay, guys," I say, kissing them on the cheeks. "Love you, see you at home."

They look a little confused and surprised.

"You don't want us to walk with you?"

"Maybe next time?" I smile. *If I let them do it once, they'll keep coming back.* My parents nod and attempt to hide their disappointment.

"Okay, hun. Have fun," my dad says.

"See you at home," mom adds, looking down. *Why does it have to be this way? I'm not trying to upset them.*

"Love you," I mumble, grabbing my backpack. I get out of the car and close the door. *Just walk as fast as I can, and don't look back. You can't see their tears. It'll ruin the rest of my day. No, Cassie, please, no. This isn't happening.* Shaking my head, I stop and turn back. My parents are still there, sitting in the car and staring at me. I wave at them with a smile. They wave back, looking so happy and excited.

Bye-bye, potential new friends! I will die alone, for sure. Continuing to wave, I send them a kiss and walk away. I look around, there are a lot of people. *I don't know any of them, which is a good sign. This is so exciting, and the best part is that nobody can guess I feel incredibly nervous. I was waiting for this moment for so long. Well, maybe it's partially because of Jake. This is the first time we'll see each other after summer camp. I'm not expecting to see him. It's a big school, what are the odds that we will run into each other right away? Technically, we can go the whole year without seeing each other. But, to be fair, I kind of want to see him. I don't even know why.*

There's a small part of me that still dreams about us. Sometimes I wonder if Jake ever thinks about me. Why? Because I think about him too. It'd make me feel so relieved to know whether he has a new girlfriend. I wonder if he still has my number or deleted it right after we broke up. Jake still follows me on social media. *Does he check it? Did he just forget to unfollow me? Is he saying that we aren't over? Because I'm totally over him.* I've got to admit I wonder about a lot of silly things. I just need one quick look to know whether he thinks about me… and maybe loves me. That will help me put any second thoughts aside.

Of course, I'm aware it's not going to change anything. If Jake really loved me, he'd do something about our break-up, but he didn't. In Jake's defense, I was the one who broke it off. So it makes a little bit of sense that he left me alone. I'm obsessing over this because when I told him that we were over, the only thing I got from him was shrugging his shoulders and saying, "Okay, if that's what you want." Who says that? Well, someone who doesn't care about you. That's why it'd never work — two bright stars in the sky, which will never get a chance to be together.

Our school is pretty big, but it's so easy to get lost. I'm happy that most schools send all the information you can possibly need to your student email nowadays. It's just amazing, but I'm still pretty sure I'm lost. I check my phone for instructions. Where is my locker? *I should have done this earlier, but I was terrified to run into Jake by accident. I wanted to delay that uncomfortable moment as long as I could. It's a little frustrating that now I'm regretting my decision.* I stop in the middle of campus. *Congratulations, Cassie, you might be late for your first class. It won't be anybody's fault but your own.* I wish I could roll my eyes harder, but it's not possible.

At least, the map is extensive. *Okay, so I'm here. The lockers for freshmen should be right over there. It shouldn't be that difficult to find, right? Ugh… I was totally going in the wrong direction. This is so frustrating.* I turn one-eighty and rush over to the spot on the map.

I quickly forget all about my troubles the second I find my locker. *Fifteen minutes to go, and I'm already here. Not bad, not bad I just need to stop overreacting and just relax. I guess the reason why I feel so tense is that I still haven't seen Jake. In a way, it would be easier to see each other and get it over with. The combination is three, five, nineteen, seven.*

Click, and the locker opens. *It really needs some decoration, so it doesn't look so sad. I don't need this book and this notebook until the break.* I'm deep in my thoughts when I hear a familiar voice.

"Well-well, who do I spy with my little eye?" Louis creepily whispers in my ear. I jump from surprise.

"OMG, Louis, you scared the hell out of me!" I say, trying to catch my breath. *Louis really got me. His voice came out of nowhere. If I have nightmares tonight, I won't be surprised.* I'd be more upset if someone else at that exact moment bear-hugged me from behind. It feels like I'm being strangled by Death. Well, that's a bit of an exaggeration. It's not Death — It's just Ally. She's one of my oldest friends and kind of my best. I think the closest description is we go way back.

"Hey, bestie," Ally says and doesn't let me go.

"We missed you. And I almost forgot," as Louis says it, he leans over and kisses me on my cheek. *Wow, that's something new — a kiss from Louis. Wow, and another one — that's way too generous.* Louis notices the surprise on my face, and he quickly adds, "Sorry. Mentally, I'm still in Paris. Two kisses, one on each cheek. It's very European, you know."

"Oh, it's the French way. Okay, okay, I'm digging it," I say. "Ally, I'm so glad to see you too."

"I can't believe I didn't get a chance to see you the whole summer," Ally pouts, finally letting me go. I smile in response. *Hmm, I wonder if I kiss Ally twice, will it buy more alone time for myself. I'll give it a shot tomorrow.*

"I missed you," she adds, staring at me with another pair of puppy dog eyes. *You see? That's why I must lie all the time. This is so unfair. Ally gets to squeeze me to death, and I have to be polite.*

"I missed you too," I reply. I notice Louis gives me a death stare. I add, "And I missed you, Louis."

My situation with my friends isn't that great. Ally and Louis are my "best friends." I'll start with Ally because she's been my friend since 2nd grade. She's a nice girl, really nice. I just don't like her. I've attempted to drift apart, but I'm incredibly unsuccessful at it. She's just too much, which isn't exactly her fault. It's not Ally — It's me. I'm just not a "best friends" type of girl. I've never wanted to be friends with Ally. Yet, she's always there when I am. She just decided to be my best friend, and she's never got the hint — I'm *not* interested. How much time should pass before Ally gives up? Unfortunately, she never has. Sometimes I wonder if I hadn't lent her that dreadful pencil the first time we met.

Then there's my second "best friend" Louis. His name's pronounced LU-EE. *Louis says his parents named him with a french word, so he'd be more aristocratic. However, I still don't buy it — I think he named himself like that to sound more unique. I've heard his mom call him Lou-Lou on more than one occasion.* I never understood why he needs to try so hard. Louis is pretty fantastic without a unique name. He always has perfect hair, and there is one more thing, which is weird to admit — he smells so amazing, like all the time.

I'm not exaggerating. It's as if Louis lives in a perfumery. I don't know how he does it, but I'm jealous. Plus, Louis is pure emotion. He screams at the drop of a hat. I'm also envious of that. Actually, I'd like to be more like him. Unfortunately, I don't know how to be myself. I can't say what I feel or think. I can't even believe I met him through Ally. Louis has always been more of Ally's friend than mine. Why? If we had a big falling out, I think he'd pick Ally over me. They've been friends since preschool. *Sorry universe, but I can't compete with that. Nobody can.* My longest friendship is with Ally, built on lies and my inability to say, "No." *My life sucks.*

"How was France, Louis?" I ask.

"I thought you'd never ask!" he starts. Louis leans on the locker next to mine. "It was Magnifique! Just fabulous, and full of adventures... with the hottest french boys."

That statement is followed by Louis's usual eyebrow work, wiggling like mad. He calls it "break-dancing eyebrows," but I'm not sold on the name. We all giggle. I mean, it's tough not to.

"We wanna know everything, with pictures," Ally says. "Right, Cassie?"

I nod because I can barely pay any attention to what she's saying. I've spotted Jake walking by with a bunch of people. *It wouldn't be so bad if he weren't holding some girl's hand. Yeah, this is not how I imagined seeing him for the first time, not with a girl. This is officially the worst day ever. I dreamed that it'd be more "Love Actually" style. My parents love that movie. So by the one-hundred-thousandth time, I started to like it too. I always imagined that Jake would realize that he couldn't live without me... or something. Instead, not only can't I keep my eyes off him, but also I can't stop freaking out that he's already got a new girlfriend! It wasn't even enough time, was it? We came back from the summer camp about two weeks ago.*

"Cassie, are you even listening?" Ally asks, annoyed. However, she sounds so far away when my eyes meet with Jake's for a second. *I was terrified to see him, but I didn't expect nothing — just nothing. We both pretend as if we don't notice each other and rush to look away. Definitely, this is not what I ever expected, and I mean ever. It was even worse than the worst thing I could imagine.*

"Are you okay? Did something happen between you two at summer camp?" Ally asks. *Ugh... I don't want to talk to my fake friends about this. The less they know, the more comfortable I feel. The reality is I don't need to talk about my feelings all the time. It's not me. I have to do my thing. I just widen my eyes as if I don't comprehend what the other person says. Then, I shake my head.*

"Who? What? Sorry, I was just thinking... My thoughts were somewhere else, you know how I am," I innocently explain.

"Yeah-yeah, doll. Sure thing," Louis says. They both give me a look. *They don't seem to be buying my act.*

"Come on. You've been secretly sighing about Jake since the beginning of middle school," Ally adds. "And it's all over your face that something did happen at summer camp."

Busted. I smile and close my locker. *I can buy some time to figure out whether there is a way not to tell them the whole truth and what pieces I should reveal.* That's why I just say, "Yeah, we dated for like a week, but you know... It was just a silly crush."

I was really trying to sell it like, *oh yeah, no biggie. Maybe there was something, but it passed. Very nonchalant type of way, so I turn to see if it worked.*

"O-M-G, are you kidding me?" they both yell at me in sync. *Well, that didn't work.*

"Whoa, whoa, whoa, guys," I say. "As I said, it was a silly summer crush, nothing serious."

I mean, what else is there to say? That I'm still in love with him. Yeah, I guess I am still in love with him. Here I am, glancing over Ally's shoulder and still hoping to see Jake looking back at me. Jack disappears around a corner. Louis catches where I'm looking.

"Summer may be over, but your crush doesn't have to be," Louis says. Ally nods. I really don't like how supportive both of them are. I smirk like *ha-ha-ha, very funny.*

The only disadvantage of constantly lying is I easily get lost in my own thoughts. Especially when all my thoughts are focused on Jake.

"Our fling is over, just like summer," I say, "but I do want to see those pictures of yours, Lou-Lou."

I used my sweetest tone of voice, which usually makes everyone forget what we're talking about. It doesn't get me out of every situation, but it's a lifesaver in most cases.

"I know what you're doing," Louis says, shaking his head with disapproval. "But I don't care because I want to brag about my slide show."

"Oh, Louis, you've got to tell us *everything*," I say. Ally rolls her eyes at me. Of course, she would. I'm okay with changing the subject.

"Okay, guys, we need to go," I say, pointing at the time on my phone.

"You aren't wrong. Let's go." Louis replies.

"Guys, this is our first year of high school! Let's take a picture before we go?" Ally suggests.

"Sure," I respond immediately. *I don't want to deal with tears or whatever* emotional crap my friends may have. I've had enough from my parents today, and I don't need more sentimental shenanigans. We squeeze together. Ally points the phone at us. I quickly glance around. Nobody else is doing anything like this. Normal people don't do random selfie sessions — *bye-bye my new friends, bye-bye my expectations, and mostly bye-bye Jake.*

"Thank you, guys," Ally hugs us. She seems so happy. *Ugh... Why is she so nice? How can she be so nice all the time?*

"Can I actually check the last one?" Louis says. *I start shaking my head — no, no, no, not this again. Last time when Louis said that, we ended up spending almost two hours retaking the same selfie over and over again. Let's be clear, they all looked the same after picture number ten. I need to jump on this quickly.* I gently hug Louis and push him away from Ally's phone.

"You always look fabulous," I say. Louis frowns. *Not today! Usually, I play along with all of this, but I'm not in the mood right now.* Ally begrudgingly nods, then she hides her cell phone away.

"If you say so," Louis says. We start moving. Ally secretly gives me a thumbs up. *Even though she's not really my best friend. Sometimes we have fun.*

Chapter 2
The "New" Guy

I don't really believe in superstitions. My life can't be determined by random events, which I have no control over. I think it's just ridiculous. For example, if a black cat crosses my path, I won't think twice about it because the cat's either going home or someone should call animal control. Not my problem — whatever happens, happens. However, I do have one superstition. I believe that the first day of high school determines how amazing or terrible the whole year will be. I remember how mediocre my first day of middle school was, just like the rest of that year. It was so dull and uneventful.

I just hope high school is going to be different. *Yet, my sixth sense is telling me this isn't destined to happen. While we're walking through the hallway, I continue fixating on Jake. I remember when I saw him for the first time. Our eyes met for a second, but he didn't notice me. To be fair, I was absolutely invisible, so I don't blame Jake. He wouldn't have been able to remember me even if he tried. Also, he was three grades above me.* I've kept tabs on him since then. I've dreamed about how we'll start dating, and at the beginning, it made sense. Jake used to be quiet, cute, and full of mystery. One of those things is still true. What happened? Well, the short answer is football. Jake had his first big win at the beginning of the tenth grade, and everything changed forever. He became a superstar. All the girls have become crazy about him, making it harder for me to dream about dating Jake.

That's why I've always imagined how I'd run into him. He'd be blown away by my awkward cuteness or something like that, and after a couple of dates, Jake would fall in love with me. I'd blush and blah-blah-blah. And boom, we're together forever. Well, perfect moments like that can't happen by themselves. Through vigorous non-stop research, I found out about Jake's summer plans. Yeah, that's how we ended up in the same summer camp. Unfortunately, that plan didn't go so well for me. At first, everything seemed perfect. We had plenty of time to hang out, explore the great outdoors. Spend plenty of alone time together, just talking. Until I dropped the "I love you" bomb and ruined it. That's why I need this year to be excellent, so badly. *Everyone loves a good redemption story.*

Ally, Louis, and I enter the classroom. I give the room a quick look over. You see, there are two conditions vital to my success this year. I sigh, with some relief, because one condition is met — I don't know anyone else in the classroom. The second thing is a little bit weird — I like sitting in the third seat in the middle row. It's my lucky day — no one is currently sitting there. *Well, I guess something finally went the way I wanted.* I love being not too close but not too far from the teacher. I rush to my spot, ignoring my friends' smirks.

"Omg, Cassie, I can't believe it!" Ally laughs and rolls her eyes at me. I've learned one trait about Ally — if you ignore her long enough, she'll always drop the subject. I proceed to follow my own advice and ignore any implications. I proudly sit at the right spot, my spot, and give Ally the most satisfied smile.

"Come on! It's high school, be a rebel, and switch your spot," she says, shaking her head. She constantly switches where she sits. My theory is it depends on how much she likes a class or a teacher. Ally totally denies it, but I know it's true.

"Some things have to stay the same, Ally," I say. Louis always sits near a window. Apparently, the sun hits his three-quarter profile, which is the best lighting for his looks or something like that. I believe Lou-Lou likes to daydream in the middle of class. One big reason why I can't sit there is that it's too distracting.

For a person who doesn't believe in superstition, I have quite a few rituals. First, I organize my desk by putting the textbook in the right corner, my pink notebook perfectly in the middle, and a blue pen at the top. It looks immaculate and geometric. Of course, I always start this way, but I always forget about it by the end of the year. It becomes unimportant as the semester progresses, but I attempt to keep it that way as long as I can.

The moment the three of us settle, I grab my phone. I've got to check something. Well, "something" is Jake's social media. I have to find out who Jake's new girlfriend is. I've never seen her before. I don't even know her name. As I start scrubbing through his page, Ally posts the picture we took earlier. The post notification brings me to Ally's page. I see the hashtags she added — #bestfriendsforever and #firstdayofhighschool. I roll my eyes.

"Already?" I say. Ally laughs.

"Omg, Ally!" Louis screams as if something horrendous has just happened. "I asked you to post the twenty-third one. You posted the nineteenth instead! My hair is totally off! On the right side! You see?! Over here."

If only I could roll my eyes any harder, I would. Without a doubt, everyone in the class is staring at us. Great, we are becoming the new weirdos. This is the first day. Why can't we be like most people who don't draw attention to themselves? I guess Louis noticed my concerns because he publicly announces, "What? Has nobody ever had a hair disaster?"

Everyone chuckles. Lou-Lou saves the day. That's why I love Louis. He can say whatever he wants without caring what other people think. I always wonder how he can be so straightforward, and I've never seen him hurt other peoples' feelings. I can't find the right words because others always get upset with me if I tell the truth.

"Okay, I'll check. I can guarantee it's not *that* bad, Louis," I say, zooming in on the picture. However, I immediately forget about Lou-Lou's hair crisis. I notice in the background of the photo Jake looking at us. *Omg, omg, omg.*

My hands are shaking. I put the phone away. *Was Jake checking me out? It looks like he was. Who am I kidding? Of course, he was! Omg, omg, omg.* I feel the warmth of a blush on my cheeks. It's difficult not to smile, but I can't show excitement to my friends. They'll have more questions, and I won't have answers for them. *Maybe, it wasn't him. The background is kind of blurry, so it's impossible to say for sure. Yeah, I bet it wasn't him! I'm just not going to think about it too much. Dammit.* I grab the phone and dive into zooming in again. It is Jake. *Maybe, it's not all over… I mean, I don't even care about him.*

"Cassie? What do you think?" Louis asks.

"Louis, your hair was perfect," I say, lying but supportive. I open Jake's page and immediately notice that he's just posted a new picture with that girl. Apparently, his new girlfriend's name is Katie Reyes. I switch to her profile, and to my surprise, she has a lot of followers. Well, it's par for the course because Katie is so pretty with her perfect blond hair and blue eyes. *I can't compete with that.* Plus, she's also a senior and a cheerleader. Now I understand how Jake and Katie know each other. It all makes sense. *The quarterback and the cheerleader are dating... How original!*

"Cassie," Ally whispers my name.

"What?"

"Look at that guy?! Do you know him?"

Without even looking up, I say, "Well, the only people I know here are you and Louis."

"He's cute. Come on, Cassie."

"Okay, Ally, but I'm telling you I don't know him," I say, looking up. I drop my phone.

"Hey, Cassie," Ally's guy says as he walks up to me. *Oh, I do know this guy. He's not supposed to be here. OMG, it's Elliot — El. Am I dreaming right now? I can't believe this is happening. What is he doing here? I wish I could become invisible right now.* My face goes pale. In a way, it's like I've seen a ghost from my past. The problem is that the so-called past happened pretty recently, at summer camp. I nervously swallow.

"Hey, El," I awkwardly smile. El stops next to my desk. I don't know how to react — I just keep smiling. El glances over at my phone.

"Cute."

I shake my head and ask, "What?"

"On your phone, it's a cute picture."

"Th-thanks," I reply, turning my phone upside down. *Does Elliot know? Did he notice that it was a picture of Jake and Katie? Okay-okay, chill, Cassie. El didn't see anything.*

"Do you have time to catch up?"

"Uh-Umm. Now? How about after class?"

"Sure."

El walks further down the aisle, and I grab my cellphone to check what picture El was referring to as cute. Luckily, it's the picture of three of us Ally just posted. It hits me that my friends are probably freaking out about El. I look at Ally and Louis. Both of their jaws are on the floor. I can only imagine what's going through their heads right now. To my surprise, they wait until El walks past us to interrogate me.

"Omg, you know the new guy?" Ally says as she secretly points from El to me.

"It's not what you think, guys," I respond. *People, give me a break. This is unbelievable, no, not unbelievable — it's a curse. I'm cursed.*

"Well, now we know why you and Jake didn't work out! You already moved on to this new guy — El, is it?" Ally continues and gives a not-so-subtle high-five to Louis. He nods knowingly, with a stupid duck face — so annoying.

"Shh... no more, no more words from you, two!"

This is too much. *What if El heard Ally? What will he think? Do I care what he thinks?* They both chuckle, but I don't find this situation worth giggling about. Then, of course, they start whispering. The worst thing about this is that they know how much I hate when they whisper, but they do it anyway. They're so good at whispering, so I can't quite make out what they're saying, just a murmur. It drives me crazy. I wonder whether Ally and Louis are pretending to have a conversation. Taking a metaphorical stand about me not disclosing every single detail of my life.

"Just quit it!" I angrily cut them off. I don't want to hear their response. I grab a textbook, open it, and try to concentrate on the first page. When I was a kid, I had anxieties about my grades and homework, so my parents wanted to help me with different techniques. Only reading used to help. I'd just read and think about words — nothing else. *Just breathe, Cass. It's gonna be alright. What is El doing here? He should have gone to a different school. Why are the words becoming so blurry?*

Chapter 3
Summer Daydreams

So how do El and I know each other? I actually have Jake to thank because he's the reason we met. It happened the same day I broke up with Jake. After the "Okay, if that's what you want" I got from him. It crushed me. *Did he ever even care about me? Did he want to break up with me, and I gave him an easy way out? He didn't even love me, did he?* I felt so lost in my thoughts and upset that I decided to go to the camp dance.

Usually, organized public dances aren't really my thing. Especially at camp, but I decided that I needed to stop thinking about Jake, and the dance seemed like such a great idea at the time. I remember sitting in front of a mirror and trying to put make-up on. I just hoped if I could put it on, I wouldn't cry. When it came to picking an outfit, I stood for a good thirty minutes staring at my clothing.

Thanks to my roommate, I picked a dress. One she mentioned, I had never worn. I nodded in response. I took it off the shelf, revealing it was my special date dress. So beautiful, a red corset flowing down into a short skirt. Everyone has a unique dress for a special day in their closet.

I thought, "I'll never get my special day, so there's no use in letting my dress go to waste." A little bit dramatic, I admit now. And looking back, I also recognize the dress did get its perfect day that night. I changed, and it was perfect. You know the feeling when you look great, the dress, makeup, hair, everything just came together. Jake and his teammates didn't go to the camp dances. They had their own parties, and you needed a special invitation to be invited. That's why I decided to go to the dance — I wouldn't see Jake, and I wouldn't think about him.

I remember everything that happened that night. I remember how confused I was that nobody looked at me or cared about what I was doing. Probably, they didn't even know who I was. I remember... I just close my eyes, and when I open them, I can teleport to that time. It's dark, and only the disco ball shines, reflecting everywhere. I'm in the middle of the dance floor, surrounded by a lot of people dancing.

For the first time, I feel free. I don't even care. Probably that's why I don't hear the music slow down. I just keep dancing. My hair moves through the air. I feel like I'm out on the ocean — being rocked by the waves. I'm strong, powerful, and brave. When I push my hair from my eyes. I see El for the first time. Tall and handsome, the lights sparkle in his eyes. He comes up to me — he smiles. I smile back. How could I not?

"Hey," he says. I couldn't stop staring at him and continued smiling.

Elliot is something blonde with perfect blue eyes and that smile. He looks rebellious and adventurous, which was exactly what I was looking for. I slow down.

"Hey," I say. Elliot just stares at me, and I do the same. It's awesome. Suddenly, he starts dancing in a weird way, goofy, definitely my kind of style. I giggle and immediately join him. *And that was how I met El. Now you tell me how it's not Jake's fault?*

After the dance, El walked me home. I think it was a full moon. We were holding hands and talking non-stop. I don't even remember what we were talking about. It was that easy with El. I didn't have to think about what to say. With Jake, it's always a battle. I have to come up with a list of topics for conversation. But with Elliot, it was easy, like breathing. Finally, we stopped in front of my room.

"This is me," I said. Letting El's hand go. He looked a little bit disappointed.

"See you tomorrow?" He asked. I shrugged my shoulders, teasing him. *Boring.* El smiled and added, "See you tomorrow."

His voice was totally different — he didn't ask me. He was a perfect distraction. Something is charming when a guy is assertive, that doesn't mean they shouldn't listen or ignore you. It's more that they care whether you're around. I felt invisible to Jake, and when he said, "Okay," to my breakup, I knew

I did the right thing. El seemed to really want to be around me.

"Sure, let's hang out," I said.

The next day El was there, and we started hanging out. The best part was I didn't see Jake during that time, and I didn't even have time to think about him. El and I were doing everything together — we skipped dinners together, snuck into the lake, we'd talk about our families, problems, schools, and hobbies. I liked hanging out with Elliot. I enjoyed myself — I didn't feel pressured to be anyone else. For the first time, I felt like someone saw me for who I was, and I didn't need to lie.

I found out that El was going to a different school than me. I thought that after camp, we'd probably never see each other again. It all felt like a dream. Now I wonder if El felt the same way. The last days of camp were amazing, thanks to El. I forgot about all my troubles. On the last day of camp, we were sitting on the dock, dangling our legs in the water. I forgot this was the exact spot where I told Jake that I loved him. I stared off into the distance, a little bit daydreaming, remembering that night with Jake.

"Okay, this is the last day of camp. You've got to tell me what's your dirty little secret," Elliot said, splashing cold water at me. I shrieked.

"Omg, it's cold, El! What are you even doing?"

"Come on, spill the beans!"

I just rolled my eyes.

"It's nothing."

El shook his head and said, "Lies." Oh, he got me. I looked away and smiled.

"Are you an expert now?"

At that moment, I noticed Jake. He was walking with another girl! It seemed like my whole world just skipped a beat. Everything came crashing to a halt. There was no longer a trace of a smile on my face. I still don't know if, at that moment, El had noticed Jake. But what did I do?

I told Elliot everything about Jake. Why? I don't know why. It all came pouring out of me, I think I felt vulnerable, and nothing made sense. I put my head on his shoulder and told him all about it. Of course, I left one thing out of the conversation, only one tiny little lie. I told him I didn't have any feelings left for Jake. El was incredible. He just listened to me without interrupting. It was easy telling him almost everything I felt. In thirty minutes, I had nothing left to say.

There was silence around us — the sunset hit the water. The moment stretched as the water lapped around our ankles. It was perfect until El said, "You know Cass... I really like you." I didn't even know what to say. I liked him too, but not the same way he wanted me. El didn't even give me time to think about what I should have said. He added, "And there's something I've wanted to do ever since we met."

El stole a kiss. *What should I do? Should I kiss him back? Omg, omg!* And then I made a critical mistake. I looked up into his eyes. The sunlight glanced off the water, making his blue eyes sparkle. *Crap.* I kissed him back. Yeah, I didn't think it through at all. However, it was the last day, and we weren't supposed to see each other ever again.

El walked me back to my room as usual. We stood and stared. I think he wanted me to say something. I just couldn't. On the one hand, I didn't want to lie to El because he was the reason why my last four days of camp didn't suck. It would have been miserable to see Jake with somebody else if I was by myself. That's why Elliot kind of deserved to hear something nice from me.

On the other hand, I felt like I shouldn't say anything. I didn't want to lead El on. *What should I do?*

"So..." El broke the silence. I felt so relieved. I couldn't decide what to do — he gave me an easy way out. "This is my number since we're going to different schools... Just call or text me when you're back."

My eyes sparkled, I nodded. I hugged El and gave him a quick kiss.

"Good night," I said and disappeared before he could say a word. I did everything I could to make it clear it was over — the perfect goodbye kiss. El didn't see me peeking out the window. He stood there, staring at the door after I ran off. It made me smile. I wanted to save the moment in my memories because

I had no plans to call/text him. We always communicated through social media, and there was no way that would change.

It's easy to ignore messages on social media. It's so easy to click off the app and forget about a message, even if you checked it. And that's precisely what I did. I ignored two messages he sent me after we got back home. Whatever happened at summer camp should stay at summer camp. Now you know how that worked out for me...

The second the bell rings, I take off. I grab all my stuff without packing it into my backpack. I don't want to talk to El. I don't want to introduce my friends to him. It should be over, but apparently, it's *not* over. That's why I do the one thing I know how to do best — run from my problems as fast as I can.

"See you later," I quickly say to Ally and Louis. *Don't look back, Cassie, do NOT look back.* I rush outside to the main hallway. Honestly, I did hear someone calling my name, but I pretended I didn't. It was Elliot, but it could have been anyone.

No matter where I am, I always try to find a safe spot nearby — a spot where I can be myself and be honest with myself. For example, it was the dock by the lake at summer camp. Technically, it was off the camp property. To get there, you had to sneak out. Two weeks ago, before school started, my parents and I came by for a tour. They had an extended conversation with the principal while I was looking for *my* spot. It was a perfect time for a search — lonely school hallways. When you wander through a school, when it's empty, it feels like you're in a zombie movie.

After an extensive search, I almost gave up. I went up the stairs, trying to get up on the roof. The door was closed. At that point, it was my last chance to find a quiet place for myself. I knew it. I sat down on the floor and closed my eyes. I felt exhausted, but when I opened my eyes, I noticed something shiny on the floor. That's how I found a janitor's key for the rooftop. I'm so lucky — they haven't changed the locks yet.

So here's my safe spot. Welcome! I've never told anybody about it. I love staring at the sky. It helps me to concentrate and go over my thoughts. Right now, I feel very nervous. *What is Elliot doing here? I knew I shouldn't have told him which school I go to. What does he want to talk to me about?* The sun makes my eyes water. I try to move a little bit, but it doesn't help at all. I cover the sun with my hand, which also doesn't save me from the bright sunlight. *Yeah, it doesn't work. I can't think right now.* I sit up.

"Oh, here you are!" I hear. *Omg, I can't believe it! My secret spot has been compromised.* It's not like I assumed I'm the only one who would use it. No, but I just hoped for some privacy for a while. I turn around to check if it's him. Yes, it's Elliot. I just can't catch a break today. I frown. *Wait, how does he know about my spot?*

"Okay, how… How did you get here?" I ask.

"Through the door, silly," Elliot says and sits next to me. I roll my eyes at him and attempt to look disinterested, implying that he's not welcome here. Of course, El being El, he hugs me. Lightly but hard enough to melt my cold attitude.

"How did you find me? It's kind of my secret spot," I ask.

"I just really know you."

"Oooh, I see, Mr. know-it-all," I say, raising my eyebrows. He smirks. I notice that El doesn't look at me at all. It's not like him.

"What's up?"

"Maybe, I get the strong sense you aren't that happy to see me," he says. I nervously swallow because it's not like he's wrong. Not at all, but he can't know that.

"No-no-no… I was… I'm surprised to see you here," I say. "I just thought..."

"You'd never see me again?" he asks as if he's half-joking. He stares at me, watching every single emotion on my face. *Just smile, Cass — smile better!* I follow my own advice and smile, shaking my head.

"Definitely, not what I meant," I say — Elliot's eyes sparkle.

"Well, you never called me back. Maybe because you lost my number?"

"No, I just got busy," I reply. The #1 rule in lying is to keep it simple. The simpler it is, the easier it is to believe. However, I don't think El bought it.

"Oooh," he says with a smug smirk.

"You could've texted me..." I say without thinking. Elliot turns and gives me a nonplussed look. I ask, "What?" He shrugs his shoulders like it's not a big deal.

"Well, maybe that's because *you* never gave me your number," El says. I don't even know how to react to that. It's a good point, an excellent point. *Hmm... What do I do next? Ah, my phone!*

"Sorry," I say, standing up and grabbing at my pocket. Pulling out my phone, I point at it. Looking very serious, I say, "Got an Insta message, El. I'm so sorry, but I've gotta go. See you around!" The plan is to say it so fast, the person won't even have time to think about what was said. And it works every time... well, most of the time.

I casually try to dash/waltz toward the exit. *This is so bad. El's definitely gonna think I'm weird.* I close the rooftop door and rush down to the stairs. I slump against a cold wall at the bottom of the staircase. I can't breathe. *Did I just use a social media message as an excuse? I'm screwed.* I hear El open the roof door. If you're not careful, the door makes the worst and loudest noise ever. I duck into a nearby bathroom. *This is where I belong now.*

Chapter 4
Jack's Diner

The main goal for the rest of the week is to avoid El, which means that I have to sneak into classes as the bell rings. It's torturous. Why? Why?! Every time I arrive, my spot is taken! This is officially the worst start to a school year ever! I can't concentrate on my classes at all. Especially in the last few minutes, I need to be ready to run away the second the bell rings.

So far, so good — I've been able to stay one step ahead of El. However, I feel so exhausted. I did not expect to find myself exercising every day for the entire week! I just can't wait until the classes are over. It's Friday, and every Friday, Ally, Louis, and I go to Jack's Diner. It's old school, from the fifties, with pink and blue neon lights, red booths, and black and white tile — it's pretty close to school. The food is okay, nothing special. The prices are great, though. There are a lot of students that go there. Sometimes we go there to study or just to treat ourselves after a long week.

But most importantly, we go to spy on high schoolers. Throughout middle school, it's how I kept tabs on Jake. The football players always go there. For the three of us, it's gonna be our first time as high schoolers. I've dreamed about this day so many times, but I'd never have guessed I'd be so exhausted.

Last bell. The last class is over. The first week is over. My nightmare is over! I immediately dart outside of school. I run until my lungs burn and my side starts to cramp. I stop, trying to catch a breath. I look up in the sky, which is so blue — bright sun. It's still too hot to be sprinting anywhere. *At least the diner is within walking distance from school. I need to go and pick my bike up on the way back. I don't even know why I can't stop thinking about El and Jake with his new girl. Too many thoughts.* Too many ideas to ignore. I'm thrilled the diner is close by, and I don't have time to dive into it too deep.

I arrive at Jack's and spot Ally and Louis. Ally, probably, drove. Ally is a year older, something to do with her parents holding her back for a year or something. We were so excited to have our private chauffeur — it's just so convenient. I wave at them. I'm thrilled because they got my favorite booth. I rush inside, and Louis is already moving, anticipating. He knows I want to sit in my spot. I always order the same thing — my favorite burger, french fries, and a milkshake. I don't remember a single time I ordered something different. So I guess I have a system where I sit and what I eat at Jack's.

Louis and Ally are talking about their first week and how excited they are for the rest of the year. I eat a fry, dipping it in my shake. Imagine telling them how I feel. *I don't know what to say to you, guys. Elliot was a distraction, and now he's in our school. However, I'm still wildly in love with Jake.* In my daydream, everything is easy. Ally and Louis are very supportive and understanding.

I stir my milkshake with a straw. Ally and Louis have moved onto a heated discussion about some TV show, the Oscars, and how it all somehow relates to the personal life of Louis's hairstylist. I just nod, giving them puppy-dog eyes and a happy smile. *I've just got to fake it, fake it 'til you make it. No one will know what's going on in your head.*

"Isn't that right, Cass?" Ally asks, staring at me.

"Sorry, what?" I respond, confused. What is she even talking about?

"That's why Jake isn't in the picture anymore..." Ally repeats. I don't even have time to respond when she adds, "And how come you get all the boys? I'm so jealous."

Louis nods, pushing his lips together, making that terrible duck face, and says, "Yeah, Ally, you're totally right. Cass is here taking all the boys, first Jake and now Elliot. I'd like to have a chance!"

I can't help myself. I start laughing — they also giggle.

"Hey, nothing is going on with El," I say, which only makes the whole situation worse.

"El? Mmmmm..." they say together.

"Since when is Elliot, El? So intimate..." Louis prods.

I just roll my eyes. What else do I have left? They keep laughing at me. I'm trying to smirk like it's cool. *I'm chill about this.* However, it's getting on my nerves.

"It's not like that. We got *friendly* at camp. I didn't even know that he's gonna transfer to our school this year," I say, and as I finish my last sentence, I feel a warm tingling feeling rush up my cheeks. *What is it?* I quickly add, "We're not interested in each other that way. Elliot and I have more of a friendship-type thing."

"So I can totally hit on him?" Ally pounces as if she's been waiting for it. Her eyes sparkle with a crazy light. I think I've seen it once before. Back when we were in sixth grade. Ally had a crush on one of the boys in our class. She used to follow him around like a little puppy dog. Honestly, it was a bit of a nice break to have her attention on someone other than me for a change. *This means she's really serious, huh? This is good, really good. See, she can have El, then I can go back to focusing on Jake.* I don't know why but her question really upset me. Maybe because I hoped I had more time to dream about El. That must be it. Ally's interested — I need to back off.

"Absolutely! You go, girl! I'm just not interested in boys right now," I say, another lie. I just need a break. At least with Ally pursuing Elliot, I don't have to spend every day running from class to class. The worst looks like it's finally over. But, of course, the actual worst happens right after I thought that. Ally and Louis both become pale, their expressions completely change.

"What?" I say and turn. It's Jake, surrounded by his group of friends. He strolls in, holding hands with Katie — the cheerleader. I turn away and close my eyes, hoping they haven't noticed me.

Jake's squad takes the biggest booth. Of course, it's located, so I have to face all of them. Jake hugs Katie. *Remember when I said I'd attempt to ignore them?* I stare deeply into my milkshake, but I look up at Jake. I just can't help it. I look up at the exact moment when Katie leans into him and kisses his cheek. *Great, this is just great.*

I stare back down at my milkshake. *Stop staring at them.* I feel somebody's eyes on me — I glance up. Ally and Louis try to play it cool, pretending not to watch my every move. It takes a lot for them to act like everything is fine. Well, I think they know me saying I'm not interested in boys is a lie. *More lies. If I didn't know myself, I'd think I was totally obsessing over my ex? Is he even an ex? Does a failed "I love you" even count as dating?*

"Are you okay?" Louis whispers, breaking the silence. I look at him, but it's just an excuse to glance over at Jake. *He seems happy. He really looks happy.* The worst is to see your ex happy because you want them to still think about you, not be busy with other girls.

"Yeah, it's not a big deal," I say. Louis doesn't say anything else — I'm very thankful. The last thing I need right now is pity.

"I don't know how serious you guys were or what really happened between you two, but it's probably weird..." Ally says. Her voice is full of sympathy, and it's almost the same thing as pity. Finally, I can't take it anymore and cut her off, "No, it's actually fine. I'm gonna run to the lady's room real fast."

They just nod. I feel relieved. I wink at Ally and dart to the bathroom. *At least, I didn't cry. I was close. My eyes are watering. I'm fine, I'm fine. But no, it's not fine. I'm invisible to him. And I hate seeing him everywhere — he's everywhere.*

The second nobody can see me, I run to the bathroom as fast as I can. Seeing Jake with someone really hurts. One thought of Jake being with someone else makes me feel so sad. And, of course, it has to be Katie. I bet they've been together for at least two weeks. It gets harder to breathe. I lock myself in the bathroom and sit down. I can barely catch a breath. I touch my chest and close my eyes. *It's okay, it's okay. Even if it's not what you were expecting, it's okay. You don't care. You don't care, Cassie.*

The pain slowly goes away, which makes it easier on my lungs. I'm exhausted. I put my head against the wall. It's cold, but it feels very comforting. My phone buzzes, helping me come back to reality. I check it right away. It's a notification from El, and it makes me smile. *He never gives up — I kind of like it.* My cheeks get red.

Hey, you. Just checking in about you giving me your number =)

Very demanding...

El would be a perfect best friend. The type of friend you can tell all your secrets to. You can discuss his girlfriend problems and your boyfriend problems. He makes me laugh. However, I doubt that he's looking for that.

I've been waiting for a while. I think I deserve it.

I don't know why, but I think it's funny. *How should I reply? Something fun like, "maybe"? Nah, that's not good enough. Hmm.* El sends another message.

;)

I roll my eyes. *I can't believe it.* I type and send my number.

Well, let's hope he's not a maniac? I think I'm pretty funny, and my humor is very awkward, sometimes inappropriate. *I can't believe I gave him my number!? I need to make sure I won't lead him on.* I unlock the stall and walk out toward the sink. On the way, I glance at my reflection in the mirror. I look tired, sad, and a little bit sweaty — not in a hot kind of way. I turn on the faucet. The water rushes down into the basin — I fill my palms. One deep breath and I wash my face. *A little bit better.* I fix my hair, and I'm ready to go and face Jake with Katie. *You don't care about him.* I nod and exit the bathroom.

So, exiting a bathroom is a whole thing for me. I'm not neurotic or anything like that, but I need to make sure I don't touch the door handle to exit. That's why I usually end up walking out of the bathroom backward, pushing the door with my foot. It's always awkward.

I bump into someone, "I'm so sorry," I say and slip on the wet tile. I start to fall over. I should really be more careful. If I fall flat on the floor, I won't even be that surprised. I don't think this can get worse. *I'm such a klutz!*

A strong arm steadies me, wrapping around my shoulders. "Oh, hey," Jake says when he realizes he's caught me. *OMG, are you kidding me? Why does it have to be Jake?* Jake holds me in his arms, looking down at me.

"Hey, can you?" I ask him, implying he should help me to stand. Jake nods and quickly allows me to stand up on my own. I smile and whisper, "Thank you, Jake."

Jake smiles, a little sheepish. I don't know what to say. There is nothing left to say. I move as if to step forward, attempting to pass him. But he doesn't shift. Instead, Jake looks down at me. It's the first time we've been alone for more than a couple of seconds since camp. We can't keep our eyes off each other — looking for answers.

"How are you?" He asks.

Wow, so casual. Good to know, Jake, good to know. I just need to be cool. It's not that hard.

"Good-good," I say, looking down. "You, Jake?"

"Good."

Silence. *Is this it? Please, tell me it's over. I just don't want to feel awkward.* We look at each other again.

"I think maybe... we should talk," Jake says. My heart starts pumping, and I nervously swallow. *What? He wants to talk? Why?* The reality is I don't want to talk about us. If we weren't done before, we are now.

"Cass, can we talk?" Jake repeats, and I smirk. It's just too funny.

"Do you really want to talk while your... girlfriend is here?" I ask, making an innocent face. Jake always tells me how much it drives him crazy.

He bristles, "Are you serious right now?"

I frown. Jake seems to look like he's about to lose it. I'm just not interested in all this drama.

"You know... I'm... I'm just gonna go," I whisper and step forward when Jake blocks my way. I look up at him like, *"what?"*

"Let's be clear. You were the one who broke it off, Cass," he says, "I just don't understand how you can end up playing the victim here. Isn't it what you wanted?

I shake my head. Honestly, this is just pathetic. I reply, "Well, I was the one who told you that I loved you in the first place." I'm proud I have something to hit him back with. Jake steps away. He looks pretty hurt.

"It's not a competition, Cass."

This is unfair. Why does Jake need to be right about stuff? Why can't I have this? I don't want to discuss why I broke up with him. I don't want to admit maybe it's not a competition. I told you how I felt because you made me feel invisible. I wanted you to notice me. And things were moving that way. I wanted to love you more than anything. However, even then, I didn't feel like I was important to you. I always feel like I'm secondary. It's always *you* than me — not us. Until I broke up with you.

My phone buzzes — I look at it automatically. Of course, it's El. *Omg, he's calling me! Who calls right when you give them your number?* I'm about to decline the call when I notice Jake is giving me a shocked stare.

"Are you for real thinking about picking it up right now?" He shakes his head. "I just can't believe you." He looks so hurt and confused. *It's so adorable.* How does it feel, Jake?

"I'm so sorry," I say, a little proud of myself. This is my best fake innocent act. "I just have to…"

"Of course, you do, Cass," he says, frustrated. "Suit yourself."

"Come on, it's my *new* boyfriend. You get it," I say and pick up the phone. The only thing I have left is to watch the train wreck — Jake looks shocked by what he's just heard. *Well, it's another lie.* I'm tired of the endless possibilities for us. I'm done. I just want to stop arguing. If Jake actually liked me, he wouldn't hang out with all those girls. But he does, and it's the end of our conversation. I should respect myself.

Jake replies, "Jeez… Cass."

"Hey, El!" I say into the phone.

"What are you up to?" Elliot asks.

Jake shakes his head. I frown at him as if to ask what's wrong.

I say, "Nothing really. Hanging out with my friends." I take a slight pause before "friends." *I'm just not sure if I can state more clearly that Jake is just a friend.*

"Do you have time to hang tonight?" El asks. He sounds very excited. I love making Jake angry — It's so easy. Just a look can set him off.

"I don't think tonight is a good time," I say. Jake gestures at me to hang up. It's cute because he's really attempting not to get mad or be rude. I ignore him, walking away. *This is not going to be easy for you, Jake.* I rush past him.

I say quietly to Elliot, "Can I call you back?"

"Uh, sure."

I hang up and hide my phone and join Ally and Louis. They don't say anything, and I'm happy about it. I glance across the diner and see that Jake isn't there anymore. *Good, he deserved that. Now he knows how rejection feels. I wonder if Ally and Louis saw us.*

Chapter 5
Doing a Dumb Thing

I lie on my bed, feeling exhausted. I'm done with my homework. My lids feel heavy, so I close them. How stupid can I be? Why was I so weird? *Stupid, stupid, stupid.* I dreamed about talking to Jake for so long, and the only thing I did was make it worse. I roll on my side. It wasn't romantic. Everything he said was wrong. Everything I said was wrong too. I can't understand why I was getting so annoyed with him. I sigh. I hear a knock on my door. I sit up — it's mom.

"How was your first week of high school?" she asks and enters.

"Good," I say, shrugging my shoulders. What else is there to say? School itself wasn't that bad. However, it was just too much personal drama. *I think I can smell lemon bars? Or maybe a lemon cake?* One of the biggest things I love about my mom is the smell of her bakery. It always makes me feel better. I used to play a game with her — guess the dessert from the scent. It was silly but my favorite game in the whole world. *Hmm, I don't even remember when we stopped doing it or why?*

"Good? Are you sure?" she prods. I nod and try to hide my eye roll. Everyone has this moment with their parents — obviously, I don't want to discuss the big dilemmas about being a teenager. *And I definitely don't want to hear my parents talk about it.* My mom's expression softens. *Okay, here goes.*

"Any plans for tonight?" she asks.

"Nothing really, just studying," I answer. Of course, this is another lie, but come on, no parent believes their kid if they say they already finished their homework.

"I heard there was a party at Jake Cohen's house," she says. I freeze for a second at the sound of Jake's name. My mom adds, "You should go, have fun."

Fun? Since when do your parents push you to go to parties, and I'm not even talking about how she knew about a party at Jake's place. I mean, she's not wrong. Going to the quarterback's house party is the opening event of the whole year. I've never been, just heard about it. In middle school, Jake also got a lot of attention, but it's nothing compared to high school. Now he's almost beyond my reach.

"Wait, how did you know about the party? I didn't even know about it!" I laugh.

"I chatted with Amber," she says.

"Mom... You know Amber is the worst!" I scream.

"I know," she says, rolling her eyes.

"And you told me how much she gossips!"

Amber's daughter Judy is in my grade. She seems very nice, a little quiet. She works as a model, which I think is very cool. Her mother is the oldest mom in our grade, and I feel like that's her core problem. Amber obsesses about her age, and that's why she constantly gossips about everyone, so people will be interested in her. And that tactic definitely works on my mom. Amber is going through a divorce, and my mom tries to help her through the transition.

"Yeah, gossiping is my guilty pleasure," she admits. I giggle.

"You have to promise me you will never tell her anything about me," I quickly add with a solemn face. "I don't want to end up like Jess."

Amber can be evil that way. She destroyed a girl's life — Jess. Jess used to be one of the popular girls. Jess was Judy's best friend. Everyone called them JJ. So the JJ's were modeling together. They always had sleepovers, makeovers, and other fun stuff. Everyone wished they had a friendship like the JJ's. Apparently, Jess was staying at Judy's place more and more. One day, Jess told Amber everything about her troubles at home, how her parents don't get her, and that she didn't want to live anymore... Amber went around and told everyone, parents, teachers, even other kids. It was pretty horrible, and Jess had to transfer.

"Promise," mom says. *I think this is it. She isn't gonna say anything else —* my phone buzzes. I quickly pick it up and check. It's El. I roll my eyes and put the phone away, then look up at mom. She's watching me.

"A boy?" she asks. *Hmm... She noticed. I need to stay sharp.* I nod in response. "Aren't you going to reply?"

"Maybe later," I say, waving my hand. "I'm gonna get back to this," I point to a stack of completed schoolwork. *You can't argue with the power of homework.* Mom looks at me a bit disappointed — she knows my game. She stands to leave. I'm surprised she's giving up so easily. Usually, she tries to get to the bottom of my feelings. Consisting of fifty percent of my mom telling me something is wrong and fifty percent of me being in denial about it. Mom turns back by a door frame. *That was too easy. Come on, Cass, you should know better.* She turns back to me.

"Hey, I know… I think something happened at summer camp."

"Mom…" I roll my eyes. Stage One — denial. "Nothing happened at camp." *By the way, Stage Two is also denial.*

"I just want you to know I'm here when," I roll my eyes when I hear the word when, "or IF you want to talk."

I smirk. What I love about my mom is that she makes me giggle. She's pretty funny.

"Thanks, mom," I say. She nods and heads to the kitchen. I grab a book and flip it open to a random page. *I wonder what El texted about? Hmm… I should concentrate on reading.* I focus on the book. *Probably, something silly like what shade of blue the sky is. No, I should read.* I glance over at my phone.

I pick it up and check it.

Hmmm, I've started getting a feeling you weren't planning to call me back…

I smile and text back.

Sorry… =)

I see text bubbles, I shake my head. He was definitely waiting for me — ridiculous.

Like the new haircut?

A pic of a new haircut is attached — the picture loads. El looks more like Jake. I frown.

Nice.

Are you going to Jake's party tonight? Should we go together?

I put my phone down on the other side of the bed. I stare into the distance. Do I really want to go to Jake's party? Short answer — no, long answer — no. I just told him I've got a new boyfriend. And I don't really want to see him all happy and moved on with that new girl. But, if I go with another guy to Jake's party, maybe he would get jealous? Short answer — yes, long answer — what the hell? *Sometimes you know you shouldn't do something, but you still do. And it doesn't matter how smart you are. You just do stupid, dumb things.* This is an example of an intelligent person doing a dumb thing because I text El back.

Love the idea! Pick me up at 6.

Chapter 6
Jake's House Party

I look at myself in the mirror. How many hours do women kill to find the perfect dress for a date? Well, now imagine how much time I spent finding the perfect dress for a fifty/fifty blend of a not-a-date and a hangout. So I went for a simple but flirty dress — lavender color with a beige cardigan on top.

I feel very nervous. For me, this isn't one but two dates. I have to look suitable for El, but not too good for him to think I'm trying hard to impress him. And at the same time, pretty enough to make Jake notice me. I know trying to make Jake jealous is a bit of a stretch, but I can dream. I think I'm mainly nervous to see Jake with Katie.

The doorbell rings, and I rush downstairs. I open the door and see Elliot holding a bag of popcorn. Even before I have a chance to say anything, I start laughing. I can't believe I just spent two hours picking my outfit.

"What?" El asks.

"Nothing," I say, having a hard time not crying from laughter. El rolls his eyes.

I don't know what Ally and Louis will do with me if they find out I'm at the party. Usually, we go to any school and school-related activities together. They've been texting me about it the whole evening, and we decided not to go. I hope I won't run into them. Otherwise, I'd have to do a lot of explaining. I wish they were with me, so I don't need to try fitting in.

Jake's house is several blocks away, so we decide to walk. Autumn weather is great for evening walks. The air is so fresh, even crisp. A light breeze plays with my hair — I run my fingers through it. I don't style it too often because it takes forever to do. I look down at the road and secretly glance at El. It's weird. Usually, we have no problem talking to each other, but not tonight. El is unexpectedly quiet. I guess he's always carried our conversations, and still, I don't really know anything about him. Everything he told me went over my head. *You should say something, Cassie. What should I say?*

I panic and ask somewhat sarcastically, "So you just bring your own popcorn to a party? Is this your thing?" *Great, Cass, why can't you be nice?* Honestly, I'm a little disappointed in myself. Elliot looks shocked with an open mouth. He immediately throws some popcorn at me. I giggle, feeling relieved. *He found it funny — It's my lucky day.* I pull the same face back at him.

"I get snacky," he says and shrugs his shoulders.

"Okay — okay! It's no big deal," I say defensively. I still can't believe I'm walking next to El. We were supposed to never see each other again but look at us now, walking along together. It's like I haven't seen him for ages. There aren't a lot of things that have changed for me, but I wonder about El. I don't feel comfortable asking why he changed schools.

I started going out with El right after I broke up with Jake partially because he'd go to a different high school. Now he's here. What was he thinking about? I can't even ask. It's a two-fold issue because I don't want to seem like I was the reason he switched schools. Even though I do. Moreover, he'd joke about me like, Oh, Cassie, would you like that I changed schools because of you? Or something like that.

I attempt to grab more popcorn, but Elliot takes the whole bag away. He takes a few and throws popcorn at me. I try really hard to catch them — we both laugh. There are moments you want to relive. Stay in. I guess this is it — Cinderella before the perfect storm. I don't know why I compare myself to Cinderella. Maybe I did it because I'm very nervous about seeing Jake. It's a pretty bold move. I'm surprised, even for me, this is too much, showing up like this (uninvited) at Jake's house after our weird conversation at the diner. *Hmm... Would he even care that I came?*

I slow down a little when I spot Jake's house — there are a lot of people. I'm not a popular girl, sometimes I wonder if people even notice me. I'm usually cautious in public. That's why nobody really knew that I was with Jake in the first place. Of course, his best friends probably knew about us. However, I doubt they even remember what I look like. Jake probably never even told them my name, which I was okay with. It was sort of what I wanted. I asked Jake if we could keep everything private until we'd know if it was going somewhere.

Look at me now. I'm about to walk into Jake's house, full of people, with a new guy. I glance at El. Should I be worried? I ask myself when I notice Katie entering the house. *Perfect blond hair, a cute little skirt, and a pink bomber jacket. Aaaaa! How can I even compete with that?* My heart pumps so hard, I can barely breathe. My face must have become so pale because El asks me, "Are you alright?" He looks worried.

"Oh, no! I'm fine, I was..." I say, feeling embarrassed. Elliot's eyes narrow, so I quickly add, "Of course, I'm fine. I was just waiting for you to finish your popcorn, weirdo."

He smirks in response. I didn't even care if he bought it or not. Do you know the moment when you have a feeling... No, not a feeling. The moment you straight up know something is a bad idea? Well, this is one of those times... I know if I go inside, it will make everything weirder.

"Oh yeah? Interesting," he says. Elliot walks to the neighbor's trash can and throws the popcorn bag away. I guess he knew I lied, or he knew it wasn't nothing. I don't understand why I reacted this way? It's not like it was a surprise to see Katie at Jake's house. She'd probably be surprised to see me there if she knew who I was. *Maybe it's all gonna be okay?*

"Is this better now?" he asks me, showing off his popcorn-free hands. I nod. *He didn't care. I'll take it — I like it.*

"Let's go," I say.

I don't like parties — especially big ones. For me, it's too many people. I prefer smaller hangouts, where you can actually talk to everyone. I decided I should just follow El's lead. From the second we came inside, El seemed like he "got" it. He drags me somewhere through the whole house. I think it's the biggest party I've been to — an endless amount of party cups with no food or snacks. As El drags me to the kitchen, I see Jake standing, surrounded by his friends. I attempt to look away before they notice me when our eyes meet. I nervously swallow and smile. Jake gives me a cold look — nothing else. *Is he mad that I came? Maybe I shouldn't have.* I run after El, faking happiness.

"Can I make you a drink?" he asks, even though it doesn't sound like a question.

"Sure," I say without paying attention. I glance over at Jake, mainly to check if he is still looking at me. And no, he wasn't. He wasn't waiting for me to give him a look. Instead, Jake's chatting away with his best friend Maison. I wonder if they are discussing me. *Nah, Jake wouldn't waste his time on that.* My eyes meet with Maison. I feel embarrassed and look away. Another hard look and I have a feeling Maison knows exactly who I am. Under different circumstances, I'd be thrilled. *Should I leave? They must have talked about me. They hate me.*

"Here you go!" El proudly announces. He snaps me out of my spiraling thoughts. I take the drink he offers with a smile. El stares at me, waiting for me to do something. I grimace and take a sip. I almost spit the second it hits my tongue. My eyes bug out so much they're ready to fall out. I put the cup down and cough.

"Omg, El, what the heck was that?" I ask, still coughing. El laughs.

"Five sodas mixed together! I call it a suicide," he says and shows me his blue-purple tongue.

"That's absolutely disgusting," I say, pointing at the cup. "It makes me want to scrape my tongue on the wall."

"No, it's not that bad," he says, giggling. "Show me yours!"

"I don't think so."

"Please-please-please," El begs. I roll my eyes.

"Okay," I say, showing my tongue, also a blueish-purple.

"Yeah, great job," El congratulates me.

We laugh when I catch Jake watching me. Jake shakes his head. I think he was waiting for my reaction, but I didn't give him the satisfaction. He leaves the room. I guess in a dream or a movie, this is the time when you run after the "love of your life" and tell him not to let you go, but I don't. Of course, I don't. I just can't. I feel a little bit disappointed — I really hoped for something more.

"It's kind of getting loud," El mentions.

"Yes, it is."

Elliot leans over the counter and looks out of the window.

"Pool?" he asks.

"Hell ya," I say.

I really need some fresh air — El leads the way. I grab a bottle of water. Surprisingly, the pool area is empty. I wonder if it's off the limits, or maybe it's too chilly for people to hang out there. Elliot already sits at the edge of the pool with his feet in it. I take my shoes off and touch the water.

"Omg… Are you kidding me!? It's absolutely freezing!" I almost scream.

"Oh, come on, you'll get used to it," he cheers me up. I try again.

"Nope, sorry," I say and sit next to him.

I watch the pool water ripple. I smile to myself because sitting by the water reminds me of the time at summer camp. It wasn't the best time of my life, but I felt alive. Not bored. I miss those times.

"We had a lot of fun, huh?" El says. I look at him, surprised.

"Yeah, it was actually a lot of fun," I admit. "I was just thinking about it."

El smirks. We get quiet again, which never happened to us at camp. It's weird to be around someone and just sit in silence. Elliot turns towards me. His eyes sparkle with happiness and hope. *Please, don't say anything silly. I don't want to think about this.*

"Cass, I need to talk to you," he says, staring directly into my eyes.

"Okay…" I say slowly. *It's not bad* — It could be anything. Talk about school or life. It could be anything.

"Cass, I..." he starts when we hear Jake's voice saying, "Hey you, guys."

Elliot and I look back as Jake comes closer. My heart trembles. I feel my cheeks start blushing. *Oh no, don't show your feelings… What is he even doing here?* El jumps out of the water.

"Jake," El says, shaking Jake's hand.

"Elliot."

Wait, what just happened? Do they know each other? I'm totally frozen.

This is great, just great, isn't it? My ex knows my other... My something? No, my nothing... Well, my fake boyfriend or? Anyways, this is fun.

"I hope I didn't interrupt anything," Jake says. El looks at me, expecting me to say something. I nervously swallow and turn to face them.

"It's fine," I say. El gives me a look like, girl, what is your problem? We were in the middle of something! Jake ignores our odd behavior.

"I actually need to talk to Cassie," he says. I turn to Jake, but before I have a chance to say or think about what to say, El says, "Umm, Cass..." He gives me a cold look. It freaks me out, and I reply without thinking, "It's okay El..."

"Okay," El says, putting his hands in his pockets. He looks pretty pissed. I'm trying not to look at him. I know I'm wrong in this situation, but it's too late now.

"Thanks," I say in a very apologetic way. *Is it working?* El ignores it, and I add, "It's not going to take too long. I'll find you ASAP."

Come on, El. He finally looks up at me and nods. *Is he mad? Well, he can't be mad at me. He just can't.* El walks away when Jake sits next to me. We wait until El gets inside in silence, then Jake gives me a hug.

"Hey, you," Jake says.

"Hey," I repeat after him. I fiddle with my curls.

"Is that him?"

"What?" I ask, confused.

"Your boyfriend..." he clarifies. He narrows his eyes, looking very suspicious. I guess I should tell him the truth about El. I start, "Oooh yeah, El... he's..."

"I actually don't care," Jake interrupts me. I stop playing with my hair and look straight into his eyes.

"Okay. Where is this going, Jake?" I ask. I think I sound cool, as if I'm totally over him. In my head, I'm begging Jack not to say something stupid. Loving him hurts more than suffering from a breakup, and I don't enjoy suffering. *His eyes are so pretty...*

"I was thinking about what happened at camp," he says, "and seeing you here now... I want you to know I really like you, Cass."

I shake my head. No-no-no, he can't be serious. It's just a little too late.

"I think I wasn't clear about how serious I felt about you," he continues. "I know you've moved on, but I just wanted to let you know."

I nod silently because I just don't know what to say.

"I hope it's not late for me to ask," he drags it out. My heart is about to jump out of my chest. This is what I wanted, isn't it? *I feel my eyes get watery. Please, don't cry. Just don't cry. Bottle it up. Hide it somewhere, somewhere deep.* He continues, "Could you give me... us another chance?"

I don't say anything. My hair falls in front of my face. He has a girlfriend, Cassie, don't forget about Katie. He moves my hair away and asks, "Cass?" I look at him, and my heart seizes. We stare at each other. Jake slides over, gently grasps my chin, he kisses me. I instinctually kiss him back. *His lips are so warm. Oh no! Not this again.*

I stop and push Jake away. "Oooh, yeah. I'm sorry, I just have to go," I tell him.

I stand up and dart away, hoping I can escape before Jake says something. Then, maybe we can pretend this never happened.

"Cass! Stop!" Jake yells. I stop. *What am I doing?* He says, "Think about it, and let me know, okay?"

It's okay... of course, it's not okay! I look back at him. His eyes light up with hope. *Oh no! Why did I turn around? Now he knows I care. No-no-no.*

"I'll think about it, but I'm not making any promises," I say with a sad smile. "Deal."

The goal is to find El as fast as possible, but there are so many people around. I dart inside, trying to spot him. Okay, it's okay. Jake likes me, and I like Jake. However, it can't work. It can't. *He's supposed to be with Katie! Why start something you know is gonna be done in a month or two. There is no reason.* I should just find El and take my brain off this...

Where are you, El? Especially when I need you. I stand in the middle of the room, surrounded by strangers. I keep looking around, feeling pretty lonely. It's the worst when you feel like you don't belong. It seems like there must be a person you can talk to when you're surrounded by so many people. I think El has already left. *It's time for me to get out of here as well. Maybe I'll find El.* With those thoughts, I leave the party.

As I run out of Jake's house, I see El walking away. I follow after him.

"Hey, you!" I shout, but he keeps walking. I frown. *That's rude — hmm... I'm pretty sure he can totally hear me. I need something bold to get him to stop.* I smirk and yell at him, "Wait for me. I know you can hear me, Elliot!"

I make sure to emphasize his full name, Elliot. He stops right away, which makes me smile. I knew it'd work — like magic! The only thing I remembered about El is that he hates when people call him by his full name. It makes him so angry. He told me why, but I don't recall the specifics at all. Probably, I should pay more attention to what people tell me. I take this opportunity to catch up with him.

El shakes his head and says, "Shouldn't you be inside, with Jake or whatever?" This is a lot of attitude coming from him. I guess it's what I should have expected. Would I be happy if Jake did it to me? No, of course not. It's so not cool of me.

"El... Let me explain, it's nothing..."

Elliot turns around and stares at her with a lot of anger. Oops, I didn't expect him to get angry at me.

"No, you know what... I was in the middle of something over there. And now," El firmly says, "I know you just don't care."

This is getting too real, but I don't say anything. Just look down, a little embarrassed. I didn't expect him to see through all of this.

"It's not how it looked, El. I'm sorry," I say. I hear El sigh.

"It was a pretty low move, calling me by my full name, Cass," he says. I smirk like — yeah, I know. El asks, "Do you actually want to hear what I wanted to tell you?"

I look up — anger has already disappeared from El's face. I feel very relieved. He takes my hand. Something is about to happen, and my heart starts pumping. Here we go.

"Of course, I do," I say, trying to make my voice sound as caring as it can be. When I get in trouble at school, my parents always help me out. They're great at smoothing any conflicts. Not like me. I'm always told that I should show people some compassion, which is a real struggle. That's why I found that I'd be a bigger success if I pretended or straight up lied. It always makes everyone feel better.

"I really like you, Cass. I know you aren't over, Jake…" El starts. It hurts. The truth really hurts. I don't need anybody to point out the obvious.

"I am," I say firmly like I really mean it. "I'm so over, Jake." *LIE*.

"Please, don't. I'm not here to pretend or play games," El explains, "I like you a lot, but I can't do this… being in between you and him."

"I'm not in love with Jake or anything like that," I defend my honor. *DOUBLE LIE*. El smirks in response. He doesn't say anything. That smirk and the silent treatment drive me crazy. I just want to yell at him that even if he's right about my feelings, it doesn't mean he's figured me out. Even I don't have myself figured out. It makes me so mad.

"I had a lot of fun with you," I say, staring right into his eyes, "but I don't think I like you in that way. It has nothing to do with Jake."

How do you like honesty now? That's why honesty is not the best policy. I proudly giggle to myself. Elliot frowns. *Did I go too far?*

"Wow, Cass," he says, shocked.

"What?"

"So cold-blooded. Damn."

"Sorry…" I apologize. *I guess I went too far.* Surprisingly, he doesn't look hurt.

"Don't be," El says. *What is wrong with him?!* He continues, "I actually think it's the first real thing that's come out of your mouth since we met. And I like it." *Ha, it doesn't prove it's better to be honest with people. Nobody wants to hear the truth, but I believe this is the first time when someone liked me for me being me. Not the image I present to the public. I kind of like it.*

"What's next?" I ask.

"I'll take you home, silly," he says, "And by the way, I think you're wrong."

"About?"

"About you not liking me that way," El proudly announces. I laugh.

"Oh yeah?"

He grabs my hand without saying a word. I like that I don't have to explain everything to El. He gets the subtext. *I wish I could love him instead. It'd be so much easier.* El turns away and drags me away. We walk together in the middle of the road, laughing without any troubles — just young and reckless.

Chapter 7
Starting from the Beginning

I lie in my bed, staring at the ceiling. It's pitch dark. I hope Dr. Seuss was right, and the reason why I can't fall asleep is that reality is finally better than my dreams. I can't stop thinking about El. I don't even remember how we got to my house. We were chatting and chatting, and I didn't notice when we were already home saying bye.

Also, I didn't really have time to process Jake's kiss. Of course, it's not the first time we've ever kissed, but it's the first time it felt natural. It was a perfect kiss — I can still feel his lips on my lips. I turn over. *This is so annoying — I don't want to think about it. Why didn't El try to kiss me? Who am I? What am I doing?*

My phone lights up with a text notification. Maybe it's from El? I check it, and no, it's not El. It's Jake. I probably shouldn't be so disappointed because the most popular boy has just texted me something charming — **Good night. <3**

I smirk and put the phone away without texting back. I don't feel in the mood. *When did my life get so complicated? It's like I have two boyfriends. Well, two guys who like me.* My phone receives another notification. I pick it up, very unwillingly. I expect to read a new text from Jake when I notice it's from El instead. I'm so excited I sit up.

Sleeping?

I look out the window. It's a full moon tonight. If somebody asked me to describe how I felt at this moment, I'd say I don't know, but the amount of feelings and their intensity is enormous. However, it's not like I like-like El. He's just a distraction from Jake. He was, but not a distraction anymore. *What should I do?*

Obviously, I cannot come up with a solution by myself, so I decide to ask Ally and Louis for their advice. I asked them to meet me at the bleachers before school starts. It was one of my favorite places in middle school. I always walk up to the top because I love the view and how quiet it is in the morning.

Ally and Louis weren't that thrilled about it, but they did agree. So I decided to grab their favorite drinks from the coffee shop and came a little earlier. That's why I feel chilly now. I sip on my green matcha tea latte, which is the only reason I can still feel my fingers.

I spot Ally and Louis walking up to me. I pretend I don't notice them and stare at the sky. *Just be cool, Cass.*

"What's the emergency? If I climbed here for nothing," Louis complains.

"French Vanilla Latte with coconut whip cream?" I offer it to him very quickly, as if I hadn't practiced saying it the whole morning — Louis's eyes sparkle.

"Oh, my-my, Ally," Louis says, grabbing his cup. He smells it, "My favorite... This must be good! Please, tell me it's Ally's favorite — cinnamon hot chocolate?"

I nod in response and give another cup to Ally.

"Jackpot!" Louis exclaims.

Ally doesn't say anything. *I feel paranoid, as if Ally already knows all my secrets, all my lies.* I wait for them to sit down and get cozy.

"To make a long story short, this is my problem," I say, showing my phone with a lot of unanswered texts from El and Jake. Louis's eyes fire up with excitement, but Ally stays silent, which is weird. Ally is the most opinionated person I've ever met, and the fact she hasn't given me a lecture is stressing me out.

"Wow, girl, this is great!" Louis says.

"Great? I don't think so..." I respond, hiding how much I love to brag about my two guys. I glance at Ally, looking for some support. No reaction. I frown. Okay, this is super weird. What's up with that?

"How... when did this even happen?" Louis asks.

"It happened at Jake's party, right?" Ally asks. *How does she know? I haven't told them about the party yet.* I nod.

Louis stands up and shouts, "You went to the party!" I barely hear him. I still stare at Ally.

"How'd you know I was at Jake's party?" I ask.

"I ran into Elliot earlier," Ally replies with a smile.

"Why are we still talking about boys when Cassie went to the party without us?!" Louis says.

I smile, still thinking about El and Ally. *Since when are they friends? I wonder what he told her? Are they close?*

"Sorry, it's just," I say, but before I can finish, Ally adds, "You should have told me about El and you."

I guess El told her enough. I don't even know how to react. Ally's kind of pissed at me now.

"I wasn't ready, Ally," I say.

"Ladies, don't start a catfight over a man. None of them are worth it. And more importantly, I just can't wrap my mind around you going to Jake's party without us!" He tries to redirect the conversation again. "And we're still not talking about it?!"

"I know, I'm sorry, it just sort of happened," I explain to Louis, who listens to me closely. "El made me go. It wasn't planned. And then I ran into Jake — I just don't know what to do."

"Who are you gonna pick?" Ally asks directly.

I take my cup and look away. I'm shocked that Ally asked me that when she knows it's a hard decision. The whole reason why I'm even telling them everything is that I don't want to choose. It'd be great if they'd make the choice for me. I don't want to be responsible for breaking anybody's heart. I feel their looks on me, waiting. I shrug my shoulders.

"Come on... You had a crush on Jake for so long," Louis says, "and let's be honest, he's a hottie with a body."

"Yeah," I admit. "I always thought I'd pick Jake, but he replaced me so fast, after..." I stop before I spill the beans. I'm not ready to tell them about my "I love you" moment from this summer. I'd better give them something good. I continue, "I just don't know if I can trust him. Jake's not the type of person who thinks things through."

"So… Are you picking Elliot?" Ally asks.

"I don't know. Do I love him?" I ask myself, "I don't think so. Is he just a friend?"

I imagine El. *Are we just friends?* Our brain is so fascinating. It can take in so many different places, different times. And mine took me back to camp, where Elliot was leaning towards me for a kiss. I can feel his soft kiss on my lips. *Is he just a friend? I don't think so… Ahhh.*

"I think I like them both," I say. I glance at Ally and Louis to check their reaction. Oh boy, and it's not great. I quickly add, "But I can't date them both, so what should I do?" I can't believe I'm asking them for advice. It's crazy. Especially since Ally is upset with me.

"Easy. You should spend time with both of them, and then you can decide," Louis suggests. I glance at Ally — she gives me nothing. This is unbelievable.

"I like it, but what do you think, Ally?" I ask her. It's time for you to let me know what you really think. Ally takes a slight pause and then asks, "I guess it makes sense, Louis. But I wanted to ask you, Cass. Didn't you spend a lot of time with both at the summer camp?"

Louis rolls his eyes at Ally, who looks so smug. I nod. It's not like she's wrong. I had enough time to figure out my feelings, but the situation was totally different.

"I guess I did," I say.

"Not like that! Summer is over. Just hang out with both of them. Casually," Louis supports me, "If you know what I mean. Seriously, don't overthink it."

"Yeah," I say. "I like it. I like it a lot. I need to text them." I grab my phone and text Jake. Louis is absolutely right. Summer is over. I need to start from the beginning with both of them, and it won't take too long to figure out who I like. Well, love.

"Oh, I just really want this for me. Drama and stuff…" Louis says, giving Ally a squeeze.

"Or you can meet someone you actually like and date them instead." Ally says. I pretend I'm too busy texting, and it totally goes over my head. I think I'm disappointed with Ally. She usually tells me everything straight, which is super annoying — not this time.

"And what, Ally? Get married? Eww…" Louis makes fun of her. "How old are you? Are you even alive? Cass, you have to back me up on this."

"No, no! Please, leave me out of it," I say, showing I'm done texting, "Done. Let's go?"

I sent a message to both Jake and El — **Hey! Want to do a Movie/Picnic night?**

"Oh, yeah, it's time," Ally stands up, avoiding eye contact with me. She really disapproves. I think it's the very first time Ally gives me the silent treatment. I glance at Louis. He nods. At least Louis doesn't judge me, and he's helpful. We walk down the bleachers.

"You must keep me posted on this," Louis whispers to me.

"Of course," I say, giving him a thumbs up.

Chapter 8
S.O.S.

Definitely, today isn't a great day for classes. I've been daydreaming the whole day. I already lost count of endless scenarios — me being with Jake, then me being with El. Sometimes my imagination takes me to where I break up with one of them and start dating the other. Yes, those scenarios are absolutely taken from the trashiest romance fanfiction. The kind you can only get online because, let's be real, it's too shameful to buy it in stores. And yes, I'm living them.

I look out the window, thinking about strolling along the beach with El and Jake. All together, walking barefoot on the sand. They are waiting for me to make a decision when suddenly I feel someone tapping me on the shoulder. I turn, wiping my eyes, so I look a bit more awake. It's Ally, and of course, she notices me being dreamy. I think dreamy is a good description. However, I'm really excited that Ally came around. She's ready to be my friend again and help me choose.

"Hey, I actually wanted," I trail off when I see Ally's stern look. It's pretty disappointing. It's like she doesn't want anything to do with me — at all. *What's she up to?* And as I thought that, Ally gives me a piece of paper.

"From Elliot," she says and goes back to taking notes.

"Ally..."

"Later," Ally shuts me down. I nod and then turn away.

I stare at the note — it's just a tiny white square, still warm. I stare at it as if my life depends on it. I nervously swallow — should I open it or not? Why does El have to make everything more complicated? If he sent me a text, I could have read it and forgotten about it. *What can it be?*

I finally open the note. It says, **Movie/Picnic tonight at 6 pm?** I feel relieved, it's charming, and it doesn't put me on the spot of picking a boyfriend. *Did I say, boyfriend?* I guess I'm excited to have a boyfriend. However, it's not going to last, so what's the point? We're all going to different ways after school anyway, and I'm not planning on my first boyfriend to be the love of my life. I look over my shoulder and see El. He's staring at me and waiting for an answer. *Yeah, not the love of my life material. Great.* I shake my head, acting as if I'm very disappointed to say no.

"Not tonight, homework," I whisper. El rolls his eyes at me as the school bell rings. I ignore it because it's the last class, and I'm happy to go home, where nobody will distract me from dreaming and studying. I'm not like your typical straight-A student. My grades aren't perfect, but they're pretty good or good enough to get into a decent college.

"Too bad," El says, walking by. "See you."

"See you."

I wait for Ally and Louis to pack their stuff in silence. It's awkward, so to break the silence, I show the note to Louis.

"Omg, this is so romantic," he says as we walk out of the classroom.

"I'll catch up with you, guys, later," Ally says out of nowhere.

"Oh," I say, surprised. We always walk from school together. She must be very upset.

"I have a thing," she explains. I nod.

"Okay, see you," Louis says in a very casual manner. *Not a big deal.*

"See you," Ally says and walks away. I nod, but I don't say anything, so she knows I'm not okay with all of this. Louis puts his arm over my shoulder.

"Let's roll," he says. We walk the opposite way. I'm pretty sure Louis is hugging me to make me feel better about Ally. And it's working.

"Do you think she is... Gonna be okay with me?" I ask.

"I don't think you should be worried about it right now," he says. I frown.

"That's a weird thing to say," I say, puzzled until I glance at Louis and notice Jake approaching.

"Hey, you," Jake says and gives me a hug, "I got your text..."

"Oh, yeah," I say. Both of them look uncomfortable. "Jake, this is my friend Louis, Louis..."

"Jake," he says simultaneously with me. I give Louis a what-are-you-doing look. Louis shrugs his shoulders.

"So yeah, Cass, I've got to run," Louis says, walking away. "See you."

"Yeah, LU-EE. See you," I say with a snobby smile, and then I look back at Jake. He seems very confused about what is going on. I apologize, "Sorry, Jake. I'm not sure what you're doing today, but we can always try to, you know..."

I mumble. I hate when it happens. Whenever I'm around Jake, like ninety-nine percent of the time, I totally lose my train of thought. Then he starts bossing me around — *do this, do that.*

"No-no-no. I have a game today. You should come," Jake suggests. I'm a little taken by surprise, and my eyebrow rises. *Game? Ahhh.... I thought this was behind us. What am I supposed to do at a game? Watch him? Am I really that girl because I hate that girl.*

"What?" he continues. I can't stop my glorious eye roll. Jake knows very well how much I hate the idea of being his personal cheerleader at his games.

"You didn't like the idea of us having a movie/picnic night?" I ask him. "I was thinking about... something more like — me and you, you know?"

"Yeah, it's game night, as you know," he explains, "and we can hang out after, with everybody."

Jake is taking a stand. He never had an issue with me not hanging out with his squad. He adds, "Unless there is a problem."

I smirk. Of course, there is a problem — I don't want to go because football is boring, but, of course, I can't say that, and I have to come.

"No, of course, not," I deny all Jake's accusations. "What time is the game anyway?"

"Six."

"Hmmm..." I mumble, making my not-excited face. I can't believe I'm about to agree to go to a game.

"Hey, I don't want to sneak around like we did at the camp," Jake says. "You should come."

It feels like a test. He really wants to make a point out of this situation. *Ah, should have texted El.* At least, a picnic and a movie sound more exciting to me.

"I'll be waiting," he adds. *You're killing me, Jake.* I nod.

"Okay," I say, lacking any enthusiasm. "I'll be there."

"See you then."

He gives me a hug. I do the only thing a person can do, which is smile. Jake doesn't notice anything fishy, or he decided not to notice. I definitely see how fast he left, so I don't have time to change my mind. Maybe that's why we didn't work out. We're just two different people who like each other. We sound great on paper, but you know who sounds even better on paper? Jake and a cheerleader — like Katie.

I'm not jealous. I'm just realistic. Katie is a perfect fit, and I'm not. She doesn't need to do anything extra. She's always at the games. They practice on the same field as the football players — she knows their routine. I have to learn all of it, and I also have to be okay with wasting my time at football games. *How many do they even have in a school year?* With that thought, I start wandering away back home. *Do I really have to? Ugh... Football. I wonder if Ally and Louis can come with me? Louis would probably like it. If only for the boys, to be fair, I should like football with that logic. So annoying.*

I have too much on my mind. That's why the plan is to rush into my room like a storm. I'm not in the mood to explain everything to my parents. They would want to give their input. And I don't want to be the one to explain to them they've only dated each other. So they have no perspective, and I'm not about that. *One-two-three.* I open the front door and run for it.

Mom definitely notices me. I can't avoid her and say, "Hello."

"Hm," mom makes this noise when she isn't satisfied with my behavior, "food in thirty."

"Okay," I yell in response, but I'm already gone. We haven't discussed the party yet, so I wonder when that conversation will happen. I shut the door to my room. At least, my parents let me close the door to my room. They don't love it, but they never say anything. I drop my bag on the floor.

My phone buzzes so many times. I don't check it, just motionlessly sit at my desk. It's been a lot. I need a moment of quietness — no buzz, no talking, no stress — just me with no thoughts. The phone buzzes again.

"Oh, come on," I say out loud to myself. I stand up and grab my phone. There are a lot of messages from Jake and El. *This is ridiculous. Can't they leave me alone? Just for a second?*

I lie on the floor, staring at the ceiling. This is the way I meditate, I guess. Sadly, it's also the moment when I realize I actually need a friend. A real friend, who gets me, and I could share things… sort of open up. We'd lie down on the floor together, share our darkest secrets.

"Cassie!" mom yells my name. I hope it's in my head until she repeats, "Cassie!" followed by something indistinguishable.

I frown. It doesn't seem like normal mom behavior. I concentrate on hearing what she's talking about. It's almost impossible to understand anything she is saying.

"What's your name?" I can just hear her ask the question, then she shouts, "Cassie, Elliot came to see you!"

I sit up. My eyes open wide. *Wait, what?* Since when does he show up unannounced?

"Coming," I yell in response. I run down the stairs as if it's the Olympics.

El stands next to my mom, chatting away. It seems like they hit it off. But, I still don't like it.

"Hey, is this a good time?" El notices me.

"What are you doing here?" I ask with a forced smile. *Okay, it's going to be okay.* I just need to get rid of him, so I can go and see Jake. I wish I hadn't texted Jake first.

"Cassie, that's not nice," mom whispers to me as I come closer. I secretly roll my eyes.

"Sorry," I say. *I didn't mean it.* "So El, I'm shocked to see you — here. Right now." Mom totally gives me a judgmental look, but I ignore it.

"I thought we could go out to the open movie night thing," El says. "Remember I told you about it?"

"Well, that sounds just wonderful!" mom replies, excited.

"Mom!? I have homework," I remind her. *I can't believe that I have to remind her.*

"I know you've already done everything," she says, which is a hundred percent not true. The only thing I've done is lie on the floor, dreaming about boys.

"Well, it's just a couple of hours," El adds to mom's point. "You'll have a lot of time to get some work done later."

Both of them, mom and El, keep staring at me, which makes me absolutely uncomfortable. I wonder if that's why I say, "Sure. Give me five. I'll grab my bag and be back."

I walk away.

"Thanks," El whispers to my mom.

"I heard that," I say.

"So, how do you know each other?" I hear mom's voice echoing. *Oh, no-no-no. This is getting dangerous. I gotta be quick.* I run up the stairs and grab my bag, and dart back down as fast as I can. On the way, I grab my phone and text to the group chat with Louis and Ally — **SOS. Elliot at my house!**

This is a great excuse to make Ally interact with me. It's not my fault El is at my house. She must have seen me saying "no" to the date. Also, they don't know about Jake's date. I just don't get why she has to be this way. As I come closer to the entrance, I hear El talking his heart out about how we met.

"And you know, we met at the camp dance, and then," El says. *Nope. This is enough.* I jump in and give him a hug and a look, which says it all — don't tell my mom anything!

"So you met at the dance?" Mom continues asking questions.

"Yes, and we're leaving, mom," I say.

"Okay-okay! Since when can't I even ask a couple of questions," she mumbles, but just loud enough for me to hear. I ignore her, "Bye, mom. Love you." It's time to go. I push El lightly out the door.

We walk along the street without saying anything. *Should I say something? Does he think I was lying to him?* Every time I glance over at El, he is looking somewhere else. I bite my lip. It's super frustrating. Suddenly, El's eye catches mine. He doesn't look away. Neither do I, but the whole situation is making me very uncomfortable.

"What?"

"Nothing… Are you hiding me from your parents?" Elliot asks. I shrug my shoulders.

"Nah, it's just… they're my parents," I say, "and they want to know everything. Sometimes I want some 'me' time, you get it right?"

"Well, I hope I didn't interrupt you from your 'me' time," he sends a wave of sarcasm my way. I giggle, but I start wondering whether I will be able to get rid of him before the game.

"Well, my dad is a musician, so he travels a lot," El explains, "and when he's at home, we mostly practice playing guitar and stuff. Everything else isn't interesting for him." I look at El again. I guess I can see a musician in him, mainly by the stylish leather jacket he's wearing.

"So you play music?"

"I'd say so," El says. I know him well enough to notice he's being modest. I stare at him.

"What?" He asks. I laugh before I can reply — my phone buzzes. I immediately check my pockets. *Where is it? Did Louis and Ally reply?*

"I guess I didn't know that much about you," I say, trying to be casual.

"Well, now you have time to find out more," he cheekily says when my phone buzzes again. I smile and nod. Finally, I found it. I check. It's a couple of messages from Ally and Louis and a few from Jake. *Should I answer? What if El will notice?*

"You can answer your phone," Elliot says, "I don't care."

"It's nothing," I reply dismissively. The phone buzzes again — great timing. I check it out, and it's another of Jake's texts — **Can't wait to see you tonight.** I frown.

"Doesn't seem like nothing, huh?" he notices. *I should probably answer. I promised Jake to come. I probably should text Louis and Ally too. Wait, what if... I have a plan!*

"Okay, just give me a second," I say and stop, "I'll quickly reply."

Elliot nods. I text to the group chat first — **Meet me at the game tonight. SOS!!!**

The plan is to make everyone come to the game with me. Then, at least, I won't have to suffer alone. And Ally and Louis can play distraction for me.

"Sorry," I apologize and put the phone away, which makes Elliot pretty happy.

"No worries..."

He doesn't say anything else. I really need to ask if it's okay for us to go and watch the game. Since El knows Jake, and he probably knows Jake is a quarterback. It's not a good time to bring it up, but here we go.

"El... Actually, I forgot about something," I carefully start, "I wonder if we can go to see the football game instead?"

Elliot frowns and prods, "I'd never guessed you were a football fan."

"No-no-no! It's not for me..." I explain, "Louis is a big fan, and wouldn't it be nice for you to hang out with my friends?"

My statement takes Elliot by surprise. It was a perfect excuse. I just need to remember to tell Louis that he's a football fan now.

"No, you're right," Elliot says. "Sounds good, but you owe me one."

"Thanks," I say. Elliot nods and hugs me. I start blushing. *Why am I feeling so happy?*

Chapter 9
Finally Myself

My plan might just work. However, doubt shadows my face like a single dark cloud creeping across the sky on a cloudless day. I make myself feel a little bit more confident because Ally and Louis agreed to come as well. It's such a relief they'll be there. Ally and Louis will distract him if needed, and the best part is that I don't even need to ask them. I will meet them by our lockers to thank them and tell them just enough information for me to have a double date. After the game, I can tell them all that I'm pretty tired and want to go home. The second I'd get a chance, I'll sneak out and join Jake and his friends.

I honestly think El could have been the most popular guy in school if Jake had already graduated. El is easy to talk to. That's why I like hanging out with him. It hasn't been that long, but everyone already loves El. Everyone wants to know him, sometimes I wish I had a personality like that, but it seems like a lot of work. I've never tried to find friends — people come and go. That's why Ally and I are friends. She's always stayed with me. No matter what. I think I'm used to it now, and I don't want anything to change.

"Hey, can you go and save us a spot?" I ask Elliot with a smile, "I've got to meet Ally and Louis first. I'll be right back. Okay?"

"Yeah, no worries."

"Thanks," I say. El still holds my hand. I look down and add, "See you in a second."

I walk away. When I'm about to turn right, I glance over my shoulder to see him again. He was already gone. I really thought he'd be waiting for me. My phone buzzes. *Oh no! It must be Ally and Louis!* I run.

They're already there, but they don't see me right away. *This is weird.* I frown — it looks like they're fighting. However, they don't sound angry. I see Louis shaking his head and saying something like, "Crap, girl! No, no, no."

"Hey, guys! So happy you're here!" I say, hugging Ally. They don't say anything in response. So, I glance at them both. I ask, confused, "Did I miss something?"

"Not at all!" Ally announces, "We're really excited to find out what happened?" They still glare at each other as if they were in a staring contest, and I can't tell who's winning.

"Let's go," I say, "El is waiting for us outside! I'll explain later."

I don't know what is up between Ally and Louis, but we don't have time for it.

"Absolutely," Ally says. I wonder why Louis is so quiet.

"Elliot should save us some spots."

We walk as quickly as we can. Partially, I think that must be because none of us want to talk about it. Also, I'm trying to concentrate on my two dates, and I don't need more issues to solve. However, Louis makes it very difficult to ignore the look he's giving me. It's about forty minutes before the first game of the year, but a lot of people are already here. It's more than I expected to see.

I can barely breathe. I feel like my heart is ready to stop. I'm excited to see Jake as well. Many people are holding posters of our school team and mascot. A lot of the posters have Jake's name written on them. I wonder if Jake thought I'd do the same.

Three of us walk outside. I look around.

"There he is," Ally tells me. She spots El before I can find Jake, so I wave at Elliot with a smile. We rush up the bleachers.

"Hey, again!" El says to me. He adds, looking at Louis and Ally, "Hey, guys!"

"Hey, El. Louis, I don't know if you remember me," Louis introduces himself.

"Oh yeah, man," El replies and shakes Louis's hand.

"Nice to finally hang out," Louis can't stop talking. I'm pretty sure he's nervous being around Elliot, which usually doesn't happen. Like ever. Louis attempts to be friends with Elliot.

"The same."

As we finally decide to sit, Ally tries to sit next to Elliot, but Louis doesn't let her and sits there instead. He gives Ally a judgmental look, which I usually find very suspicious, and I usually start asking questions. Not this time. This time I let it slide because I carefully observe the football field, trying to find Jake.

Nobody says anything, and it's kind of awkward. Elliot glances at me, I should start a conversation, so everyone can be a part of it. I would, but I still can't spot Jake. I want him to see me here, maybe get a little bit jealous...

"So I've heard you're a big fan, huh?" Elliot says to Louis, who has a tough time hiding how confusing the question is for him.

"What?" Louis asks.

"That you're a big football fan?" Elliot replies.

Louis glances at me like *Cassie, what is wrong with you? At least give me a heads up when you're going to lie.* He wasn't wrong. I totally forgot to tell him about his new hobby.

I interject, "Of course, that's the whole reason we're here!"

I finally spotted Jake. He's warming up and casually chatting with Katie. *Usual. Oh, Jake, you'll never change... I'm not jealous.* It's just ridiculous to ask me to come, so he can flirt with her. Just date her already, I think, and I totally forget El and Louis are still there. I look over and add, "For the boys, right?"

Louis takes a second as if he can't believe I've just said that but replies, "Ah, yeah! Honestly, Elliot, I don't care about football... but BOYS." His voice fades out partially because I'm being a witness of Katie putting her hand over Jake's shoulder. The worst is that he lets her. She's totally flirting with him, or am I crazy? He always does this to me, so frustrating. It doesn't matter.

"Yeah, right, Cass," Louis says. I nod, looking down. Louis notices Jake and Katie and gets off my back. He gives me that surprised look like he wants to scream at me, *"OMG, have you seen that?!"* I shake my head and roll my eyes.

It gets windier. I guess the summer is officially over. It's not too bad during the day, but evenings feel so much cooler. I shiver a little when Elliot takes off his jacket and puts it on me.

"Oh…thanks," I say, a little surprised. El smiles. I put my hand on his shoulder, just like Katie did. I am pretty sure Jake saw it. I hope he did.

"Let's take a selfie?" Ally suggests while we're staring at each other.

"Sure, why not," I say as the four of us slide closer together. Ally holds the phone, trying to get everyone in. I look at Jake quickly. He's still talking to Katie. I roll my eyes. *I can't believe it. No, wait. Yeah, I totally believe it.* Ally counts, "One, two, three." I put my head on El's shoulder, and this time I know, Jake has noticed me. I did that right when he was looking my way.

At least, I got back at him, but it doesn't make me feel great. This is not how this should be. However, it's Jake, which means it's exactly what I should have expected. I frown. *This is ridiculous — Jake will never change. It's just a waste of my time, and stop hoping for a fairy tale.* I quietly say, "Do you guys want to get out of here?" I'm pretty sure nobody heard me except El.

"Yeah, of course," he says and tells Ally and Louis louder, "guys, do you wanna get out of here?

"Oh yes," Ally says. Louis nods as well and supportively states, "Of course, I'm a little disappointed, but alright. There are gonna be so many more games."

"Let's roll," El says. We all stand up and move through the crowd. The game is about to start. That's why people aren't that happy we're walking by. I glance towards Jake the last time. He stands next to Katie, and both of them stare at us. Well, me. I don't look away. It's not like I started this. Jake shakes his head and joins his team at the run almost right away. And there is always something more important than me.

This is the last time I'm looking at Jake's back. I just need to move on, and I am moving forward. Decided.

I'm extra quiet. We walk together, weirdly in silence. I guess everyone is in their own thoughts. Even Louis has never been so silent. He's usually the soul of any party or hang. I wish I could talk to him, but it's getting harder and harder not to think about Jake. What is it about him, which drives me absolutely crazy? When he looks at me… I want to kiss him. I want to be with him. However, I can't just take a leap of faith and give him my heart. I did it once… So yeah,

I'm not going to make the same mistake again. I'm smarter than that.

As we're walking away, almost all of our school loudly cheers for our team. It sounds like Jake made a touchdown. At least, the first game is going well. I guess, but it hurts. Am I really not worth losing a game? I know that's selfish, and deep down, I'm happy nothing can throw Jake's game off. He works very hard to be the best. *Hmm... Did he even notice I left? Did he care at all?*

We come to the parking lot. Honestly, I don't even remember how we got there. I look in the sky. The sun comes out of clouds, which usually makes me smile. Not today, though. Even a bright sun seems so dark? I feel a huge wave of sadness catching up with me. El glances at me as if he wants to know what's next.

"Okay, guys, I'm gonna go home," I say.

"Okay," Ally agrees. El looks very confused and shakes his head.

"Wait, what?" El asks, "Come on, it's not even late."

"We have nothing else to do," I explain to him.

"Technically, something is going on. I've got a plan," El proudly announces. "Let's walk to my car near your house."

"Where are we going?" I ask.

"Surprise," El says and winks at Louis.

We start walking towards El's car. I didn't know he had a car. I haven't even started getting a permit, but what's the point of having it if I can't drive by myself until next year. *Hah, that means El is a year older than me. Interesting.* I wonder what car Elliot drives. *We should have driven here instead.*

"Here it is," El says and points to a red Jeep Wrangler. "Get in, guys."

Honestly, it's pretty cool. My parents always had boring economy class cars, so this is kind of fun. I don't really care where we're going now. Ally rushes to sit in front, next to El, which is also unusual. Louis and I are in the back seats. My eyes sparkle when El drops the top of the Jeep. El turns on the navigation, and I realize we're going to my favorite place, the beach! We're going to the beach!

We drive, and there is something very freeing to travel with the top down. I can feel the wind. I notice Ally gives El so many looks, which he just ignores. *I wish Jake would ever do that. I really need to stop thinking about him.* I glance at Louis.

"Let's do something crazy," I tell Louis and grab his hand. We raise our hands in the air, and we start giggling together. My hair goes crazy, with no thoughts and pure freedom. I stand up and arch back, staring at the night sky and a few stars. It's beautiful.

"Omg, Cassie," Louis says. I shake my hair, and it feels great. He carefully joins me. I love that about Louis. He doesn't overthink things. He always supports my crazy ideas. *Sometimes I wish I could be more like him. He doesn't care about what other people think or say about him. He lets himself go loose. I believe he thinks I'm just like him. That's what I call having an imagination. I pretend in the moment I am that way as well.*

"Just be careful," Elliot tells us. His voice sounds concerned, which I find very cute.

"We're free!" Louis screams against the wind.

Louis and I help each other to sit down. All my problems feel like they've been swept away by the wind. Maybe that's why I hug Ally from behind. I know she didn't expect it.

We park by the beach. El helps me to jump off the car. It's even chillier by the ocean. I look around and close my eyes. The air is so fresh. I might just get drunk on it.

"Oh, we're right on time," El says and grabs my hand. He brought us to the bonfire party — it's pretty incredible. I have never been at one. I have heard about it before. My interest was limited because I never thought I could be here. El says hi to a lot of people, and it's definitely not his first time here.

"I've been here a couple of times this summer," he explains.

"I see. This is pretty cool," I say. The wind becomes stronger. I glance at El — I should probably give his jacket back. It's getting freezing, and I don't want to get him sick. So I start taking it off and add, "Let me give it back."

"Oh, don't worry about it."

"Are you sure?"

"Absolutely."

I guess that's what happiness means. It's being surrounded by people who enjoy your company. I notice there are about thirty people, but I don't know anyone else. Everyone comes up to El, shaking his hand, giving him hugs. *Is he popular? Wait, that can't be, right? Or can it?* I take my shoes off, staying a little bit further away from the crowd. *Am I trying to get his attention now? Was I wasting my time to get Jake while El was here all along? Who is that?* A random girl comes up to Elliot and gives him a kiss. *No-no-no! I'm not going to fall into the same trap. El isn't Jake. He's always been interested in me — only me.* As I'm thinking about that blondie, El finally remembers about me.

"Hey."

"Hey."

"Are you okay?" he asks.

"Yeah," I say as if I don't understand what he's implying. "Why?"

El shrugs his shoulders, "I don't know, let's go and join everyone."

"Okay..."

"Cass, sometimes I really don't know what's going on in your head."

Honestly, neither do I, but that's a totally different story, not for next time, though. We all sit around the bonfire. I don't end up next to El. By my own choice. I sit next to Louis — it's safer. I'm not desperate. A couple of other girls and guys join us around the fire. One guy passes a guitar to Elliot. I think his name is Alec or Alex. *Hmm...I should start remembering peoples' names.*

Growing up, my parents have always read me a lot of fairy tales. I don't even remember if I liked them back then. Later, of course, I was watching Disney movies non-stop. Not anymore. Why? It's just not realistic. At least, that's what I told myself over and over — not realistic. However, my heart totally drops when El starts playing the guitar. I guess I'm not Cinderella. *El is, and I'm the prince, who is blown away. Kind of unfair.*

I put my head on Louis's shoulder, but I can't take my eyes off Elliot. To be fair, nobody can. He is the center of attention, and the only thing I want is for him to look at me. I know it's stupid — I should probably take some time to find out how I actually feel before jumping into a new relationship. *However, isn't this the whole point of being young?* My eyes finally meet with El's. This isn't bad, and he knows it.

Now I understand why he didn't want to go to the football game. He's just not that type of a guy. But hey, I'm not your typical girl either. I guess it could work. Why not? It feels right, and I don't believe in "a perfect moment." Even though I could never imagine myself experiencing one, here I am...

"Hey," Louis brings me back down to reality. I look at him, realizing that he's been watching me. How long has he been spying on me? Okay, this is not the time for conspiracy theories. Just be normal.

"What's up?" I ask, trying to be nonchalant about it. Lou-Lou whispers to me, "If he's the one, you should probably talk to Ally about it."

I keep my face straight, but I can't stop thinking, okay, what the hell? Since I need written permission from Ally to date someone.

"Why?" I ask Lou.

Louis shrugs his shoulders and smiles mysteriously. Oh, no-no-no! That must be really bad because when your gay friend doesn't want to tell you the answer/gossip, you know that you're in deep shit. However, he gives me a hint, obviously looking at Ally. She can't take her eyes off El, just like me. I'd describe it as full of love, but when did that happen?

Oh yeah... Probably, when I told Ally I was totally okay for her to hit on Elliot. What was I thinking? I feel like the whole universe is turning on against me. It's so unfair because I don't know why it's doing that to me. What have I done wrong? I'm a nice person, not perfect. Still nice. I'm always trying to do the right thing, but it works against me. *Well, I guess I have to deal with this....Ugh.*

"Hey, do you wanna take a walk with me?" I ask Ally. *Who asks that? I'm so weird sometimes. Why can't I be normal?* It's hard to avoid looking straight at her. I just wish I hadn't said anything about El. Then, I wouldn't be in such a weird situation.

"Of course!" she says and puts her s'more down. She sounds pretty excited. *Ugh...I don't like bringing people bad news.* I don't want to hurt anybody, which is incredibly difficult. How can anybody be perfect all the time? I honestly believe it's not realistic...

We start walking away in silence. The ocean is so beautiful and calm tonight — the full moon reflects on the water. It's definitely getting close to the wintertime because it gets dark so quickly. *Yeah, I'm analyzing the weather, so I won't have to talk to Ally. She deserves better, you know. I don't know how to be her friend. She picked me to be her friend. I wish she wouldn't.* I notice Ally glancing at me with confusion in her eyes. I don't blame her, I'm supposed to start the conversation, but I don't even know where to start.   It's just uncomfortable—a hundred percent.

"So, what's up?" She breaks the silence. I feel so relieved that I didn't have to.

"I just wanted to tell you," I start, but I don't want to finish that sentence. I feel so hopeless. Ally is so lovely. I have to be brave — just be brave, Cassie. Isn't it what your parents always tell you? Be bold, and be kind. It's definitely easier to say than to do.

"Is this about, El?"

O-M-G. SHE KNOWS! How does she know? Am I that obvious? I look at Ally. I'm absolutely terrified. However, she doesn't look mad. Not mad at all. *What game is she playing? And if I had to put my finger on it, I'd say her voice sounded full of... pity. Does she feel sorry for me, or is it about El?*

"It's okay, you know," she adds, " from the first time I saw him, then your reaction... I've noticed you have a history."

It makes me feel a bit better about bringing her "bad news," and I apologetically say, " I'm sorry, Ally. I totally underestimated the thing with... Elliot. I truly didn't mean to."

Before I could finish my sentence, she cuts me off, "Oh, you pick him?" She sounds surprised. What did she expect? I can't pick Jake because he isn't a choice anymore. I'm not going to make the same mistake over and over — I'm not stupid.

"Yeah, I made my mind up," I mumble, feeling ashamed of myself. I know I've been exploring my options, but as Lou-Lou says, "it's the normal course of discovering yourself." Unfortunately, I don't quite remember what exactly he said. I think he'd say something like that. At least, I hope it's what he would say.

Suddenly, Ally stops and stares at me. *Is she going to punch me?* I'm mentally prepared to close my eyes and take it. But, instead, she gives me a hug out of nowhere. When she squeezes me, I realize how wrong I am about Ally. She's so nice. Too nice. Why does she keep hanging out with me? I'm not even half as nice. *Crap.*

"Hey, I'm so happy for you," she says and lets me go.

"Thanks," I awkwardly whisper. *If only she knew what I was thinking... I don't think she'd be my friend anymore.*

"I'm just happy you made a choice, you know."

The weirdest part is that she means it. Even though she has a crush on Elliot, she's actually happy for me. That's pretty insane.

"Yeah, I know. I just..." I can't even finish, but I'm not going to keep it inside me anymore, "I'm sorry I didn't tell you the whole story. I didn't think it'll come up, and things were happening so fast. And honestly, when El showed up at the school out of nowhere? I mean, who does that, right?"

"I'd say it's kind of romantic, though."

"It is, but I thought we were clear that it was just... We weren't supposed to be serious."

"Well, maybe it's a good thing. You seemed a little tense during the game."

I know what she's referring to. *Was she watching me at the game?* I'm not stoked about that. The more people know, the more they can use against me.

"Oh, yeah. Jake," I say, staring at Ally. I watch her every move. She is playing some kind of game. It really bores me, "It's over. For sure. Have you seen Katie flirting all over Jake? And he was happily eating it up. I couldn't believe my eyes. It's like, why invite me if you're going to flirt with another girl, right? Finally, I can't take it anymore."

"But you do like-like El, right?"

"What do you mean?"

"You are serious about him?"

"Of course," I reply, a little irritated, I might add, "I made my mind up."

"That's great. I just want to make sure because El is better than just being used as bait," she says. That hurts! I can't believe Ally could even think that way about me! She doesn't even know El that much. Or does she? I should find out more about that.

"It's not like that."

"I know. It's more like food for thought."

"Yeah, totally get it," I say, but in my mind, I'm more like, "What the hell, Ally? So much judgment! Aren't you supposed to be on my side or at least pretend that you are? I'm doing it, and it's not that hard."

"A-ll-y!!" I hear Lou-Lou's voice. Oh, Louis, you're my hero today. We both look back and see Lou-Lou waving at us. "Come here!"

That's a relief. I need a second to process all of what happened — Ally giggles when she sees Lou-Lou. If I wasn't so pissed at her, I would be totally giggling with her. Louis is holding five sticks of s'mores. I'm pretty sure he wants Ally to take a picture of him. She is like a pro, taking perfect pictures.

"Let's go!" she cheerfully says.

"I actually want to take a second to clear my mind."

"Really?"

"Yeah, I need a second, and I'll be right back. It's so peaceful here."

"Okay, but you know what? You're missing out," she says, pretending to take pictures of me. Yep, I don't want to laugh, but I can't help it.

"Ally, please stop. It's just too funny."

"Okay…"

I smile, but the second she walks away, I feel so empty. *Why did she say that? Am I missing something? Maybe, she's right — and everything I do is just about getting back at Jake?* I come closer to the ocean and sit down on cold sand. I can finally breathe. *I felt like I was so close to putting the whole "Jake thing" to rest. But, of course, Ally must ruin it. Why did she say, "It's not the time to doubt myself. I'm going to be okay. I don't even know if El still wants to be with me. It seems like there are a lot of girls interested in him. Maybe he's already moved on. Who knows?*

"Hey, you!" I hear El's voice nearby. My heart starts beating. It feels like it's trying to get out of my chest like a bird attempting to escape its cage. I can't take a break today. From one rollercoaster to another. Elliot adds, "What are you doing here, alone?"

"Just hanging out. Thinking, nothing special."

El sits right next to me, "What are you thinking about?"

"How hard life is, you know. And life, in general."

"Life...That is so specific, Cass!"

We both laugh — it's so easy to talk to El because he's actually listening. I never have to explain things to him. With Jake, it always goes the same way "why do you feel this or that way" followed by "well, how was I supposed to know?" And then, I want to yell at him, "Why do I have to explain everything to you?" It makes me mad even thinking about it, but sometimes I wonder whether we have the passion, which is lacking with El. I never want to yell at him. He doesn't even give me a reason to. Could I call that love?

"I dunno, I've just got a weird feeling..." I don't even know why I'm saying it. I'm not interested in having an honest conversation with him.

"What is it?"

"It's nothing."

"Come on, it's okay," he calmly says, and I suddenly feel like I can be myself. Maybe, just for a few minutes, it can't hurt.

"It's like I'm going through life, and I'm just a passenger on a train," I start my confession, "Things happen, and I don't have any say. The train stops. Some people board, some people get off. I'm always there, sitting by myself. Just watch as the train passes countries, cities, people. And I'm just sitting and waiting for something to happen."

I glance at Elliot, and he's not judging me. He seems to get it. At least, he's trying to understand how I feel. That's why I continue, "But sometimes, I see myself doing things. It's not quite me, maybe evil me."

" I doubt it. You aren't evil, don't judge yourself so hard."

"Wait," I stop him, "It's like I'm watching myself from a distance. Often, I don't know who that person is. That person does things that are expected of me. But it's not me, you know. It's like being a stranger to yourself. I'm so sorry. I'm mumbling again about something silly…"

"Oh, no-no-no. I get it," El reassures me. I don't know why, but I believe him. It's the way he said it — there is so much pain hidden in his voice. You can't fake it. You have to feel it to know it.

"Are you… Have you ever felt yourself, then?" El asks. *When did this conversation become so real? I wish the answer would be easy. Have I ever felt myself? That's a good question. Damn, Elliot, you're good.* I look away. Maybe he wants to know who I actually am? Maybe. I've been here before, but perhaps I'm a little scared because I always feel like I'm stuck in somebody else's story. I'm a side character, who randomly pops by, so the main cast can lash out at me. I give them advice, they nod, listening very carefully. However, they already know what they are going to do. Not what I offer, they'll do something else — I'm like what the hell, but it always works out for them. But maybe, just maybe… This is the time I am myself because everything seems so clear like never before.

"I guess today," I say, "right now. It's like I don't have any other random thoughts."

When I say by random thoughts, what I actually mean is Jake. I haven't really thought about him or Katie. I glance at Elliot. His eyes are so warm and understanding. But, he also has that dark spot, hidden somewhere deep. Maybe he likes me because he thinks we're so similar. He thinks he knows me now. Lol. He has no idea who I am.

Nobody does. It all starts at school — it's the worst. All the teachers think they can just look at us and know whether we're worth their time or not. So smug. Sometimes they believe their students are idiots, but teachers aren't better than us. Because we have time.

However, I think we'll fall into the same trap. We'll be just like the teachers someday — putting people in boxes. Wrapping them, so they all look alike. When people do that to me, I always want to tell them, "Don't forget to tie a bow on top. I deserve it. I've been working so hard to please you." But I'm scared I'll end up just like them.

"Good, I like the person in front of me," Elliot stares at me. *Wait, I think he actually means it... Oh man, I want to kiss him. I really do.* We've kissed at the camp, but this is something different. How so? I don't want to kiss him to get attention from Jake or to forget Jake. It's not about him at all.

"Let's get out of here. Other people should also get a chance to spend time with the real Cassie," he says and stands up.

WTH? This is the moment for a kiss, so why doesn't he? What went wrong? Okay, I need to stop being so insecure. The guy switched schools for me. It's kind of weird and romantic. I wonder why he did that? I take his hand, and we run towards the crowd. It's like I'm in a Taylor Swift music video, and I don't want it to stop. I'm so happy.

Chapter 10
Back At Camp

Elliot and I sit on the dock. I put my legs in the water, moving them back and forth. I'm trying not to look at him while he patiently waits for me to start the conversation. *Why do we have to talk about it?* This is the second to the last day at the summer camp. It's almost over, just like us. We are over after this. I think it's obvious. However, I can't tell him directly.

Boys can do whatever they want, and it's totally okay. Look at Jake, for example. He can ignore my feelings, and when I broke up with him, he moved on immediately. However, when I started to see Elliot, the whole summer camp had been talking about that. Nobody wants to shame a guy, even though he is the one who didn't feel the same way.

And here I am, trying not to hurt a boy's feelings. He must have heard about Jake and me. I mean, there is a chance that he didn't, but I don't buy it. I already know the end result. Everyone is going to think I'm a terrible person. This is so tiring because girls can never win. If you're too nice, you're boring and plain. If you do what you want, you're a bitch.

Please, don't tell me it's not quite that because it is. You see, I've done the right thing before, and there is nothing good about it. I told Jake about my feelings, but honestly, I know for a fact he didn't want to hear it. We broke up. And then, as you know, I met El.

"So, what are your plans when you go back home?" El asks. I don't leave him a choice because I really don't want to tell him that he's just my summer fling. I wish I were a boy. They do it all the time. At least, Jake did.

"I don't know," I mumble, "I'm kind of excited to see my parents."

OMG. What is wrong with me? Parents? Really? I need to come up with a comeback, I've got to save myself, so I add, "Probably, meet with my best friends — Ally and Loui. Loui went to Paris this summer."

"Oh, that's so cool."

"Yeah."

Silence. This is so uncomfortable.

"What about you, El?"

He shrugs his shoulders, "I don't know. I thought maybe we could go to see a movie or..."

He notices that I'm not too thrilled about the idea. I'm trying really hard to make it simpler for both of us. We've been hanging out for a little over a week. There is no way he thinks we're serious.

You see, Jack and I is an entirely different story. I've been into Jake forever. I used to always imagine how it would be like to be with him, date him. Even before he knew me. We had a story, which shouldn't have ended like that... I guess I can't predict everything. Well, I'm pretty sure you can't predict that your possible soulmate is just not that into you, right? I know it's ridiculous, but I used to hope for a different ending to our story. And El? I don't even know who he is, and he doesn't know me. We could be a thing, but I don't have any energy for imagination left. I gave everything to Jake. It was wrong, and it's not going to happen again.

"Maybe," I cheekily say. However, when I glance at Elliot, he already knows what's coming next. Ugh. "It's not like that..."

"Umm."

"Really."

"So what is it? You have a secret boyfriend at home, you forgot to mention?" he says it like it's not a big deal like everything is a joke. I must know that I'm an expert at that.

"No-no-no. There is no secret boyfriend. It's just..." I really attempt to drag out the sentence, hoping something clever comes out, "I don't want it to be hard, you know?"

Dang, Cassie. It's so like you. Instead of telling the truth and being ruthless, I'm lying. Oh, I wish I were a boy. Elliot seems to be confused, which is good — there is a chance I can get away with this.

"What do you mean by hard?"

"Well, I know that we live nearby, but we're going to different schools," I lie through my teeth, "I just don't want to continue this because when school starts, it'll be difficult. My friend Ally was dating this guy from a different school, and it didn't end well. I don't want to be hurt, you know."

Well, the truth is I came up with that story. Ally's never dated anyone from a different school, so it didn't go south. Of course, I'm a liar, but at least nobody will get hurt this way.

"So you don't want to see where this goes because we go to different schools?" he wants to clarify. Bingo, this is my way out. I sadly nod.

"I know it's stupid, but if you switch schools for me..." I say, but I immediately realize it's a bad idea, so I add, "but that's crazy."

I genuinely believe it's the most embarrassing moment in my entire life. I should have stopped after calling it stupid.

"Maybe I will."

"Maybe you should," I say. I feel so relieved that El took it as a joke. We both giggle.

"Well, don't be surprised if I do."

"I won't be."

El leans closer to me, and we kiss. *One, two, three.* Just right on schedule — Jake and his buddies usually do their runs at this time. Today isn't any different. I know he'll see us... It's our spot. He used to kiss me here too. This isn't a payback, and I'm not trying to hurt him back. I just want him to know I'm moving on, just like him — nothing else.

Chapter 11
Just The... Three of Us?

Elliot parks the car in front of my house. It's just us, which makes me even tenser. Since our conversation, he is just normal. It's always like that with guys — you open up, and they behave like it's not a big deal. Well, it is a big deal for me. After what happened with Jake, I decided that I'd never let my guard down. It just feels like that day at the dock, and I have only one word for it — uncomfortable. There is no other way to slice it. I don't know what I expected.

I guess I can make a move. Elliot always makes a move, and I play catch up with him. So it would make total sense that he wants me to do something... Anything. I can't blame him.

"El..."

"Yeah?"

"About that thing you asked me..." I start, "Yeah, let's do it."

However, it totally goes over Elliot's head. He seems so confused. I can't believe I have to be more specific, so I give him a "flirty" look. Something clicks.

"Wait..." he realized, "Are you talking about being my girlfriend?"

I nod. Honestly, I feel like a fool. Do guys ever feel the same way? And the feeling definitely gets worse when he cheekily adds, "Oh, you're so silly, Cass."

"Umm, is it more like a yes or..."

"Of course, it is," he pulls me into a kiss. No, there is no way it's like it was at the dock. *Not even a comparison — so much better.* I don't even know what to say when we stop. And the only reason we stop is that I get a text from mom. She's just wondering where I'm at.

"It's pretty late, so-o-o..." I say. I don't want to go. I want him to stop me. I want to kiss him again.

"Give me your phone?" El softly demands.

"What? Why?"

"Just trust me."

I stare at him because I need more information. He rolls his eyes at me but adds, "Pretty please?"

"Okay," I pass my phone to him. His eyes sparkle, and he starts working his voodoo magic on it. The weirdest part is that I don't even care what he's doing. I'm just happy to be around him because I can be myself. There are no other games — it's just us.

"Here," he returns my phone. I immediately noticed that Elliot's contact is changed to Boyfriend with a heart. A picture of us, we took at the bonfire. It's cute, very cute. He always makes me smile.

"Well, it's official now."

"I guess so."

"But I do have to go. As much as I love that you've met my mom, I'd like to save the introduction to my dad for later."

"Okay, give me a second."

El gets out of the car and opens a door for me. I get out and stand in front of him. My heart is beating so hard as if it's trying to escape somewhere.

"Bye," I say, but it sounds like I'm posing a question.

"Good night, Cas."

"Good night," I look back, and I feel so scared. I don't even know why. Maybe everything is just too perfect, like the weather before a storm. To be completely honest, I'm pretty sure I'll screw this thing up. I don't know how, but it's a matter of time.

"I'll text you," he says right before I open the front door.

"Can't wait."

I enter the house, leaning on the door. I'm trying to catch a breath. People usually tell me that I should wait before entirely giving my heart to someone. It's easier to say than to do.

"Hey, you're back. We called you, hon," my dad says. He sounds a little concerned. *Crap.*

"Sorry, I lost track of time."

"Next time, text us?"

I nod and quickly add, "Of course, again, sorry."

"How was it?" he asks. My dad always makes it easy to talk to him. Sometimes I wish my parents would yell at me, so I wouldn't have to care about it. It's not their style, though. By being so reasonable, they make it impossible for me not to feel bad. Dammit.

"It was pretty great, but we didn't end up staying at the game."

"Oh, mom told me that you, guys, re-routed to the beach," he says. Oh yeah, I almost forgot about that.

"Yeah, it was nice, hanging out with friends."

"Are you hungry? Mom left you food in the fridge. You can microwave it," he offers.

"Nah, I'm good. I think I'm going straight to bed."

"Okay."

"Good night."

"Good night, dad."

My room is on the first floor, and my parent's master bedroom is on the second. I run into my bedroom, jumping on my bed. I immediately check my phone, hoping I'll see a text from El. It's pretty disappointing — no message. *Well, that's fine. He could still be driving home. Hmm… I don't know where he lives. I should probably ask.*

I go to the bathroom and start taking my make-up off. I look at myself in the mirror, and the only thing I see in the reflection is a disappointment. Not so much with El, but with myself. I shouldn't have been so naive, expecting him immediately to text me. Maybe he won't, but El isn't like that. He always keeps his promise. I hear a text notification, and my heart starts racing.

I quickly take off my eyelash, leaving the second one on. *He texted, he texted, he texted.* I rush to my phone, but it feels like a heartbreak because this text isn't from Elliot. It's from Jake. Disappointing. Ugh, I'm not even interested in what he has to say. I put the phone away and march to the bathroom to fix my other eye.

Hmm... I wonder what Jake has to say. Probably, excuses — excuses, and more excuses. I finally get the second eyelash off, then sigh. *Maybe I should check his text. Maybe it's important.* I look at myself in the mirror and tell myself off, "No, no, no. I have a boyfriend now. You, Cassie, can't text another guy like it's not a big deal."

I wash my face off with cold water, but it doesn't help calm my curiosity.

"I'm just not going to reply, Jake texted me," I explain to my reflection, and the best part it agrees with me. "So I'm not going to do anything wrong by checking my own phone, and it'll be so annoying to see an unchecked message. Decided."

I rush back, checking it — **I'm very disappointed you didn't stay. I was hoping you'd come back.** *OMG. Of course. Of course, he'd say something stupid like that. What did I expect?*

I roll my eyes as hard as I can. Jake's disappointed. He is disappointed with me. Right. I don't remember asking for his opinion. Maybe I'm disappointed with him. Why does he get to text me, spreading his disappointment when he was the one who started flirting with another girl. Was I supposed to sit and watch them until the end of the game, and then he'd pay attention to me?

I put my phone further away and get under the blanket. I close my eyes, attempting to find peace in my heart. *It's in the past, so the only thing left is to let it go. Technically... Dammit.* I sit up and grab my phone — the game is on:

Ummm, seriously, Jake?

It's silly, but it makes me feel like I'm in control. My heart starts pumping when I see bubbles. Jake's replying. Even though he and I are over, totally over, I'm finally getting justice for myself. How? I'm wasting as much of his time as he's wasted mine.

Yeah, seriously

Haha, lol — I quickly type.

What's so funny?

I wasn't the one who was flirting with that cheerleader, but nice try — I send, followed by a smiley emoji. *That will show him.*

I wasn't. Are you jealous?

Were you? But FYI. I'm not. — I angrily type in response.

I'm jealous. I'm not, idiot. Why do guys get to say that? The fact is that he was flirting with Katie — he was. That's just a fact. They can't just put a sticker reading "jealous" on girls as if we're the crazy ones.

I thought it was clear I am serious about you — he replies. I shake my head. *Yeah, right. However, I'm always left alone, looking at your back. I'm tired of running after you. It's tiring.*

It didn't look like it.

Meet me tomorrow at the field. I want to talk to you.

Well, that's interesting. Why should we meet up? To talk? Everything is clear now. What else is left to say? I don't even know what to say. There is no need for this.

It's Saturday.

I know. See you at 10. Don't be late — Jake texts and adds, **You owe me that.**

I guess it's not wrong to see Jake because the only reason why I'm meeting up with him is to say we're over. For good. I'm tired of these games, so I text back — **Fine, see you then.**

The next morning I noticed that El texted me as he promised, but I was asleep. He wished me good night, followed by a red heart. I don't want to reply to him until the situation with Jake is resolved. It shouldn't take too much time. So I'll keep it short. *Maybe El and I can meet up afterward? We'll see.*

I carefully pick my outfit. I don't want to give Jake the wrong impression. Therefore, I wear black jeans, a t-shirt, white sneakers. Very simple. I'm with El now. No make-up, hair up in a tight ponytail.

"Hmm… It's easy, Cassie. You just need to tell him the truth," I say in front of the mirror. Why am I so nervous? I continue my monologue, "It's not that easy to say everything. I know, and I also know that you don't want to hurt his feelings…"

Oh boy, I think that might have been a lie. Deep down, I'm a little excited.

Jake's hurt me so many times. Why is it a problem if I hurt him? However, I'm better than that.

"I'm just not gonna mention some parts. If it doesn't come up, what's the point of mentioning it? I need to let him go. It's time," I say out loud. I check the time. It's already 9:30 — shoot.

I walk back and forth near the bleachers and glance at the field. Jake is there, but the problem is that the whole football team and cheerleading team are there. That's not what I expected. I thought it'd be just us and nobody else.

I feel like a fool. Jake is being Jake, and I should have known better. This is so like him, but what am I afraid of? He wants to talk in front of everybody? Fine, it's his choice. He never cares about my feelings, so I don't have to either. I bravely rush toward the bleachers, but halfway through, I turn around. *No, I can't do this. It's just too embracing, and I don't want to deal with this. If I don't want to, then I don't have to. Just walk away, and don't look back.*

"Cassie! Cas-sie!" Jake shouts. I freeze. *Oh boy. I guess I'm dealing with it now — Crap.* I turn back and see Jake's already coming up to her. I walk up to him, he gives me a hug, "Where are you going? You're late…"

"Sorry," I say, but I don't think that's the problem. I almost immediately noticed Katie staring at me with her friends in their perfect cheerleading uniforms, perfectly matching makeup, curled hair in a ponytail. It's 10 a.m, and they all look so perfect. The whole entourage could take up to a few hours. *Well, if I knew that we'd have a company, I'd wear something fancier, but Jake didn't notify me as usual.*

"Hey, everyone!" Jake loudly gets everyone's attention. "Most of you know this is Cassie, but one thing you don't know is we're dating."

"What?" Katie slips, but I don't blame her. I want to yell "what" too. WTH, is that why he asked me to come, so he can announce this? I think it was clear that we needed to talk… I was supposed to put us to rest. Maybe, there is a different definition for "dating." While I'm wondering how I can spin this, Jake makes everything worse by adding, "She's my girlfriend."

Yeah, he just said I'm his girlfriend. I awkwardly smile, trying to keep my jaw-dropping. My eyes meet with Katie's. Surprisingly, there is no hate, just confusion — me too, sister. Jake's teammates clap, cheering him up like God. Crap. How did I get here? At least, this IS the worst, and I can still fix it. I'm just going to talk to him right after.

"Congrats, guys," Katie starts. *Oh no, I know that tone and intonation. This isn't good.* "So you're going to the Homecoming Dance together?"

This is terrible, horrible. How am I supposed to fix this now? Hey, Jake, no to Homecoming. Why? Oh well, I actually came here to break up with you because I needed to tell you I already picked El. Sorry, I hope we can be friends. Oh crap. I'm screwed. You see, if I were a boy, this would be a problem. Probably, his teammates would cheer me up just as much, and I wouldn't have to feel bad.

"Yeah, why not? Right, Cass?" Jake asks, but we all know he isn't really asking, and I can't really say anything, but "Of course, we are. I can't think of a single reason why not…"

Here it is. The trap. What happened? Katie is good. I underestimated the damage she could do to me. She saw an opportunity and sealed it. I would do the same. She locked me into something I didn't want, and she knew it from looking at me. I should be more careful. Oh, Jake… Why not? Well, maybe I already have a boyfriend. Nah, that can't be that.

"Great, that's a date," Jake says, breaking my train of thought. However, I can't catch a breath today because my phone starts ringing.

"Sorry," I offhandedly mumble, glancing at the incoming call. It's Elliot. My hands shake because his caller ID says — **Boyfriend <3**. I'm not good at this. Why does it always have to go wrong? Why couldn't it just work like I plan? This isn't supposed to be complicated — meet with a guy and tell him, "Hey, it's not working. Let's stay friends." We both nod and never talk again. How hard is that?

"Are you okay?" Jake notices that something is wrong. *Come on, Cassie! You can do better. Keep your face straight.* El keeps calling.

"Sorry, it's nothing. Parents, you know," I say, sending El straight to the voicemail, "But I should probably call them back."

"Okay, we actually have to practice unless you want to wait until I'm done."

"I have a math test on Monday, this week went over my head, and..."

"Don't worry," he stops me and kisses me on the forehead.

"Text me later?" I ask. This is a huge relief. I give him a hug goodbye and dart away like my life depends on it. I don't even look back, even though I probably should. Happy couples always want to look at each other for as long as they possibly can. At least, that's how I feel about El. It's upsetting, though. I've been dreaming about this moment since middle school. I don't even remember how many times I've imagined Jake calling me his girlfriend. I imagined hearing those words so many times, and here I am. Disappointed. This is supposed to be the moment. Life is very disappointing.

I run into a school bathroom and lock myself in, attempting to catch a breath. It finally got to me. *Omg, omg... Cassie, what's wrong with you? Crap. You've just become Jake's girlfriend, and from yesterday you got a boyfriend. Oh no-no-no, that's wrong. I should have said something... anything would be better than what I've done. Am I a bad person? No, I tried to do the right thing. To be completely honest, I feel like I'm kind of a victim here. I didn't want Jake to say that, or I didn't even expect this to happen. What was I supposed to do? I should have embarrassed him in front of everyone... I don't want to upset anybody. This is just wrong.*

Yesterday I felt like I was the happiest person on this planet, and look at me now — I officially have two boyfriends. I guess Lou-Lou will be proud of me. Will he? Ally will kill me. I can't blame her. Honestly, I even understand if she feels that way because I would feel like her if I really like someone. And who am I kidding? El is definitely worth it — he's pretty amazing. I wish I were amazing too. I take a deep breath.

I have to tell Jake the truth. Hey, Jake, I need to talk to you. He'd say, "Okay, go ahead." He'd look concerned, and I'd take a deep breath. Then I'd start explaining, "I'm so sorry, Jake. I didn't want to embarrass you in front of the team, and you calling me your girlfriend is very flattering. I love it, but I kind of already have a boyfriend. It's Elliot. Remember him? You, guys, have met before." Ugh... I'm so screwed.

I walk out of my hideout, realizing there is no good way to tell Jake the truth. It doesn't matter how long I'm hiding. I start washing my hands, then washing my face. *I wish I could just be a different person. Only who? I don't even know, but I want to be someone who never gets themselves into a situation like that. What is wrong with me?* I exhale, and I'd call it "disappointed exhale." I consider myself pretty smart, but how the hell does an intelligent person get herself in such a conundrum.

"Cassie, right?" I hear Katie's voice. She's never talked to me, but I know that voice way too well. *She knows my name but tries to downplay it because realistically, she shouldn't be talking to a nerd, isn't that right? However, if you want to play, Katie, I can play.*

"Hello to you, too?" I turn off the water and look over at her.

"You know why I'm here," Katie states as if it's a verdict, which is super annoying. Why do girls always do that? For example, look at Katie, coming at me, thinking she has everything figured out. My biggest problem is that she treats me as if she knows me, but she has no clue who I am or my struggles. I wonder if Jake mentions how he didn't say "I love you" back. I don't even need to ask to know that he's never mentioned it, and he won't. However, she gets to tell me off. Great. I love "female solidarity."

"Actually, no...not really. Katie, right?"

It makes Katie almost lose her cool, so she smirks at me. Her face starts blushing. Oops, she's pissed.

"I'm gonna say it once. Jake is an amazing and sweet guy," she quietly says. Bingo, I was totally right. She thinks she really knows Jake. A fantastic and sweet guy? I wouldn't call him sweet — after all, he did break my heart this summer. *Come on, Katie, we both know that calling Jake "amazing" is a little bit of a stretch, even by your standards. We both know he's stringing you along. Would an amazing guy do that to you? Look at you, you're the perfection, but I know it's easier to make me into the bad guy.* I try so hard not to roll my eyes as

Katie continues, "And if you hurt him, I'll make sure you…"

"You'll find me and murder me in my sleep?" I interrupt her before she has a chance to finish her thoughts. Maybe that is too much, but I just couldn't handle this anymore. This is ridiculous.

"You know what," she starts as I prepare myself for another tirade. "I don't know what Jake sees in you, but I'll be watching you."

Katie gives me a staredown and darts away. That sucked. This is not going to end well for me. There is no way it's going to end well. She's totally going to kill me in my sleep. Right?

Chapter 12
Decision Time

I walk back home, I'm not even in the mood to ride my bike. I usually ride it to clear my mind. Still, recently I've been feeling that I'm overthinking everything without any positive results. The more I think or plan, the worse it gets. I guess not riding the bike is my punishment. I know it's not how anything works, and it doesn't matter how I try to spin the whole situation. I need advice, but who should I call? Maybe Louis can help me with my dilemma, but without telling Ally. It's still a maybe. *Lou-Lou and I are pretty close. It's not a betrayal if we don't mention it to Ally. He might do that for me. Not quite for me — Lou-Lou enjoys drama a little too much. Well, that's not fair. I've noticed that Louis never puts himself into somebody else's drama. He's never in the middle of the drama. However, I'm sure he loves imagining himself in one through other people's mess. Unfortunately, I have to admit that my mess might just do the trick. I should give him a call.*

When I go to the kitchen, I'm so in my own head that I don't even notice my parents. Unfortunately, another horrible mistake was made today.

"Hey, honey. Is everything okay?" dad asks me. I look over and see mom and dad sitting on the couch and reading books. *Oh no, they know something is wrong. Of course, they don't know what precisely, but they'd like to know what's up. Ugh... Today is Saturday, and they have a reading brunch. At least, that's what they call it. If only I could roll my eyes harder because they both sit and read something, not together and not even the same book. They just read next to each other. I don't get it, and I've even attempted to join them a few times. However, it makes them happy, so who cares if I enjoy their thing or not. I should have remembered they'd be here, though.*

"Come here," mom adds. "You look a little... sad. What happened?"

As I walk up to them, mom puts her head on dad's shoulder. They are so perfect — it's so intimidating. My parents have been together since high school.

I can't even imagine them in high school. However, that's not my point. My actual point is that I'm torn between two boys. *I bet you, mom, have never dealt with that. I wish you would help me, but I know you can't. Even if I tell them, I think they'll be confused or heartbroken that I could behave like that.*

"You two… ARE just too happy," I playfully say. My parents smile, but I can just see this isn't going to cut it. "Everything is good."

They glance at each other, and I don't have to be a mind reader to know that my performance hasn't satisfied them.

"Seriously," I add as if it could make a difference.

"You know we love you very much," dad says. This is bad. How do I know that? It's like knowing the lyrics of an old song. Sometimes you even want to forget its words, but you can't. It's exactly what's happening to me now because my mom is about to add, "So much, honey, you know you can tell us anything?" Then I'm going to awkwardly nod and come up with some stupid excuse. My parents will know I'm lying, but they will respect my privacy. Here it goes.

"Cassie, honey, we love you so much. You know you can tell us anything?" mom asks.

"I love you too," I respond, trying not to sound like a broken record, "honestly, it's nothing. Ally and I had a fight, you know, but I think I might get Louis involved. He'll know what to do. So no worries on my front, we'll resolve it."

My parents both nod, which is very confusing, I have no idea if they're buying it or not, and I really need them to believe this story because I can't tell them the truth. I know one thing for sure — my parents could never understand having two boyfriends. It's not their style.

"What's the fight about?" mom asks.

"She likes El, and when El and I started dating, we had a fight over him," I mumble without even realizing what precisely I'm saying. I can't believe I've revealed so much to them.

"You and Elliot are dating!?" My mom gets really excited.

"Who is Elliot?" my dad asks.

"He transferred to our school this year, but we met at the summer camp," I clarify.

"Ally also liked Elliot, oh! That's very unfortunate," mom says. *This could actually work, and my parents won't ask more questions.*

"I know, but hopefully Louis will help us to figure it out," I add. "I think I'm going to call him. Can I go to call him?"

"Sure, honey."

I dart away from the living room. I just want to hide in my bedroom. My whole world is upside down. *I feel trapped. The worst thing is I've done it to myself. I am the entire reason why in this mess.* I close the door to my room and jump on the bed. I dial Lou-Lou, but he doesn't pick up my call, leaving me with long beeps on another end.

"Hey, this is your favorite person in the world! Lou-Lou," he laughs as he says it, "okay, I'm joking around, but please, leave me a message, so I can get back to you as soon as I can. Love ya."

If I could roll my eyes any harder, I would, but this is not the time to be picky over my limited number of friends. I guess I have no other choice. That's why I start talking, "Hey, Lou-Lou. Just calling you. I wanted to ask you if you can drop by? Alone… I think I got myself in a… situation. Ally can't know. Anywho, hope to see you soon. By-y-ye."

I drop down on the pillow, close my eyes, trying to catch my breath. Sometimes it really helps me visualize my problems. I go over and over what exactly I feel. *I wonder what I would tell Jake if he was here? Probably, ugh… who am I lying to?*

"To be fair, our thing was first," I hear Jake's voice. Great, now I'm talking to Jake in my mind. I'm officially going crazy, but Imaginary Jake's point is actually good. If we started dating earlier, I should give us another chance. Oh my gosh! What am I thinking? This is insane.

"But we had a lot of fun, and you said you felt like yourself," I hear Elliot's voice, and he also makes an excellent point. Honestly, my heart is full of relief because I should do the right thing, and the right thing is to break up with Jake.

I look over at the window and imagine Elliot standing right next to it. Jake sits on the armchair in the corner. They both stare at me, but they aren't angry or upset with me. I even think they understand my struggle.

"Elliot makes a good point," I say out loud. "I should be with a person, with whom I feel myself. It's so difficult for you, Cassie, to be yourself. You should appreciate that."

"Maybe we just didn't have enough time," Jake analyzes our relationships, "it's not fair. You and I haven't found our groove. We need a little bit more time."

I sigh. I can't believe how many excuses I can find for Jake, and I don't even love him anymore. I just can't let the idea of us... no, not us. Let me try this again — I can't let the idea of being with Jake go.

However, I'm happy. Until Imaginary Elliot stops my train of thought by adding, "Cassie, I hope you aren't buying this bullshit. If a guy wants to be with you, he will find a way to be with you. Look at me — I switched schools for you. I actually want to be with you. This 'we need a little bit more time' is a hoax. Jake could never find time for you."

OMG. I'm going to go insane. I sit up, trying to shake this whole thing away. I hear a doorbell ring, then it's followed by mom announcing, "Honey, Louis is here!"

I jump off the bed, rushing downstairs. Louis is already on the way upstairs.

"Hey, you," Louis greets me with a bit of irritation in his voice. I attempt to ignore it and give him a hug.

"Why didn't you call me when you were on your way?" I can't ask Lou-Lou. It's a double negative because he has no reason to be upset with me. *I haven't even told him my problem, and he's already pissy. Should I be worried?* We're about to come into my room.

"I did."

"Really? I don't think I got any calls..."

"Really?"

We sit down on the bed and check my phone — five texts and six missed calls. Oops.

"Sorry, I think I just blacked out. I'm in so much trouble," I explain and hug Louis again. "You don't even know how happy I am to see you."

"Cassie is extra nice, damn, this must be serious," he analyzes. " Go on."

"I can't tell this to Ally. I think she'll kill me," I start, " but I don't know what to do, Lou-Lou. El and I decided… We're officially dating, you know?"

"That's great, Cas. Congrats."

"Thanks."

"So what's the problem? I talked to Ally. She's totally cool with it."

"Yeah, the only problem is that Jake introduced me to his team as his girlfriend."

"Wait, what?"

"I know. It happened so fast, and it was out of nowhere. I freaked out and didn't say anything."

"Okay. You have two boyfriends now," Lou states it again as if he hopes it'll make more sense. "What were you even doing with Jake and his team?"

"Well, he texted me last night saying something like I owe him an explanation."

"Cassie…"

"I know, I shouldn't have gone, but I honestly was going to break it off and tell him that I started dating El," I explain. "I didn't have time to open my mouth about how I already became Jake's girlfriend in front of the whole team and cheerleaders. How bad is this?"

"Pretty bad, Cassie. Ally would kill you."

"No doubt, but I swear this wasn't my intent. I didn't see it coming, and then Katie made it so much worse when she asked whether we'd go to Homecoming together."

I roll my eyes. I really don't like Katie. Louis looks totally shocked, making me wonder whether it's a good idea to fill him in.

"Please, tell me that you haven't officially agreed to go to Homecoming, the first and the biggest social event of high school, with the most popular guy in school?"

"Well, when you put this that way," I mumble, hoping for some kind of silver lining.

"What were you thinking? How are you planning to keep this a secret from Elliot?" Louis asks. It's a very fair question, and the honest answer would be that I haven't thought it through. I haven't thought about the consequences but isn't it a little too late to wonder why. It's time for damage control. I shrug my shoulders and ask, "What should I do?"

"Umm... It's very easy, Cassie," he replies, "You have to break up with one of them. Girl, it is impressive to have two boyfriends. Hell ya!"

"I mean, it's not like I was trying to have two boyfriends," I explain, "It just happened. It's not that bad, right?"

Lou-Lou moves his head from side to side while I'm dying of waiting for him to say something nice. Louis is such a cheering person. He always finds a way to look at things positively. That's exactly what I need right now. I'd even say the only thing I need right now. My heart is about to jump off my chest when I see Louis's smirk. He gets that smirk only when he has something good. He raises his hand up, ready for a high five. Instinctually, I follow his lead, not expecting to hear, "High five for sluts!"

Right when I'm about to high five, Louis inches away from me, but the second I hear the word "sluts", I hopelessly drop my hand.

"Well, and you know why it's wrong," Louis explains. Well, I'm totally screwed. When your best friend, who usually finds a positive side in everything, can't cheer you up, you know you have a problem. A real problem...

"I can't break up with Jake right away. Maybe after Homecoming," I wonder out loud.

"Wait, am I getting this right? You're considering breaking up with El."

"No. Of course, not."

"So, are you planning to date both of them? AND go to the Homecoming Dance with both of them?"

Yeah, Cassie, you didn't think this through. I can't break up with Jake, and

I'm definitely not breaking up with Elliot. And let's be honest, I can't pull off two dates at Homecoming. *I'm not that smooth. I wish I were.* I sigh and slump down on the bed.

"Maybe one of them will get sick, or I'll get sick, Aaaaaahh!" I put my hands over my face. "I haven't been lucky. Maybe if I get sick and kiss El, he'll get sick," I continue spewing nonsense, but it makes Lou-Lou giggle. At least, something is normal.

"O-m-g, Cassie," he says, "You're gonna be an old cat lady."

"Totally."

Louis lies next to me. We both quietly stare at the ceiling.

"I'm so jealous of you. I wish I were you even for a day," Lou-Lou admits.

"Why?"

"I don't know maybe the idea of having two people be into me at the same time or maybe the thrill of it."

"Well, that's why I..."

"Oh, no-no-no! You still have to break it off," he interrupts me.

"But how?"

"I don't know. But you have to break it off."

"I know."

"No, Cas. I'm serious."

"Okay-okay, I will," I say, but then I make a huge mistake by looking at Louis. *He's judging me. He's totally judging me. What? He thinks I won't break up with Jake? Well, I know how hard it can be to break up with a person. I've already broken up before.* I immediately add, "I'll totally break up with Jake."

"Okay."

"Come on, I'll break up with Jake tomorrow."

"Sounds like a plan."

"I'll even text him."

"Okay."

"Right now…"

"Okay."

"It's done," I say as I send the text — hey, can we meet tomorrow?

"Okay."

Louis gives me a suspicious look as if he's skeptical whether, actually, I'll go through with it.

Chapter 13
The Nomination

Well, Louis was right. A hundred percent. Am I so predictable? It's hard to think about anything while I'm sitting next to Jake at the movie theater. He texted me back, telling me he'd pick me up today. I can't believe he kept his promise because anytime I wait for Jake to show up on time or go on an actual date, he's never been there for me. I'm still surprised that he showed up on time. I feel like it's finally different. Why is he perfect on the day when we're supposed to break up? Jake gently puts his head on my shoulder and continues playing with my hair. This is bad. I can't do this.

It's our first perfect date, a real one. We were sneaking out partially because of me during summer camp, but I still stand my decision. I couldn't let everyone know we were a thing before we'd start dating. Since Jake freaked out when I prematurely said, "I love you," I'm sure it was the right decision. But, honestly, I still can't believe us being on a date is even possible. Why? I guess I've been underestimating Jake. I really want to tell him the truth, but maybe I should see this through.

As Louis said, I should have dated both of them, and I'm doing what I'm told. I know that's not exactly what he said, but if you think about it, you'll see that's what he actually meant. Maybe my Imaginary Jake is correct, and it's our second chance to spend more time. Katie was always there, standing in between our love. Love? Maybe, he hasn't actually said that he loves me. At the camp, Jake wasn't ready, and anybody would understand that. While I'm trying to find any possible excuse to answer why it's okay to be with Jake, El texts me. I don't check it, but being discreet is kind of difficult.

"Is everything okay?" Jake asks.

"Yeah, it's mom," I reply. "You know my parents always want to know where I am."

I pretend to be interested in the movie, and I have to act because I've seen it already. With El… *Yeah, I know how wrong this is, and I can't even imagine what Louis could say about me actually dating both of them. He was pretty ruthless yesterday. Honestly, I start wondering whether Ally and Louis are just jealous of me. My life is so perfect, so how can't you be jealous of me? I'd say precisely the same thing, "Oh, this is so wrong." Of course, I would. How couldn't I? It's easy to be judgmental if you could never imagine yourself in a situation like that. In a million years, I thought two people would be interested in me, which is kind of sad. After Jake couldn't say love you back, I wasn't even sure anybody would be able to love me back. Why can't I enjoy this for a day… or two.*

I feel every moment. I feel like everything moves in slow motion, so I relive this over and over. It's selfish, but I love it because I can see the whole movie two times with two boyfriends. El and Jake are incredibly different, like day and night. That's why I never have to worry about meeting one while being on a date with another. Jake and I go to the baseball game. I'd call us basic, but that's mean. Who am I lying to? If we were in a romantic comedy, I'd be the main character's sister, having a third baby. Jake would hang out with his buddies from high school, remembering his past glory. Well, it sounds depressing, but the road to that disaster must be fun. I know, I know I'm mean. I'm just trying to process the whole thing. I sound very comfortable having two boyfriends, but I'm not. I can't even kiss Jake. That's why I asked him to take everything slowly.

In contrast, El and I are a hundred percent opposite, where I'm the main character and finally get to find the right guy. Sometimes I wonder if being or feeling like the main character means so much to me? I guess El and I are more romantic. We're more on the same page. Going to see baseball is fun, but it wouldn't be my first choice. I have no complaints with El. He always surprises me, and it's always memorable and exciting.

I guess it can't get more sophisticated than that when you're seventeen. I'll never forget the time he surprised me and took me to a fair. I remember it as if it's happening right now. We're driving together — I hold El's hand.

"Where are we going?" I ask. "We've been driving forever... I honestly start wondering if you're planning to murder me?"

"Okay, this is ridiculous, Cass," El says, shaking his head. "You're ridiculous. At the most, we've been driving for forty minutes."

"And still... You haven't told me where we're going."

"It's a surprise."

"You know I don't like surprises," I say, but I can't ignore the prideful smirk on his face.

"I think you'll like this one."

"I hardly doubt it."

"Well, I'm willing to take that chance."

"Good luck."

In retrospect, I should have known El would never behave so stuck-up if he wasn't sure I'd love his surprise. In thirty minutes, he parks the car in front of the annual fair. Yes, I can be totally wrong because my heart fills with happiness when I see so many bright lights. I look over at El, and he knows immediately I love it.

"Let's go," he softly says. I nod, and we both get out of the car. I can't take my eyes off El, he could have rubbed it in my face that he was right, but he's better than me... I stare at the ground while my mind dives into self-pity and self-hate. The second the self-pity train leaves self-hate station, it's unstoppable. *This is a huge mistake. Only a fool like me would think she deserves to be with someone like El. He's just too good for me, and I'm definitely not good enough to be his girlfriend. Cassie, you have two boyfriends, what's now? You have no plan. You're a horrible person. How can I do this to El? How will he react when the truth is out? Oh yeah, you hope it won't get out, but deep down in your heart, you know you won't be able to hide it for too long even though you're doing a great job now. However, you aren't wired to play games, and you know it.* As much as I'd love to continue hating myself, I can't when El takes my hand.

"Are you okay?" he asks. *His hand is so warm.* I look up, and all my worries disappear, which I often say... but I guess it always surprises me because I can't stop thinking. I'm not a control freak, but my parents always tell me that all my actions have consequences, which leads me to overthink. Of course, no one can describe my double dating situation as overthinking. However, I genuinely believe I'm in this mess because it takes me forever to decide anything. By the time I'm ready to make a decision, it's already made for me. The whole reason why I haven't broken up with one of them is to see who I want to be with. Wait a second, we can't forget Jake made me his girlfriend without asking me.

"Yes," I reply.

"Are you sure?"

"Absolutely," I say and lean into a kiss. "Let's go?"

"Yeah."

Imagine a perfect date? Two weeks ago, I wouldn't be able to, but now... I think I can. We play arcades together, then air hockey. El lets me win, but it doesn't stop me from jumping in happiness after getting a final goal, which leads us to get a giant pink bear. Usually, I'd be like, "Man, this is pathetic... A giant pink bear? Really? Are we in a cheap romantic comedy? And again... Really?" Look at me now. Holding that giant pink bear isn't making my soul die. It's nice. I'm officially happy. You must be, right? I don't see any other explanation of how the hell I look so excited and end up on a Ferris Wheel, sitting with Elliot and the giant pink bear. When the wheel stops at the top, I look over the fair, and it's so scenic. By that, I actually mean it's so romantic. El just drives me wild. I can't control myself. I reach to kiss El again, which is becoming a problem.

Why? I'm supposed to have rules to follow, so I won't get caught dating two guys. If my 'adventures' become public, I won't be able to live with myself. I think I'll have to switch schools for sure. I can never find a good lie or excuse to transfer schools for my parents. I go over millions of potential scenarios, but unfortunately, my parents find out the truth in every single one of them. However, you can't transfer to different parents, and they will know what I've done forever. That's why it's essential to follow the rules. As I've already mentioned, Jake and I are going very slow #nokissing, so I usually attempt to be fair. The no kissing rule is generally applied to Elliot. However, it's impossible to find a reason not to kiss Elliot, so the rule with El is that I don't kiss him. We also agreed that we wouldn't kiss at school, which was easy to explain to him. Anybody could buy into the idea that I'm a very private person. Well, even if El didn't believe me, well, he agreed to it. I sometimes guess things just work out. However, as much as it's fun, it's been so hard juggling my boyfriends at school. Since Jake is our football star, I've become the center of everyone's attention. It's been two weeks since I started dating both Jake and El. It's been a lot of work...

Every day requires following a strict schedule. It's just exhausting. Probably, if someone mentioned this as a reason why I shouldn't date two guys, maybe I wouldn't have in the first place. One mistake could ruin everything. Like being late, even for five minutes, could result in a collision of two universes. Metaphorical, of course, but I have too much on my plate.

For example, my day starts with me getting to the school parking lot at seven-thirty. Jake and his buddies usually hang out there. *How else will you be able to rule high school if you don't spend an unreasonable amount of time hanging out in the school parking lot right? Anyways...* I usually spend about fifteen, twenty minutes before I need to run to El. The best part is most days it's only fifteen minutes. But it always feels like torture. The guys always talk about girls — *ones I don't like* — cars, or sports — *you already know what I think about that.*

Sometimes I wonder what's even the point of trying so hard because no matter how much I try to fit into Jake's life — I always feel like an outsider. There are a lot of times I imagine myself somewhere else. Too many times. It's like I'm looking out of the window while cool kids are playing dodgeball outside. *Yeah, I'm a passive observer.* There are some benefits of being out of it. One of them is that I noticed Katie's been watching my every move like a hawk, which isn't helping with my confidence. She reminds me that I have to be incredibly careful every day because I'm walking on very thin ice. One wrong move — I'm busted.

"Jake, I gotta run. See you later?" I ask.

"Do you want me to walk with you?" Jake asks, but we both know that he's polite. He wants to stay with his buddies. I always pretend to be touched and excited about the idea, but then I politely decline by going through a list of reasons he should stay. Jake always agrees without even hearing me out. I could come up with almost anything, and he'd buy it.

"I'm meeting up with Ally and Louis," I start to explain, but before I can even finish, he says, "Oh, then see you at lunch?"

"Yeah, I'll text you?"

"Sounds good."

I think Jake doesn't really care about my friends. Funnily enough, if he was my only boyfriend, it'd be driving me crazy. I'd be so upset. But, hey, I can't be too mad because I met El, Ally, Louis at around seven forty-five. That's my favorite time. It's easy. I'm finally myself, and I can forget about my double-boyfriend problem. My life gets easier since Jake and I don't have any classes together. It's easy to avoid him in between.

On top of that, I've learned all the classes, so I don't have to run into him. However, it's been nerve-racking as time gets closer to the Homecoming Dance because, in our school, we have to choose a Homecoming Queen and King. Jake is nominated for obvious reasons, and it's not making my life any easier. Since I'm his so-called girlfriend, I've been nominated too. Usually, I'd be so happy, but I know I got this nomination because of my boyfriend. She's also nominated, which isn't even a surprise. Katie is the most popular girl in school. Without Jake, I'd have to wait until she graduates to become a Homecoming Queen. That's the best-case scenario.

Also, Katie's been staring at me, sparkling with happiness as if she attempts to tell me something with her eyes. It's very unsettling. I've actually started suspecting she might be behind my nomination.

I remember that day. I didn't have enough time to hang out with Jake. Let me describe it. It's Monday, and I'm running late. *Okay-okay, just text Jake. You just need some stupid excuse. He won't even care.* But, of course, that wouldn't work with El, like Sherlock Holmes — he always asks a lot of questions. So as I rush to the entrance, I text Jake.

Hey, sorry. Louis emergency, see you later?

I carefully wait for his reply, and within a few minutes, I notice the texting bubbles. As I'm walking, I see people are giving me weird looks. I don't need extra attention because I'll have to pay more attention to what I'm doing. This week hasn't started so well for me. The reason why I'm late is that I've been having nightmares nonstop. I woke up in the middle of the night, sweating like a pig. *What was that nightmare about?* Oh, ha-ha, very funny. Obviously, it was about my two boyfriends finding out. During the day there is no problem. I can totally control myself and shut down any bad thoughts, but at night... Yesterday was terrible. It wasn't a lot of fun to watch Katie revealing my secret in front of the whole school. I nervously swallow. I still feel shaken up by how much people were hating on me. Of course, it's well-deserved... I wish I could just shut it down.

Cool. I hope you'll be excited...

Reading that text makes me so confused. I just want to scream something like, "This raises more questions!!! I have no time for this."

I forget to reply when I see that Ally and Louis are already there, chatting away about something.

"Hey, guys."

"Well, hello, missy," Louis says with such a sassy tone.

"Hi," Ally says, staring at me like WTH.

"What's up?" I ask, full of confusion.

"What do you mean?!" Ally and Louis yell at the same time.

"Okay, what are you two talking about? I have no idea..."

"You're nominated for Homecoming Queen!" Ally reveals.

"Please don't tell me you have no idea that you got nominated for Homecoming Queen!!!" Lou-Lou almost yells at me. *Oh great... This is just fantastic. It's another thing I have to deal with. Well, it explains Jake's text and that everyone stares at me.*

"Me?" I ask. I don't even know what the point of asking is. I guess deep down, I hope it's another nightmare I'm about to wake up from. I wish.

"Oh my gosh, Cassie! Yes, you are!" Louis responds, rolling his eyes. He hasn't put two and two together, which is fascinating. If the situation was reversed, I would be already yelling at him, spewing the truth to anyone and everyone who'd listen.

"Wait... How did this even happen?" Ally asks. That's a good question, but who even cares. It's a stupid dance, and it's a stupid title to make popular kids even more popular. I don't want it. At all. That's the truth.

"I don't know, and I don't even know how that happened," I say. Still, you don't have to be a genius to see Ally and Louis continue freaking out about this, so I add, "Stop freaking out. It's a stupid title for stupid people, and only stupid people care about this. Chill, you guys."

Yeah... It feels great to say it out loud. I'm finally free, but then I glance at Ally and Louis. Both of them look shocked by my words and hurt, and that's why I don't tell people what I actually think. People want to hear what they want to hear. There is no reason to upset them more than they already are. I bet Ally and Louis just would love to be nominated, and they're trying to be excited for me while I'm ripping their dreams to shreds.

"Sorry, guys," I apologize for something in a perfect world I wouldn't have to, but whatever. "I didn't really get to sleep last night. I'm kind of cranky and annoyed."

"Oh... We got so excited for you when we heard," Ally says.

"And it's so rare the freshman gets nominated," Louis jumps on the same train. "That's so rare, you know."

I wish I could just tell them the recipe to become nominated — step one: date the most popular guy in school, step two: get nominated. It's that easy. Maybe, you can become nominated if you're already popular or exceptional in some way... No, I can't even do this because there is no other way.

"I'm just so tired. I wish I could exchange it for some sleep," I say, and it makes my friends giggle. I can barely concentrate, wondering where Elliot is.

I glance at my phone. It's already 8:05, which isn't good for me. El is late, and it's getting closer to the time when Jake and his squad roll up to school. Just to hang out more.

"Have you seen, El?" I ask.

"Nope."

"He's running late. His dad came from a trip last night," Ally replies. I frown, wondering how she knows about it, but not me. Are they friends? Is Ally still into El? Why didn't El tell me? Are they closer than we are? Should I be worried about it? My train of thought is so far gone, but all my worries disappear when I see Jake and his squad have already started walking away from the parking lot. Crap.

"I think we should just go," I offer.

"Are you sure?" Lou-Lou asks.

"He might be a few minutes late," Ally adds to his point, which is very reasonable. However, I haven't got enough sleep. I'm hiding that I'm dating two guys... and on top of that, I've just found out Ally knows more about what's going on with my favorite boyfriend than me. Can I even have a favorite boyfriend? Ugh... I really need some sleep.

"No, it's fine. He texted me. Did he text you, too?" I snap.

"No... but..."

"No, buts. I'm his girlfriend, I'd know," I explain with a passive-aggressive tone. "Let's go?"

Ally and Louis share a WTH look, but I ignore it, which isn't too tricky. We enter the school, walking through the hallway in silence. My locker and Louis's are pretty close to each other, but Ally is almost on the other side. I feel a little relieved when she leaves. I grab a history book from my locker.

"Hey," Louis comes up to me. "What's up with you?"

"I don't know, Lou. Maybe I freaked out that Ally knew more about my boyfriend than me."

"Wait, you didn't know?"

"Yes, I didn't know. Okay?"

You know how there is a saying, "before it gets better, it gets so much worse first." I'm going to admit I thought it couldn't get worse for me. But, I immediately know it's about to get worse, so much worse for me, when a group of cheerleaders approaches us.

"Cassie, do you need any help with your campaign?" one of them asks me. She looks familiar, but I don't know her name, or maybe I don't remember. Who knows at this point. Jake and I don't spend time with his groupies. However, I could have met them. My main problem with those girls is that they look so damn similar. Let's call her Amanda.

"And this is not optional, by the way," another one announces.

"No thanks," I decline the offer, which apparently isn't an option.

"But Jake told us..." Amanda starts mumbling, but I stare and say, close your mouth with my eyes.

"I don't know why Jake would say anything about me, you, but, ladies, we," I say as I point at Lou-Lou and me, "are running late. Have a nice day. Let's go, Loui."

I take his hand, and we pass the girls, who are so confused that they won't say a word in response. Lucky because I can totally believe that Jake could ask them to help me be picked as Homecoming Queen. We walk up to Ally, who looks suspicious. Loui doesn't say a word to me, which is even worse. I can't even imagine what he's thinking right now. *Has he figured it out? Can I trick him?*

"Wow, what did they want?" Ally asks. She's already let it go. There is some good news, I guess.

"Nothing interesting. Jake must be feeling petty if he thinks I can be tricked so easily," I downplay the whole thing. Still, I'm not sure whether it's working because Ally and Loui aren't giving me any indication of how good my performance is.

"To be fair, Jake's always been such a player, so we shouldn't be so surprised," Ally says, rolling her eyes at me. I nod.

"Yeah, it's ridiculous," I say and quickly glance at Louis, wondering whether he's about to become another problem.

"Hey, all of you," El comes up to us from behind. "Sorry, I'm late."

El puts his arm around me. Uh-oh, it's not a good time for this... Jake is about to enter the school, and I don't want to explain that to anyone.

"No problem, how is your dad?" I ask, taking his arm off. His jaw almost drops. *I know it's a surprise to you, El. Maybe you should have told me instead of Ally.*

"Yeah... It's fine," he mumbles in response, not looking up at us. At least, he's playing the game. Ally glances at El, then at me.

"Shall we?" I ask, hinting that it's time to go.

"Yeah," El agrees. It's a perfect diversion because nobody wants to have a conflict in the middle of school. It's much easier to move on, so all of us start walking away.

The whole way, everyone stays silent. It's uncomfortable. It's hard for me to concentrate. My mind goes back and forth, wondering if someone's already noticed El's hug. However, even if people saw it, it doesn't seem to be a problem. El and Ally enter the classroom when Lou-Lou puts his hand on my shoulder.

"Cass," Louis says. I look over and immediately know that I was worried about the wrong thing. I need to play this cool, and I'll get away with it.

"What's up?" I ask, very nonchalant. I've noticed people believe me more when I'm lying, which is very disheartening. When I tell people the truth, they don't quite buy it. They just stare at me as if they ask 'really?' with their eyes. I used to be upset about it, but now... Well, I decided to take advantage of the situation.

"Can you come with me for a sec?" Louis asks me.

"Sure."

Lou-Lou pulls me over aside in the hallway. I know exactly what this is about, but I'm interested in how he's going to approach this. I immediately take

TATI VOGT

a mental note it's going to be easy because Lou-Lou looks totally freaked out. He's very uncomfortable talking to me. That means it's totally about my nomination and Jake.

"Did you..."

"Of course, I did," I assure him, "I talked to Jake, and I thought it sank in, but I think he can't just let it go…"

You see, the secret of lying is that right before you're accused of something, you know you've got a hundred percent done. You don't let the accuser finish their question. For example, Louis was likely to ask me whether I've broken up with Jake. Well, that's a "yes" or "no" question, so what have I done? I've answered a different question, and if things go wrong, I'll say, "I've never said I broke up with Jake, and I did talk to him. That's a hundred percent truth. The next step is to quickly change the subject. I'm a master of varying subjects, at least, I would like to think that. However, either way, I've circled back to the conversation of me being Homecoming Queen skillfully. The last step of the deception is to downplay the whole thing as if you have no interest in whatever. In my case, it's being Homecoming Queen.

"Really? I don't know. That doesn't quite make sense," Louis questions me, but I'm ready to play this game.

"I don't even know their names. Jake is just messing with me," I say, rolling my eyes.

"Okay," Louis says, but he's not totally sold on it.

"Honestly, I'm also super weirded out that I'm nominated for a Homecoming Queen. Isn't that so ridiculous? Look at me."

Sometimes to make people believe me, I start downplaying myself or my appearances, and it always works.

"No, why would you even say something like that. You will be a perfect Homecoming Queen."

"It's not going to happen. It's just another Jake's prank," I say, even though deep down I hope it's true because otherwise, it means Katie is on me, and she's good at this.

"Come on, even if it's true, that's going to be a lot of fun," Lou responds with a bit of jealousy in his voice. I get it. He's probably never going to be nominated, which is unfair. Then he has to make me feel better about it. Life is unfair.

"Really? I think the Homecoming Dance is kind of stupid."

"Oh! Come on, it could be a lot of fun. We'll all be dressed up, dancing. I guarantee that," Louis claims.

"Whatever, Lou-Lou. I'm not going to get it anyways. Our school is hooked on Katie anyways."

"Let's go… You know you're such a pessimist, Cass," Louis replies to my fake whining, and we go to the classroom.

I don't know, but recently I feel like Jake and I are falling apart. The more we spend time together, the more I feel like he could be an excellent friend. Jake has shared a lot of his thoughts with me, and it makes me very scared. I don't want anybody to get hurt, but it's clear that someone will get hurt if I don't fix this quickly. It'll be on me…

Jake and I sit in front of the ocean, staring in the distance.

"So, Jake, what do you want to do? Are you planning to become a football player after you graduate?" I ask.

Jake shrugs his shoulders, replying, "I love football, but who knows. I'm just trying to be the best I could be. I'm not sure whether I want to go to college and get a degree in economics or I should take a shot in sports. It's so competitive, and to be honest, I'm not so sure I'm that good to make it in a professional world."

I nod, trying to show support. However, I'm a little bit disappointed. I always imagine Jake being a successful football player, and I'm his wife, waving at him from the packed stadium. I guess I would never think that Jake doesn't have a plan.

"Are you worried?"

"Well, everyone is. We're graduating this year. Whether you're a soccer player or a straight-A student, it's going to be a new chapter of our lives. It always worries some, but it's exciting."

"I guess..."

"Are you worried?" he asks.

"No, I'm not worried at all. I have a few years, right?"

"Yeah, that's why I think it's a good idea to go and get a degree. Football can help me with it, and hey, it still might work out differently."

"That's awesome...I don't know what I want to do. I don't love what I do, you know..."

I've had a very similar conversation with El. I guess it's been enough time to figure out... a lot of things. I finally can admit I want to be with El. Jake and I could be really good friends, but whatever image I've created isn't who Jake actually is. He's a person, and I need to let go of the idea of him. I genuinely care about Jake, and that's why it's time to accept the reality.

In the same conversation, Elliot replies, "That's okay. You can't know a hundred percent what you want, or it's impossible, Cass."

"I dunno. Is it okay?"

Elliot gives a severe look, maybe even concerned.

"Hey, are you okay?"

"Yeah, why?" I ask. I'm a little bit confused. What does it even mean? Are you okay?

"I don't know. You recently seem so exhausted," El reveals. He's right. It's been exhausting — dating two guys is a lot of work. At least, it's more than they show in movies.

The Homecoming Dance is right around the corner, and my hopes are really high that El won't be attending. We've recently talked about it, and El also thinks it's stupid. We agreed we wouldn't go as a protest. That conversation had happened before I was nominated for Homecoming Queen. It's changed things — I've been popping up everywhere. I've even been bringing cupcakes, cookies, and other treats to all the school clubs, hoping that bribing them will pay off and I'll win the Homecoming Queen. Yes, maybe it's not the right way to win, but who cares. I still have to campaign anyway. My schedule is so tight. I have been doing it on autopilot. Honestly, I'm not surprised El noticed me not paying attention. The worst thing is when I assumed that El wouldn't go to Homecoming.

Chapter 14
Visions of Boyfriends Dancing in My Head

I haven't seen El or Jake for a few days because I had to catch up on my homework. How I haven't slacked off is a pure mystery to me, even more than the question of how I haven't gotten caught dating two guys. Jake has an important game, so he hasn't really cared. Elliot, on the other hand, has asked me to go on a date on Sunday. So, of course, I've agreed, which luckily hasn't become a problem.

I've caught up with everything I needed to on Saturday, so I'm pretty excited to go out. I sit by the window, waiting for El to pick me up. He hasn't told me about where we're planning to go. It's kind of exciting not to know and not to be worried about the plan and time frame. It's nice and freeing.

El pulls over in front of my house, and I rush downstairs.

"Bye, mom and dad!" I say.

"Bye, honey. Remember, we're going to Angela's tonight," mom says, "Your dinner is in the fridge, just microwave it when you come back."

"Sounds good!"

"And don't be too late," dad adds.

"Okay, b-y-e," I say, closing the front door.

"Hey," I hear El's voice from behind.

I look over and see him smiling at me.

"Hey," I tell him in response and give El a hug. I'm so happy to see him. It's like getting an exceptional coffee or cookie after you've done so much work. He stares at me as if I should notice something. I even start wondering if he's had a haircut.

"I'm really happy to see you. Let's go?" I ask him.

"Not so fast," he says.

"What is it?" I ask, very seriously. My heart drops because I'm scared he could have found out the truth, and it's ugly.

El rolls his eyes and raises his arm, revealing a black blindfold to me. I smirk and joke, "Okay, be honest, El, are you planning to kill me?"

"Jeez, Cass!"

"That's not an answer," I tease him.

"Of course not," El says, "but it's a surprise, so it's okay if I cover your eyes?"

"A surprise?" I ask, implying again. He knows I'm not a huge fan of surprises, especially when dealing with two guys and the homecoming queen nomination.

"I missed you, so I wanted to do something special for you."

"Oh! That's so sweet, El," I warm up. "I will put this on, but only in the car. Not a second earlier."

"Deal."

We go to his car. El opens the door for me. I quickly turn off my phone. I don't want to get any weird texts from Jake or from his friends. El takes a seat next to me.

"Ready?" he asks, leaning closer to me.

"Ready or not, right?" I say. I'm used to being in control. That's why not knowing where we're going is driving me crazy. It's even worse, especially because I have to wear a blindfold. I won't even be able to guess where El's taking me.

"Come on, Cassie. It's not that bad. It's like you don't even trust me," El says, "and it's very upsetting."

"Okay. Let's do this. Put it on," I say.

"Do you trust me?" he asks, giving a long stare. *Ugh, why didn't I just put the stupid blindfold on immediately? So I wouldn't have to have a silly conversation with El. Do I trust him? The reality is that he shouldn't be trusting me. I'm the bad guy here, and if I was honest with El, I would just tell him that he shouldn't trust me.*

"Of course, I do."

"No, seriously, Cass. This is important."

"I know, and I am serious. I trust you a hundred percent," I reassure him.

"Good," he says, giving me a small kiss. "Should I?"

I look down and shake my head. I can't even hide how upset I am.

"Nah, I'll do it myself," I say, taking the blindfold, but El stops me.

"Are you okay?"

"Yeah, I'm just... I've been studying a lot, and I think it's been catching up with me," I say. *It wasn't the truth. I hate myself right now because I'm worried about who might see us instead of enjoying this moment. I can just imagine Jake walking up on us around the corner, and I know he wouldn't say anything for a while. He would judge me but wouldn't say anything. I guess that's my personal hell.*

"Let me help you, silly," he says and puts the blindfold on me. "Done. Let's roll."

"Okay."

El turns on the radio, and we drive away. I'm worried that I could fall asleep the whole ride because the blindfold over my eyes makes me feel so cozy. I've decided when an opportunity to rest presents itself, I'll take it. I think we've been driving at least for forty minutes, and I'm becoming more nervous.

"I know I said I trust you, but I'm about to fall asleep," I start explaining, "so I just want to check in whether we're almost there or I can take a quick nap."

"Almost there," El replies.

"Like ten minutes away or..."

"Five minutes, Cass," he says, rolling his eyes. Of course, I couldn't see it, but he usually does when he uses his sarcastic tone. *Hmm... I really know Elliot, even though we don't talk about his family. I don't want to ask because I truly believe he would speak to me if he needed to tell me if it was the time. Yeah, it was frustrating when Ally knew something, I didn't, but hey, I have a huge secret. It's just not my place to judge someone else. It wouldn't be fair. However, I know El's dad has been at home for a while now, but honestly, El seems even more upset about it. It's upsetting.*

"We're here, just like I promised," El says as he parks the car. "And look at you, you're fine."

"I had no doubts," I say. "Can I finally take this blindfold off?"

"Not yet. Please, wait just a little bit longer," El asks me. "I promise it's worth it."

"Okay."

El jumps out of the car and helps me to get out. I always hit my head, but El catches it before it could happen. We slowly take a few steps — I feel so awkward. It seems my legs feel so weak. Now I wonder if I should have worn sneakers instead of pumps.

"Just a little bit further," he reassures me. "You're doing great."

I think we're probably not too far away from the car, but it feels like it's been an entire eternity. Until suddenly we stop, I smile.

"Ready?" El asks. I nod.

El carefully takes the blindfold off, and my heart skips a beat from excitement. I can believe my own eyes. It's already dark, with quite a few stars in the sky. We're standing in the middle of a small lantern festival. People are preparing to release their lanterns over a lake. It's just breathtaking.

I look over at El, who has been watching me. I want to say so many words, but all of them don't seem to describe my joy. So instead of saying anything, I lean in and give him a kiss.

"I guess I don't hate surprises anymore," I say. El shakes his head.

"I told you, you would enjoy it."

"How did you even find this place? I love the lanterns," I say.

"Well, I know you love Rapunzel, and it gave me an idea to check the lantern festivals," he starts explaining. "The big ones usually happen in February, but I found this one…"

"I love it," I don't even let him finish.

"I'm glad," he says, giving me a hug. "Let's get to work."

"Yeah, let's do this."

El has everything ready. I help him to put a blanket down on the ground, then we unwrap the lantern. I have never done this before. I've only seen pictures. It's mesmerizing, and I hope one day I'll be able to go there to experience being a small part of something big. Honestly, I don't even remember when I mentioned it to El. However, who even cares because I feel so happy being here with El. We write each other's initials and draw a heart on our lantern.

"On three?" El asks.

"Yeah. One."

"Two."

"Three," I say as we let it go, watching how our lantern is slowly going up. El hugs me. There are about a hundred lanterns up in their air, and I can't take a picture. This is the time to mention another strict rule I have — not taking any pictures with El or Jake. It's vital because it's so hard to control where it could end up or who is going to notice a photo you're tagged on. Probably, I would just go insane or have gray hair from worrying about it every second. However, don't people say that rules exist to be broken, do they?

I pull my phone out of a pocket, and I take a couple of selfies with El, then several pictures of the view. I really want to post it, but I can't. That's a big no-no. Some rules can't be broken under any circumstances. It's like Pandora's box — once it's opened, there is no coming back. Breaking rules overall isn't that great. Look at me now. It's hard for me to recognize myself. I used to be the definition of a goody-two-shoes. What happened?

When I look at El, I can't stop thinking that I should enjoy this until it lasts. I know my lying and juggling boyfriends will come to an end soon. I've started worrying that it's going to happen sooner rather than later. I should have dropped out from the 'homecoming queen' nomination, and I really should have broken up with Jake…

"Do you want to sit? I actually have some coffee," El asks while I'm deep in my thoughts.

"Yeah," I reply, and we both sit. I don't know what *El is staring at me as if he is about to ask me to marry him. This is too much. I need to stop this. Why is he so cute? Oh, he looked away… I guess that's what you wanted, so why are you so disappointed, Cassie? Well, I don't know the answer because I don't want to know.* The whole time I can't stop staring at El, and suddenly it hits me. *I'm in love. O-M-G, I'm in love with El.* Just like that.

"What's up?" El asks me. I shake my head.

"Nothing."

"Okay, weirdo," he smirks. "I was actually wondering… Will you join me?"

El takes two tickets to the Homecoming out of his jacket. This is literally the worst day in my entire life. *What happened? I was so happy a second ago. I attempt to smile and not look as if he's sentenced to death. Okay-okay, that's just an enormous exaggeration. It's not that bad.*

"Homecoming, hah?" I repeat. I don't know what I expect to happen by repeating the obvious. "Never imagined you as a 'homecoming' type."

We both laugh, but then El gets serious. *It's not good, not good at all.*

"Aren't you nominated for a Homecoming Queen?"

"That's just shallow and derivative. I wasn't planning to go…"

"Wo-o-o-w, Cassie. Wow."

I can see so much disappointment on his face. *Yeah, what else was I supposed to say? The only reason I was nominated in the first place was that I was/am with Jake… And you shouldn't have bought those tickets.* El frowns and asks, "So… Are you?"

"Of course," I say before he could even finish his question. I give him a hug, and after that, I don't remember what happened. I don't even remember how we drove back or anything until now. I'm opening the front door.

"Mom? Dad?" I enter, turning on the lights in the house, "Are you, guys, home?"

I close the door when it hits me. They're out tonight. It's a little bit disappointing. I'd love to spend some quality time with them without thinking about boys. I sigh. I hear several text notifications because I already know who is texting me. However, I glance at my phone just out of curiosity, and I was totally right — all seven texts from El and Jake.

I shake my head and take my boots off. Even by looking at them, I know they'll need some deep cleaning. I should have worn sneakers. I hear another notification. What the hell?! I check it.

"Can't wait to see you tomorrow," Jake texts, followed by a kiss emoji. I don't reply, taking off the jacket. I hear another notification. *Okay, Jake, this is too much.* I grab the phone, but it's El, to my surprise.

"Can't wait to see you soon," El texts, accompanied by a kiss emoji and a heart one. *What is this? When did all guys become the same?* I roll my eyes, and I make an easy decision to ignore it as well.

"I just need a break — no Jake, no Elliot," I say out loud, putting the phone away when I hear El's voice, "So what are you planning to do? How long are you planning to avoid this problem?"

The second I look over, I see Imaginary Elliot sitting on the stairs. Ugh... My mind is messing with me. Great. I roll my eyes and march towards the kitchen. How do you escape your own mind? You just ignore it and hope that it's not going to catch up with you. I look around the kitchen and quickly notice mom's note for me on a fridge — Dinner is inside. We love you. I smirk. She knew I'd forget to eat.

I open the fridge and stare at what is inside. The problem is I'm not too hungry, but I probably should snack on something.

"Mom, I'm not hungry," I say out loud and close the fridge. "But I'd love some tea. Yeah, tea sounds nice."

I turn on the teakettle and go to pick out the kind of tea I want. It's almost a tradition for me — I pick the tea and then grab a cup, which I find fits my mood and tea. Right now, I feel so exhausted. It's been a long evening. I slowly go over the tea — breakfast, green, fruit. I stop when I get to chamomile tea.

"That sounds like the one," I say, putting it aside. I walk to the cabinet with cups. I automatically grab the first cup I see when I hear how El clears his throat. I almost broke the cup. Luckily, I catch it and turn around.

"I'm not going anywhere," Imaginary El states, standing right next to me.

"Of course. Why would you?" I rhetorically ask and continue to make my tea. I feel very annoyed at myself. *Why can't I just shut this down... Once and for all.*

"Maybe, because you just want to be with me, that's why you can't shut me down," El responds to my question. Nobody likes a know-it-all. I don't even look over and pour boiling water into my cup. I notice the tea bag is ripped. Ugh, this is frustrating.

"Nothing goes your way because you need to break up with Jake," Imaginary El isn't dropping this conversation.

"Really? It looks like you have everything figured out," I snap.

"You already know this, but for some reason, you don't want to admit it to yourself."

"Well, I guess your job here is done," I say and leave the kitchen with my tea. Deep down, I don't want to admit that Imaginary El is right. I'm not ready for it. Right now, the only thing I really wish I could do is to rewrite this story. I would be so free.

As I come closer to the stairs, I become more nervous to see Imaginary El again. My heart can't stop beating so quickly. I guess it was fun to date two boys initially, but recently it's been draining. I feel so guilty. I wonder if boys ever feel guilty when they date multiple girls or whether it's as tiring as it seems to me.

Imaginary El hasn't shown, even when I enter my room and turn on the lights. I was pretty sure he'd pop up. I feel so relieved that he hasn't already appeared in front of my face. I highly doubt he will. I put my cup on a nightstand and stare at the distance. I really want to reset the whole thing because starting to date both of them was a mistake — no other explanation.

You need to stop feeling so bad for yourself, Cassie. It's going to be alright. I get comfortable in the middle of the bed and reach for my tea. I hear Imaginary Jake's voice, "So you're gonna break up with me before Homecoming?"

Right on time, Jake. Of course, if El disappears, Jake will show up. It makes so much sense. I sit up and see Imaginary Jake sitting next to me on the bed. It takes all my energy to pretend that I don't see him. Jake leans close to my ear and whispers, "I was promised a date…"

I nervously swallow, moving away from him. I sarcastically reply, "Jake, you never miss a party. Even if it's a self-pity one."

"Don't change the subject."

"I did agree to go with you, but to be fair, it was weeks ago," I explain and look at Jake. I wish I didn't because Jake's eyes are so sad. My heart feels like it's about to break into thousands of pieces. This is exceptionally unfair because I can't stop imagining us sharing the stage as Homecoming King and Queen. *Maybe I can figure something out, so I can still go.*

"We all know you want to go with me," Imaginary El protests, hanging out by the window. "Jake, we agreed we wouldn't use puppy-dog eyes on Cassie."

"You know that I'm right here?!" I protest. They both give a pointed look.

"Come on, Cass, we're basically you," El explains, then points at his body, "and don't let this trick you."

"Hey, we also agreed not to use our bodies," Imaginary Jake protests.

"Well, I guess we're even now," El replies.

It's not that much fun watching my Imaginary boyfriends bicker over things not related to me. And they're products of my mind. I should be in control.

"You know what," I start, but I won't get a chance to finish.

"Wait a second, don't give me that look, Elliot," Jake interrupts me.

"Come on, you can't be serious," Imaginary El blows him off.

"Yeah, I have to break up with Jake," I say out loud. It's finally quiet. I look around, and there is no one else in the room. *If you think about it, that was easy. Just be honest, Cassie. Be honest.*

I put the cup away and grab my phone.

Hey, Jake. Let's meet tomorrow at Jack's Diner around 6:30 p.m. I need to talk to you.

He replies almost immediately.

Sounds good. <3

I put my phone away. I don't feel so weird, maybe even relieved because I can finally breathe. *This is it. I'm doing it. I'll be free. I am free.*

Chapter 15
The Break-Up

Weirdly, I haven't slept so well in a while, and I haven't felt so happy. The whole day I've been doing just great. I even start wondering whether I should have done this much earlier. Well, hey, I'm here at the diner now. I'm about to fix everything and go to the Homecoming with a guy I love. And yes, probably I won't win, but being there with El is more important than a stupid title.

I check the time. It's already 6:43. I'm kind of getting hungry. I only ordered a glass of Coke, and I paid for it. Why? So I could run away if things don't go well. I've never broken up with anyone before. Not like that, at least. *The last time I broke up with Jake, but he let me do it first. It was polite. I'm not breaking up with him a second time. He would break up with me because I said I love you too early. You could technically say that he said I'm his girlfriend too early. Oh no-no-no. He's going to freak out. He's going to yell at me. He might not care that much. I hope he won't cry. Do boys cry over a breakup?*

I can't spin it any other way, but I'm just panicking. I sigh and spin ice in my glass. I check my Instagram, there is nothing new. This is typical Jake. He says many words, but it'll be a different story when it comes to doing. *That's why you're breaking up with him, Cassie.* I smirk at myself. *You can do it, Cass, but don't buy into his cute puppy-dog eyes. You'll be just fine.*

"Hey, babe! Sorry, I'm late," Jake pulls me out of my daydreaming.

"Hey," I look up and put the phone away. I immediately notice that he sits in front of me, not with me. Interesting. That has never happened before. *What does this mean? Could it mean... Wouldn't it be amazing if he breaks up with me right now?*

"Is everything okay, babe?" he asks. I nod, looking down at the table. I think I need to pull it together. Jake is here, and it's time, to be honest.

"I wanted to talk to you," we say at the same time. I look up at him, very surprised.

"Oh, me too, isn't it hysterical?" he asks. He's never been so right because we've never thought about the same thing, and I'm not even mentioning saying something at the same time. Both at the same time? I'd say one word — impossible.

"I know..." I try to sound enthusiastic.

"What do you want to talk about?"

"No, you go ahead," I say. I'm not delaying the breakup. I just want to make sure that he's not about to tell me something horrible. What would I do if I broke up with him only to find out that his grandmother passed away? I will never forgive myself.

"Okay," Jake agrees and reaches for something in his pocket. "Since you've been nominated as a Homecoming Queen, I got us tickets."

Jake puts two tickets on the table. I don't know what has just happened, but I can't take my eyes off the tickets. I think it finally hits me. I'm screwed. I should have gone first. Those tickets are exactly the same as the ones El gave me yesterday. What are you going to do, Cassie? You can't break up with him now...

"Are you okay?" he asks me, a little bit confused.

"Yeah, sorry."

"As I was saying," Jake continues to mumble, "I really hope we'll be the couple who wins the Homecoming nominations together."

"Are you kidding?" I hear Ally's voice out of nowhere. Oh, no-no-no! Ally is the last person I want to see right now. I turn my head to the right and immediately notice Ally grabbing her stuff from a few tables over. She's absolutely furious, and I have to admit I've never seen her so mad.

"Mmm... excuse me?" Jake asks. He sounds a little bit offended, but Ally behaves as if she doesn't hear me. She rushes up close to me and asks me, "So...the couple? Really?"

"Ally," I slowly start. "It's not..."

"You must be kidding me," Ally interrupts me. She runs away, shaking her head. I can barely breathe because my heart is pounding. *Does Jake figure it out? Is Ally texting Elliot right now? OMG. This is so bad, this is so bad.*

"Cassie, what the hell is that?" Jake asks me. "Is she your friend? What's her name."

"Ally, it's a miscommunication," I explain. "I promised to go with her to the Homecoming, you know. Give a second, okay? I need to talk to her."

"Should I come?" Jake asks.

"No, it's okay. I'll be right back," I say and take off.

"Okay," Jake says, but I'm already gone.

I run as fast as I can. I need to talk to Ally —— I have to. Maybe I can explain it to her just like I've done with Jake. Ally is pulling back from a parking spot.

For a second, I feel relieved because she couldn't text El, even if she wanted to. I still have a chance. I need to make her talk to me.

"Ally! Stop..." I scream as I stand right in front of her car, blocking her way. Ally glances at me through the mirror. I can feel her angry glare on me. Ally shakes her head.

"We have nothing to talk about, Cassie."

"Please, Ally. Please, I'm begging you," I scream. Ally's voice sounds so cold, she seems to understand what was happening back in the diner. *I'm screwed. There is no way out. I'm going to lose Elliot because Ally is in love with him. There is no way she won't tell him.* I think I finally understood what it meant. The tears start rolling down one by one, and I can't stop them. Eventually, Ally turns off the car and gets out.

"So?"

"I know how it looks, and I'm not going to say it's not what it looks like," I say. "I know it is wrong, but to be honest, I was about to break it off."

Ally laughs in response and then adds, "To be honest? Haha... Oh my Gosh, Cassie. This is so like you. Yeah, you know it didn't look like you were about to break it off. Although, to be honest, it did look like you were about to go on another date. Now you...being nominated for a homecoming queen out of nowhere makes a lot more sense. There is no way a freshman would be nominated unless... Well, you know what you need to do."

"Ally, no-no-no. It's not like that. I swear," I reassure her, but I can barely even look at her. I can't stand her disappointed glare, and I know this is just the beginning... My house of cards is about to fall.

"I can't believe you'd do something like this to Elliot. What were you thinking?" she yells at me.

"Please-please, you can't tell him," I beg her.

"Oh, no! I won't, but you will."

"Wait, what?"

"And Jake."

"What?"

"You have to tell both of them. Please, don't pretend that you don't understand."

"Ally..." I say. I need to fix this, and I need to do it fast. I start explaining, "I don't want to hurt anyone. I just want you to know that. It's never been my goal."

"You know, Cassie, it's not about what you want," Ally states. "And let's be honest, it's all about what you've done, and what you've done is terrible. But, you know what is absolutely the worst? I'm pretty sure you don't even have a clue why I'm so upset."

She stares at me, waiting for my response. I don't even know what I can say, but only because it seems like anything I say just makes me look like a villain. Don't take me wrong, I know I'm not perfect, but I'm not such a horrible person Ally wants me to be.

"No, Ally, I know," I start.

"No, Cassie," she stops me. "Just stop. You don't need to say anything. Just do the right thing... So I won't have to."

That's the only thing she says before she gets in the car and drives away. I don't stop her. What's the point? Ally gives me a stare at the end. It's the "I-am-serious" type of stare as if I need it. I roll my eyes when I'm a hundred percent sure she can't see me. However, it doesn't matter how snarky I am right now because this is bad. I know, Ally. She isn't one of those people, who say, and then don't do anything. If she says something, she actually means it, which is an obvious problem for me. *All my dreams are shattered. El won't forgive me if he finds out. Louis was right. I'm going to die alone. Hmm, what could change her mind? Can anything change her mind? Wait.* It finally hit me — not something, but someone. I can't believe I haven't thought about it. Louis can talk Ally into anything. I have no idea why, but I don't really care about the reasons. I pick up the phone and dial. It goes to voicemail. No biggie, I need to go back to Jake anyways.

"Hey, Lou-Lou, hope everything is good," I leave a message as I walk back to the diner, "I'm calling you because I need a... Umm, I guess I need to use your superpowers for fixing things. I really need your help, call me back. Ta-ta, love."

I walk back and find Jake waiting for me. *At least, he's ordered some food. Remind me, Cassie, what did you want to tell him? Oh, you tried to break up with him. Yeah, it's not going to happen — not today.*

"Hey, what the hell happened?" Jake immediately asks, and for a second, I consider breaking up with him, just like I've planned. Then maybe I can spin that Ally is coming up with the crazy shenanigans to break El and me I. Ugh... I've done some stuff, but that would be just too far. Even if I've never felt like Ally is my friend, I can't do that to her. She believes we're close friends, so I have to honor it.

"It's nothing, just a misunderstanding," I'm trying to downplay the situation. "Sorry about that."

"Cass, that didn't sound like nothing, and it definitely sounded like your friend... What's her name?"

"Ally."

"Ally doesn't even know that we're dating."

Jake gives me a pointed look. A thousand lies cross my mind, and any of them could work. However, I'm so exhausted...

"Honestly, Jake, I was so scared to tell you..."

"Please, don't even finish. I know."

That's it, he knows. That's good. At least, it's going to be over in a second. It's about time. I awkwardly say, "Yeah?"

"I understand why you wouldn't tell your friends about us. I was a jerk to you at the camp, and you didn't want to tell your friends before we were a sure thing," he states. Wow, this is just insane. How did he even get there? Should I tell him the truth?

Jake puts his hand over mine and says, intensely looking at me, "I hope it'll change soon."

"I don't know what to say," I mumble.

"Don't, it's okay, Cass," Jake reassures me as I get a text from Louis. I glance over it. Louis is asking when he should come over.

"Hey, can you take me home? I really need to talk to Ally about this," I ask.

"Sure. Give me a second."

I nod as Jake goes to pay for food. *I haven't eaten at all today. Hmm… I was so nervous about breaking up with Jake that I wouldn't be able to take a single bite. And now… Oh well, now I feel nauseated.*

"Ready?" Jake asks. I nod again, and we both walk off.

The whole ride on the way to my house, Jake and I spent in silence. I guess it's been working out for me, but deep down, I know I'm running out of time to make everything alright. I'm falling deeper and deeper into a rabbit hole, and soon… there will be no way out. I text Louis to come to me around seven o'clock. At some point, he replies, "Sounds good." I try really hard not to worry too much. The worst is in my head, which is making me so paranoid. I can't stop thinking about what if El will be there when Jake drops me off. Maybe I want it to play that way because it's not the case. When Jake parks in front of my house, I secretly monitor the area. Even though I'm still waiting for El to pop out of nowhere, he's not around. I lean over to open the door and say, "Bye, Jake. I'll call you later."

"Can you wait for a second?" he stops me.

"Yeah, sure. What's up?"

"So... Have you decided?"

"Wait, what are you talking about?"

"Will you come with me for the Homecoming?" he asks. Oh yeah. The Homecoming. I almost forgot about it. Then I make the biggest mistake by looking at Jake. His eyes are so warm as I answer, "Yeah. Of course."

Why did I agree? Who knows at this point.

"Great."

"See you."

I dart out of the car before Jake leans for a kiss. I don't deserve to be happy. On a scale between zero and a hundred of being a horrible person, I wonder where I am on that scale. Probably a hundred means that you're an evil person like a killer. Where should a soul killer be?

"Bye, Cassie," I hear Jake's voice in the distance. I look back for a second and wave, "I'll call you later, okay?"

Jake thumbs it up, sending me an air kiss. However, I'm already gone. I'm trying to sneak in so I don't have to chat with my parents. They always immediately know that something is up with me. Honestly, I can't have them knowing what is happening with my love life. Why? Well, they will be so disappointed in me. I can't see the disapproval on their faces because I never live up to the expectations. When they went on their first date, mom and dad knew that they would spend the rest of their lives together. What would they think about me if they found out about Jake and Elliot? Yeah, exactly.

"Hey," I announce that I'm at home.

"Hey, honey," dad says. I look over and see dad prepping for dinner. However, sometimes to

"Where's mom?"

"Oh, she's dropping some stuff for Wendy? I think," he says.

"Okay," I say. "Actually, I forgot to ask you, guys... Louis is going to come over, is that fine?"

"Of course," dad replies. "Do you think he'll stay for dinner?"

"Umm... I don't think so."

"Well, I'll cook extra food just in case."

"Sounds good."

I rush to my room, randomly checking my phone. Louis can come any time. I hope that he can fix all my problems, but deep down, I know I'm the one who has to take charge and do the right thing. I drop dead in the middle of my bed, staring at the ceiling. I don't know how long I've been doing that before I hear the doorbell.

"I got it," I yell, jumping off the bed and running downstairs.

"Okay!" dad yells back.

I sprint to the front door like an Olympic champion. Well, that's an exaggeration, but I'm doing the best I can. I open the door, and Louis enters.

"She knows," I state before Louis has a chance to say anything else.

"I know."

"I'm so screwed," I say, staring at the floor.

"Not here, Cassie," Lou-Lou says and demonstratively looks towards the kitchen where my dad is. "Hello, Mr. Fuller."

"Hi, Louis. How is everything going?"

"Good."

"Dad, we're going upstairs," I cut their chit-chat, and I grab Louis's hand, dragging him upstairs.

When we enter my bedroom, I lock the door. Louis makes himself comfortable on my bed, lounging on my big heart pillow.

"This is bad," I say while I'm pacing back and forth. It makes me so focused. I'm just in the zone of fixing things.

"Well, you should have broken up with one of the ways before this happened," Louis says as he catches my death stare, "but probably you already know that."

I want to roll my eyes, but I totally understand that I can't give too much attitude to my last ally.

"Well, I'll just have to break up with both of them. That's going to be a safe bet, right?" I ask Lou-Lou.

"Are you kidding me?" Louis shakily asks me in response. "You can't break up with both of them now. Homecoming is tomorrow!"

I know he's right. He's right about everything. I can't believe I've waited for so long to break up with Jake.

"I should just tell them I'm sick," I start spiraling, "then move, change my name, dye my hair, go into witness protection."

Louis giggles at my statement and says, "Yeah, I don't think the police give out new identities over heartbreaks, but I totally get what you're going for. Good try."

"I know, I'm just... crazy," I explain and sit next to Louis. "Did Ally say anything to you?"

Louis makes a weird face as if he knows something I shouldn't.

"What?" I ask.

"Well, I'm trying not to pick sides here..."

"Louis, you're here... now. If you ask me, you have picked," I tell Louis.

"But, Cassie, I didn't ask you," he replies with a smirk. I know that smirk. Lou-Lou is ready to spill the beans.

"What did she say?"

"Without going into the details, the situation as it stands is she'll tell Elliot if you don't..."

My heart is just broken. I guess Ally is the one who seals my destiny. It's over — I look down, feeling so devastated. There is no way out.

"This is so unfair," I start. "I was literally trying to break up with Jake. What was she even doing there?"

I ask, but Louis just goes silent. I even look at him a little bit confused, but instead of an answer, it comes across that Louis is mad at me.

"Are you kidding me right now?!" he angrily asks. Louis quickly notices by my reaction that I have no idea what he's talking about. He shakes his head and continues, "She meets her tutor there every Friday!"

"Oh yeah," it hits me, "crap."

"This is the problem with you. You live in a different universe, where you're the center of it. It's not reality. You're not the only person here. Your life would be so much easier if you listen to others. At least, sometimes."

"Point taken. I suck," I agree with Louis. He's right. I'm a horrible person. I just have to face it. "I'm not going to Homecoming."

"Hell, no! You'll be a social pariah for the rest of the year. Okay-okay, I'll help you."

"Why would you do that?" I ask him with so much desperation in my voice.

"I think that could be fun to be your wingman," Lou-Lou explains. "And we'll figure out Ally stuff later. I promise she's not going to bust you during Homecoming. I have a plan for your double boyfriend problem."

"Really?"

Louis nods in response. The happiness rushes through my whole body, but I'm so sure about Ally's situation. I don't believe she's going to let it go that easy. At least, I wouldn't.

"But Ally was vivid with me," I start.

"I got you, girl. Promise, you won't have anything to worry about," he reassures me.

"And you mentioned you have a plan?" I hesitantly ask.

"Hell yeah."

Chapter 16
The Homecoming Dance Part 1

When Louis leaves, we've decided what Lou-Lou and I will do, which I'll tell you all about in a bit. It all makes sense, and I'm pretty sure it's going to work. I have to admit Louis's wingman skills are just top-notch. However, my heart isn't in it. In a way, I feel like I should do what Ally demands.

Anyway… Lou-Lou had left before the dinner, and I wasn't that hungry. I know it's probably suspicious to my parents that I skipped it, but tomorrow will be a big day. I need to refocus because, for Louis's plan to work, everything must be perfect, or the whole school will find out my secret. That will be my worst nightmare. What would people say? I know they won't say anything good, and then my parents will hear some rumors. They won't believe it at first, but they will. Everyone will know that I'm a terrible person. Most people aren't great, and nobody is perfect. Everyone can just hide their deep, dark nature, but mine is going to be known. It's going to be in front of everyone, right there to judge me. So yeah, tomorrow will be a crucial day.

I haven't eaten anything since lunch, and I finally feel like I can eat something. I wander downstairs. When I get to the kitchen, I don't even know what I want to snack on. I go through every cabinet and find nothing I'd like. That's how my tedious journey brings me to the fridge. I know how terrible it is to stand in front of an opened fridge, but hey, we all do that sometimes. I grab a jug of milk and turn around when I see my mom getting me a glass of milk. *What the hell? How long was she there? OMG…*

"Are you okay, honey?" mom asks me. I shake my head.

"Yeah, sorry, mom," I reply, "You just scared me. I didn't see or hear you."

"Oh, sorry. I didn't mean to."

Mom sits at the dining table while I pour milk into the glass. I quickly notice that mom is kind of staring at me, which usually means we're about to have the talk. *Great. Did they find out? No-no-no, Cassie, this is not the time to let your anxieties take over you.*

"Dad and I..." she starts. Yep. Here it is. "We wanted to ask if everything is okay? You seem a little tense."

I immediately feel relieved. They have no idea about Elliot and Jake.

"No, I'm good," I say, but my mom gives me a skeptical look. I need to give her something before she starts, so I add, "There are a lot of people who say that, but I don't know why. I'm okay."

I grab the glass and sit next to her. Mom smiles and explains, "I don't know, honey. We noticed you've been stressing out a lot."

I roll my eyes. Usually, it works so well because I'm only snarky with them when everything is going well.

"No-no-no," mom stops me. "Don't."

"I'm fine. Really."

"Well, then... If everything is fine, please, explain this," she states. "Your dress and shoes came in, and you haven't asked about them at all or tried them on. That's not like you."

Oh yeah, she's right. I ask my parents to get me something special for the Homecoming because El asked me to come with him about a week ago. I was so excited, but I was getting less and less enthusiastic the closer it was getting. Maybe I just felt like... I don't know. I guess the truth is that I don't want to choose because I'm scared to make the wrong choice. I know I love El, but...what if I pick him? Will he get bored of being a good boyfriend and break up with me? Jake broke up with me, then he crawled back to me. I didn't break up with him earlier because I felt very safe having plan B.

"Omg, I totally forgot about it!" I yell, trying to make myself sound excited. *Did she buy it? Was it enough?*

"Do you want to try it on?" mom asks. I guess it worked.

"Let's do it."

"That's more like you."

"Where is it?"

"In the living room."

We both stand up and wander there. The second we enter the room, I see two beautifully wrapped boxes. I can't even hide the enormous amount of excitement. I glance at mom as if I need her permission to open them.

"Come on, what are you waiting for?' she asks.

"I don't know," I say and start unwrapping the first box. I slowly untie the bow and open it. I'm excited like a kid waking up on Christmas Day and running downstairs to see what Santa brought them. I can't believe my own eyes when I open the box because it's definitely the most beautiful dress I've ever seen in my whole life. It's an ivory sleeveless A-line dress with embellishment and glitters on the front and back. When I unfold the dress, I see the flounced organza skirt.

"Do you like it?" mom asks. I put the dress back and look at mom.

"I love it."

"Oh good, dad and I wanted to get you something special for the dance with Elliot. You, guys, are going together, right?" she asks.

My eyes become watery. I can barely hold myself from bursting into tears. I can't cry right now. It's going to be hard to explain, Cassie. Keep it together! I nod.

"Yes, we are. Thanks, mom. I love the dress so much."

"Try it on," mom says with a smile on her face. I do, but I feel like I don't deserve the dress. I don't deserve the nomination. However, I still put the dress on, which is making it even harder on me. It fits me perfectly. It could make anyone feel like a princess.

"This is too much, mom. It's probably too expensive and where would I wear it after the Homecoming? We should return it, and I'll wear some other dress I already have," I say. That will be fair.

"Oh no, hon. Don't worry about it. Wendy told me you got nominated, and you didn't even tell us!"

"It's really not a big deal."

"Come on," she gives me a severe look. "What's going on with you?"

"I don't know. I think the whole Homecoming Queen and King is kind of ridiculous," I explain. "It's the twenty-first century. Picking a king and a queen is another way to divide people. You know."

Mom doesn't say anything. She just smiles, which is suspicious by itself.

"What?" I ask.

"You're so funny."

"I'm serious."

"I know. Do you want to try on the shoes?" Mom ignores me. "I want to see the whole look in case you decide to return everything."

"Okay," I say, opening the shoe box. However, the second I see the shoes, my destiny is sealed because there is no way I'm returning them.

"Or not. It's up to you, but I would love it if you keep it."

I run up to mom, and squeeze her a tight hug. She seems a little bit surprised.

"I'm taking this as we're keeping all of it," mom teases me.

"Thank you, mom."

My mom made me so happy and excited that I slept like a baby the night before, totally forgetting my troubles. However, as I open my eyes, I mentally go back to it, so the first part of the plan is to tell Jake I'll be late because I promised Ally to go with her.

Yeah, if she finds out, she'll be so mad at me, but Louis has reassured me that it's okay multiple times. Jake wasn't super happy about it, but he agreed to that. Louis insisted that Elliot should take me to the dance, and since he's the one who will have to make Ally decide not to bust me, I've agreed to everything.

The whole morning I'm running around like a crazy person, trying to figure out what will be the best make-up. To be completely honest, I'm not that great with make-up. Therefore, it usually takes me forever to find the right look. I wish I could just ask Louis to help me with this, but I know that would be too much. Lou-Lou is right. I haven't been the best at listening and paying attention to others. However, I have to do better for everybody, so I know Louis is planning to do something fabulous for Homecoming. He's planning to do something similar to The Rocky Horror Picture Show, which I'm apparently scheduled to watch. I don't quite even know what that means, but I know one thing for sure is that it's vital to Louis. He's really saving my bacon here, so it's vital to me too. I remember that his make-up is going to take forever because it's going to be a masterpiece.

I've been putting make-up on and off, but I'm going with a natural look. And I decided to go with loose curls for my hair. It's simple and easy, but it doesn't take anything away from my spectacular dress. I thought I had so much time, but when I hear the doorbell go off, I'm barely ready, putting the second shoe on my right foot. *Hell ya, I finally feel like Cinderella.* Last look and I nervously swallow. I'm so not ready for this. I can't even believe I'm in this position. I was such a good girl through the whole middle school, having a crush on a guy who didn't even know my name. And look at me now. Cassie, you have two dates, and one of the guys is that boy who didn't know your name.

I run downstairs, which is hard to call a "run" because the shoes my parents got for me are high heels, and I'm not used to wearing them. I guess it's like running in slow motion. My parents open the door for El, even before I could go down the stairs. I feel a butterfly in my stomach when I see him. I guess this is it. I'm finally the main character in my own story. Yes, maybe it's a stupid romantic comedy, where a guy stands down there and falls in love with me all over again, but I love it.

I gracefully walk to Elliot, and he helps me step off the stairs. We can't keep our eyes off each other.

"Cassie, you look fantastic," the first thing El says.

"You too," I reply, attempting not to stare at him.

"Picture time!" both of my parents yell. In normal circumstances, I would hate this, but I love this right now. It's a perfect distraction. I'm a little bit nervous about El, but since both of us, Elliot and I, think that these types of events are kinds of lame, I might have a chance to get away with 'a murder'.

"Okay, guys," I say to my parents after I've taken over fifty pictures. "We gotta go. I want us to come, not in the middle of the dance."

Sometimes I get paranoid about what mom and dad will post. Can you imagine what would happen if they posted a picture with El and me? However, we've made an agreement that they won't post anything without asking me, so fingers crossed.

"Okay-okay, the last one," dad asks. I roll my eyes and shake my head.

"Sure thing," El says. "Maybe you can drop them for my parents as well."

"You see, Cassie," mom adds.

"Only if it is going to be the last one," I insist, "I bet you've got too many."

"Okay, say cheese," dad directs us.

"Cheese," El and I say at the same time.

I turn to El and command, "Let's go."

He nods, and we both start walking outside. My parents follow us out. I'm pretty sure if they could, they would try to come with us. That would be a disaster, don't you think? My high heels are so tall, it's a little bit difficult to walk. I usually wear high heels, so I've always had mom get me something over eight inches. However, I have to admit that I should have practiced before the Homecoming. Thanks to El, who helps me with such an easy task as walking. He opens the car door for me as I sit.

"Bye, guys," I look over and say to my parents. They wave at me, looking so excited for me. *Hmm... I wish I could be as thrilled as they are. I should have broken up with Jake long before, but mistakes were made.*

"Have fun, kids!" My parents shout as we're driving away. "Don't be too late!"

El and I get quiet. I quickly check my phone, and we're running a little bit late from the original schedule, which Louis created for me. I see the text from Lou-Lou, and he's asking if we're getting close.

"Is everything okay?" El asks me.

"Oh yeah," I say, looking away from my phone. "Lou-Lou is already there, and he's just wondering where we're at. He already got there. I think he's nervous."

"Isn't he with Ally?"

"Honestly, I have no idea," I say, looking at the window.

El nods and picks up the speed. We haven't said a word the rest of the ride, partially because I'm a bundle of nerves. When El parks the car in a totally full parking lot, it finally hits me — this is it. One wrong step might just destroy everything between El and me.

"Ready?" he asks.

"Yeah."

"You seem really nervous. Is it me or…"

"Yeah, your hotness made me lose my mind," I cut El off. He rolls his eyes at me.

"Okay, then."

"I really don't want to win the nomination for Homecoming Queen."

"Who cares, Cass? We're here to have fun," El calms me down. "Trust me, it's all going to be okay. Let's go and find Louis."

He's right. I need to stop worrying too much and start with small tasks like finding Louis. He promised to help, so everything should be just fine. I hope so.

Chapter 17
The Homecoming Dance Part 2

Our Homecoming traditionally takes place in the gym. It's decorated so well that our regular gym has become unrecognizable. I was skeptical about the whole thing because our gym isn't some cool venue that could make anyone feel special. However, I was wrong. It looks very sophisticated. The music is playing very loud. I can guarantee my hearing will be lost for a bit afterward. A buffet is full of salads, sides, entrees, and lots of delicious rolls. There are an enormous variety of drinks. We also get special glasses, which we can keep afterward, which is kind of fun — the champagne glasses for the ladies and beer mugs for the guys. Of course, the champagne is non-alcoholic ginger ale, and the beer is the root beer. I find that's cute. The whole vibe of the dance is pretty magical, which makes me excited for a second. However, everything has to end when Louis shows up out of nowhere. I even get startled because the gym is packed and pretty dark.

"Hey, guys!" Louis screams over the music. He looks absolutely fantastic, and I mean it. His make-up is flawless.

"Hen, man," Elliot says. They shake hands, and then Louis gives Cassie a tight hug.

"Be careful. Ally is already here," he whispers in my ear.

"I thought you talked to her," I whisper in response. Still, I'm pretty sure Louis couldn't hear what I'm saying at all because he quickly moves on, "Okay, beautiful people, we have to take a few selfies."

"Lou-Lou, not you too," I complain, "my parents made us take so many pictures…"

"Not even a conversation, missy. I didn't do all of this," he says, pointing at his costume. "I already had to tone down my Dr. Frank-N-Furter look. My parents insisted that would be too much. Can you believe this? It's the 21st century, not the 1950s. So the least you can do is to take a selfie with me. What do you think, El?"

"Sure, why not?"

Sometimes Louis is such a drama queen. Maybe he should be nominated for the Homecoming queen. He would play that part much better than me. I believe he deserves it more as well.

"Yeah, Louis, let's do this," I agree.

"That's the spirit," Louis says, getting his phone out like a magician. "Okay, guys, get closer."

I should just attempt to have some fun because I'm already here, and I don't have complete control over the situation. I glance around the space, hoping to spot Ally. Instead, I spot Jake and his entourage near the buffet tables. It wouldn't be that bad if there wasn't one more person with them. Of course, it has to be Katie, who is shamelessly flirting with my boyfriend. Elliot is my boyfriend, but this is inappropriate because she's supposed to think that Jake and I are dating. I know I shouldn't be jealous, but I don't understand why Katie drives me crazy.

"Smile, Cass?" Louis asks me.

"Oh yeah," I reply and put on a smile. However, when I notice Katie putting her hand on Jake's shoulder, and the worst is that Jake behaves like he's single. After Louis's few attempts to get a perfect selfie, I add, "I'm so sorry, guys, I'm gonna run to the bathroom."

"Should we get a drink?" Lou-Lou asks El.

"Sure."

"I'll be right back," I promise to El and give him a small kiss on his cheek. Three of us split up, and even though I'm walking towards the bathroom, I have no intention of going to the bathroom. The second El and Louis disappear in the crowd, I change my course towards Jake.

I wake long enough before I come up to Jake's table. They've just finished discussing something, so that's my opening.

"Hey, everyone. How are you all doing?" I ask, taking a seat in front of him. I really want to give Katie a look down, but I'm better than that. Jake's eyes sparkle with happiness when he sees me.

"Good," he says.

"Hey, Cassie," Katie says. Her eyes are locked on me, which makes me very uncomfortable. She's definitely showing that I don't belong here.

"Oh hey, Kate."

"Actually, it's Katie."

"So sorry, I totally forgot," I say with a smile on my face. I couldn't forget her name, and she knows it.

"No problem."

"Hey, do you want to get a drink?" Jake asks partially because he wants to change the subject, but that can't happen. *El and Louis are getting drinks. I can't let this happen. Well, that's going to be so awkward. Hey, El. Remember Jake? Jake, do you remember El?* I've noticed that all of them are staring at me. *Oops, I might have been thinking for too long.* I nervously swallow.

"A drink?" I say to drag out the time, hoping I can come up with something clever. Why is it so hard to concentrate? Come on, Cassie, you can do better.

"Yeah, are you okay?"

"Totally. I actually wanted to do a loop, you know, " I reply. A loop? What the hell does it mean?

"A loop?" Katie speaks up. If only I could just get rid of you, Katie. I would be so happy. You have no idea.

"Yeah, there is so little time to make an appearance before everyone votes."

"Are you sure, babe?" Jake asks me. His voice is full of confusion. *Okay, Cassie. Turn on your brain. Think, think... What does the king of the cafeteria care about?*

"I just want to make sure people will vote for me. I really want to be a queen next to my king," I reply. Not bad, not bad at all. I'm pretty sure it's a pretty good excuse, but the only question is left unanswered — did Jake buy into my bullshit.

"Well, then," Jake says, "of course, go. That's important."

"Thank you, babe," I say, sending him an air kiss. I notice Katie goggles at

Jake and me in total disbelief. I run away from them, hiding in a hallway. I'm trying to catch a breath. Even though the first part went pretty smoothly, I'm a step away from failing. I just need to stay sharp to pull the whole thing off. Take a deep breath, Cassie. It's time to go back. Hmm… I really miss Elliot. He's my anchor, so I have to complete this game. If I get away with tonight, I promise I'll break up with Jake first thing in the morning. Ugh… I should have stayed at home.

"Hey, Cassie," says a girl, who I don't even know.

"Hey," I awkwardly reply, wondering whether I should have recognized her.

"I don't know if you know me," she starts talking at me, "but I want you to know that I voted for you. Honestly, I love you and Jake together. Good luck."

"Thanks. I really appreciate it," I say as the girl walks away. I shake my head, thinking that I'm a horrible person. I have to find El.

I walk back into the gym towards the area with drinks and almost immediately notice Lou-Lou and El chatting and drinking. They are obviously having fun. I'm pretty sure they've stolen the champagne glasses, which are supposed to be exclusively for girls. El always makes me smile. I feel relieved. I just want to run away with him. Ally is right. I've done something terrible, and I should have known better.

I walk up to them, but very carefully because I'm terrified of getting caught. The guys are chatting about something, and they don't even see me coming up to them.

"So, who is the lucky guy you took to the dance?" I overhear El ask Lou-Lou. My heart just melts because El cares about my friends.

"Oh, I didn't know we were that close…" Louis cheekily replies. If only I could roll my eyes harder…Why? I know one thing Lou-Lou loves this so much. He adds, "It's complicated. He's not from our school, you know…"

"Hey, what are you, guys, drinking?" I ask as I come up.

"Well, hello, stranger, " Elliot says in response.

"Cassie, honestly," Louis starts, " El is a catch."

"I know. Louis, please, don't steal him from me," I facetiously beg

Lou-Lou.

"Honey, it's going to be hard."

"Do you want some punch?" El asks me.

"I would love some. Thank you."

"Of course."

Elliot walks away as I get closer to Louis. Before I start chatting with him about everything, I wait until El is away from Lou-Lou and me.

"You, little minx," I say, pinching him a little. He giggles as I continue, "How are we doing?"

"Good. I just saw Ally."

"And..."

"You tell me," he says as he looks over. I follow his glance and immediately notice Ally dancing with our classmates. She's so free and happy. Honestly, I feel so bad. I wish I would have done better, so we all can enjoy this time. I smile, and I'm ready to go and talk it through with her.

"Just don't remind her about the whole thing," Lou-Lou whispers. I think he's read my mind that minute, and since he's a good friend, he brings me back to reality.

"Yeah, when you say something, it always sounds so easy," I'm sarcastic, which happens very often. It's my defense mechanism. Louis knows it — that's why he shakes his head.

"Oh, my queen of sarcasm," he says, petting me on my back. We both watch Ally have fun.

"Sorry, I stole this from you."

"Nah. Not a big deal. Honestly, I would be so bored without your shenanigans."

"Do you miss the times we could just hang out together?" I ask, but looking at Louis's confusion, I clarify, "without the boys, you know."

"Cassie, look at me," Louis tells me, and I do. "It's all gonna be alright."

"I hope so," I hopelessly say as Elliot comes back. He passes a glass full of punch to me. I take his hand and ask him, "Do you want to get out of here?"

"Sure," El answers. "What about Louis?"

"It's cool," Lou-Lou says. "I'm going to join Ally. Someone has to rock the dance floor."

I take El's hand, and we walk away. He looks confused and surprised at the same time.

"Where are we going?" he asks me.

"It's a surprise," I tease Elliot as we walk.

"A surprise from a girl, who hates surprises," he teases me back.

"Burn," I giggle, dragging him outside.

It's already pitch black — a few stars are sparkling in the sky. A light wind plays with hair. It's finally quiet. We walk towards the bleachers, and it feels like time has stopped. I take off my shoes. El shakes his head.

"What are you doing?" he asks me.

"Just give me a second," I stand, facing away. "Catch me if you can!"

I start running, leaving El behind.

"Wait, what?" he yells, but it's too late. I'm already far away. I look over to make sure El is chasing after me. Of course, he does. Even though El isn't a football player, he catches up with me very quickly.

I run up and sit in the middle of the bleachers. El joins me almost right away. Elliot glances at me as I'm catching my breath.

"Cassie, what's going on?" he asks. I nervously swallow. *This is surprising. Does he know? I just need to find out what he knows...* I shrug my shoulders.

"What do you mean?" I casually ask.

"Since when are Louis and I best friends?"

"Who said anything about best friends?"

"Come on, Cass."

El gives me a skeptical stare. Maybe it's a good time to tell him the truth... Yes, it's time.

"It's just Ally, we're having an... we're fighting," I say instead. *Where is that coming from? Why the hell did I involve Ally in this conversation between El and me?*

"And how is it even related to me or to us?" he asks. I can hear the skepticism in his voice, and I've got to admit it's an excellent question. What is your plan, Cassie?

"She's…" I start saying, and it's too late for me to stop, "she's in love with you."

Omg…why did I just say that? I quickly realize that I've done something horrible.

"What?!"

"She's in love with you, and it makes me uncomfortable…" I say. Omg, I repeated it. However, before I can even think this through, I add, "because I love you."

At least, that's true. I feel incredibly vulnerable. This is the first time I said since Jake rejected me. Elliot looks at me, but he doesn't say a word. It's freaking me. *Did I freak him out? Omg, Cassie, why can't you wait until a guy tells you I love you first? How hard is that? I make the same mistakes over and over. It's time to learn, Cassie.*

It's getting chilly. *This is so embarrassing.* I stare at the metal floor when El leans closer to me and kisses me. It's not an ordinary kiss. It's the type you see at the end of a romantic comedy. For a second, I've forgotten about all my problems and mistakes. Everything has become crystal clear to me.

"I love you too," the first thing El says after the fairy-tale kiss. My phone buzzes. I got a text. Welcome back to reality. I don't need to check my cellphone to know that it's from Lou-Lou. Everything good always ends at some point.

"Sorry," I say and quickly glance at the text. It is from Louis as I thought. He reminds me that I'm running out of time, and I should go back inside because Jake's becoming suspicious. It's almost over.

"Are you ready to go back?" El asks me.

"It was from Louis."

"I figured he seems a little lonely tonight."

"Yeah…"

I put my high heels back on, El helps me to walk down the stairs. We quickly come back. The whole time I can't stop thinking about how Ally got into this mess. If she finds out, she'll kill me. Literally, I would have done the same thing if she did that to me. I'm a lousy friend. How likely can I get away with two huge secrets? How will El behave around Ally? I really screwed up this time. I've done some bad stuff, but this... This is on a different level. I feel like I have a panic attack.

"El, I need to run to the lady's room," I tell him. "I'll find you in there."

"Okay."

Chapter 18
The Homecoming Dance Part 3

I rush inside into the bathroom and lock myself into one of the bathroom stalls. I close my eyes, hoping that everything that has just happened is a nightmare, and I can wake up. *It is a nightmare. What have you done, Cassie? How could you? Please-please, let everything be a dream. If it's a dream, I didn't hurt anybody.*

A few tears drop on my cheeks. If it was a dream, that would mean that I didn't hurt anyone. However, the only thing I have done so far is to hurt a lot of people. None of them deserves this. They will never forgive me.

I wipe the tears away from my face. *Stop pitying yourself. Take a deep breath. You're going to be okay.* I grab my phone and text Lou-Lou — I screwed up in a big way... I don't know what even the point is. I need to go through this night, and it will be over soon. I get out and wash my hands. Luckily, my tears have destroyed my whole look. I grab a napkin and start fixing my make-up. This could be worse, so don't be so upset.

"Hey," I hear Ally's voice right next to me. I turn around, and here she is.

"H-hi," I mumble in shock. Ally is the last person I was expecting to see. I can't catch a breath.

"Chill, Cassie," she says with a smile. "I'm not gonna destroy you tonight."

I nervously swallow. My eyes become watery again because I already know what Ally's about to say. I want to yell, "Oh no-no-no, please don't say it." But, I don't want to hurt her...

"We're still friends, you know," she explains.

"Don't, please," I beg her, shaking my head. Ally is actually a lovely person. Unfortunately, she's about to say something she'll regret. I won't be surprised if she hates me forever.

"Even if I think it's wrong, I'm okay with you doing this your way," she continues anyway, then she gives me a hug. She shouldn't be touching me. *I'm a traitor.* You'll be coming back to this moment over and over. You'll know that I already threw you under the bus. Ally, you're much better than that.

"Thanks, Ally."

Ally nods. I feel like I should say something meaningful, so she'll know I care about her if the truth comes out. However, I don't know what I can say.

"And now this is the time to announce Homecoming KING AND QUEEN!" Ally and I hear a DJ's voice through a microphone.

I roll my eyes, but Ally smiles and tells me, "Go, you might just get it after all."

She seems really happy for me. This is torture.

"I know," I say with disappointment in my voice. I leave the bathroom. The only thing I'm hoping for is not to win the nomination because it will be finally over, then El and I can just escape.

The gym is packed, and everyone's eyes are drilled onto the stage. A guy from a media club, I think his name is Erik, is opening an envelope and dramatically takes out the note. I feel like I'm about to have another panic attack because my heart is ready to jump out of my chest.

"Ladies and gentlemen, this year, the Homecoming King is..." Erik drags the announcement out, "Jake Thompson! Congratulations, Jake!

Everyone goes wild, clapping, whistling, and yelling. I would be surprised if Jake is picked and brought on stage like a rockstar. Unfortunately for him, he has to get to the stage on his two feet, and I'm barely breathing. Please, let it not be me. Pretty please. Even if I never get a chance to be a Homecoming Queen, I don't want to win right now. I glance around, trying to spot El or Louis in the crowd, but I don't have too much luck. Erik passes the Homecoming sash. I roll my eyes. Personally, I think the sashes and the titles are incredibly overrated. At least, there are no crowns because that would be the worst.

"Thank you so much," Jake says as he takes the microphone. "This is so unexpected. Thank you again to all of you. Love you, the Mountain High!"

I shake my head. OMG... Unexpected? Really? Sometimes Jake's such a poser.

"Thank you, Jake. And now we'll find out who won the title of Homecoming Queen this year," Erik says as he grabs the second envelope. After that, everything has become blurry. All the noises sound so far away.

I totally freeze when Erik announces, "It's Cassie Fuller! Cassie is this year's Homecoming Queen!"

My mind tells me that it's time to run away, but my legs aren't listening to me. I wonder what people, who were struck by a bolt of lightning, feel like. I won, but it doesn't feel right. I can't even recognize myself. Who am I? What is going on? You're a homecoming queen? I'm something I thought I could never be. I hear how people are cheering for me, clapping. However, I can move even for an inch. I feel like someone pushes me towards the stage. There is no way out.

When I walk up on stage, Erik helps me to put the homecoming sash on. I attempt to smile. Isn't that what normal people do in a situation like this? Jake passes the microphone to me while I'm trying to spot El. However, the bright lights are blinding, and I'm not able to recognize anyone.

"Thank you so much," I awkwardly say, and people clap for me before I even get a chance to say anything else.

"And now join our king and queen in a slow dance!" Erik announces as a DJ switches the music. Jake comes closer, takes my hand. The light is dim, and a spotlight finds us in the middle of the stage. This is happening. Okay, it's not too bad. I'm dancing with a guy who won the Homecoming King nomination. It's a tradition for a king and a queen to slow dance in front of the school. Therefore, I must dance with Jake because I'm this year's homecoming queen. This is not weird at all. I nervously swallow when Jake pulls me closer.

"We did it!" he whispers into my ear, but I can't concentrate at all because I see El everywhere I look. "Cass, are you okay?"

"Yeah," I say as Jake leans over for a kiss. I stop him, "What do you think you're doing?"

"What? Cassie, you just need to let this go."

"Jake, you just don't understand," I explain. "You're about to graduate, and

I'll still be right here by myself. Who knows, maybe you'll be dating some hotshot in college? People will stop discussing you when I'm around... I just don't want to be that sad girl."

"Wow, Cass," Jake replies. I glance at him, and he looks shocked.

"Sorry, I didn't mean to freak you out. I'm not used to being the center of everybody's attention. I don't know what got into me."

"I just didn't realize that," he starts explaining, "you're so worried about these things. I think we should discuss it."

"That's a great idea, but can we do that tomorrow or on Monday? Does Monday sound good to you?"

"How about now?"

"Please, Jake. This is not the time."

"Okay-okay."

At that moment, the song ends. Suddenly, the lights come back. It's nice to get away from the spotlight. I'm about to find out what El is thinking about this. I step away from him, mentally preparing myself for something to go wrong. I'm ready for almost anything.

"Thanks."

"And Monday sounds great to me."

"Deal," I agree with a smile.

"Let's go," Jake says. "Ladies first."

"Thanks."

As we walk up the stairs, Jake lets me go first. For a second, I feel like I can do this. *Maybe I can get away with it tonight. Why not? In the history of humanity, people have gotten worse than adultery.* However, it doesn't matter how optimistic you can be. Sometimes it's just over. When I turn away from Jake, I see Elliot standing at the bottom of the stairs.

"Let me help you," he says, offering his hand. I can't take too much time thinking about what the right decision is. I take his hand and carefully walk down. It all makes sense. Even if El hasn't figured this out, there is no chance in hell Jake won't know what game I'm playing. I cannot afford to have a chitchat.

"Congratulations, guys!" El says, giving me a hug. Then El and Jake shake hands just like they did at Jake's party. I know one thing for sure, I'm dead. I've never felt so nauseated in my entire life. I notice how Louis and Ally are running up to us, but it's too late. Nobody can save me at this point, and to be completely honest, I don't believe I'm not a very lucky person.

"Thanks, man! We're so excited," Jake replies. He gives me a pet on my back. I glance at Elliot, who rolls his eyes and tells Jake, "Yeah, we're too!"

I glance at Jake, and he looks baffled. I shut my eyes closed because I can see how a few questions are crossing through Jake's mind, and then something crazy happens.

"JAAAKE!" Mike yells. "Come here, man!"

I've never felt I can get along with any of Jake's friends or teammates. It's always been awkward. I feel like a bit of a child around them. Maybe that's why I hate Katie so much. She's so confident and can believe I might be saved by Jake's teammates. Elliot rolls his eyes at Jake while he looks over at Mike.

"Give me a minute," Jake screams at his teammate, then he looks over to El and me.

"Awesome. Sorry, man, I have to go and thank everybody else."

"Yeah, sure thing," El says.

"I'll see you in a bit, my Queen!" Jake says and kisses my hand. I nod, forcing a smile. *Am I going to get away with this? In a way, I feel even more disappointed than I thought before. Who knew that both El and Jake would be so self-involved, so they wouldn't even notice that they date the same girl? Ugh... I don't even know why I'm upset. Shouldn't I be happy my secret is safe?*

"Can you believe this?" El asks me when Jake walks away. "Football players, always thinking every girl's their girlfriend!

"I know, right," I carefully agree with him.

"Congratulations, babe."

"Thanks. Can you get me something to drink?" I ask El. "I'm so thirsty."

"Of course."

El gives me a quick kiss on my cheek, and then he walks away as I'm hoping to catch a break.

"Omg, girl," Louis says, running up to me with Ally. "You got away with it. High five!"

"I'm happy for you," Ally says. "This is a perfect sitcom moment."

"It's like we're in an episode of Friends," Lou-Lou utters. Still, even though he's amusing, for some reason, it's not getting easier to breathe, and I don't feel less nauseated.

"Sorry. I need to get some fresh air," I cut the conversation short and rush outside. First, I must clear my head.

Chapter 19
My House of Lies Finally Falls

I want to run, but I don't know where I should run. It's about a forty-minute walk from school to my house. I am panicking, even though everything is still under control. I've made a mess everywhere. Every part of my life is meaningless because it's entangled with some kind of lie. It's my fault — I know it. I guess I always knew. It started with Jake hurting me, but after that, it's all on me. My pain created so much pain for others. I did Ally so bad, and it's a matter of time for her to find out. I'm ready to give up.

I take the sash off and throw it away in a garbage can. *I'm not a real queen.* The only reason why I was even picked is that most people thought I'm Jake's girlfriend. I go barefoot — my feet bring me back to the bleachers. I'm pacing back and forth. Usually, it's beneficial for me to get my thoughts under control. I'm just a joke now. Why am I freaking out so much? El and Jake have no idea, so I shouldn't be so worried. The truth is I'm trying to find the way out, find my way back to myself. I don't believe this is who I am.

I'm not a bad person. I just can't get a hold of myself. I can't get a hold of the situation. Everyone gets lost, but I'm disappointed in present-day Cassie. I don't like that girl. I can't believe Ally and Louis have been giving me so much slack. I don't deserve it, and I won't deserve their forgiveness or El's.

Why haven't you broken up with Jake? Cassie, you knew where it all leads to, but no, you wanted to have some stupid drama in your life. You thought you'd love the drama, where you're the main character. What does that even mean? Well, let me break it down for you. Cassie, you're a stupid little girl. I hope you're happy now. However, it doesn't matter how much I can yell at myself in my head because I'm in the same situation I was a minute ago. Honestly, I want to see some kind of a sign to break up with Jake. Every time I want to drop the hammer on him, something will stop me. I didn't want to give up on my dream yet, and look at me now. Communication has always been a huge issue for me.

That's why I wanted to see the sign that I'm doing the right thing.

"Hey, you," I hear Jake's voice from behind."What are you doing here?"

I look over my shoulder. Jake is approaching me. Is this the sign I've been asking for? As much as I am scared, I'm finally sure the time has come to get myself back. Look forward, Cassie, don't be stuck in the past of your mistakes.

"Okay, I can't do this anymore," I say, stepping closer to Jake. That's definitely not a conversation he's been expecting. I feel like everything has become clear to me, and I can't believe it took me so long.

"Okay. What's up?" Jake asks me.

" I need to tell you the truth. No, I must tell you the truth."

"Okay."

"I should start by saying, I really care about you," I explain.

"Cassie!!!" Ally's voice echoes through the whole stadium. Have you ever heard a lion roar? If I were a betting man, I'd guess that Ally has already found out. I look over and see Ally running towards us. She is absolutely furious — I can't even blame her. The worst is that she's not alone. She's dragging Louis and El along.

"You told Elliot I love him?!" she screams at me. Oh yeah, I've been reliving this nightmare in my head so many times, I imagined what I'd say. I was so wrong. This is so much worse than I've ever thought, but that was before seeing Katie walking up to us. Great. I feel like everyone had too high expectations for me, and I couldn't get there.

"Umm…" I can barely make a sound. *What am I supposed to say? Yeah, Ally, that's exactly what happened. I just need to buy some time*, "I can explain…"

"No, no, no… Are you kidding me? You can explain?!" Ally screams at me. Honestly, I've never seen her so angry. If there are levels of anger, I think everyone can agree that Ally was about at Level 7 — furious, and now… It's about Level 10 — blind rage. However, it's not going to help me. She's about to act on her anger and tell everyone the truth. *Ugh… I can't do anything about it.*

"Ally, please. Don't," I beg.

"No, Cassie, that was too far," she explains. "Enough is enough, honey! Your game is over."

People say that when you're in a car accident, the time will go in slow-motion, and you might see your whole life in front of your eyes? Well, I'm going through that right now. Ally turns to El and Jake and says, "She is dating both of you."

"Ally, please. I'm about to..." I stop in the middle of my sentence because it doesn't matter anymore. My secret is out.

"I can't believe that you tried to use my feelings to do... THIS CRAP! Was all of this worth it, Cassie?" Ally continues to scream at me.

My tears start rolling down my face. I want to say something, but I can't. I step away, looking at Jake and Elliot.

"No-no-no, Cassie and I, there is no way" Jake denies the truth, and he glances at El.

"Omg, really, Jake?" Ally sounds astonished. "You can ask her yourself."

"Cassie, is this true?" Jake asks me. He gives a pointed stare.

"Elliot..." I nervously say. I look over at him, hoping he and I are still together. However, his eyes meet me with a cold glare. *It's over.*

"Yeah, Cass, is it true? Please, tell all of us the truth if you don't mind."

"I never meant this to happen," I start telling the truth. "I'm so-o-o sorry."

"I can believe this..." El breaks an awkward silence. Ally wants to give him a hug, but he doesn't let her. Sorrow crosses Ally's face, and I think she just realized what she's done.

"Wait a second," Jake says, "Cassie, is that what you were about to tell me?!"

"Yes! You have to understand it's not the first time I was trying," I'm explaining through tears, "and at the diner, and when I came to see you at practice. I was about to tell you the truth so many times!"

I've never seen so much disappointment in anybody's eyes. Katie runs up to him, giving him a hug. This is so embarrassing — I'm such an embarrassment.

"Cassie, this is... I was actually concerned about you," Jake says, shaking his head. "You know I'm gonna go."

Katie takes his hand, and they both rush away from me. I'm supposed to be smarter than that. I wish I could blame this on others, but I'm finally getting what I deserve. I'm surprised Katie has kept her mouth shut the whole time. I guess I expected she would yell at me that I'm a horrible person. The silence is even worse than the vocal punishment.

"Jake," I yell at his back, but it doesn't matter anymore. I look over at El and mumble. "El, I didn't want any of this to happen. I'm so sorry."

"You know, Cassie. My dad always says that life is a road, which goes both ways," El says with a cold look in his eyes.

"El, I'm so sorry."

El, please, don't look at me this way. I can see in his eyes that he wants me to stop. How many 'sorry' should I say for you to forgive me?

"I wish all of this wasn't true, Cass," he says. But it is true. He shakes his head and turns away. I want to run after him, but there is nothing else to say. I don't want you to give up on me. However, I let him walk away.

"I thought you were my friend. How could you?" Ally reproaches.

"I'm sorry, I don't know why I said that. It wasn't on purpose, I swear."

"This is very disappointing," she replies and starts walking away.

"Ally!" I call for her, but she doesn't say a word. I glance over at Louis. He's totally frozen. The only thing you always wanted is to help me and for all of us to have some fun. However, Lou-Lou, you made a huge mistake helping me.

"Let's go, Lou-Lou," Ally commands him. Louis looks at me and nervously swallows.

"Louis, please!" I scream as my tears roll down my face. However, I know nothing I do or say right now. Lou-Lou looks over at Ally and nods.

They both leave. I didn't want to hurt anybody. I got caught up in this thing, and I got lost in it. However, what goes around, comes around. It's time, it's time to pay for what I've done...

I sit down on the bleachers, dropping my shoes. My first idea is to cry this whole thing out, but I quickly realize that I don't have a ride home. I don't think El would like to see me any time soon. He will give me a ride because he's a nice person. However, I'm pretty sure I won't be able to be next to him, so I've got to figure out my own way home. Of course, the idea of calling my parents has crossed my mind, but they will ask a thousand questions about what happened between El and me. My parents are the only people who won't know right now. I can guarantee half of the school has already found out about my "adventures." Mom and dad love Elliot. What will they think about my actions? That's why I really want to keep it a secret. They won't see me the way everyone else is looking at me with their constant disapproval.

How am I getting home? Sometimes I leave my bike at school. Unfortunately for me, this is not one of those times. I only have two friends who could give me a ride. So yeah... It's not a viable option.

"I have to walk," I realize, and I finally feel kind of okay. I'm in this, and I need to find my way back. I'm not sure how exactly I'm supposed to do that, but walking back home is a start. I've never walked from the school to my house, but there's a first time for everything, right? So I pick up my shoes and start walking.

It's like a walk of shame. After ten minutes, my excitement runs out, and the temperature drops. I wish I would have grabbed a jacket. Ugh... I can't believe I was so sure I'd get away with the plan. *Sometimes, Cassie, you surprise me.* I'm so stupid. Should I text El?

I know it's a bad idea, but I feel like he isn't hearing me. If only I can find the right words, maybe he can understand me, and hopefully, he will be able to forgive me. *Or perhaps you'll push him further away because he doesn't have enough time to process your betrayal.* I wish I could go to the beach right now. For some reason, I feel so calm near the ocean. Maybe it's the sound, maybe it's the water... All my thoughts usually fly away, so I won't be waiting for a text from El. I want him to ask how I'm getting home, and I'm scared. I'm terrified that he won't ask because it's the sign that we're over — for good. Sometimes life outplays you. I wanted a sign. Well, I'm getting it now. It's crystal clear.

I finally get to my street. At this point, my feet are freezing. I might even catch a cold. Would that be nice? The front lights are on, but I'm pretty sure my parents have already fallen asleep. I grab my phone and text them in a group chat that I'm a few minutes away. They don't bother me too much when I'm over-communicating.

I open the front door and carefully tiptoe upstairs. Right before I'm about to close the door to my room, I hear footsteps. No-no-no. I'm shutting the door down.

"Honey!" Mom says with a sleepy voice. Today is the worst day. I wipe my eyes and move my hair around, so I don't look like I've just had a forty-minute power walk. Even though the gym look is similar to an afterparty look, I can't be too careful. I open the door ajar and only show my head.

"Hey, mom!"

"How was the dance?"

"It was great," I reply with excitement in my voice, "but I'm so tired."

"Did you win?"

"Win what?"

"The homecoming queen nomination..."

"Oh yeah. I did."

"Aren't you supposed to get a tiara or a sash?"

"I did," I say. "It was a sash, and I lost it immediately. Sorry, I didn't realize it was important."

"Well, is that important to you?"

"No, not really. Can we finish chatting about it tomorrow? I want to take a warm bath. I feel a little under the weather."

"Okay, hon."

I close the door. Why can't I say the right things today? Now she knows something is wrong, and I don't want her to know. Tears roll down my face again. I take the dress off and leave it on the floor. I should take better care of it, but I blame the dress for all my problems right now. If it wasn't so pretty, I would skip the dance, and I would be okay.

Instead of the bath, I drop dead on my bed under three blankets. I cover myself from head to toe and stare at my phone as if I'm trying to break a curse of not getting any texts. I text Ally again that I'm very sorry, then I text Lou-Lou, saying that I'm sorry, and I screwed up this time. Then I text to El that I got home, and I'm so sorry.

I didn't mean to behave like a jerk. I've made a mistake. Well, I've made quite a few mistakes. I put my phone on the nightstand. I know they won't reply — it's okay. I go back under the blankets. I close my eyes, and the tears go down on my pillow like a river.

My phone suddenly vibrates, and my heart is about to jump off my chest. Oh, hope is such a funny thing because you have it until the very last minute... I hesitate to check it. Who has relied on me? I want it to be El. No one has an idea how much I want it to be him. I check my phone, and, of course, it's Lou-Lou.

Yeah, you did ;(

My heart crumbles. I drop the phone on the floor. I cover my eyes. *Please-please, let it be a nightmare. Please. I knew it's not El, but I still hoped. I've always rushed into things. I fell in love with Jake by looking at the guy. I didn't even know him. He didn't know me. I was watching him. Yes. I was watching him and creating a thousand scenarios to become a part of his life. I was following the idea of him, the dream of my first love. Isn't it supposed to be romantic? However, the reality is, as it stands, Jake is his own person. He's not what I've imagined. Whatever I created in my head isn't him. I didn't want to let go. Jake is a person, not an idea. I've been chasing it for so long, I missed the real chance for love. Now I can't stop thinking about El. I won't be able to get through this.*

"It's going to be alright. You will be okay anyway," I tell myself even though I know it's a lie.

Chapter 20
I Know What It Means To Be Alone

I don't know how or when I fell asleep, but it's the following day. I'm awake, meaninglessly staring at the white ceiling. I'm not even sure if I'm a hundred percent sharp. Have you felt like you wanted to stay asleep for a while? Maybe it's a long shot, but I wish I were the Sleeping Beauty. Then I could only wake up if El forgives me. Wouldn't that be nice? Ugh… Look how many problems all that dreaming brought into my life.

I roll over on the side of my bed and pick the cellphone up from the floor. I glance over the notifications, but it's not surprising that I don't have any new ones. I check my texts in case it was a nightmare. But no, it wasn't a dream. I shake my head, trying to erase my memories. Suddenly, it hits me that probably the school has already found out. People are probably tagging me to the endless amount of pictures.

I quickly check my Instagram account. Nothing. *Hmm… Good, that's actually good. I should be happy.* Instead of relief, I kind of feel disappointed. Has the school posted anything? I go to the school page, and I click on the picture of Jake and me on stage. I guess I'm lucky that our school policy isn't allowing anyone to comment on posted photos. I don't even want to know what everyone would say about me. However, tomorrow is Monday, and I'll have to face the aftermath. The idea of pretending I'm sick has already crossed my mind a few times, but it'll only delay something I need to deal with now. At least, it's not Monday.

A little bit later, I drag myself out of bed and wander downstairs to grab some food. Mom and dad are already sitting and drinking coffee.

"Good morning, sunshine," dad says. "How was the dance?"

"Good. I'm still kind of tired, you know."

"You, guys, came back pretty early last night," mom states, passing me a bowl.

"Thank you. Yeah, it was kind of boring."

"But you won!"

"Oh, dad!" I roll my eyes at him. "Do you really think it was fun to dance with a different guy at the last slow dance?"

"Okay-okay."

Dad continues staring at his newspaper. I don't even know why he still buys the actual newspapers since you can get everything online anyways. It's so wasteful, but it makes him happy. I giggle as I pour milk into my bowl of cereal.

"But we didn't hear Elliot's car," mom starts implying.

"Okay, you two, this is ridiculous," I say. "I thought you were asleep because the lights were off. So I asked El to park further away, then we walked, and here I am. Does that answer all your questions, your honors?"

"We didn't mean anything by that! We're just so excited," dad defensively explains.

"I hope you don't mind if I eat in my room?"

"Sure, hon," mom allows me.

"Thanks, guys. I'm also planning to finish my homework while I'm eating."

"Wonderful."

I walk back to my room, thinking about my new lie. *I guess this lie is a part of the previous ones. The problem with lying is that it's hard to stop after you've started. I have to be honest with myself and stop the circle of madness. I have to start telling the truth, and it doesn't matter how difficult the situation is. Can I even do that, not to lie all the time? Is it even humanly possible? Everybody lies, but it's usually something small. It's not like me... Nobody lies like me. Yeah-yeah, I know there is a difference between meaningless lying and the type of lying, after which close to you, people stop talking to you. I know, but it's been so hard for me to stay in line. How hard can it be?*

I enter my room, quickly check my phone. There are no notifications. I guess unnecessarily checking the phone can be my new "hobby" instead of lying. I already finished my homework, so I flop on the bed and stare at the ceiling. *It's weird how mom and dad were interrogating me. How do they always know when something is wrong with me? It works so well as if I'm holding an I-am-in-trouble sign. But I think I handled it well. I'll tell them later. I'm just not ready to tell right now. I'm not prepared to let them down. However, I will say to them, I promise.*

I feel like the day has gotten away from me because I realize it's time to go to sleep. However, I don't think I'll do so because I'm so nervous about tomorrow. Tomorrow I'll see everyone. I can stop driving myself crazy imagining every single scenario. Some of them are cruel. People can be very hurtful. In every scenario, I always end up crying on the roof. I'm scared I'll have to change schools. Isn't it ironic that I might have to switch schools after Elliot transferred here for me? I agree with people who say that life is full of surprises.

I don't remember when I fell asleep or how my alarm went off. Yep, today is going to be the worst day in my life. How can anybody be prepared for it? You see, I'm the type of person who prefers not to know such things. It's paralyzing to know today I'm about to have the worst day. I wish I didn't know.

I stand up and start getting ready. My hands shake. I can't let fear take over, so my first rule is not to worry too much and react to things as they come. Everything has already changed, and I'm about to find out how it's going to affect my day-to-day routine. Honestly, it's tough to stay positive, but I'm trying to. However, who knows? Maybe after everyone finds a new black sheep, I'll finally be able to be me. Since the beginning of high school, I've felt like I have to do what everyone wants to, not be such a party pooper all the time. It could be precisely what I need. And other lies I tell myself. Ugh. I roll my eyes at my ridiculousness.

"You're going to be fine," I tell out loud, staring at my reflection in the mirror. "You don't have a choice but to be okay."

"Cassie, are you coming down?" Dad loudly shouts for me. I almost forgot that I need to get to school. My dad has been giving me a ride to school because El usually gives me a ride back home. I have been riding a bike several times from my parent's perspective, but they might get suspicious.

"Give me a second. I'll be right there!" I yell, quickly finish my make-up. People will hate on me, and the only thing I can do is look good. I don't know why, but it makes me feel like I'm taking away their power. Their words will never reach me. It's stupid. It's crazy to think that looking good is that important to me. I'm already a straight-A student, but I put the value of my looks before. However, I wouldn't get an A in friendship or in being a good girlfriend.

I run downstairs, checking a clock on the wall. It's only seven-thirty. That's kind of early.

"Dad! It's only seven-thirty," I protest.

"Just making sure that you're not still asleep."

"Thanks, but I'm not coming with you today," I say, attempting to sound nonchalant.

"Really?"

"Did you, guys, break up?" mom asks. How do they always know?! I'm not ready to tell them the truth.

"Yeah, mom, we broke up. Is that what you want to hear?!" I lose my cool. Hmm, I'm not at school, and I'm already going insane. I catch my parents giving each other worried glares. This is unfair to them because they want to help me. I know that. I need to change the subject. I quickly come up with an explanation, "El's car broke down or something. It's going to be in the shop, at least, for a week. Not everything is a conspiracy theory."

"Sorry, honey. We just assumed..."

"I'm sorry, it's been very frustrating because El is very popular," I explain, "and the girls are just waiting for us to break up. I don't usually let it get into my head, but apparently, I'm not doing as well as I thought."

Technically, everything I've just said is true, one way or another. But I'm not sure if I will be okay because I'm a live wire right now. Where have I lost a piece of myself? Will anybody be there on another side? I guess I'm about to find out, but I have a feeling that nobody will be there for me. I wasn't there for anybody...

"Oh honey, don't worry about it," mom says. "It's all going to work itself out. I believe you'll make good choices."

Yeah, mom, I wouldn't be so sure about that. I can't roll my eyes any harder because she shouldn't believe in me. I don't deserve your trust, mom.

"Thanks, guys."

I walk back to my room and just wait until the last minute before I've got to leave the house in order not to be late. As I leave the house, slowly rolling the bicycle, I realize I forget to have breakfast. My stomach makes a grumbled noise, but I don't feel hungry, just nauseated. I couldn't have anything even if I wanted to. That's how my body responds to stress. Any time a big test is about to happen, I can't eat. However, it doesn't stop my stomach, which actively tries to kill me.

I ride the bicycle the whole way to school. I've found my music playlist with sad break-up songs. I created it during summer camp, right after Jake and I broke up. *Who knew I would need it again, but who knew that I'm so bad for everyone around? Who knew I would be so misunderstood? I want to beg for everyone's forgiveness, but it's too late because they already know I'm a lost cause.* Music and physical exercise really help with clearing my mind. You see, Cassie, this could be good for you. You can spend more time doing things you actually like.

When I get to the school entrance, I jump off the bike and stare at the distance. *This is it. I'm about to find out how much everyone hates me.* I take a deep breath and lock my bike to the station. Interestingly, even though I encounter quite a few people, I don't even hear a whisper about my personal fiasco. It's weird, but I guess it's okay. My heart is beating as if I'm about to die from a heart attack. I can't even look straight. I'm ready for the upcoming hate. However, when I walk up to my locker, I still don't notice anything strange or different. I secretly scout the hallway while I'm organizing the locker by taking down the pictures of Ally and Lou-Lou. People give me odd glares, but otherwise, nothing is strange. I don't even know what I've expected. I guess I was so scared to see a "slut" sign on the locker. I haven't thought what if everyone at the school could ignore me. I assumed I was a little bit more important than that. It's wrong to feel disappointed. I know it. *Why am I holding these pictures? Oh yeah... I should probably get rid of those, or should I keep them? Ugh, this is so annoying. This isn't real.*

Suddenly I hear Ally's laughter followed by Lou-Lou's personal anecdote.

"I swear that happened!" I hear Lou-Lou insists on something. My muscle memory takes over for a second, but I stop myself right on time. *Poor Louis, nobody reasonably believes in his ridiculous adventures, but I used to entertain him by pretending I did. I remember one story he told us. He accidentally got locked in a shopping mall overnight with another guy, who he's been kind of stalking. Louis can be so weird for someone who's such a confident person. I have asked him why he couldn't just come up to a guy and ask him out. And his response has always been ridiculous. He always says it's not romantic, and he's not planning to waste his teen years on such nonsense. Louis always points out he has the rest of his life to ask people out usually. Even thinking about this makes me smile. Ally always tells me that I need to stop encouraging him, but I don't know I enjoy Lou- Lou's romantic values. Maybe that's why he tried to help me. I wonder what they're chatting about.*

The school bell rings, and I glance at the pictures for the last time. I'm not ready to throw them away. At least, not yet. I close my locker and wander through the hallway to the math classroom. Students rush to their classrooms. Nobody even looks at me. *Do they even know? To be fair, I should be concentrating on El because I'm about to see him for the first time after the dance.* When I get to the classroom, I just stand in front of the closed door. I can't do it. I can't.

"Are you coming in, Cassie?" our math teacher, Mrs. Jenkins. She carries so much in her hands. It looks like she's been buried with work the rest of the weekend. *OMG, I just got very lucky. Nobody will do or say anything to me if I enter with our teacher.* My eyes sparkle with happiness, and I finally feel calm. I hope he hasn't expected I wouldn't show up at school.

"Oh yes, of course, Mrs. Jenkins. Let me help you," I offer.

"Thank you, Cassie."

Mrs. Jenkins lets me take a couple of books and two huge files with our homework. I open the door as we both enter the classroom.

"Good morning, class. I hope everyone had a good weekend," Mrs. Jenkins says as the whole class goes crazy, but not about me. "Okay, Cassie, you put this here. Thank you so much."

I nod and quietly follow her instructions. *Is El looking at me? Yeah, Cassie, you should know better. It doesn't matter if he is or not because he's not going to forgive me. Would you forgive Jake if he did that to you? The honest answer is no, but I've recently started realizing that I might have been judging people too hard. I should cut everyone some slack. However, I promised myself not to fixate on unnecessary issues I wouldn't be able to resolve. Right now, I can solve one puzzle by finding a seat, which usually is taken care of for me. Interesting. Ally and Louis permanently save me a spot next to them.* I look around, and there are only two empty seats on different sides of the classroom. One is next to Ally and Lou, and another one is next to El. *Of course, it has to be this way. Can you believe this? I can. I feel like someone made me into a joke. Oh! Wait, that someone is me!.* Honestly, I don't know what to do. I feel like my hands shake, but I can't stop it—panic bubbles within me.

"So everyone had fun at the dance?" she asks as students yell, "Yes!"

While I'm deciding what the right choice is, El picks up all his stuff and sits with Ally and Louis. I silently march there and unpack. There are so many feelings boiling inside me, I can't even count. This is insulting. El has made a choice for me. Maybe it's a sign. I couldn't have made a choice between Jake and him, and now he's showing off. Look how easy it is to choose. I know, El. You don't have to rub it in front of my face.

I have been fighting my need to look at El the whole class. That's why I'm so surprised when I hear the school bell again. If someone asks me what we've learned in the past hour or so, I won't answer. I haven't listened to a single thing that was said in class.

"Has everyone understood on which topic I will be concentrating on in the test tomorrow?" Mrs. Jenkins asks as everyone nods. "I'll be posting the homework online. Thank you."

Mrs. Jenkins always tries to end on a good note. It seems to me she kind of feels bad for torturing us. She's a wonderful teacher, but Mrs. Jenkins knows that she makes class extra hard. There are quite a few students who can barely keep up with the workload. We always attempt to run away from the classroom as quickly as possible. Louis hates math, so the whole way our next class, he complains about Mrs. Jenkins. However, I'm not in a rush today.

Even though nothing wrong has happened yet, I'm trying to be mentally prepared for people to start coming up to me. It'll happen. It's just a matter of time. As I pack all my stuff, I peek at El, hoping our eyes meet. However, the reality could be brutal. He isn't looking at me. Ally and Louis are about to leave, but El stops them.

"Hey, guys! Wait for me!"

"You're so slow, El! Speed it up," Louis teases him. El rolls his eyes. Three of them leave while I still stay in the classroom and wait until I'm the last one.

The rest of today has been going very slow and quiet. Now I'm sitting on the roof, finishing my lunch and watching clouds in the sky. The days are getting colder. I don't know how long I can hang out here — I might have to find a new place. *It's uncomfortable around people. Everyone has decided to ignore me. Honestly, I didn't expect this reaction. It's even worse than anything I imagined in my head, but I guess the crime fits the punishment. In the beginning, I was wondering whether everyone found out or not. However, I overheard people talking about it while I was picking up my lunch in the cafeteria. I should start making my own lunch. I'll save the money, and I can eat on the roof. I don't enjoy feeling the looks burning into my back. When I was at the cafeteria, I saw Jake. He didn't look at me, which wasn't a surprise. I don't know what I've expected — I should be relieved. There is no problem. Maybe I want to be punished, so we all can move forward. I'm scared, but I need to be mentally prepared to spend the rest of high school. Hopefully, I can graduate earlier. It's also odd not to hear your name out loud—only Mrs. Jenkins called me by my name today. On a typical day, people call for me at least thirty times a day.*

Suddenly, it's almost nothing. I'm like a ghost now, and it's weird.

I hear the school bell. It's time to go back. It's better to be late than sitting among my classmates, who hate me and don't say anything. I wish they would say what they actually think. Have I already mentioned this silent treatment is the worst? If it's supposed to drive me crazy, it works. All the worrying catches up with me because I'm ready to fall asleep during the last class. It's biology. I know Mrs. Levinson's class is traditionally scheduled at the end of the day, and she complains about it all the time.

"I thought you're better than that, miss Fuller," she says as her voice wakes me up from a quick nap.

"We all did," I hear a male voice mumbling. I battle the urge to turn around and find out who has just said it. *Of course, someone saying that is more than anything wakes me up. Here it is. At least, it's something. Right? I don't know who said it. Honestly, I don't even want to know. Maybe it was El. What if it wasn't him? Maybe I know it wasn't him, but I still want to believe.*

"Shh! Quiet, please," Mrs. Levinson commands.

I don't remember what happened afterward, but I find myself walking back home. There is no way I'll walk to school tomorrow, so I'm rolling the bike next to me. How should I react to that? They all thought I was better than that. People always expect too much from me. It's not my fault they overestimate how good I am and get disappointed. It's weird when someone starts believing in me. I genuinely try to do my best. However, it never works because I can never keep up with building pressure.

It's been a couple of weeks. One day turns into another, and so on. The weekends aren't as exciting, but on a positive note, I admit I have more time for homework. Nobody expects me to know what it means to be alone. I didn't know what being alone actually is before. I used to have a choice not to pick the phone up, and now... My friends don't respond to my calls. I've tried to reach out to Lou-Lou several times. During any conflict between Ally and me, he usually breaks first. Louis always says, "You two will make up, so I'm just speeding this up."

I guess there is nothing to speed up this time, and we all know what it could mean. Unfortunately, Ally doesn't plan to forgive me any time soon. I've texted her a few times as well, but without any positive results. I wonder if she'll be able to forgive me.

Next time I hear them nearby, I'm trying to catch their attention. Ally and Louis come up to her locker, chatting about something. It's hard to listen to what exactly they're talking about, but I'm pretty sure they're discussing last weekend's party. Of course, I wasn't invited. I'm not asked for anything. I tried to get into some clubs, but nobody wants me around, which is understandable.

"I know — I know, El was so crazy," Ally says, opening her locker. My heart drops. It sounds like he's having a good time without me. He's got so good at avoiding my presence in the school after we ran into each other a few times. For a while, I've hoped that it meant something. El makes sure our eyes never meet. He always disappears before I can even get close to him. Recently, I've seen him around new girls. I've heard some rumors here and there. I know I shouldn't be jealous because I'm the whole reason why it's happening to me. I understand that, but it's been heartbreaking. *Cassie, get it together! You're not here to be upset about El. You're making an attempt to reconnect with your friends, and they also hate you. Ugh.*

"Come on, Lou-Lou," I mumble while I'm spying on them. "Look at me. I only need a second."

Louis feels that I'm staring at him, and he looks at me. My eyes sparkle with hope and happiness, but I haven't realized yet it doesn't mean anything. He drops his glance down as if he's ashamed of seeing me. However, it takes a different turn when he taps Ally on her shoulder, totally compromising my plan.

"Hey, look," he says. At least, I think that's what he says.

"Whatever," Ally announces, shrugging her shoulders. I know she said it, so I'd hear it, and I did. Everything is on purpose, and it's done to remind me that I'm an outcast now. The funniest thing is that I will never forget it. I haven't realized how crappy it could be. Ally locks her locker, walking away and saying, "Let's go, Louis."

She doesn't look back to check if Lou-Lou follows her. Louis lets her walk a little further and mimes, "Sorry."

"Please, Lou-Lou," I whisper.

Louis shakes his head and follows in Ally's footsteps. He looks like a little dog, following his owner. Ugh... This is unfair to him. I hurt his friend, and I don't matter anymore.

"That was cold," I say out loud, but then I shake my head. "You're just upset with yourself, Cassie. get over yourself."

I pick up a history book, and some old pictures fall out of Louis, Ally, and me. I totally forgot about them. I wonder if it's a sign I've been waiting for so long. It's time to let go. *Nobody wants you around, Cassie.* I lean down and start picking them up. My tears splash a photo of the three of us smiling. I don't even care who sees me like that. *Have you ever felt like there is not enough oxygen in your lungs, no matter how hard you're gasping for it? Well, that's how I think, and I deserve it.* I pick up all of them and decide not to throw them away. It is an obvious sign, but I'm not ready to let go. I'm holding onto something, which is over. How many people do actually stay friends after high school? Actually, not that many. Fewer than one in ten friendships lasted into high school, and only one percent of friendships continued to the 12th grade. I'm just part of the statistics. My friendships aren't that special. Maybe I'm not as unique as I would like to be. It's more complicated than I expected because I feel so lonely around here for the first time in my life. I've never been surrounded by so much silence. There are no silly comments from Ally and Louis. These are the moments I never noticed, and it suddenly hits me. *Ally and Louis were my friends. They had always been around me, and I lost it. My head was totally busy with boys. And don't take me wrong, I'm sorry, and I want to apologize. However, I'd do anything to have Ally and Louis around. They always know what the right thing to say is.*

Jake has started dating Katie, which isn't even that surprising. She's always been all over him, and he needs an ego boost after me. That's mean and very unfair to both of them. I need an ego boost, but honestly, I'm happy for Jake.

He's moved on. As much as I don't like Katie, she's a better choice than me. He's handling everything well, so I'm not worried about Jake. He's in good hands. Katie's even tried to talk to me a few times, which is so annoying. Why does she have to be so perfect? Not only does she get to save the guy, but also does she know that I'm a better runner. It doesn't matter what she wants to say. I don't need that. I guess I'm ghosting her just like El ghosting me. There are a few times I've already made several unsuccessful attempts to talk to him. He still needs space, and I should respect that. However, I couldn't stop keeping tabs on him from a distance. He's been spending more time at the library, which is an easy place to spy on anyone.

The hardest thing is I see both of them in my head because everything I see reminds me of Jake and El. Mostly, El through. I miss him so much. It's killing me. Maybe that's why I imagine them everywhere I go. I can't even go to the beach by myself because I relive being on the dates with Jake or El. Only this time, neither of them talk to me. I will never forget those days when I didn't even have time to think about who I would see that night.

"Do you want me to come over tonight?" I remember saying to El. "I think I can make that. Can you give me twenty minutes? I need to check with my parents."

"Okay."

I remember how annoyed I got when I noticed that Jake was calling.

"Can I call you right back?"

"Sure."

"Okay, bye," I answered, "Hi Jake. How are you?"

"Guess what? I got two tickets to the movies."

"Well, you didn't give me a chance to guess," I replied.

"Cass, you're so funny. What do you say?" He said.

"Ugh... I think I'll say yes. Just let me check my calendar," I miss the times I was trying to come up with an excuse. "Umm...Yeah, it's not going to work tonight."

"Really? Is everything okay?"

"Yeah, I have a test tomorrow."

I remember those times. However, it's weird to be surrounded by nothing but silence. My phone barely makes any noise. Everyone in school has already unfollowed me over time. Apparently, it's not enough torture for me because El and Jake have started interacting with each other, but not me. I feel like my own mind is betraying me. I'm supposed to be in control of it. It's so frustrating because I can't stop thinking about what I've done and not make any changes. I'm reliving the same moments over and over, knowing the horrible outcome. The feeling of guilt is overwhelming. Sometimes I don't feel like I can live like that, but I come to the identical conclusion that I must live with it, carry it through my whole life. I will remember the moment in time when I made a wrong decision and will try my best not to make the same mistake. Of course, it's even more upsetting because I already knew how it could end up, but I wish I knew how much I hurt everyone.

However, the boys don't care about my feelings. They've been torturing me more than ever, so when I enter my room, I'm not even surprised that El and Jake are already there. You think they'd say anything to me by this point, but no. They just sit on the edge of my bed, playing video games. Together. *Oh well, that's something new. What do they think they're doing? They've never been cooperating. Since when have they decided to have fun together? Whatever. I know it's not real. I just don't know how to deal with it. I did something wrong, and it's going to define who I am for a few years. Ugh... Why was I so stupid?*

I put on my bag and start changing. I glance at them, but they don't even try to look at me. I don't know why, but I feel a little bit insulted. It's obvious that they don't care about anything but their stupid game. *What is he even playing?* I secretly peek to find out which game they're playing. It's some kind of racing game. I can't roll my eyes any harder. *What are you even doing in my head if they have no intentions to talk to me?* To be fair, I can't stop thinking about the whole thing. I go through the day, trying not to think about it, but I have to face I miss Ally, I miss Louis and El. I also miss my friendship with Jake. Of course, who knows if he would like that. I miss it all more than I ever expected. I used to believe I'm an incredibly solitary person. However, I've never been so wrong because I miss being around people, experiencing new things together, and going to the beach. Even going to my favorite places isn't satisfying because I see my friends everywhere I go. Any time I go to a new home, I wish I would be with El or Ally. I feel incredibly lonely when I see groups of friends having fun, and Ally and Lou-Lou are always there. I know it's not true. My mind just loves to play games with me.

I carefully sit in the middle of my bed. *At least Jake and El hang out with me. Even though they don't talk to me, they're still around me.* I feel a little bit better. The second I relax, Jake and El startle me by loudly cheering. I jump off the bed, but they don't even see it because Jake is too busy throwing his console on the floor.

"Yes!" El screams.

"Dude, you cheated!" Jake says through laughing.

"No, Cassie did!"

"Burn! That's a good one!" Jake high fives El. "But this time, you're the one who cheated. You've learned from the best."

This is so embarrassing. I want to talk to either of them, but it seems impossible now. I feel disconnected from everyone. I don't even know where to start because everyone sees me as a joke. I've made too many mistakes.

"I don't know what you're talking about. I won fair and square."

"Let's go again!"

"Oh really? You want me to kick your ass again?"

"Wow. Rematch!" Jake demands, picking the console from the floor.

"Okay, but you already know the result."

"Excuse me," I say, drawing their attention. *Yeah, it's pretty childish and desperate. I will never talk to either of them in real life if I can't even make the Imaginary Jake and El chat with them. This isn't real, so it should be possible for me to have a normal conversation. I have to take charge of my life, and this could be the first step. It's time to do so.*

"What?" they ask at the same time without even looking at me. I'm not even worth looking at. That hurts as if a thousand knives go through my heart.

"What do you mean what?" I resent it. " What are you two doing here?"

"Chilling. Right, Elliot?" Jake replies.

"Absolutely, brother!"

They high-five each other.

"What is wrong with you two?" I ask as tears roll down my face.

"Nothing is wrong with us, Cassie," El starts, but still not looking at me. "A better question… Hmm, Jake, help me out here."

"What is wrong with you?" Jake asks a rhetorical question. Jake and El stare at each other, then they nod with a smirk.

"It's exactly what I was thinking."

They high five again. *I just want to kill them. Now they can understand and agree with no words. Isn't it great?* I really don't know why they bother me so much.

"Okay," I say, "No, you know what? I'll tell you what's wrong with me. You two! Why aren't you leaving me alone?"

"Cassie, the only reason why we're here is that you need to talk to us," Jake explains.

"But we don't want that. We're done with you. If we have to be here," El continues to build on Jake's point, "at least, we decided that we'd have fun."

"Great. Just get out!" I yell at them, but when I turn around, they're already gone. The room is empty. It's just me. I drop on the pillow, face first. *Ugh… Get out of my memory. I just want to be okay…*

Chapter 21
Just Tell Me What To Do

It's another day, but everything is the same. I think it's been almost a month. Christmas is close, just like a winter break. I've been so upset, I almost forgot. However, I'm counting on the days left. I love the holidays — Christmas is definitely my favorite one. There is something magical about going to the mall during this time. It's a little crowded, and everyone is on edge before Christmas. However, I don't mind people at all. It's the only way I can feel like I'm a part of something bigger.

I love shopping for Christmas gifts, wrapping them. Of course, I don't need to buy that many gifts, but I'm happy with what I got for my parents — the first US edition of George Orwell's book "Nineteen eighty-four" for mom. She loves that book so much, she reads it at least once a year. I've read it as well. It's interesting, but I'm always fascinated by how much my parents' generation is so scared of the government. At the same time, they are less worried about all these big corporations taking advantage of people and collecting data about us. I've got a wake-up light therapy alarm clock for dad. I think he'll enjoy it because he always tries to turn off the alarm on the phone. It drives mom crazy, so I hope a sunrise simulation will help him. I have a lot of pride in picking a perfect gift for everyone. I can't wait to see their faces when they unwrap them.

To be completely honest, I've bought gifts for Ally and Louis — a matching set of friendship bracelets for Ally and me, and the eyelashes Lou-Lou has been dreaming about. I don't even know why I got them because there is no sign that we'll ever patch things up. My heart is still full of hope, but it's getting harder and harder to believe that it will be okay.

I'm walking back home from the mall. All the neighbors have already decorated their houses, and it's a lot of fun. My family put our decorations up very early, and since I've had so much time, it looks better than usual. I think mom and dad noticed that I've been intense about it, but they haven't said anything. I really appreciate it because I'm not ready to discuss it yet.

I haven't been so excited in a while. Finally, I'm about to start wrapping the gifts. It's just pure joy. I put shopping bags on the concrete to open the door, attempting to find the key in my purse.

"Hi, guys! I'm home," I announce as I enter the house. My parents are in the middle of a conversation.

"I don't know how long I will keep it together with Wendy," mom explains to dad.

"She's a train wreck, just ignore it," dad says, and then he addresses me. "Hi, honey!"

"How was shopping?"

"It was so fun, guys. I got everything I need," I let them know and rush upstairs.

"Do you want something to eat?" mom yells.

"Later!" I stop immediately after saying it. *They will follow me if I don't explicitly tell them that I'm about to wrap the gifts. I'm pretty sure I'm running out of time before they would like to have a conversation with me.* I put all the bags on the floor and run downstairs.

"Mom, dad," I address them. They both look up at me. Their eyes are full of confusion. "I'm about to wrap your Christmas gift. Is it okay if I let you know when you can come into my room?"

"Honey, you know you can just put it in a Christmas bag. We'd love it either way," dad says.

"A bag?" I double-check with him.

"Yeah," he starts, glancing at mom. "You've done so much decorating the house."

"We just want to make sure you know that you don't have to do anything else if you don't have enough time."

"What mom's saying," dad jumps in. *Oh yeah. They're definitely getting more suspicious, and if I'm not careful, they'll start poking at my story.*

"Mom, Dad," I say. "Don't worry about it. You know how much I love doing it."

"Okay," mom says as dad nods with a smile.

"Okay, I need to get to work," I tell them. "I'll be late, you know?"

"Sounds good."

I go back to my room, where I organize everything I need to wrap the gifts. It's my ritual. When everything is ready, I start with mom's book. Usually, it doesn't take too much, but it doesn't seem like I can get anything right this time. My hands shake when I grab scissors, and it's even hard to cut the paper in a straight line. It's a little disappointing because I want it to look just perfect.

When I finally finished with my parents' gifts, I quickly realized it's already dark outside. Three hours have already passed, and I have two more to go — for Ally and Louis. Maybe taking a break would have been the right decision. Still, I immediately jump into doing them, which has rapidly become my personal hell. I've already picked the wrapping paper, but it doesn't seem like a good choice with the color of ribbons I've got left.

On top of that, I can't make it look good. This is a disaster. I don't know why, but this is the moment when I couldn't pretend that everything is okay anymore. Tears burn my eyes, my lower lip trembles. I'm tired of feeling ashamed — I'm not happy. Then, as I collect all the pieces of wrapping paper, someone knocks at the door.

I jump off the bed, wiping my tears away, and open it.

"Hey, come in," I say, walking back to the bed. When I get there, I hang a fluffy pillow. However, no one enters the room. It makes me look up to check whether it's mom or dad. It's mom. She's just standing in the door frame. I wonder if she's already noticed that I cried.

"Are you... are you planning to come in?" I break the silence first, asking mom the question. Interestingly, she isn't rushing to answer.

"Are you okay?" she asks me instead.

"Yeah, I'm fine," I reply with a smirk. That's not true, and mom knows it. Mom enters the room, closing the door behind. Here it is. They want to know what it's up to me. I've run out of time, and I didn't even notice. While I have an emotional revolution, mom is taking a seat next to me.

"Do you wanna t-talk about it?" she asks me. Her voice just sounds as if she's begging me to open up. She doesn't know yet that this isn't worth her time. I'm supposed to be better, smarter than that.

In a way, I genuinely hope mom already knows about the whole situation. However, what if she has no idea what's up. I need more time to figure out what kind of conversation she wants to have. I wish I could talk to you. *So yeah, mom, you're right. I'd love to talk to you, so I can tell you all about how I lost my friends, Jake, and El before I even had a chance to realize how much I'd need them.*

"No-o-o. I'm good, thanks," I reply.

"Okay, hon," mom says, "but you should know that we're here."

Mom stands up, and she's totally ready to leave. It makes me so miserable, so I break, "You, guys, are just so perfect."

Even though I sound a little bit frustrated, it's enough for her to say. I notice she frowns. Mom sits back as my tears roll down. I secretly wipe them away. I'm pretty sure she saw it, but it doesn't stop me from adding, "and I'm not. I'm not perfect at all. I'm just scared if I tell you, you're gonna hate as much as everyone else like Elliot, Ally, Louis."

"We aren't perfect, and we don't expect you to be," mom explains. *What's that supposed to mean? I'm sorry, I don't believe it even for a second.* I shake my head.

"Yeah, sure."

"Plus, I don't believe you could have done anything that will make me or your dad hate you," she explains, but I only roll my eyes.

"I highly doubt that."

"Try me."

Mom softly wipes tears off my face. I shrug my shoulders, then I spill the beans. Even though I'm scared to look at her, I still tell her everything from the beginning to the end. I've included my summer heartbreak.

"I just got stuck in those lies, and it was harder and harder to tell the truth without hurting someone. I really didn't mean to hurt anyone, but I guess it's a little too late for that."

Honestly, I have no idea what she's thinking right now. I want to yell, "Just tell me what to do!" I don't, but I need to hear advice from someone. This time I strongly consider following through if my mom offers me any solution. I'm desperate, and I can guarantee nobody better than they know me.

I really want to get my life back. Of course,

"Well, it seems to me it's not as difficult as you want it to be," mom says.

"Unfortunately, I don't think my situation isn't that easy."

"You need to tell all of them the truth."

"The truth?" I rhetorically ask. "The only thing they see in me is that I'm a liar, and the worst is... They aren't even wrong."

"Cassie, you know, I have a feeling that you're just scared to show people who you actually are."

This is disappointing. I expected so much more. To be fair, anything would be better, but the idea of me being myself. That's why I'm in this situation in the first place. She doesn't want to see reality because it's ugly. I'm a horrible person who should never be the same. Some people say, "Fake until you make it." I think it applies to me. Maybe if I fake being a good person for long, I might become one at some point. However, I should never be myself.

"I don't even know who I am. You know, there are a lot of times when I'm an observer. It's like I'm watching a movie, and I can't do anything about it. Unfortunately, by doing that, I've become a villain in my own story. I have no idea who I am."

"Of course, you know! You're the sweetest person. I know it. Listen, we all make mistakes. That's just unavoidable," mom explains. "But it's what you do with it. It's a lesson, not a life sentence. Just ask yourself whether you've learned from this experience. And if the answer is yes, and you know you won't do anything like that again, maybe it's the time to start forgiving yourself."

"Even if I do, I don't think it's going to help me with my friends. They'll never listen or believe me, and honestly, I can't even be upset with them for that.

Every time I say I'd do something, I never did. I lied and lied. They're not going to buy that I've changed."

"You just have to keep trying, and who knows, maybe some of your friends will be able to forgive you. If not, it's also okay because, at the end of it, you've learned your lesson. When you make new friends, you won't treat them the same."

"Yeah…"

Mom leans over to give me a hug. I put my head on her shoulder. I feel relieved. However, nothing has changed. I wish Ally and Lou-Lou would forgive me, so I wouldn't have to talk to my mom about it. However, the whole conversation has gone better than I expected, and mom doesn't seem to be angry with me. She still loves me, even though she knows everything.

"It's going to be okay."

"I doubt I'll make new friends at school. Everyone knows, and nobody talks to me," I say. "I might have to switch schools."

"Well, let's see."

She's right. It will be hard to do in the middle of the school year. I nod in response, looking absolutely lost. *How long can I deal with this? How long does everyone plan to ignore me? Yes, I deserve it. Yes, it's better than bullying. But, it doesn't mean it makes it easier because there is no end to it. It's awkward because nobody wants to be my partner in any experiments. That's definitely the hardest part to be persona non grata. Isn't it ironic how Louis said that I would be a social pariah, but going to the Homecoming was what made me one? Well, I'm the whole reason why I'm in this mess, but I can't stop wondering what would have happened if I stayed at home that night. I would have broken up with Jake the next day. I believe I would have done the right thing, but it doesn't matter anymore.*

"But if the situation doesn't change, we'll seriously consider it," mom says out of nowhere. "I promise."

"Thanks, mom," I say, but for some reason, it doesn't make me feel any better.

"Laila!" dad shouts. "Wendy is calling you!"

"Are you okay?"

"Yeah, mom. Go. I'll be okay. At some point," I jokingly say.

"Okay, but I'm here for you."

"I know."

Mom leaves, and I look around the room. Why am I not happy? Mom promised I can switch schools if I need to. The truth is it's not what I actually want. I want my friends back. Of course, it would be nice if El and Jake could forgive me, but it's a pipe dream. It's good for me to stay realistic and grounded.

I go back to wrapping Ally's and Louis's gifts. *I know it's not a bad dream, and that fact will never change. I have to face reality, and mom is right — I should be more active to make amends with them. She did mean that, right? I've been watching them, and I've kind of tried to talk to them. However, I can do better. I'm sure of it. The only question is how. Well, I haven't come up with a plan. Maybe that's why I started wrapping their gifts.* I don't know how long I've been working on them, but when I've noticed the sunrise, I go to bed. *Tomorrow...Well, technically, today. I guess I should start my plan for reconciliation today.*

Chapter 22
Stop Stalking Me

As much as I like my idea of having a plan, I still don't know what I should do even when I wake up. You know the feeling when you're thrilled to start something, but then you feel disappointed because it's not a simple task. Well, welcome to my life. I wanted to show up in front of Ally's house to beg for her forgiveness, and if that isn't enough, I will attempt to bribe her with a Christmas present. It looks absolutely amazing, so I'm pretty sure my plan is rock-solid. However, there is one issue, I'd say a tiny one, but it is kind of a deal-breaker. I don't have Ally's address.

Yeah-yeah. I know what you think, but to be fair to me, her family has recently moved. She invited me over to her new house a few times, but I've been busy. With El and Jake. This isn't great. Therefore, I need a new plan. It hasn't taken too long to figure out that I need Louis, who doesn't talk to me. As far as I remember, he needs Ally's permission to have any contact with me.

On the contrary, today is my lucky day because it's Sunday. It means only one thing. Well, it means a lot of things, but in my case, it means Louis is at his art school. If I haven't mentioned that Lou-Lou wants to be an animator, I'm sorry, my bad. He's working on his painting, and honestly, he's pretty good. Louis even drew a fun design, which he printed on sweatshirts. There were a lot of us. Three of us were matching during the holiday season.

I've decided to show up at Louis's art school, but obviously, the odds aren't on my side. I'll have to improvise, and I'm not that good at it. I need some help, which I'm hoping to achieve by wearing the sweatshirt Lou-Lou got me. Maybe it's low, maybe it's wrong, but I'll take anything. Even if it's a nostalgic factor. I guess it's the best I could do, and yes, I've tried to locate Ally's house by myself. I've gone through every picture on her social media, hoping to come across a tag with her address. Therefore, I don't have a choice but to ask Lou-Lou for help. I'm so mad at myself for not paying any attention. I feel trapped by my own ignorance. It doesn't get easier, and the non-stop crushing guilt puts extra pressure on me.

My biggest problem isn't even to make Lou-Lou talk to me. It's not on top of the priority list. I don't remember which exact class he's currently taking. It's either drawing or illustration, which are both scheduled for today. The only thing I know for sure is that Louis has already started working on his university portfolio, and those two classes play a vital part.

One of these classes starts at twelve in the afternoon, and another one is at six pm. I came on the campus at eleven am, so I could find the right classroom. I ride a bicycle the whole way, but I quickly realize it won't be an easy task when I park it on campus. Louis's class is at the community college. It's really chilly outside, so wandering around the campus doesn't sound like a good idea anymore. However, it's too late — I'm already in. I don't know how long I've been trying to find the art department before someone approaches me, "Hey, can I help you?"

I turn and see another teen. He reminds me of Jake — I don't know what it is. It's something about that sadness in their eyes that makes my heart melt.

"Umm. I think I'm good."

"Okay, but you do look like you're a bit lost."

"Yeah, I'm good."

"Okay," the stranger says. He's ready to leave me alone when I stop him, "Actually, you're right. I'm totally lost."

"Where are you going?

"Art department. Room 392."

"Oh. Advance drawing?" The stranger asks with surprise in his voice.

"Yeah. Why?"

"I'm taking it."

"Really?" I ask, unable to hide the chagrin.

"Oh damn, is that so disappointing?" the stranger asks through laughter. I shake my head, thinking the opposite. How can anyone be so unlucky? Why, out of all the people, does it have to be Louis's classmate? I'm not supposed to be invasive of his life. Only then might he tell me Ally's address.

"No, no," I say. "It's not that."

"Are you joining our class, then?"

"Oh, no. I'm actually visiting a friend."

"Let's go. I'll walk you there. Maybe I even know your friend."

"Thanks. Probably, you do."

We both walk — I let him go in front of me. I can't even hide my happiness when we enter the art building.

"Cold, hah?"

"Well, I've been wandering around the campus for a while," I jokingly add, making Cole laugh.

"I'm Cole, by the way. "

"Cassie."

"Nice to meet you, Cassie. And what's your friend's name?"

"It's Lou-Lou."

"Lou-Lou?" Cole asks as if he can't put two and two together. I roll my eyes because there is no way he doesn't know who Louis is.

"Really? Louis Frazer?"

"Oh yeah, the quiet kid."

"I guess you could say that," I agree with Cole, even though I have no idea what he's talking about. How could anyone call Lou-Lou quiet? He's always at the center of everyone's attention. No matter what the price is, and I mean it. When we enter the elevator, I'll add, "He doesn't expect me, though."

"I bet he'll be thrilled to see him."

"Yeah."

The elevator door is opened, and I immediately notice Louis in a group of people. My heart is ready to jump off my chest. I feel so uncomfortable. I haven't talked to him, and it's about to change. He looks miserable, even lost. I've never seen Lou-Lou quietly standing around anywhere.

"Hey, guys!" Cole says as everyone looks at us. My eyes meet with Louis's, and he's not too happy to see me. It's disappointing because he doesn't say a word to me. We walk up to the group, and Cole adds, "Louis?"

Cole comes up and gives him a hug. If I didn't know Lou-Lou, I would think that he was scared to look at Cole. However, when I see how much his cheeks are blushing, it hits me. Lou-Lou really likes this guy.

"Can we talk?" I awkwardly ask Louis as everyone's eyes are on him. *Wow, this complicates things. Obviously, I wasn't supposed to know about Lou-Lou's crush. He must be so angry at me. I shouldn't have shown up like this — I should have texted.*

"Sure," Lou-Lou grabs me by my arm and says, "I'll be right back, guys."

"Cassie, I love your shirt, by the way," Cole notices.

"Thanks. Actually, Louis..."

"Don't," Louis stops me, dragging me away from his friend group. "Just follow me."

When we walk far enough for anyone to see us, his smile will immediately fade, and his expression will become ardent. *This isn't good. Louis can't even pretend for a second that he doesn't hate me — probably, he can. But he doesn't want to. Hmm... That's weird. Why wouldn't he want me to say it? Especially when he obviously likes the guy. This isn't Louis, I know. He's always confident around people. What has happened to him? I've missed so much, I guess.* I nod and follow him.

"Cassie, what the hell are you doing here?" he asks the second we go around the corner.

"I came to talk to you, but you and Cole, hah?" while I'm asking Lou.

"Stop."

"Is Cole aware of your crush?"

"Stop."

"Wait. Does Ally know about this?"

"Stop."

"Oh my gosh. Really?"

"Why are you here?"

"I told you I came to talk to you. Is this not a good time?" I ask him with my innocent tone of voice.

"Yeah, but I'm surprised that you could even notice it," he says, but he quickly adds, "it's shocking you can pay attention to somebody else. And it's not yourself."

"Burn."

Some people say that words hurt, but I understand he's just upset with me. I'd be upset with me too. Interestingly, Louis gets that snarky only when he's nervous. "I'm not supposed to talk to you anyways. You should leave."

"Hey, I want to apologize to you in person."

"All the messages you've sent aren't enough?"

"Are they enough? You, tell me."

Louis looks down at the floor. We all know it doesn't matter how many texts I've sent.

"I'm truly sorry," I start my planned speech, "my behavior was totally unacceptable."

"Yeah-yeah, I get it."

"Will you ever be able to forgive me?"

"Ugh, Cassie. You have to sort this stuff out with Ally first. Okay?" he explains, ready to take off.

"I need a little help with that," I ask him, but the second these words leave my mouth, Louis's facial expressions totally charge. I'm pretty sure this is the first time Louis is about to get mad.

"Help? Are you kidding me?!" he yells at me through laughter. "After you've humiliated Ally so much? You're unbelievable. No, Cassie. No. I'm sorry, but I can't help you."

"No, that's not what I meant."

"Oh really? Do you really think you can just show up like this... I don't understand you! What are you thinking about?"

"Can you text me Ally's home address?"

"Wow. You don't know your best friend's address?"

"You're my best friend."

"Really?" he asks, rolling his eyes at me.

"Yeah," I mumble in response. I feel like it's a trap, and it's too late to escape it.

"Really?"

"Yes."

"Then please, tell me what my home address is."

Silence. Yeah, here it is — the trap. I don't know his address, and since knowing your friend's address is a milestone, you should achieve it.

"I don't know."

"Yeah, that's what I thought. Cassie, my class is about to start. I've got to go."

"Okay," I agree with him, but I take his present from my pocket, "this is for you."

"Ugh. I don't think so."

"It's something you'll enjoy, and I know it doesn't change anything. You've made my Christmas special a few times."

Louis gives me a skeptical look but carefully takes his gift.

"Thanks."

"Bye."

"Bye, Cassie," Lou-Lou says and walks away from me.

My plan has failed, but I'm not too upset. I've officially apologized, which means I've done everything I could. Even though it's disappointing that I couldn't get Ally's address, I'll be okay. I'll come up with a new plan. I'll be okay.

When I unlock my bicycle, my phone buzzes. I don't rush to check it because I don't think it's anything important. Probably, dad wants me to pick up some bread on my way back home. So I frown when it buzzes again.

"Okay. Mom or dad? Hmm... Maybe, it's grandma," I say, and I almost drop my phone when I see Ally's address. It's Lou-Lou.

Good luck. I love them btw. I can't believe you remembered :P

My tears roll down my face. I can't believe it worked. If Ally can forgive me, I'll be the happiest person. I've realized that if I have Ally and Louis by my side, I will be able to survive the rest of high school. It won't matter even if everyone else hates me. This is the first time in a long time when I feel like, finally, something has gone my way. It feels good to do the right thing.

Bubbling with happiness, I copy the address to a map app. Ally's house is about forty minutes away from the campus. Ugh, I wish her house would be closer. I'd better be going. Deep down, I'm a little bit worried about seeing Ally. She's not as easy as Lou-Lou, who was so distant with me. *Honestly, I didn't expect Louis to text me. I was a hundred percent sure our conversation was over. I don't think Ally will ever be able to forgive me. Isn't that sad? Ally was so into El. I bet she believed if only I could be out of the picture, she'd be with El. However, nothing has changed between them since we broke up. I'm so relieved, but I could only imagine how I'd be feeling if I were Ally. I hope she'll listen to me.*

Chapter 23
Hello, My Old Friend

Sometimes time goes by so quickly. I've noticed it only happens when I'm about to do something I don't want to deal with. Well, it's time to apologize, face to face. I was even excited about it, but all the excitement instantly disappeared, especially when I get off my bike in front of Ally's house. Wow, her family moved into a beautiful home. I should have definitely come over more. No wonder Ally's been inviting us all the time.

I jump off the bike, but I can't move. I freeze. My whole body goes through the shock, reliving the dreadful Homecoming dance. It feels like my lungs are running out of oxygen. *Come down. What is the worst that could happen? Ally has already said everything, and it can't hurt as much the second time, right. At least, I hope. She might yell at you, close the door in front of your face. I can totally deal with all these things. Easy.* Even though thinking about those things really helps me calm down, I still don't feel like facing Ally.

I pace back and forth in front of her house. I'll go when I have a perfect speech, which will depict how I feel in under thirty seconds. I assume that's how much time I have before Ally shuts the front door in my face. It's not enough time to describe even half of how I feel, and I'm pretty sure it's not enough time to make Ally forgive me for everything.

"Ally, I'm sorry," I mumble under my breath. "No, I should say hi. What if her parents open the door."

There are no words in the world, which can describe how sorry I am. I have one chance in this, and it's terrifying. I want to run away, but it doesn't work so well for me, and I know that from experience. Plus, this uncertainty drives me absolutely crazy. I need to know one way or another if Ally could forgive me. Suddenly, I feel brave and confident I can do this. I just have to tell Ally how it is. I rush to the entrance and fiercely ring the doorbell.

My heart drops when I hear footsteps. I nervously swallow because I don't feel so brave anymore. *Cassie, run.* Even before I have a chance to act on that thought, Ally opens the door. Her eyes are locked on me, but I'm not sure what her stare means. She hasn't been expecting to see me on her doorsteps.

"Cassie?!" She states the obvious. However, she quickly realizes that I'm not a ghost, and Ally starts shutting the door just like I'd expected. I prevent Ally from closing the door. I should probably say something, but I've forgotten all the words in my speech.

"I know you're upset, and you should be, but please, give me a chance to apologize," I say, looking down. Ally lets go of the door. It's working. Happiness crosses my face as I add, "I really miss you."

Okay-okay. I've done everything I could, for now on, it's on Ally—blood races up my cheeks. I feel so embarrassed. I follow Ally's glance, and she looks at my sweatshirt, which makes her smile.

"Nice touch," she says. "Come on in."

"What?" I ask to double-check because I can't believe Ally even considers letting me inside.

"Come in."

I carefully enter her house. I know it's just the beginning of this conversation. We haven't discussed anything. I should have prepared this part as well, but it should be more difficult.

"Are your parents at home?" I ask her as we walk through the gorgeous house. I can't believe I've never found time to come over.

"No, my parents and brother James went to the movie theatre," Ally explains as we walk upstairs.

"I see."

"It's almost unbelievable that you're here, Cassie," Ally implies something.

"Agree, I had to ask Louis for help."

"Oh."

"I wasn't the best friend, hah," I state. We stop in front of a closed door. Ally opens it.

"Come in. This is my room."

"Thanks," I say, entering the room. Ally sits on her bed, and I take a seat by a desk. I'm picking on my nails, wondering how I can naturally get back to my apologies.

"So you've talked to Louis."

"I wouldn't count it as a conversation. Lou-Lou was very clear he wouldn't tell me anything," I clarify. I've caused so much pain, and I can't let Louis be in between my emotional problems.

"And here you are."

"Well, I'm here because," I start changing the subject, "Yeah... So, I'm, I wanted... I want to tell you I'm sorry. It wasn't cool of me."

"Are you kidding me? It wasn't cool of you?" Ally doesn't find me as amusing as Louis.

"Okay, I know what you want me to say. Yeah, you're right. My behavior was unacceptable, and I can't believe you let me in because I've been treating you like you aren't my real friend. I don't know why you're so nice to me."

"Wait, what?" Ally stops me. "You didn't think of me as your friend?"

Is that the only thing she heard? Ugh, this is so annoying. You see, that's the problem with people. You open your heart to them, then you say nice things about them. Will they hear them? No, no. People just concentrate on only one negative thing. However, I promised myself that I'd tell the truth no matter what.

"Yeah. It's stupid," I say with sadness in my voice, "I'd behave as if you aren't my real friend. I'd lie to myself that I didn't want to be your friend, and you were the one who was into best-friend things."

"Oh wow. Cassie, why are you telling me this?"

"Because I want you to know how stupid I was. It's not true, and it's never been the reality. You were my friend, who I treated terribly. I think that's why I told El about your feelings. I thought it was okay to tell Elliot about your feelings because you weren't my real friend. It didn't matter how many mental gymnastics I had to do because it was convenient to think that way. I'm sorry. I was such a bad friend."

"Is this the first real... honest thing you've told me?" Ally asks.

"Kind of, I think so," I answer. Maybe it's too much, but I'm tired of sparing everyone's feelings all the time. I look down and continue, "I'm sorry about that too. And... I wanted to ask you to consider giving me another chance to be your friend? A real one this time."

Silence. I'm waiting for Ally to reply with something. Preferably, it's a simple answer like yes or no. I carefully look up as Ally comes up to me and gives me a tight hug.

"I can't believe it took you so long to apologize," she says.

"Sorry," I reply as we both hear the doorbell ringing.

"Louis must already be here."

"When did you even text him?"

"I didn't," Ally tells me, then she checks her phone. "Oh yeah! It's Lou-Lou. After you paid him a visit, he texted me that he'd pop by."

"Of course, he decided to join us."

We run down the stairs and let Louis in. He looks so excited, and he immediately asks, "So beautiful ladies, are we all cool and chill?"

I give Ally a grateful look, and she smiles.

"Yeah, Lou-Lou, Cassie, and I are good."

"Thanks, Ally."

"Yay!" Louis screams and gives us a hug. "Okay, let's go upstairs. I want to put on my Christmas gift. Thanks for getting two sets!"

"Christmas gift?"

"Yeah, Cassie got me one," he says. Ally rolls her eyes at him.

"At least, now I know what it takes for Louis to sell me out!" Ally teases him.

"I can't hear you, Ally!"

"Actually, this is for you," I tell, passing the gift to her.

"Ah-ha, here the bribe is," she teases me.

"Not a bribe. If it was, I should have led with it," I explain. Ally gives me a hug and carefully unwraps the gift.

"Thanks, Cassie."

My eyes sparkle with happiness when Ally sees the bracelets, and her face lights up. She immediately puts it on her arm, then she steps forward to me.

"You don't have to share it with me, you know," I say, backing away from my friend. "You can give it to Louis. I know we weren't on the best terms."

"Don't be silly," Ally says, putting the second bracelet on my arm. "Let's go. I want to see what you got for Lou-Lou."

A little later, three of us lay on the bed, totally dead. It's hard to even move. Yes, we had a lot of pizza, and yes, we had too much soda, then we had ice cream. My vision is blurred. Luckily, this time it's not caused by unshed tears but by overeating. I look at the window and notice it's already dark outside. I should text mom and dad. Let them know I'm at Ally's. I grab my phone.

"Are you texting El?" Louis asks me out of nowhere. It's weird because I assume they've been hanging out with him. *Wouldn't they know I couldn't even get a chance to talk to him even if I wanted to? This doesn't make any sense.* I turn around, facing Lou-Lou.

"No," I reply. "I'm just letting mom and dad know where I'm at. No one else talks to me. Well, now you do."

"Have you talked to El or Jake at all?"

"No," I answer. I notice Ally and Louis look very suspicious, as if they know more than they're telling me. "I was thinking to apologize to both of you first, and after the trial run with you, I'd go to talk to my exes."

"If that worked with us, it doesn't mean it'd work on Elliot," Ally says. "He's pretty pissed."

"Well, I don't think anyone can talk to El. He went batshit crazy."

"What?" I ask.

"Shhhh," Ally stops Louis. "Stop exaggerating, Louis. El didn't go crazy. He's just having fun."

"Having fun?" I ask because I have no idea what she's talking about.

"Umm…"

"El's dating around," Louis finishes for Ally.

Yeah, it's not what I want to hear. It would be okay if they told me about Jake. He's with Katie, and I'm not even upset about it. However, I can't say I don't care. I do. It's not the same thing with El. I'm not ready to accept that El has started dating. I'm even talking about dating around. What does that even mean? I've already heard rumors about El and numerous girls, but it's easy to ignore the reality when it ignores you.

"Sorry," Louis says.

"No, it's okay."

"I just can't believe you almost got away with dating two guys!" Ally changes the subject.

"Or going to the Homecoming with both of them! You were so close," Louis adds, then he compliments himself, "I'm such a great wingman."

"I know. But you have no idea how many times I was close to breaking up with Jake," I say, shaking my head.

"Oh yeah?"

"How many?" Louis asks.

"Too many. Times. Okay, I'll tell you my favorite one," I say. My eyes sparkle with happiness. *This is the first time I'm talking about my side. Everything is still my fault, but it's nice to share my story with my friends. Keeping all those secrets made me into an incredibly lonely person. When the truth got out, it became easier in a way. I didn't have to look over my shoulder all the time, but it wasn't the same without the ability to discuss my secrets with friends.* I can finally tell them everything. "Remember the day when we went to the beach, and I told Ally that I had picked El?"

They both nod.

"So next day I came to see Jake, so I could break up with him," I explain, "but before I could even open my mouth, he introduced me as his girlfriend in front of the whole team."

"No!?" they both say.

"Yes, it's true. I never forget being shocked and thinking whether it's time to spill the beans. I couldn't say a thing."

"Is that how you became Jake's girlfriend?"

"Yes, it's literally the worst," I reply. "It was killing me. Of course, Jake couldn't call me his girlfriend before I've made a decision to break up with him. Why couldn't he do that at camp, you know? I used to think I'd do anything to have Jake call me his girlfriend. It was so important. Yes, I always get what I want, but it always takes a horrible turn. I inevitably end up hoping that my dreams will never come true."

"To be fair, I don't know what I'd have done in your place," Louis admits.

"Oh, come on, Louis. You're just saying it," Ally stops him.

"No, Ally. Remember, it's Jake."

"Jake isn't my type."

"Jake is everyone's type." Louis states.

"I have to agree with Lou-Lou on this one," I pile up.

"You wanted to break up with him!"

"Yeah, and it took me forever to do it. That's the point."

"You two are unbelievable, but I can see your point," Ally finally agrees. "Yeah, I'm not sure I'd have done the right thing."

"I understand why I've done certain things, but in the end, I know it wasn't worth it," I reveal another secret. "I missed something important, which was in front of my nose, but I couldn't see it. I almost lost you, and I definitely lost El."

Tears sting my eyes. I hadn't noticed when I started crying how one by one, teardrops slid down my face. My heart aches every time I think about El. I can't believe that I did it to myself. Then, Ally and Louis give me a group hug. It makes me feel a little bit better.

"I need to know something, guys," I say — Lou-Lou and Ally nod. "You, guys, have spent time with El since the Homecoming. I have to know if you think he can forgive me."

"Cassie, it's not our place," Ally explains.

"One way or another, but please, tell me what you think," I beg them.

"Cassie, we honestly don't know," Lou-Lou answers.

"And when we talked about you, El never said a word."

"Sorry, but Jake was the reason why nobody said anything about the whole Homecoming thing," Louis reveals to me. "How cool is that?"

"Yeah, Jake is a good guy. Thanks, guys."

"Oh, come on. Don't be so sad," Louis says, giving me a hug.

"I don't know what you're talking about. I'm fine," I say, getting a little defensive.

"No, you aren't fine, but you will be," Ally adds, also giving me a hug.

I feel so frustrated with them. I don't even know why. Technically, Lou-Lou and Ally are absolute. I'm not okay. The reality is catching up with me. I did an excellent job at avoiding it. It suddenly hits me — our story is over. That's my reality. *El and I will never be together. There is no point in crying about it. It's over. It's disappointing and heartbreaking, but I shouldn't have expected anything else. How could I have been so naive to think El might forgive in a few months? I broke his heart in a million pieces. I get it. He's just trying to find all of them to put himself back together.*

Of course, everyone loves Jake because he's so nice, thoughtful, and noble. If he tells everyone to leave me alone, they will listen to him, no questions asked. However, I can't imagine what I would have to go through if he didn't do that. I can guarantee his football team would have done something. At least, there would be posters with something like "slut" on it. It's sweet of Jake to help me out, but I wish he wouldn't do that. Maybe El would have forgiven me by this point.

I don't even remember how I got home, but I can't fall asleep. Sometimes it's easier not to know things. I recall having a meaningless conversation with my parents. I've told them that I'm friends with Ally and Louis again. They probably think I'm doing fine, and it's partly true. However, I won't have the same success with Jake or El. I feel like in my situation the cheating is worse than telling your best friend's secret. Both are undeniably bad, but one is worse than another. I just have a bad feeling about everything else. I wish it wouldn't have to be this way.

I guess it's challenging to face the repercussions of the choices I've made.

It's partially because I was getting away with so much. I felt like it'd always be like that. I was too cocky. I know one thing for sure: I will never be so ignorant. I wish I could just purchase a little bit of luck because I need it, like more than anything right now. I was so scared to make the wrong choice that I didn't decide on a time. I could have been happy with El since summer, but I wasn't ready to let go of Jake. If only I could go back and have a do-over, I would just pick El. I would have been so happy.

Chapter 24
My Broken Promises

Well, it's Monday. It's another day at school. At least this week is the last one before winter break. All tests have already been completed, the grade is in. Maybe I didn't do so well at the love front, but I've got all As this semester. At least, it's something to be proud of. I guess there are two things — my grades and that I made amends with my friends, which has been fantastic. I don't have to hide to eat my lunch. I can just join my friends. Of course, it's not about eating food with Ally and Lou-Lou, but it's one thing that made me realize how much I have missed them. Overall, I think it's been better than it was in a while.

Even though the first couple of days were weird, I found a way to deal with it. A lot of people at school have been staring at us. Some still do. However, it doesn't bother me anymore. I try to. I'm just so happy I have my friends by my side. Real friends. It was weird to think even a month ago. I didn't even believe that we were even close. Thanks to them, it's been getting easier to see El with new girls every day. It's not only about emotional support. The guilt is a compounding feeling, so it's not a surprise that I've felt so horrible. Since Ally and Louis forgave me, I've seemed to be better. Not great, but better. I don't deserve to be better. At least until I apologize to both of them in person. I've been asking myself the same question over and over — why is it so important to me. I guess the answer is simple. I've made many mistakes this year, but I don't want to continue that path. Being a good person is a lot of work, and apologizing is something a good person would do. Of course, good people don't ask for forgiveness, but that's what is supposed to happen. There is no other way, so that's what needs to be done.

This conflict with El brings me back to the summer. I have an idea about how El feels because I felt the same way when Jake and I broke up for the first time. I was obsessing over Jake. Nothing really mattered. It was just such a bad time for me to meet El. We were doomed to fail from the beginning. Well, I was.

The hardest part is seeing me in him because he's been going through the same patterns. It's not a good path, and I know where it leads. I want to be there for him, but I've done enough. Since I can only be a spectator right now, I've been thinking about the beginning many times, going through every detail. I can almost certainly say that I remember every moment when we were together. Isn't it love? If so, why can't I answer a simple yes or no question — have I ever used him to make Jake jealous?

The reality is I don't want to answer that question. It doesn't make me look good at all. I'm trying to escape the real world as much as I can. To be fair, it's partially because my honest answer doesn't fit into the narrative. Everything that happened was a big misunderstanding. Misfortune mixed a tiny splash of miscommunication. Isn't that the recipe for a Molotov cocktail? For me, it is because all together, it brings me here. I still don't want to admit that some squeaky voice was yelling the truth somewhere deep down, but I shut my ears. I didn't have to hear it — that annoying voice told me that I was making one mistake after another. Where is the line between a misfortune and a strategic decision? What if it was an active decision to use El to get more attention from Jake? These questions rip my heart into a million pieces. I've got to face that as much as I want to believe everything is an unfortunate coincidence, it's not realistic. Maybe I haven't been so innocent as I want to be — built-up in my mind.

If you think about it, forgiveness isn't that easy to achieve, and I can say it from my own experience. I wasn't so quick with it either. I couldn't believe a single word Jake said. I will never forget the moment when he proudly stated that he had changed. It took a lot out of me in order not to laugh in his face. I couldn't believe it. Sometimes you even want to trust someone, but it's not the most straightforward task in the world. Ironically, it takes so much time to warm to someone who has broken it once. If anyone breaks my trust, I'll take forever to let anyone off the hook. I'll make a point out of that. I can see why both of my exes might not be able to forgive me. The fact is it takes a lot of work to forgive somebody, so I shouldn't be expecting too much from Jake and Elliot.

I'm still nonplussed by attaining both of my friends' forgiveness. It still feels a little bit surrealistic. I've never felt so uncomfortable before, but it was such a huge letdown. It wasn't even that hard to attain their forgiveness, and then they behaved like nothing had happened. I don't get me wrong, I'm not bragging about it, but I wish Ally and Lou-Lou would have created a million complicated tasks. They should have made me work hard to earn their trust back. How can they let go just like that? The main reason why I even think about it is that it makes me feel I don't deserve their forgiveness. Funny? My friends are nice, and their behavior has raised suspicion. As much as I love to be a detective, nobody can live experiencing so much distrust. I need this emotional baggage to be dropped like a bad habit.

However, it's easier to say than do because I regularly wonder whether Ally and Lou-Lou have actually forgiven me. I have to admit it's a little bit ironic that I'm the one who is worried about other people's honesty. It's like the universe is laughing at me, but if I've got to admit it in a way, I wanted to get caught. It's the one explanation why I didn't run back home. Something in the back of my head told me to get out of there before I got caught. I decided to ignore it, hoping it would work itself out. As far as I remember, I was so tired that day. I wanted to be free of my lies and secrets, but I couldn't do it myself, so I used Ally, who did all the dirty work, instead of me. She was an actual victim of circumstances who got caught in the middle of my drama.

However, I've decided no matter what the universe is planning for me, I'll be ready for it. I know the odds aren't on my side — I definitely don't deserve Jake's and El's forgiveness. That's just a fact. Jake didn't let anyone bully me or even say a word, regardless of the betrayal. It was so big of him. I want him to know that I appreciate that. Deep down in my heart, I hope he's found an excuse for my behavior and forgiven me. It's a long shot, but it's fun sometimes to dream. At least, I can see that potentially happening with Jake. Not with Elliot, though. It's totally a different situation with him.

I've thought over and over about what the ramifications of our conversation could be. Still, there is no scenario where he forgives me. He has been nothing but a perfect boyfriend. The most heartbreaking realization is that Elliot was the whole package. I can't believe I couldn't see it earlier. In retrospect, I should have known that he's always been the one, but it feels like I was under a spell. It doesn't change my sad reality — I can't come up with a single reason why he'd ever forgive me.

During the blowup, El gave me such a cold glare. It was full of disappointment, mixed with a flare of contempt. To all the seriousness, I'm not sure he'll ever be able to look me in the eyes ever again. Those memories still give me chills. So, inevitably, I always walk away from any opportunity to have a tête-à-tête with El.

Recently, a perfect opportunity came across for me to apologize to him. I remember it was early morning. I was standing at the parking lot when El parked not too far away. There was not a soul around, except us. I nervously turned around and tiptoed away from him. I could have made an attempt, but I didn't. I froze. It never occurs how terrified I am to see his cold gaze again. I was ready to give up on that idea. However, my romanization of Christmas always makes me believe that everything will work out in the way I need it to. I'm not saying Santa Claus is real or anything crazy like that. Still, I totally buy into the idea that good spirits bring luck during holidays. It gives me hope. Maybe there is a possibility that in some universe, El and Jake will forgive me on the spot with no questions asked? Realistically, no way will that happen, but I'm willing to settle for something a little worse.

The uncertainty drives me crazy. Who knew that it could be torture in itself? You don't realize how necessary knowledge is for your sanity. I'm only fifteen, and it shouldn't be any of my concerns. People say that sometimes you have to lose someone to know how much you need them. I hope it's not true because it's kind of depressing. I'm more a love at first sight type of person, but that's what was holding me back. I hope one of them will be able to forgive me at some point. Every time I see them around, I always imagine how my next attempt to have a challenging conversation with Jake and El could go. Inevitably, they end up yelling at me. It happens in every single conversation I have with both of them. I've noticed El always yells at me a little bit more than Jake, which is understandable. Despite everything, I've made a promise to myself that I'll apologize to both Jake and El before the end of winter break.

Initially, I wanted to do it before the last day of school. I've thought about it a lot and realized that I'm in a very delicate situation. It'll be worth it because I can let Jake and El be rent-free in my head. I have talked about it too much, but the imaginary boys aren't too much fun to be around. They're mean. Yes, they only state the truth, but it doesn't make it less acceptable. Recently, they've mentioned that it doesn't matter how good my grade is. I won't feel good about myself until I apologize to both of them. Again, they aren't wrong.

My goal is set, and I need to get ready to make that happen. I want to start next semester from a blank space. It frustrates me that I'm using the word "ambitious" in that context. My working theory is that if I can resolve my issues before a new year, I'll be able to move forward. If not? Oh well, there is always next year, right? It's not like I'm a senior, joking. I want to get some kind of resolution because I don't want to be haunted by my past. It's so funny how you're okay, but a second later, you make a wrong choice, and you're immediately a bad person. I can't move on until I get their forgiveness, and that's why I've been watching Jake and El. I've spent a reasonable amount of time learning about their schedule, trying to figure out when is the best time to talk. Of course, it's a bit selfish, but I have only one chance with it.

I don't want to rush into anything because I want to have a productive conversation. The biggest surprise is that I could use "not rush into anything" and "productive conversation" in the same sentence. I'm just a loser. I'm willing to believe anything instead of facing the truth. I'm just terrified Jake and El might never forgive me. What am I going to do then? I honestly think I can't live with such crushing guilt forever. It's already been too long. I was so upset when Jake couldn't say I love you back. I felt like my heart was broken into a million pieces, and I immediately broke up with him. The problem is I don't even know if we were dating last summer. To be completely honest, I can only imagine how both of them feel. Even though Jake's never cheated on me, pure jealousy guided my thoughts — and constant fear of losing him. It was even true, and I was losing my mind. They had to go through because of me.

As much as I dream about being forgiven by them, I've been mentally preparing myself for the worst. I'm not as naive as I used to be, which is good because it has become a problem a few times. As a result, I can even think about asking for El's forgiveness without a panic attack. Any time I begin to work on what I should say when I get a chance, I'll end up having one while Jake and El are endlessly yelling at me. I should add they haven't been nicer, only ruder. They've been telling me that I'm the worst thing ever happened, and it's not even the most hurtful thing they've ever said. Despite all my fears, I've decided to start my apology with Jake. In a way, he's a safer bet. I don't mean it as a bad thing. I just don't want to be discouraged by starting with El. It'll be soul-crushing.

Jake made the whole school leave me alone, which means he doesn't hate me, right? Well, it's not as bad. On the other hand, El just hates me. If it's not hated, then he's definitely angry at me. Even though Jake hasn't tried to talk to me, it seems more realistic to talk to someone who still cares about you. I've texted Jake a few times. He's never replied to any of my messages, just like everyone else. El hasn't shown any interest in me, but Jake secretly helped me even after the blowup. I think it makes a lot of sense to start with him. It might be a good idea to give El as much time to cool off as possible.

The biggest issue with the existing plan is that talking to Jake is more complicated than any mission in a spy movie. He's always surrounded by people. It's insane. The only time I've seen him alone was when he went to the bathroom, and that's where I draw a line — I'm not going to the men's bathroom under any circumstances. I've already known that he's always the center of attention, but I've never realized that Jake spent a lot of time with me. We went on many dates. It never occurred to me it was such an undertaking from his side. I've started to feel discouraged because I think it's the right time, but it's impossible to catch him alone. To be fair, since Katie is a captain of the cheerleading team, they can spend even more time together. Jake drives his buddy Chase and Katie home. Chase and Jake live on the same street. If one of them goes somewhere to hang out, another one always joins. It's a vicious cycle.

One day, something that I didn't expect happened. Our team is going to the semi-finals for the first time in eleven years, and luckily, it's a home game. The whole school is buzzing about it because several scouts are coming to see Jake. He's probably freaking out about it. Can you truly be ready to play the most crucial game in your life? I remember Jake was telling me that the scholarship was the only way for him to go to college. It's too much pressure. Katie probably helps him mentally to prepare for that day. It's good. I would even know where to start. If I were still with Jake, I'd be useless. I've never dreamed about anything like that, so it's hard for me to relate to something I don't understand. Therefore, Jake and Katie are good together.

The good news is that it can be my only chance to talk to Jake. Some athletes have rituals. Of course, Jake has one as well — it's going on the field to train early in the morning for the last time before the game. He wakes up at five am., so he can be on the field by six. He never misses it. I should know that. He dragged me on the field before a few important games, where I always fell asleep on the bleacher. Every time I ask Jake what are the reasons why he had to pick such a torturous ritual. He always laughs at me, and then he explains that the only way for him to find peace within himself is to train alone. Who knows what that means? I still don't know, but at least I don't have to guess the answer to that question. I need to talk to him, and it's the only way. I've been looking for such a moment when Jake's going to be alone, and I'll finally get a chance to talk to him. Of course, it crossed my mind that showing unannounced can be considered as bad juju. Jake used to invite me to come over for such an occasion, so I hope nothing has changed. If I've got to defend my logic, I'll remind him that he used to say that I brought him good luck. It's going to work. It must work.

It means I have to wake up very early. Nothing can be worse. To tell you the truth, I'm not a morning person. I'm always sleepy, and I hate that I'll have to ride a bike to school so early. My parents are okay with me going to school, but they were precise in their instruction — don't wake them up. I don't blame them. I wish I could sleep in, but it could be my only chance to talk to Jake before winter break. I have no choice.

Chapter 25
You Know I'm Sorry

The fifth alarm goes off in a row. I think there are ten alarms in total. Yeah, I'm not messing around. I can't be late. I'm lying on top of the bed, struggling with such a basic task as keeping my eyes open. I've never expected to be defeated by jeans. Every single attempt to put them on has ended up with me falling back to sleep. Hopefully, I've set enough alarms. Everything is an impossible task in the morning because I'm just not a morning person. I wipe the sleep from my eyes, but I'm not ready to sit up. I feel how heavy my eyelids have become. I wish I had dressed up last night. It'd buy me fifteen to twenty minutes of sleep. *You can't be late, Cassie. You know how important it is. Ugh. The voice of reason in my head drives me insane. If only it wasn't right all the time, it would be so much easier to ignore.*

Despite all the sleepiness and inability to keep my eyes open, I leave the house as scheduled. Mom and dad are still asleep, but I left a note on the fridge in case they'll wake up before I come back. However, I have a sneaking suspicion it's not going to happen. The road is empty. It's hard to keep my mind off Jake. Even though I have a good feeling he'll be at school, I still don't know whether I'm right. If he's there, I'll finally talk to him because nothing can stop me now. I'm riding a bike while it's showering. *Of course, the weather has to match my mood. I can't stop thinking that next year I'll be able to drive. I won't have to be worried about the cold winter wind and rain blowing right in my face. If I haven't already been halfway there, I would totally run back home. What can be better than your warm bed? At least, I'm not sleepy anymore. Is he going to talk to me? Will he be training when I come? Will he be alone?* My heart races faster as I get closer to school. *Just don't think about him. You don't know how he'll react. It's going to be okay.*

Honestly, it's been extremely nerve-racking. I've gone through every scenario in my head, but I have no idea what today's outcome will be. You think you know someone, but once in a while, people can surprise you. Jake probably didn't expect me to cheat on him. He's always looked at me as a cute little girl, and he probably thought I wouldn't be able to do anything like that. But, you can never be too confident. Even though I'm pretty sure I know who Jake is, I can't tell exactly how he'll react towards me. No matter how much I've thought out every single detail, I can't say that I'm a hundred percent sure what is about to happen. Rarely, I imagine Jake forgiving me, but it's not as satisfying because I never feel like I deserved it. Every time it seems too easy.

I've been waiting for the moment when I can find out all the answers to my questions. One way or another, I will finally know whether Jake and I can be okay. Being in a state of constant uncertainty has been defining my entire world for a while. It's been frustrating, but somewhere on the way, it became the new normal. I didn't even notice when that happened. Deep down, I'm scared. *I'm not ready to know that Jake will never talk to me. However, it doesn't matter whether I'm ready or not.* I jump off the bike and walk through the empty ally. Technically, I don't need to leave my bike at the parking lot, but if Jake's car is there, that means he's here as well. He cares about his car so much, he'll never keep it overnight at school. No matter what, and I hope today isn't an exception.

Jake's car is the only one there, and it's parked in its usual spot. There isn't a soul at this hour at school. I'm pretty sure our genitor isn't even here. The whole building has a spooky vibe, especially with such gloomy weather. The wind makes a humming noise, which will make you believe in every horror movie. If a ghost or something supernatural shows up in front of me, I won't even question it. Just think, "That's right on time." Without any surprises, I quickly walk through the campus on my way to the soccer field. I wish I could slow this moment down. I don't even care about the wind, but I need as much time before I have to talk to Jake. I'm excited about it. At least, I should be.

Sometimes my world falls apart when Jake walks away from me. It doesn't matter how much I'm trying to get him to talk. He continues to disappear in the distance. I just need to stay positive. It's important. Otherwise, I won't be able to have a conversation with Jake. I've finally realized what I've got to do for me to forgive myself. It's a vital step to move forward. Since I apologized to Ally and Louis, my life has gotten so much better. In their case, they've forgiven me, but it might not happen. Who knows, maybe I'll get lucky? If not, then I'll try again and again. I'm getting used to the idea that the boys might not be able to forgive me. But, I have to do my best, so if things don't go well, I know I've done everything I could.

As I wander up to the bleachers, I see Jake is running laps. It's time. I go down the stairs, experiencing a sense of déjà vu. It reminds me of what happened about a year ago. I was with my mom, going to the principal's office because there was a mix-up with my documents. I remember how annoyed mom was at the whole situation. She was supposed to be somewhere, and the papers shouldn't have been a problem. We were standing in a hallway in front of the principal office, waiting for our appointment. I'll never forget that moment when I saw Jake after two years. He's changed a lot — he's definitely got taller. Two years seemed like an eternity to me. Jake was with a group of friends — they were congratulating him. He just became captain of the school football team, and he looked so happy. I was so in love with Jake. He used to be in the center of my universe. Partially, it's a big reason why it's been so hard for me to let go of Jake. Loving him has been a long chapter in my life, and now it's over. It wasn't too long ago I was dreaming about our first kiss. Look at me now — I don't feel this way anymore.

When I walk upon the field, something interesting catches my eye. To be more specific, it's someone who I wouldn't guess in a million years. It's Katie. She's there, and I don't know what to do. I feel like I'm an idiot. *Of course, she has to be here. Katie is always right next to me at my low moments. Ugh, boys. Jake is so predictable. Look at him. He used to tell me that I'm the only person he could ever bring to his secret rituals. He made me feel so jaded when I didn't believe him. Now I feel a little validated for not buying into that crap. I wanted to believe him — I wanted to have our thing. It's just never real. The second we break up, he replaces me with Katie. It's unfair to Jake.* Sometimes I wonder if we all say things just to get what we want or if our feelings don't last for too long. Even though I'd love to blame everything on Jake, I know it's not his fault. It's not just him. It's everyone, including me. At the end of summer, I thought I'd die from how much I love Jake. I thought my love was forever, but even my feelings have changed.

Honestly, I haven't been in love with Jake for a while. *Have I drastically changed? I have no clue. I think my personality has pretty much stayed the same. I'd like to believe that I grew up, but is it enough for Jake to forgive me? There is no point in wondering what could happen. I've got to do this.*

"Hey, Jake, Katie," I say to both of them as I walk onto the field. They give each other a concerned look.

"Hey, Cassie."

"Hey," Jake says, coming up to me.

"Can I talk to you, Jake? Alone?" I ask. "If it's okay with you, Katie."

They both look at each other again. It makes me irritated. Jake and I haven't had that. We could never understand what the other person meant just by looking. Maybe we weren't that good together.

"Yes, it's fine with me," Katie replies after Jake nods.

"Are you sure, babe?"

"Yeah, it's fine. I'll go get coffee from the car."

"Sounds good. The keys are in my bag," Jake explains.

"Okay."

Katie leaves. Wow, these two are so in sync. I feel a bit jealous, and it's not about seeing my ex-boyfriend with his new girlfriend. We've never been together like that. It always felt different. They remind me of El and me. I'm not sure how to even describe it. Jake and I never click. We're always off — if I go to the right, he'll go to the left. I look down at the grass. I don't know where to start because my thoughts are racing.

"So, what's up?" Jake asks as he takes off the helmet.

"I want to apologize," I start. "What I've done is horrible, and understand if you can't forgive me. I want you to know I didn't intend to hurt you. Everything got out of hand too fast. I'm sorry I created my own idea about who you were.

When the dream and the reality became in conflict, I wasn't brave enough to tell you the truth. And I know it's not an excuse, but I truly tried to tell you the truth. Please, don't hate me."

"Cassie, I don't hate you," he says, "but I'm going, to be honest with you — I really don't get you."

"Yeah, I was a kid, who needed to grow up," I reply as my tears roll down my face. *Oh, Jake, I can be a mystery to myself. I'm doing things half thinking, and it's not going so well for me. I don't even know why I feel so emotional right now.*

"Come here," Jake says, offering me a hug, which I need so much right now. Crying has never been a part of the plan. It's nothing but humiliating. I want him to see how much I've grown. All these tears make me look like a bit of a child in his eyes.

"I'm so sorry, Jake. Do you think you'll be able to..."

"We're cool, Cassie," he cuts me off, "I mean, you and I. Not like in the past, but there is no issue between us."

"Okay, it makes a lot of sense, but I have one simple question?"

"Go ahead?"

"What does it exactly mean?"

"Ugh, what are you implying?"

"I'm not implying anything, but I have something on my mind."

"Okay," he states. This is not how I imagined our conversation going. I'm here to find peace. Jake isn't attacking me.

"Okay," I repeat after him. *I'm behaving like a child.*

"What's on your mind, Cassie?"

"I wonder if I can say hi to you when I see you at school? Or it's more like I'm telling you that we're cool, but let's pretend we don't know each other in front of everyone else?" I ask, trying to sound as if I made a joke. But, deep down, I'm scared Jake is just saying that we're cool, so I'll move on. Jake and I used to be pretty close, and I hope he's telling me the truth.

"Are you serious, Cassie? I can't believe you," he says, shaking his head.

"Of course, you can say hi, weirdo."

"Okay."

"Okay."

"You guys seem great together."

"Thanks?"

"Sorry, I don't know why I'm so weird."

"Cassie, just relax. Next fall, you'll be a sophomore, and I'll be in college. There is no problem," he explains. For some reason, I really hate how reasonable Jake is. I can't blame him. He's about to move forward.

"Yeah, you're right. You will be in college, and I'll be here. Everyone is going to remember me as a cheater."

"Come on, people quickly forget things."

"Oh really?"

"Yes, I'll see. Next year people might start saying that I've cheated on you instead."

"I guess. I hope Elliot will be one of those people," I snap. It's unfair to Jake, but he seems to be happy. I can't quite talk to Ally and Louis about Elliot since they all are still friends. Of course, Jake isn't the best person to hear about my heartbreak with Elliot. It's definitely a long shot.

"Oh no! You're on your own there!" he jokes, then adds, "But most people won't remember about the whole thing between us. They will barely remember me by the end of summer. When I say barely, I actually mean they won't remember me."

"You're just saying that. I will remember you."

"Well, I hope so."

"I've missed you."

"Cassie, don't start this. It's not a good idea."

"Sorry."

"So, are we good?" Jake asks. Weirdly, I know what it means. When Jake wants to go back to whatever he's doing, he always says, are we good. It's a sign the conversation is over.

"Yes, we're good, but before I go, you have to say one last thing," I bravely demand.

"Sure, but if it's about helping with your love life, I'm telling you now that I'll pass. There is no way I..."

"No-no-no," I interrupt Jake before he can finish his sentence. "It's not like that. My friends told me that you told everyone in the school to leave me alone. I want to know why you'd do something like that for a person who betrayed you?"

"We're cool, Cassie," Jake mumbles.

He still cares about me. Silence's the only answer I'm going to get out, Jake. Even when we were technically dating, I would call our relationships more like a close friendship rather than being in love. Once Katie mentioned that she didn't understand what Jake had seen in me. I don't know why, but it's stuck with me. I always wonder what Jake sees in me. It's a mystery I'm never going to solve.

"Okay. Then I guess, bye?

"Are you coming for the game?"

I shake my head. Maybe he'd like me to come, but I have to be honest that watching his game is literally the last thing I want to do — like ever. Jake knows me better than that. Everyone knows how much I don't care about football. He rolls his eyes at me.

"Isn't it bad luck to have your ex at the game?" I tease him. "Especially when you already have such a supportive girlfriend?"

"Ha-hah, you're right."

"You see, that's why I had a problem with you. Maybe you shouldn't ask other girls to show up for you. You should work on that," I joke around.

"Really? I can't believe you, Cass."

"What?"

"You just begged for my forgiveness, and look at you, already giving me relationship advice?"

"Okay-okay, I went too far. I'm begging you to forgive me!" I say, though, laughing. "I'm going to go before I say something stupid again."

"Okay, weirdo."

"Bye."

"Bye, Cassie."

I give Jake a hug. It was our last hug and our last conversation, and it was the second type of, we're cool, because the next time I said hi to Jake in the hallway, he pretended that he didn't see me. Now and then, it crosses my mind. I wonder if he didn't mean that to happen, but that's what inevitably ends up being. Honestly, I'm not even mad about it. Still, I genuinely hope that he's right about everyone forgetting about the last Homecoming.

As I'm picking up my bike, Katie is walking by. I hoped that I wouldn't see her on the way back. Unfortunately, my luck has its limits.

"Oh, Cassie. How was it?" she asks. Even though she's been so nice to me, I can't trust her. Why can't she leave me alone? I can't fall any lower at this point, and Katie has already got everything she could possibly dream about. However, it's never enough. She always comes back for more.

"I think we're good, but you know. It's hard to say," I mumble, shrugging my shoulders. I hope I'm saying what she wants to hear.

"I wanted to talk to you earlier..."

"Yeah," I'm trying not to let Katie finish her sentence, but she smiles and keeps going with her thought, "But you always found a way around it."

"Yeah. I'm so sorry about that," I don't let her finish the sentence. "I just wasn't ready to discuss how I was, but I really appreciate the thought."

Katie is pitying me. *Ugh, I don't need this today. I have no problem with her, but she's just like an angel sent to judge me nonstop. She doesn't know a thing about me, but she isn't aware that I'm happy I'm not with Jake. I don't like that she assumes I'm miserable without him. It's not the truth — the only reason I'm even remotely upset is because of El. He's the one.*

"No, it's cool. I wanted to tell you that Jake was always fine with you, even after everything. I'm glad it all worked out, and you, guys, can put it behind."

"You're so nice," I say. The second those words leave my mouth, I feel embarrassed. I don't understand. It came out of nowhere. Hating on Katie has never brought me anything but bad luck. I'm so tired of playing games. Objectively, she's a friendly and caring person, and she should know that.

"Thanks?" Katie carefully says as if she's asking a question.

"No, seriously. I wish I could be more like you. You're always nice."

"Thanks, you're fine too. You know."

"Yeah," I mumble. "Well, no. It's fine, though."

"Nobody's perfect."

"Thanks," I tell Katie, and then I check the time on my phone. "Sorry, I've got to go."

"Yeah, me too. See you around."

"Bye."

We go in the opposite direction. Interestingly, Katie and I would never have a conversation if it wasn't for Jake. I know girls like her. I need time to think about everything. So, I walk my bike next to me, trying to crack Katie's code. *What does she mean by saying nobody's perfect? I guess it's so easy for her to judge. She's probably never done anything wrong. I can guarantee Katie has never had such an issue. Even by looking at her, nobody could imagine her cheating. It's a different story for me. Everyone thinks they've figured me out.*

I remember how much I used to feel like nobody sees me or nothing I do matters. Well, there is some good news — I don't feel this way anymore. I want people to forget about me. Overall, the conversation with Jake and Katie went well. It doesn't seem to me that they're still upset with me. Of course, it's a relief even in itself. Why was it worse? He didn't yell at me. I should be happy about it — however, I'm not. I'm incredibly far away from being happy. It makes me scared that it means it's not going to be the same with Elliot.

"Jake went easy on you, hah?" I hear Imaginary El's voice. I look to the left — he walks on the other side of my bike, staring at the cellphone.

"You're talking? To me?" I ask him.

"Sure, why not?"

"What changed?"

"I don't know. Maybe my buddy Jake isn't as strong as I thought. There is no other explanation."

"Yeah, of course. There is no other explanation. Not even a single one," I say. I want Imaginary Elliot to keep talking to me. It's been a while since we had a chitchat, but thankfully he breaks the uncomfortable silence, "It sounds like you can think of something."

"I don't know. Maybe Jake realized that everyone made mistakes. It doesn't make me a bad person."

"Is that what you tell yourself to go to sleep?"

"Wait a second. Do you disagree?"

"Yes."

"So I make one bad choice, and bang — I'm a bad person?"

"No, it's more like you've made too many mistakes, and bang — after a month of dating two guys, guess what? You're a bad person."

El's going to torture me, but he's never letting this go. He's just waiting for a perfect moment when he can get his payback. I'll have only one chance to change his mind, and I can't blow it. Therefore, I should really work on what I'm going to say. I can't let myself mumble again. I can't believe it worked with Jake. Unlike El, he's already moved with his life. That's why it wasn't a big deal, and he was willing to forgive me. Even though El has been dating around, I wouldn't call that moving on. It's hard to stay positive, but I still believe something I can say will change his mind. Yeah, I need to come up with a heart-melting, life-changing speech. It's not too much pressure at all. All these thoughts have been racing through my mind. I haven't even noticed when I'm already near my house. I just need a small break. I've been fixating over this for a while, but it's not productive. Worrying about it hasn't helped me to find the right words. Since this morning, I've done so much exercise, and I feel like I'm ready to go straight to bed. When I open the front door, I immediately smell fresh-made coffee. *Maybe I don't need a nap.* It means only one thing — parents are awake, and they're about to have breakfast. *If only I was hungry....*

"Hey, honey," I hear mom's voice. "How did it go?

"Fine. I apologized to Jake, and he forgave me."

"Oh, that's good, right," dad asks as he comes up to me.

"Yeah, but who knows if he actually meant it."

"Join us for breakfast?" mom suggests.

"Okay."

I go to the kitchen and put oatmeal in a bowl. We always eat it for breakfast during the weekends. As my parents always say, it's not great, we don't eat healthily all the time, that's why they double down on Saturday, Sunday, and some holidays. It's not that bad because they've left Christmas and Easter out of it. Mom passes me a cup of coffee and adds, "Of course, he meant. Don't worry about it."

Yeah, I know she's right. Frankly, I do feel better. It's pretty annoying how good it feels to do the right thing. I can finally enjoy spending time with my family, my friends without constantly thinking that I'm a horrible person. However, it's not over...

Chapter 26
The Last of Them

The only one I haven't gotten a chance to apologize to is Elliot. It's been stressful for me to figure out when I should do it. Well, I'm attempting to convince myself to do so. First, I want to ask El for his forgiveness. That's not the problem — I'm terrified. That's the truth. I can't breathe when I see him. El's forgiveness is so important to me, but he won't ever be able to do that even if he tries to push himself into letting go of the amount of pain I've caused. So I can't ask for too much. I'm not sure if El did the same thing to me, I would be quick to forgive him. Maybe or maybe not. *Maybe, I'm just not ready, but what if I'll never be able to talk to him? Am I always going to feel this way?*

El also shows that he doesn't want to see me, so it feels like having a conversation out of a window. That's why I've become his shadow. I've been hoping that I'll be there when he's alone and in a good mood. Apparently, it's an uphill battle because it's always one or another — he's either alone or happy. The semester is about to end, but I haven't got any closer to this task. Ally and Louis have gone to a few parties with him, and they generally tell me when it might be the time. Nonetheless, it never ends up in success. I've been looking at him from far away, just like I'm doing right now.

I'm standing behind the tree at the parking lot, spying on El. That's my life now. For some reason, he's running late. He gets out of his car, looking absolutely miserable. It seems like something terrible has happened. What's wrong? I was planning to have a confrontation right now, but it might not be the right time to do so. El looks miserable, chatting on the phone with his dad. They don't have the best relationships. Yeah... Approaching him is out of the window now. El used to tell me all about his dad. He's always angry with him. He wants to impress him so much, and from what I've heard, El never could. I wish I could find the right words to help him or cheer him up, but I never could. In a way, it's my parents' fault. But, it's not their fault that they are always so supportive.

"Dad, I don't know what exactly you're saying. It's insane," El yells.

Cassie, you shouldn't be here right now. It's time to go. If he sees me, he'll get even angrier. Who needs to see your ex-girlfriend when you're having an emotional argument with your dad, who you love more than anything? Well, it's the obvious one — nobody. I want to move, but my body refuses to listen. This is paralyzing.

"Really?! Maybe I will. Okay, then."

As soon as he hangs up, he immediately turns back and goes towards the car. *What is he doing? Is planning to skip school? No, that's not El.* As soon as I think that, he sits in the car and drives away. Honestly, it feels like I'm still asleep because one thing I know for sure El doesn't skip school. It must be serious. Today is not the day. I wish I could run after him, but I'm not even sure where he's going. I highly doubt he's driving back home. I turn around and wander towards the school. What else am I supposed to do?

My thoughts are racing. I can't concentrate on anything at all. Luckily, since it's deep down, I hope he'll show up. He won't, though — I know that. I can still hope. The whole day I've unsuccessfully tackled thinking about El and wondering where he is. It sounded like the conversation with his dad got away from him. I wish I could be there for him right now. The worst part is that I can't even mention it to him any time soon because I shouldn't have been there. It wasn't my place to overhear it.

Finally, it's lunchtime. Louis, Ally, and I go through the hallway to the cafeteria. I'm on autopilot through the motions. I can barely hear what my friends are talking about.

"Hey," Louis says as he pinches my hand.

"Ouch!" I scream from pain. "What the hell?"

"Sorry, not sorry. What's up with you?"

"Did you really have to pinch me? It's so painful," I complain.

"But really, Cassie, what's on your mind?" Ally asks me.

"It's El. You know," I answer, wondering whether I should tell them the whole story. And I can forget about getting El's forgiveness if he finds out that I'm the one who is spreading gossip.

"Didn't you plan to talk to him today?" Lou-Lou asks.

"Yeah."

"It's a shame he didn't come to school today," Ally says.

"Ally, do you think he didn't get himself out of bed after the party?!" Louis asks. There is so much excitement in his voice. It makes me sad, but just for a second. Even though I want to be a part of it, I know it will not happen, which is understandable. Nobody talks to me except Ally and Louis. They're the only people who actually interact with me. Yet, they have no idea what Elliot is going through, and I do.

"Yeah, I don't think it's what it is," I say, trying to sound nonchalant.

"Wait, how would you know that it wasn't the party? Did you talk to him?" Ally promptly asks me with a note of skepticism in her voice. Of course, the intelligent thing to do is shut up because telling them about El's argument with his dad isn't a good idea. I have one rule — never gossip. My friends behave as if I'm never going to be a part of El's life, and nothing can change that.

"No, El didn't tell me anything about the party or anything at all. I haven't got a chance to talk to him," I reply, staring at the floor. If I avoid their glares, maybe, they won't notice that I'm trying to cover up the truth.

"What do you know?" Lou-Lou grills me.

"Nothing."

"I don't buy it. What about you, Ally?"

"Come on, Cassie, spill the beans."

"Is that why you were late for school?"

"OMG, guys. It's not a big deal. Forget about it. El might still show up."

"Okay-okay, Cassie."

"We didn't mean to upset you," Ally says, putting her hand on my shoulder. "I can't even imagine how difficult it must be."

"Yeah, exactly what Ally said," Louis piles up on the point.

It's kind of cute that they're supportive. *They're lying to themselves and to me right now because neither of them can even comprehend how I feel. Neither Ally nor Louis is the type of person who could consider dating two people. It's never going to happen in their life. Both of them are better human beings than me.* Ally and Lou-Lou aren't buying it, but they don't continue grilling me over the secret. Probably, they're pretty sure El will tell them later. I'm incredibly thankful that Ally and Louis have forgiven me. I'm so happy about it. Truly. Yet, there is one tiny thing I wish I could change — I wish my friends would stop pretending that they've always had better relationships with Elliot. Yes. Maybe it's the case now, but they're *fools if any of them thinks it's always been that way. No-no-no.*

No one has ever been as close to him as I used to. El doesn't tell people about his issues with his dad. I'd say he doesn't quite talk about any of his problems and concerns. El always looks at the world with a smile. I used to be the only exception. It's crazy to think that it wasn't such a big deal. At least, that's what I was telling myself. It was a big deal. I can't believe I couldn't see it before. If only I listened to what El was telling me more carefully, I would know what to say. It's killing me that I can't fix it for him.

I suddenly get a feeling of deja vu, similar to right before the conversation with Jake. When I notice a silhouette, which reminds me of El, all my senses tell me to run after him. The idea that I've just seen El right now is insane. It hits me that he is in the school — to be specific, at my secret spot. *Of course, where else could he go?! Ready or not, but it's time. Maybe I've caused so much pain, but it won't matter if I can fix everything.*

"Sorry, I totally forgot about something. I have to go," I say and take off without waiting for their response. Maybe it's crazy, but I haven't been so confident in a while. He must be there. There is no other way. We all do bizarre things sometimes, so there is a slight chance it could be true. I hasten to get upstairs as fast as I can.

When I get upstairs, I put my hand on a door handle. I'm hesitant to open the door. It's funny because I should be finally ready to do this. Why can't I? My heart beats, almost jumping out of the chest. Overall, I'd say I have a good feeling. But, in the back of my mind, I can't stop wondering what if I'm wrong? *What if I'm not, and he's there? Is this the right time? Stop, Cassie. You need to come down — deep breath.*

I shut my eyes with the hope of finding peace. Instead, my whole body is trembling. I'm not ready to go there and face Elliot.

"One, two, three," I mumble. "He's there, and I'm ready."

No matter what happens, it's time to put this behind. I open the door and walk outside. There is nothing. No one else is around on the roof, just me. Honestly, this is a huge letdown. It's been a long shot, so why do I feel like all my dreams are shattered? The wind picks up, and a cold gust hits my face.

Everything seems so unrealistic. I don't even understand what I expected? *I'm such a fool for believing El's here. Unbelievable.* I slowly wander to the edge of the roof and look around. It's been long enough for me to be honest that I miss El like crazy, and seeing him so upset on top of that is just torture, in my opinion. I wish someone would come up with a time machine, so I would have an opportunity to redo many things.

Time is an interesting thing. It could drag like a turtle, but it also can surprise you by getting away from you. I can't believe we're almost halfway through the year. Sometimes you look around, recalling something, which used to be so vital to your life. However, you can't even remember what's so great about it. I feel this way right now — kind of. I'm looking around, and I can't call up what's so special about this roof. I used to be so proud of the opportunity to sneakily come here. I felt so special. I guess it was the only place where I was able to get away from my day-to-day life. It was so easy for me to get lost in my thoughts when I was here. It was so special to me — it hasn't been the same, though. I've avoided coming up here. There are so many reasons why I can't be here as much, but the only one I care about is that El and I used to eat lunch here once in a while. Being here is a constant reminder of us. So many things have changed, and unfortunately for me, a lot of them haven't worked out for the best. The school bell rings, which means it's time to go back inside. *How long have I been here?*

Chapter 27
Moving On

There are only three days left before the winter break, so I'm running out of time to accomplish my resolution. If I want to fulfill my wish to apologize to everyone, I'll have only a few days to achieve that. Together with the time limit, it's been nerve-racking to see El around. I've seen El around the school, and he looks good as usual. It doesn't seem like anything is wrong. He smiles more than ever. It's weird. Who knows, maybe he's made up with his dad, and there is nothing I should be worried about? Yet, I have a sneaking suspicion that he's putting on a happy face in front of everyone. It's a little bit surprising, but of all people, I should really know that looking "fine" and actually feeling "fine" are two different things.

Ally and Lou-Lou have attempted to get El talking as a favor to me. He swore nothing was going on, which is a blatant lie I'd say in his place. Thus, I don't buy a single word. My friends just couldn't crack him. Now Ally and Louis look at me as if I'm a crazy person who will come with anything to get more information on Elliot. It's upsetting when your friends are a little skeptical of you. Even though I know what I've seen, and Elliot's pretending that everything is okay.

I've kept my taps on him. I've noticed that he's been more around people, making it more difficult for me to approach El. I feel like it's happening on purpose because I secretly believe that Ally has already told him about it. He knows I'm planning to talk to him, so he makes sure that he's always with other people. I can't bring myself to come up to him in front of other people, and El is a hundred percent aware of it. Therefore, it's not complicated to prevent me from approaching him.

The whole first day out of the three days left, I was only watching Elliot like a hawk, but I didn't get an open window to make contact with him. He was alone for only a minute in the library, which was weird by itself. Who goes to the library at the end of the semester? It's truly shocking how many girls go to the library, so they could talk to El. He's getting so popular. I'm pretty sure he's going to take Jake's place. I would take Katie's spot as the "it" girl in school if I didn't screw it up. Frankly, it's not the most important thing to me. I still think the whole school's popularity is silly. I just want to be closer to Elliot in any way I can. Sometimes I tell myself he'll forgive me if I become popular. But, of course, I shouldn't think this way because it's very toxic. It doesn't matter that I miss him so much because he's changed a lot. Whether I'd like it or not, he's different now. El even goes by Elliot now. At least, that's how everyone's calling him.

It seems like the longer I wait, the further I get from El. I feel like I'm observing him from a glass wall. I'm lying in bed right now when I suddenly realize I'm invisible to him. That's exactly how I felt when I was with Jake, but Elliot is better at ignoring me. The fact is that he knows me really well, so he's aware of how much I suffer when people neglect my presence. It's even worse with El. He scorns me on my account.

It's the second day, and I've already announced to Ally and Louis that I'm about to talk to El. I thought it couldn't get worse, but it can. I'm standing next to the locker, surrounded by my friends. Louis is blabbering about his crush from the art course when I hear Ally whispering something. In a furtive manner. Ugh... This is another annoying thing. I wish they would just talk about El because this half measure isn't working for me. I immediately figured out it's about my ex-boyfriend. So what's even the point? Just talk normally.

"Shit," I hear Louis swear. That's interesting. Louis loves to swear, but he has a rule, which he never breaks — don't use any curse words at school. I can guarantee Louis is terrified to slip and say something inappropriate to a teacher. There are a few teachers who can't get Louis's approval under any circumstances. I don't even think he's wrong, but Louis can be incredibly salty. If he ever lets it go, I hope I'll be around to see it.

"No, it can't be," Ally whispers. "Shh. Be quiet."

They're killing me sometimes. I'm right here, and they can see me. Also,

I'm not deaf. This has to stop.

"So, what's up?" I ask as I continue to tidy the locker.

"What do you mean?" Ally asks with an innocent tone of voice. I don't even need to look at her to know that she's trying to act surprised even though she always says things I could hear.

"Come on. What is it about El?"

"No, it's not that," Louis explains.

"Let's just drop the pretense," I say, closing my locker and turning around. "What's up with El?"

I feel a wave of apprehension and an accelerated heartbeat as I turn around. My eyes spot El walking with a girl. She's naturally pretty. Dammit. She's making my ex-boyfriend laugh. *Uh-oh.* This is really bad. I have a terrible feeling. I've seen him around girls, but this is the first time anyone makes me nervous.

"He's been hanging out with Emma a lot," Ally adds. "They posted the selfie yesterday, so it's the second day in a row they're hanging out."

"See, over there? They're walking up right now."

"Yes, I see," I say, doing my best to hide the heartbreak in my voice. "They look cute together."

"Are you kidding me?! You two were the best couple," Louis gasps as I look down. I said that to get some empathy because I don't feel like I'm not getting enough of it from my closest friends. I want them to say something nice about me, which is ridiculous. Undoubtedly, he's only starting his tirade, and I'm so excited. I feel like my soul fills with happiness when Louis abruptly stops.

"Hey, Ally," El greets, waving at us. "Hey, Louis."

Now everything makes more sense. Hearing El's voice freezes my whole body as if someone dumps a bucket full of ice water over my head. It feels horrible. Ally and Louis wave at El and Emma as they say hi to each other. Not me, and I get it. El avoids me. Emma and I haven't been introduced. I don't know what to do, which is my personal hell. In a way, I feel like El is doing this on purpose. Maybe he wants me to go through the same thing as he's already experienced. Should I say hi?

On the other hand, it's not a bad idea to keep it quiet. Is that what El wants from me? To be quiet forever? My mind is racing, working hard on solving the dilemma. However, by the time I conclude that the right decision is not to say anything, Emma and El are already gone. Here it is. Nowadays, it's Elliot's favorite thing to do to me — acknowledge my friends or people around, but not me. It's absolutely driving me crazy. At this point, there is no way he doesn't know that I've apologized to everyone except him. It's only logical he's next. Maybe that's why he doubles down on ignoring me. His grasp of my personality delights me. It's a bit sad because as much as I want to get back together with El, we aren't dating. I've got to watch him hanging out with other girls.

I turn back to my locker, opening it up again. That's the only way for me to hide my tears rolling down my cheeks. Ally and Louis stay quiet. It's obvious I'm crying, and they don't even know how to react.

"We're sorry," Louis tells me, putting his hand over my shoulder. Finally, I'm happy Lou-Lou has acknowledged how upset I am. I need my friends right now. Even if they believe it's been a long time coming, our friendship will require unconditional moral support. Have you ever felt disappointed in yourself? Well, that's how I feel now. It's partially because I can't keep my emotions under control. I used to think that if I finally accept everyone's hatred is justified, I'll feel better. To be fair, it's been easier, but I can't escape the regret.

"No, it's not your fault. You weren't cheating on him," I reply. "I deserve it."

It's the sad truth. I deserve this, and it doesn't matter how much I suffer. Unfortunately, it doesn't guarantee El's forgiveness. I was wrong when I thought that I'd need my friends' support. Right now, I wish I would be alone. This is too embarrassing to be around people. It feels like my heart attempts a painful escape through my throat in front of everyone's eyes, and it's not something I'd recommend seeing.

"I've got to tell you something," Ally says, interrupting my unstoppable train of thought. She gives me a light hug before I can reply.

"What?"

"As a couple, you and El were much cuter together."

A few tears roll down my face. I wipe them in secret. I don't want to make my best friends even more uncomfortable than they already are. *Why can't I stop wondering whether El and Emma are dating? Yeah, this one is going to be on my mind for a while. He's so ready to forget about my existence like a nightmare. It's not surprising that he wants to get that point, but I haven't expected my ex-boyfriend to move on from us so quickly. It just hurts. Maybe I should look into the B plan.*

The whole story behind a different approach starts when Lou-Lou has asked me a few times whether I have a B plan if El and I will never get back together. I was shocked when I heard that for the first time. Up until this moment, the entire idea has seemed crazy to me. However, it could be time to reconsider. What has El been telling my friends, so they must have an intervention about our breakup? Maybe he's already decided that he'll never forgive me.

"Yeah, Ally is totally right," Louis adds, "You and El were much better together. Hands down."

"Thanks, guys," I say and join them in a group hug. It even makes me giggle, despite feeling incredibly discouraged. *We were cute. El and I were great together. I just honestly hope I won't have to think about us in the past tense. We'll get through this. We will date again. I know how silly this is, but them saying all these things already makes me feel better. They give me hope, and I don't need anything else. It's so great to have good friends.*

As much as I would love to talk to El today, but it must wait. First of all, I've been too emotional, and on top of that, I've got to find out more about Emma. Since I have one chance to talk to El, I must be prepared for everything. Therefore, it includes digging personal information about Emma. It needs to be done because if they're already dating, there is no reason for me to be worried about approaching El. It'll be over very quickly — I'll apologize, and it's over. On the other hand, if they don't see each other, it will complicate things. I prefer the second option, which means I still have a chance.

From the first time I've met Emma, jealousy has been guiding my thoughts. As much as I struggle to change my feelings, I continue getting the sense that I'm losing Elliot. It's been happening faster than I expected. I've started wondering what I'll do if I can't catch up with him. What if I'm too late? What can I do in that case? Does it mean he's over me?

All my lies are getting back at me, and it's hard for me to be a spectator. It seems I've played my cards, and now my only purpose is to observe the consequences of my actions without the capability to alter anything. I hate it so much. Everyone makes mistakes, but I hate the outcomes of my mistakes. I can't believe my platonic love towards Jake used to make me so blind. Chasing after the idea of Jake clouded my ability to analyze, so I couldn't see the difference between real love and an imaginary one. It's not an excuse — at least, it's not a good one. Even though it's the sole justification for my actions, my inability to see the right person in front of my own nose is troublesome. Mom always tells me that if I can't restore everything, I'll have to accept it. Withal, I'm not ready to do so. I will pursue El until I can visualize us being together in my heart. I've promised myself if one day I wake up and can't imagine us dating, I will let it go. I hope it won't come to that.

Chapter 28
The Old Me

Tomorrow is the last day before the winter break, so I'm out of time. It's safe to say that I'm officially out of time. Since I got home, I've invested the rest of the day researching Emma. Mostly, I've been going through her social media, hoping to find out more about whether she could be El's type. Deep down in my heart, I'm terrified that El is about to fall in love again, putting our relationship aside. That's the entire reason why I've been obsessively scrubbing through her accounts. I wish someone would stop me, but I've got smarter about not getting caught. Instead of confessing all my feelings and craziness to my friends, I've shut it down.

Here I am now, lying in bed. My eyes are bloody red from excessively staring at my laptop. As much as I've counted on my intelligence to stop, it hasn't happened yet. In addition, I don't think I'm capable of quitting my research at this point. I'm too deep. Emma seems nothing but friendly. Nothing bad. It makes me wonder what people think when they look at my social media. Probably — oh, she's a cheater who seemed so nice. Oh, that's so sad. It's a different story with Emma. I'm getting to the point when I feel like I want to date her. How can I be mad at El? If or when they start dating, El will be in good hands. *This is so unhealthy.*

That thought persuades me to close the laptop and finally go to bed. It's easier to say than to do. Even the complete darkness in the room doesn't help me with falling asleep. It's partially because I can't stop thinking about what I should do. There are a few words I'd like to say in my mind. It'd be something like, "Dear mind, please stop thinking so much. I need to get some sleep. Now." To be fair to my mind, I know exactly why I can't sleep. My mind wants me to have a conversation with El tomorrow. Even though he might reject my attempt, at least I'll try.

Usually, it won't be a problem, but it is now. After checking out Emma, I don't have too much confidence in myself. There is no way El will talk to me, which is a bad attitude to have. As a captain, you can't have your soldiers not believing in a victory. On the other hand, I've made a promise to myself to apologize to everyone I've hurt. The old me would absolutely have done that, no doubt. However, as much as I'd love to go back to my previous behavior patterns, I can't. If I have to be completely honest with myself, I've got to admit that I haven't been happier than I am now. Being true to who I am has been making me feel so amazing. I don't want to lose that. I guess I have no other choice, but I have to talk to El tomorrow.

The next morning I leave early, even though I'm incredibly sleepy. Luckily, it's the last day, so everyone, including the teachers, is relaxed. So it doesn't matter if I fall asleep during class. Of course, that's an exaggeration, but in all seriousness, I'm going to school earlier than usual because I need to come up with a plan, which isn't a great idea. As I walk up to the entrance first, I realize that I should have slept in — I can't focus on anything.

I go to the parking lot, hoping I can catch him right away. At least, I know exactly what I want to say. After over a hundred unsuccessful speeches, I've finally come up with one, which Imaginary Elliot has approved. He even said he could consider forgiving me. Of course, it's not real life. However, there are a few things, which I'm not expecting to happen. It absolutely blows my mind when I see Emma getting out of El's car. *OMG, I can't come up to him now. They must be dating. It's the only explanation why he's driving her to school, and I'm okay with everything. There is nothing wrong with El and Emma seeing each other. I'm totally OK with that. Why would I? It's not like it makes me feel like I'm dead inside. Not at all.*

Every muscle in my body isn't listening to me, preventing me from running away. I can't afford to be seen like that. I just need a second to process the new information. Everything's okay — I just need a new plan. I wander through the classroom, feeling absolutely shocked. I pick the furthest seat from a teacher and start working on my next step. El shows up a little bit later, alone. As far as I remember, Emma must have English instead. Yeah, I know her schedule too. El always makes sure he picks the furthest seat on the opposite side of me. He does it so sufficiently, it's almost impossible to catch his eye.

It's American history class, but my mind is somewhere else. But it's no big deal because our teacher is doing an overview of what we've already learned. Therefore, it's okay that instead of paying any attention to the teacher, I'm assessing during the entire class whether I should still do this or not. A big part of me wants to put a kibosh on plans A, B, and C. Go forward with plan D. It's basically to forget about apologizing and move on, not making the same mistake ever again. I'm not on El's radar, and it's obvious he'd rather I don't try to talk to him. Maybe it's the way to go. It's rare for high school couples to continue dating after they graduate, so what is the point of pushing for something, which may or may not happen. So then, we can break up. I should just let it go because there is no point. *Why is it so hard for me to do that?*

I'm pretty sure if any other person in my place would follow my advice and let it go. At least, I hope so because that's the right decision. Not me, though. I've decided that I'll get this over with and apologize to Elliot right after the class. Despite any logic, I think it's time. I can guarantee he's already dating Emma. By atoning for my sins, I'll finally get the closure my soul craves so much. Also, since he seems more cheerful and overjoyed these past days, I might succeed at my mission.

When the school bell rings, I immediately start collecting my things and putting them in my backpack. My hope is to catch him before he leaves the classroom, but to my surprise, El is already walking out the door by the time I collect all my stuff.

"What are you rushing for?" Louis asks, slowing me down.

"I'm trying to talk to El. Excuse me," I reply and run after Elliot without waiting for my friends. *I haven't expected El to dart off so quickly. That's something new. Maybe I wasn't as sneaky as I thought, and he noticed me glancing at him.*

The hallway is expeditiously bustled with students. I notice El and run for it. It's a little crazy and incredibly embarrassing — I'm aware of it. However, the truth is that if I don't do it now, it'll never happen. I'm not that brave. It's been pretty exhausting to avoid Elliot. To be fair, he's been doing all the work to shun my presence. Therefore, I bet he might be willing to put the whole thing to rest. It doesn't take too much time to catch up with him at the end of the hallway. Just in a few seconds, we're already walking next to each other, shoulder to shoulder.

"El? Can we talk?" I ask him, murmuring the words. I'm dragging my feet with these apologies, and it's so uncomfortable. At least, the faster you get it over with, the sooner it's going to be over. In a way, I can't believe that I'm walking just a few steps away from El. I haven't got a chance to be so close to him since Homecoming. *I can even smell his cologne. Not in a weird way.* It immediately brings me back to the time when El and I were together. *We used to be so happy together. I can't believe I screwed this up so badly.*

Not knowing whether he's heard me or not makes me very uncomfortable. Also, I've felt like I'm stuck in a limbo, in which El gives me a silent treatment. Welcome to my personal hell. I'm surprised that El hasn't even glanced my way once. It's odd. He must be mad at me. Well, there is a tiny chance he didn't hear me. But, in all seriousness, there is no way he hasn't heard me.

"El?" I carefully call for him one more time. This time I'm watching El's every move to make sure he hears me. As a result, it becomes clear to me that El indeed hears my every word. Even though frowning isn't a reaction, I'm looking forward to it, but it's still a reaction to the sound of my voice. Honestly, I'm relieved Elliot isn't looking at me. I don't think I can survive seeing the crushing disappointment in his eyes. Unfortunately, I'm not ready to face one of my biggest fears yet.

"Elliot, can we talk? It won't take too much of your time," I say as I continue staring at him. It becomes apparent to me that El can hear me. It means he's pretending not to listen to me.

"I know you can hear me. Can we talk?" I demand, sounding a bit irritated. It's El's fault because he still hasn't said a single word in response to my requests. Everything is happening in slow motion. I notice how other students point at me. It's probably funny to see a girl chasing a guy who is so not interested in her. *Honestly, I didn't expect him to ignore me as if I don't mean anything to him. My heart skips a beat from that thought. But, of course, it's not entirely about me. It shouldn't be. Ignoring me could be the way El's dealing with the pain I've caused him.*

El goes down the stairs, leaving me behind. I don't follow him because I notice Emma at the end of the stairs. I feel like my whole world starts breaking into a thousand pieces from the realization that he doesn't care about me. Is this it? Are we done just like this? Should I run after him? Even if I run after El, it doesn't mean he'll even hear me out. Who knows, maybe his life's got so much better without me? It bothers me so much that Emma is part of his life while I've got to watch El from the arrears. I miss being a part of his life. If it got better, it would explain why he's been staying away from me.

"Emma, you're already here!" I hear El's voice in the distance. Even though I know it's a bad idea to look at them, I still do. I see my ex-boyfriend, who I love, giving Emma a hug. Then El apologizes, "Sorry, you had to wait for me."

"No worries, shall we?" Emma says, followed by some giggling. *El hasn't even said anything you need or want to giggle about. Maybe I don't need to worry that much about Emma because I know he hates girls who behave like this. El even told me about it, and that's one of the biggest reasons he likes me. Well, he used to like me. Okay, Cassie, you aren't going to cry. You just turn around and walk away from here.* Unfortunately, it's easier to say than to do. I feel like I'm glued down to the floor. I can't believe my own legs betray me by stealing an opportunity to remove myself from such an embarrassing situation. Seeing El with Emma makes my entire body so numb that I have no other choice but to watch my ex-boyfriend. *No one cares about my feelings. Even if I love him, I'll still have to watch him flirting with his new girlfriend. Of course, she has to be incredibly pretty.*

"Let's go," El says, and both of them leave. The time stops, and I don't know how long I've been standing in the middle of the hallway. I've never felt de trop before, and it's weird.

"Cassie! Are you okay?" Ally asks, running up to me. It feels like she wakes me up from a long sleep by giving me a hug. *Ugh... It's pretty pathetic, but I really needed it because I'm absolutely frozen. How am I supposed to react to El ignoring me?* It seems there is no correct answer. No matter what I do, El won't change his mind, and we'll never be together ever again. When Louis comes up to Ally and me, I notice that he looks worried.

Nobody knows how much I wish I could pretend El hadn't heard me. At least, even for a second, my life would be so much easier. However, I couldn't buy into the whole premise even if I wanted to. It's challenging for me to accept that El's heard me and proceed to ignore me. He made an active choice, and that's what is so upsetting.

"Yeah, I'm good," I say, and it's not even a lie — kind of. *I've expected El to behave this way, and as much as it hurts, I've got to admit I should have been ready for it. I just hoped for the best. Now I know it was childish of me to believe in it. I need to grow up.*

Lou-Lou joins us in a group hug. They don't believe me at all. However, they don't bother me with a million questions, but both of them understand how everything saddens me. I appreciate it. Ally and Louis attempt secretly to exchange their looks. I'm pretty sure they don't want me to see how shocked they are. *It's interesting they also haven't expected El to ignore me like that. Maybe this isn't the right time.*

As much as I'd love to fulfill my Christmas resolution, I don't think it's a viable option anymore. I've got a feeling that El hasn't made up with his dad, and he's taking me out because I'm an easy target. It must be the only explanation. Of course, it's disappointing to hit such a huge setback. I can stay persistent at approaching El today. Still, it means publicly chasing after a guy who absolutely enjoys ignoring me in front of the whole school. I'm out. A hundred percent off. I can't do it. I can't do it. I'm not ready to give another shot at this.

I've put too much pressure on myself. Let's face it — I was able to apologize to everyone except El. He's shut my attempt to have a reasonable conversation by ignoring me. I didn't expect that I would feel so hurt by El's actions. I've been stressing myself out about apologizing to El, and my expectation is too high. It's time to lower the bar, and I should work on plan B, as Louis's already suggested.

Rest of the day, I stayed quiet at school. Ally and Lou-Lou aren't leaving me alone, even for a minute. I'm pretty sure they're waiting for a colossal meltdown from me. It's insulting, but I don't say anything. Even though I'm not as upset as they think I am, having them around me is nice. They have a very calming aura, which is the only reason why I'm going through the day like nothing has happened. Of course, I wouldn't go rogue or anything like that, but it would be so much harder without my friends.

"Are you gonna be okay?" Louis asks me as both of them walk me back home.

"Yeah. I know how it looks, and I know I shouldn't be okay," I start my explanation, "but I am. Really."

"Okay," they both mumble.

"But promise, you'll call if you need to talk to someone," Ally asks.

"I promise, but it's not that big of a deal," I say, rolling my eyes at those two. "I'll talk to him later."

"Sounds good."

"Talk to you soon, Cassie."

"Bye, guys."

"Bye."

As they leave, I walk into the house. My parents are still at work, so it's nice to be alone. I go to the kitchen to make myself a sandwich when I notice Imaginary El. He's rarely come nowadays, so it's a little surprising that he's showed up. *No matter how happy I am to see him, I decide to ignore him. Yeah, his behavior really got under my nerves. Nobody can tell, right? If I can't give real El a piece of my mind, I'll get the satisfaction of telling off the one who is haunting my imagination.* As I think that, I open the fridge, picking up all the ingredients for the sandwich.

"Wow, I see how this is," Imaginary El starts the conversation. *Ugh, if only it was as easy to talk to the real one, I'd be already forgiven today.* Instead, I follow El's patterns of behavior and ignore the imaginary one. He doesn't quit, "So now you don't speak to me. Good job, Cassie."

I put a sandwich on a plate, and leave the kitchen, pretending I don't hear him. Sometimes I enjoy eating in my room. My parents are never excited about it, but they allow it with one rule — clean up after yourself. When I walk into my room, the Imaginary El is already there, sitting at my desk. I sit on the bed, waiting for him to speak up. It's a matter of time.

"Oh, come on. I bet you have quite a few questions for me," Imaginary El says, swinging his legs back and forth. I've also noticed the annoyance in his voice. *Hmm... even Imaginary El has attitude issues too.*

"It's not like you know the answers to my questions," I say, throwing him a bone. I don't want him to disappear. Obviously, I'm aware this conversation isn't real, but there is no way I'll get an opportunity to confer with El. Therefore, I'm taking what I can get, even if it's an imaginary conversation with my ex. Yeah, I know how pathetic I sound right now. I'm not proud of this.

"Wow, try me," Imaginary El teases me. "Who knows, maybe I'll be able to provide the information you seek?"

"Yeah, I get what you're saying, and thank you," I reply as if I'm not totally sold on his idea, "but no."

"Really?"

"Yeah."

"May I ask you why?"

"Sure. You see, you're nothing more than a product of imagination," I explain it to him, "so you can't say anything that I don't already know. You're probably planning to say what I want to hear, so what's even the point?"

"Wow, Cassie, you're mean."

"I'm just telling the truth."

"I hope it's working for you well."

He's right. I don't understand why I'm so snarky with him. It's another thing which is going so well. I need him around, so I can talk this through with someone. The Imaginary El is perfect for this task. What is wrong with me? Why am I arguing so much, attempting to hurt him back? And for what? It's not like it's making me feel better. It just annoys Imaginary El. This conversation is getting away from me. I think he wants to leave me again, which scares me. I'm not ready to say bye. I need a few more minutes.

"I actually have one question for you," I announce and instantly notice a smirk at the left corner of his mouth. I recognize that smirk. It could mean only one thing — he thinks he's figured me out, and his evaluation of my personality is accurate. It's offensive because he doesn't even comprehend how wrong he is.

"What is it? I'm surprised you even want to ask me something because I don't know anything useful. Is that what you told me?"

"Okay, I'm not going to ask you."

"Whatever. Ask me or don't ask me. I don't care," Imaginary El says, shrugging his shoulders.

"Do you think you will ever be able to forgive me?" I ask him, staring down at the floor. I feel so ashamed of myself. Even if he isn't real, he's become a person I can talk to about El. I hate the idea of discussing my love life with my parents. It's weird. I'm thankful to mom for the talk we had, but I'm not a massive fan of this becoming an everyday thing. I'd love to tell Ally and Louis how I feel, but I've been such a burden to my friends. I can't become a piece of baggage they have to carry around.

My friends are already doing a lot for me. Look at today — both of them walked me home. Even though they don't have to do that, they always make sure I'm alright. It'll be too much if I dump my issues on them. Especially if it's something regarding Elliot. They've tried to help me before, so it's not a good idea to involve them again. Becoming a better friend is important to me, and I can't be trusted. However, it's a different story with the Imaginary El. Having a discussion with him is safe because it can't hurt anyone, and I can finally get heard.

"So, the second I open my mouth, you don't say a word. It's so you."

"I was just thinking how I should answer. Jeez, you're so demanding."

"And?"

"Cassie, I don't know," Imaginary El explains, "I'm not ready to forgive you now. And as the Chinese proverb says, when the wind of change blows, some people build walls and others build windmills."

"What the hell that's supposed to mean? No, let me answer for you. That's something, which could be interpreted into a million different things. It doesn't actually mean anything," I scream at the Imaginary El. I can't recall a moment in my entire life when I've ever felt so angry. Imaginary El disappears shortly after I yell at him. I don't blame him — who would want that? Well, it's safe to say that Louis and Ally were correct, thinking it was a matter of time before I'd lose my cool. I thought I was better than that.

I lie down on the bed and stare at the ceiling. This is not the winter break I've expected to have. It will be quieter because Lou-Lou will ski in Utah with his family, and Ally's family has planned a Caribbean cruise. I still hope something will change, and El will decide to talk to me. I had an idea to show up in front of his house. It worked on Ally, so why shouldn't I give it a chance again? I can only imagine how weird it's going to be if I show up at El's house. It was different with Ally because we've been friends forever. That's already been pushing my boundaries. Such behavior is absolutely inappropriate towards El — I haven't even met his parents. What will I do or say if I show up unasked at his house and his parents open the door instead of El? I can't say, "Hey, I'm your son's ex-girlfriend. I must talk to him because I broke his heart. You see, I'd love to let him know how sorry I am."

Yeah, it wouldn't end in success. I think it's pretty pathetic. If only I could get El's forgiveness as a Christmas gift, it would be the best present I've ever received. I wish life would be that easy. However, it isn't that simple. Nothing can work like that. For a few days in a row, I couldn't entirely fall asleep. I couldn't stop thinking about how much I want to fix everything. Nobody will be able to continue to live like that, so it's time to face El might never speak to me. Taking a closer look at the new information, I've got to be prepared to give up on getting back with him. The only problem is that putting it aside doesn't solve the underlying problem. To get closure, I must apologize to El. However, it has to wait.

Chapter 29
Nothing Matters Anymore

Winter break has been a bit anticlimactic. Unfortunately, I still have a secret Christmas gift I got for him. I expected it, but it's been nice. I've spent time with my family, and my decision to put my obsession with El aside is hands down the best I've ever made. On top of that, I think it's unfair to make other people as miserable as I am during the holiday season. It should be a magical time of the entire year, but I feel like I've never felt sadder. Even when nobody talked to me, I've always had the hope I'd make it right eventually. Now I'm forced to face the reality that I won't be able to make it right. It's like at the end of a video game, the sign says Game Over, and I'm ready for such an unfortunate outcome. Christmas is the time of happiness, hope, and sacred dreams. It used to be everything to me. I feel like I've robbed myself of it. Nothing I've wished for has become true, but it's not a surprise. I get it. I was very naughty this year and etc., so, understandably, I don't deserve my wishes to be fulfilled this Christmas.

I've been pretending that I'm fine the whole time, and it's been so much fun to be lazy. However, it's been slowly getting under my skin. Ugh, I wish I could stop caring about my issues with Elliot. I wish I could start over, but it's not realistic. It's harder to keep smiling. The truth is I can't bring myself to approach El once again. Even the entire idea of walking up to him again is languishing, and I feel as if I'm having a panic attack every time I imagine approaching Elliot. Honestly, I've felt incredibly devastated after my first attempt to start a conversation with my ex-boyfriend. It was soul-crushing. Honestly, I've used up all my energy not to let all the memories creep up on me. I don't even feel like I have had enough rest during the winter break.

Deep down, I'm aware I should have already quit chasing after El and move on with my life. Yet, I can't quite let it go like this. I'd love to believe it's all about the apologies because I would be emotionally done by now. Otherwise, I'd be already satisfied after sending over fifty texts to El, but the reality is that

I'm not. I'm not over. I have to achieve closure for everyone's sake and sanity. That's why apologizing over text isn't enough for me. I've got to admit I'd love to talk to Elliot just like I've done with everyone else. I've successfully reconciled with Ally and Louis. I can even say that Jake and Katie are okay with me. Everyone else hasn't been too hard on me. But, of course, El isn't everyone else, which is the explanation for his entire behavior. I don't think it's in his plans to let me off the hook so quickly. Frankly, I hope El will transfer to another school, and I fear the idea of him staying, which puts more pressure on our next conversation.

Anybody would fail at finding a silver lining, but not me. I'm good at doing that because I've already seen one. I admit it's a little flimsy, but the total embarrassment El caused me seems to be my punishment. Maybe, he'll forgive me soon, and it's a part of his elaborate plan. I believe that people should face their fears, so I've made another attempt to talk to El two days before Christmas. I even rode a bike to El's house. *I was so close to just going for it, but I turned away at the very last minute. It didn't seem like the right move. Of course, it's partially because I started to have a panic attack even thinking about it. The decision to walk away wasn't so difficult to make. I had no other choice.* Even though I've felt crushed since that happened, I've stayed in good spirits. I think I've done well. The holidays are already emotionally draining, and there is no reason to add any additional stress to other people. Someone has to enjoy the holidays. However, even my parents have had such a rough time doing that as well. For them, it's started since my grandparents from both sides came. I love when my grandparents come to visit us, but I wish I could say the same about my parents because both of them always seem on edge the whole time.

Honestly, I've felt a little lonely these days. I can't wait to go back to school because Ally and Louis have just returned from being out of town for the entire winter break. They seem so excited and full of happiness. Lou-Lou has fallen in love with the Utah ski resort. He couldn't stop talking about it. As much as he's tried to sound extra enthusiastic about the holidays, yet I immediately detect something weird in his voice. I'm pretty sure Lou-Lou's been hiding that he's missed going to the art school because he's craving to see his crush. To be fair to Louis, I also have a secret — I can't wait for school to start again, so I don't have to be alone. It's embarrassing, especially when Ally had such a fantastic time with her family. If she told me that she didn't want to come back home, I would totally believe her and fear that I would never see her again. They are the only people who have stayed in contact regularly. Everybody else in school avoids me. Overall, it's been getting better at school, but most classmates have been distant. The girls in school just hate me. Once or twice, I overheard them discussing how stupid it was not to choose one while I was in the bathroom. I had waited until my classmates left. It's easy to judge "pick El over Jake" or "pick Jake over El" when you have a crush on one of them. However, no matter what, I can't wait to go back to school.

Partially, I'm so eager to start the new semester because I miss being able to see El around the school. Even if it happens only from a distance, it'll already make me happier. Plus, I've been having the same nightmare over and over from the beginning of winter break. It's about El and Emma, and their relationship is getting stronger and more serious. I've been staring at their social media accounts every day. I'm not even sure what I'm looking for while I've buried myself by attempting to find a meaningful explanation of every single picture Emma has posted. It's just madness, especially since she's also been out of town. I've been looking for a sign to figure out what El's up to, but he hasn't posted anything for a while. It drives me so crazy. On top of that, he hasn't reached out to me, which isn't a surprise. I can't believe I've been expecting that to happen.

Chapter 30
A New Semester

Tomorrow is the first day when school starts, and I'm over the moon about it for obvious reasons. I've already picked the outfit I'm going to wear if I decide to walk up to Elliot. I'm going to fulfill my plan, and the first thing to do is have a conversation with him no matter what. Well, I'll definitely do it before the summer break. There is no rush, right? Yeah, it's a bit too much. On the positive side, I'm absolutely thrilled to hang out with my friends. We've already discussed our plans for this week, and we're going to see a movie this weekend. Even my parents have noticed that I'm incredibly eager to go back to school, but anybody in my shoes would feel the same way.

Of course, I can't describe this Christmas as a total failure because it hasn't been all bad. There are a few good things, which came out from the winter break. Ally has been on a cruise to the Caribbean. We've been video chatting all the time. It's become our regular thing to talk before we go to sleep. Even after Ally came back home, we continued to call each other. I believe it's our new tradition to video chat on the dot at nine o'clock. I've got to admit it's been a lot of fun, and I feel like we've started to develop a deeper connection by doing it. The best part is that we discuss everything, except boys. It's our one rule. Well, it's more like an unspoken rule, but we've never talked about love life, and it's stuck around. Indubitably, I'd love to discuss how El's doing with Ally because she knows more about his life than me. However, I don't want to compromise the time we've been spending together. My sixth sense tells me it might be over the second I start talking about El. Opening that can of worms isn't a smart move if I want to have a best friend type of relationship with Ally. Overall, it's been freeing. Since we haven't talked about boys, I'm able to chat without overthinking every single word I say. Honestly, I've been enjoying it a lot. I feel like I can finally say I know Ally. I hope she feels the same way.

It's almost nine. I'm ready, sitting in PJs. I'm counting minutes until Ally calls. It's the most exciting part of my day. Of course, I'm planning to dial my excitement down right before the chat. I can't be too happy to go back to school because that would be weird. Normal people aren't excited about it. Why is it so hard to be normal? Maybe everybody feels the same way. When I see that Ally's calling, I immediately answer as I roll over on the bed.

"Hey, Cassie," Ally says. She waves at me as I join the video chat. Ally smiles at me when I notice that Louis is also a part of our evening conversation. What is Louis doing here? I'm so surprised to see Lou-Lou, who has joined us on the video chat. I don't know why, but I feel a little insulted. After all, I've been under the impression that it was our thing, and it's exclusively between Ally and me. I may have built it up in my head. For the first time in a long time, I feel that we've reconnected as friends. I want us to have our thing, it'll be good for us. Of course, I've considered these nine o'clock chats could become that. What are you going to do if Ally doesn't feel the same way?

"Hey, what's up, guys?" I say. It takes a lot of energy out of me to hide my frustration and disappointment in my voice.

"Hello, Cassie. I missed you so much," Louis says. He also waves at me with a smile on his face. At least, he's happy to see me, and it's a good feeling. Very few people light up from my presence, and I'm adding my parents to the whole count. Lou-Lou and I have been in touch, but not as much as Ally and I have. Not on purpose. It's just happened partially because of a lousy phone reception Louis had at the ski resort. I've been under the impression Ally hasn't been in touch with him as much, but apparently, that's not the case. I don't know what's so upsetting about it, but it makes me feel left out. My mind has immediately taken me to some dark corners of my soul, and I've started wondering whether my friends have forgiven me or not. What if they've pretended to condone me? What am I supposed to do then? Ugh... Even my consciousness loves to tease me by playing mind games. Why else would I think that my friends were lying? I'm just driving myself insane. I just need to take a deep breath. There is no reason for them ever do something like that to you.`

"I hope Cassie, you don't mind that Louis joined us," Ally states. Hmm...

Ally, I wish you had asked me about this before you made a decision all by yourself. However, it's a little late for that. I'd like to be a part of the conversation instead of dumping the decisions on me. It's the worst when your feelings aren't being considered.

"No problem," I say with the voice of an angel, so nobody can even notice how upset I am by that. "The more, the merrier! Right?"

"I can't believe we've got to go back to school tomorrow," Ally says, changing the subject. Maybe she knows I'm not so happy about Louis joining us. What is the point of

"I know, it's so annoying," I blatantly lie.

"Are you sure that is annoying?" Lou-Lou asked me with a cheeky voice. *I wonder if Ally asked him to join the video chat with a purpose. It's a little disappointing because I've felt like we've made a lot of progress in our friendship. Especially since we haven't talked about a boyfriend at all. It's possible she asked Louis to join us, so he can ask something she doesn't feel comfortable with. If they want to spice this conversation up, they're going to get it.*

"What do you mean?"

"Well, aren't you excited that you'll finally get to see El after all this time?!" Lou-Lou explains. I can just see in his facial expressions that he's shocked by my response. He's actually rooting for me. This is so cute. I'll take any emotional support I can get. Both of them have been very clear that they want to stay out of my situation with Elliot. It's a little surprising because I've never thought that either of them could even let me talk about him.

"Come on, Louis! You've promised me not to open this conversation," Ally tells him off. Oh! This is so touching because it means Louis is the one who insisted on joining us. I feel so relieved. I have absolutely the best friends.

"I mean, I think I can officially say I've moved on," I announce. I'm a little shocked by myself because I don't like how defensive I'm getting over this. I'm over El. It's just I hate feeling like I'm a loser in front of everyone's eyes.

"Really?!" Lou-Lou screams as if his dreams are being shuttered.

"Seriously? What happened?" Ally wonders.

"Nothing, guys. I'm moving on," I say more time even though I don't completely understand what I mean by that. If my friends don't ask too many difficult questions or answer most of their questions, I might get away with my statement.

"Does this mean you're not planning to make him talk to you?" Louis asks with desperation. "To be completely honest with you, Cassie, I've always hoped you, guys, find your way back to each other."

"What's even the point of trying if I already know his response? And girls should have respect for themselves and let it go if they're publicly ignored."

"Well, that wasn't planned," Lou-Lou says, his voice sounds as if he spills the beans by accident. Still, he's deliberately saying something to reveal new information to another party.

"What is that supposed to mean?"

"Louis, this is too far," Ally steps in,

"I'm sorry, but I think she should know," Loui protests. I'm aware of what's going on, but I might find out more about El if I continue looking confused. At least, it seems like he has a plan, which is absolutely the best news I've heard in weeks.

"I can't believe you, Louis. This is not okay."

"Well, Cassie is our friend too."

"Guys, what are you even talking about? Can you, guys, fill me in?" I ask, attempting to

"Do whatever you want, Louis."

"Cassie," Lou-Lou slowly starts explaining. My heart skips a beat because I'll finally get a chance to find out about El's plan. As they say, that curiosity killed the cat. It's too true. I understand it now since curiosity has no boundaries. It's killing me too. I feel like I want to yell at him so he'd spit the truth out. He adds, "As far as I know, El wasn't supposed to ignore you like that."

I smirk in response. Yeah, if that is what Ally doesn't approve for him to share, I'll have to

"Yeah, you know it's okay. I've even thought the same, so it's not news to me," I tell them. I totally feel disappointed. I've expected to learn additional information about Elliot.

"Well, he mentioned that he could consider forgiving you…"

"Louis! You can't count that!?"

"Why?" Louis asks Ally.

"Because he was drunk that time. Remember, the next day, El came to us and said it had meant nothing?"

"El is drinking and getting trashed!" I exclaim, even though it's not the most fascinating piece of information. Nevertheless, it means Elliot still thinks about me, and it gives me hope for our reconciliation.

"OMG, Ally. It's preposterous. Look at this as it is. He was drunk, of course, he meant it," Lou-Lou disagrees with Ally. However, both of them continue to ignore me, which I'm not too mad about. Recently, I've been in the center of every conflict, so it feels nice just to watch other people argue with each other. The best part is that they can't be mad at me because they've started this. Since I got caught dating two guys, I haven't been interested in discussing my love life. It never ends well, which is my fault — I can't take basic advice. I always ask for a piece of advice, and I invariably do the opposite of what has been recommended. It drives everyone insane, and other people's feelings get hurt. As a result, I have no other choice but to make a difficult decision not to talk to my friends about my love issues.

"No, Louis. You just want more drama, but it's very straightforward — Elliot was drunk, and he felt vulnerable. It doesn't mean anything."

"No, Ally. Why else did he drink? You're the one who doesn't seem to get it. When people are wasted, they always tell the truth. That's a known fact. Google it."

I know it's horrible that El's turned to alcohol to find out all the answers, but I can't stop thinking about it. I guess I have a chance to get back with El. The fact is that I've felt like it's never going to happen. If I have to be completely honest with myself, it's not a good sign. There is no way it's a healthy way to deal with heartbreak, and I'm really worried about him. I know it sounds pathetic because anybody in their right mind could only say that everything is my fault. If I really cared about Elliot, I wouldn't be dating two guys to avoid this exact situation. They would be absolutely right, but I still do care about him. I wish I could say this is going to bring us even closer. However, this isn't one of those things, which make you stronger. It's absolutely the opposite situation because not everything makes you stronger.

Interestingly enough, a lot of things could weaken you — a lot. In my situation, for example, it's absolutely destroying everything we've had with Elliot. Yet, here I am, grasping for any hope I get. Finally, I've received the hope I was looking for. It makes me a little sad that it's under such unfortunate circumstances.

"Whatever, Louis," Ally says as if she wants to be clear that this conversation is over. The only concerning part is her ice-cold tone of voice. I heard the same tone last time, right as Ally told me off in front of my soon-to-be boyfriends. Yeah, it's definitely a bad sign, and that's an accurate description. It's striking to me that Ally could use a threatening tone of voice towards Louis. I guess she usually doesn't have to because Lou-Lou capitulates faster, and, surprisingly, he isn't backing off from the fight.

"No, Ally. El's still in love with Cassie, and Cassie loves him. It's meant to be, they're meant to be," Louis reveals. "We should help them."

Lou-Lou's words are so touching and romantic. However, as much as I love Lou-Lou's speech, I've been watching how Ally's face blushes from agitation and frustration. Apparently, nobody should ever mess with her or make her angry, which is the most valuable lesson I could get without being a bad guy. I don't want to hurt people again in my life, but I have a long way to go. To be completely honest, I'm terrified of Ally's aura. So, even though my heart is about to stop from hearing Louis's words, I don't understand what's the big deal.

I guess Louis has always picked my side. As unfair as it is, Louis is just like my knight. In a way, I love it, and I'm also ashamed of it. I have a deep desire to be on Ally's side, but Louis makes it so hard for me. Why is it so difficult? If I were Ally, I would also be bummed out. Everyone wants to have the type of best friend who chooses you all the time without any questions. I wish I could be more helpful in this argument, but happiness has clouded my thoughts. We've got a chance — a real one. It's not only in my head. Maybe, everything is worth the struggle, tears, and disappointment.

My mind immediately takes me to my dream world, where all my dreams come true. For the first time in forever, I feel happy, and it's getting harder to keep myself from tearing up.

"Okay, I'm gonna go," Ally starts saying goodbye. I don't blame her. "See you tomorrow at school."

"Ally, wait. I'm sorry."

"Really?"

"Cassie is El's lobster. You can't deny that," Louis explains. It's the cutest thing I've ever heard. My heart's just melting.

"What did you just say?" Ally asks through laughing.

"They belong together."

"Are you kidding me? It's what the media wants you to believe. There is no such thing, and I think it's crazy to base relationship advice on popular sitcoms."

"Why? Why not? It's the truth. People are exactly like that."

"No, most relationships are so codependent and so unhealthy. It's not something anybody should be seeking," Ally explains. She has a point. Even if we get back together with El, it might not be such a great idea. I've never thought this through. Maybe, I should listen to Ally more. She might know a thing or two.

"Ally, don't make it personal. This isn't about you."

I have to admit that the only thing I wish I did differently today is to make myself popcorn. I feel I'm in the middle of a soap opera episode, and things are getting noticeably heated.

"I've never said it was about me? You're just gossiping," Ally says, "El is our friend, and you use his weakness for quick chit chat. It's kind of low even for you, Louis."

It feels like Louis has entered a staring competition with Ally. Surprisingly, both of them are incredibly intense about this, which is just shocking. What has happened to them to be so sore about a small and innocent lie? It's not like it's groundbreaking news to me. Maybe there is something specific about this gossip. Still, I've got a feeling that I'm the spectator of people proving some meaningless point. Something tells me that they have resolved their issues with each other since Homecoming, and now it's about to happen again because you can't be running away from the argument forever. It must be hard for them since it's been a clear cut — I'm the one who has made more than enough mistakes. I was responsible for everything, but it looks like Ally and Louis are still blaming each other. Louis helped me even though Ally didn't approve of the whole thing from the beginning. Of course, it wasn't Louis's fault that he believed in me. I understand his argument about how he can be held responsible for my mistakes. I should have done better. Technically, that's true.

It's been a while since anybody said something. It's getting even more uncomfortable, and I've started to believe that Ally and Louis have totally forgotten I'm here. I'm not offended or anything like that. However, I'm still here, and it could be a good idea to remind them about my existence. I would like that in case I'm about to say something, if I regret the second the horrible words leave my mouth. Maybe I should cough? Is that enough of a signal?

"You're just jealous," Louis says. I glance at Ally and immediately see how sad she gets. It's not cool of Louis. We all know Ally's crush on El has passed yet. It's already devastating when a person you really like doesn't feel the same way. I'm of all people should know exactly how it feels. What if she loves him like I was with Jake? Lou-Lou isn't making it easy on her either.

"Okay, I'm going to say 'bye' right now. Before we say something, we'll regret even more than what has already been said. So... bye," Ally says as she hangs upon us. Wow, I can believe she just dropped out, not giving us a chance to say a word — silence. Lou-Lou and I are still on the other ends, secretly glancing at each other. Neither Louis nor I say anything. It looks like we both are scared to open our mouths because it's just uncomfortable. Louis has crossed the line with Ally, but I know one thing that these two don't ever stop talking to each other. That has never happened. They just pretend like there has been no fight. I've always wondered whether they ever get to talk to each other.

"Thanks, Louis. I really appreciate your support. I'm sorry I've made it so hard to do," I say. There is nothing else I can say to make Louis feel better. He won't. I can guarantee the conversation has gotten out of his control. There is no way Lou-Lou has picked a fight with Ally on purpose.

"Yeah, of course. I feel so bad for upsetting her. I should have known better. You know, it's such unfortunate timing," he says, and the weirdest part is that I can't crack what Louis's implying. I don't know what he means by that, but it doesn't sound great.

"I think I know what you're talking about. However, would you mind telling me what you mean to ensure we're on the same page?" I suggest it. I need to catch up with everything as quickly as possible. When he finds out that I don't know the information, Louis might not tell me what it's all about. However, if this trick works on him, I'll be proud of how quickly I've come up with this idea to get more information. Honestly, the entire situation is a little bit upsetting because I've got this feeling deep inside that it's something I don't know, but I should have known.

"Well, she's probably told you. If not, you'll probably find out at some point," Louis starts explaining. The more he's talking, the more confused I get. Louis continues, "Ally's parents have been thinking about the divorce. I don't know the full story, but that's just it. Ally isn't adjusting to the idea too well."

This is shocking for many reasons, but the worst of all is that Ally hasn't mentioned it. I don't even deserve an implication that something is wrong. I just feel depressed because we're supposed to be friends, and real friends tell each other about their personal life. Even if they disagree, all their issues should work themselves out. I guess my earlier behavior has caused too many scars, and I'm unsure whether we can repair the damage. I can't express how hurtful it is to realize that you aren't as close to someone as I think we are. There is no other explanation why she hasn't shared anything with me. Deep down in my guts, I keep hoping that maybe she wants to pretend that everything is okay. Sometimes people don't share their feelings, so they continue lying to themselves, and I've been there. Everyone has secrets, which they do anything to hide.

"I actually didn't know that," I reveal to my friend. Maybe it's not such a great idea to tell him that, but I'm not playing "friends" anymore.

"Oh, Cassie. Don't take it personally, and don't you dare read into this! Probably, she wasn't ready to tell you."

"Thanks, but it's hard not to take it personally. Ally and I have been video chatting the whole break, every night. There was not a sign in her voice that something was wrong. And now you're telling me she wasn't ready to tell me yet? She hasn't forgiven me. That's the only explanation."

"Wait, how did you even get there? Ally's totally forgiven you. I swear."

"No, she hasn't. It has to be it because why else hasn't she told her close friend? I know the answer to that question."

"Cassie, slow down. I totally understand how you feel, and I'd also feel the same way in your place," Louis explains, "but everyone wants to feel normal. She told me about it."

"It doesn't mean anything, Lou-Lou."

"Ally needed to tell somebody, and I was there," Louis mumbles. "She was thinking about it, but when she called you the first time, you looked so sad..."

It suddenly hit me — Ally was taking care of me. *It's a little shocking and disappointing, but I'll survive. Overall, it's not such a big deal. A lot of people won't even think twice about it. I thought we were making progress. I truly did. Apparently, I'm such a massive train wreck, so everyone has to tiptoe around my feelings. How bad of a friend am I to end up like that? I wanted to cheer up Ally, but I don't stand a chance.*

"She didn't want you to know. Yet, she was probably planning to tell you tomorrow at school. As Ally explained it to me, she continues to pretend that nothing's going on with her family until she tells you. You see? There is no issue. It's a misunderstanding mixed with deep denial. However, that's a story for a different day."

"Yeah. I'm sorry, Louis," I apologize. It seems to me that he's trying really hard to make me feel better. Unfortunately, it's not going to work this time. "I don't know how upsetting this is for Ally. However, it makes me feel that we're not that close."

"Sorry, I really didn't mean to upset you. I even told you that you'd have found out about it later. Please, don't read into this. I'm begging you. I can't fight another battle. Please, do me a huge favor and let this go."

"It's not that easy," I start saying before he cuts me off.

"No, Cassie, it's easy. Let it go, and done. Please, pretty please."

"Okay," I give up. I don't want to get into all the reasons why I've decided to let you, but the main explanation is that I'm trying to be a better friend, and it's a part of it.

"Thanks. Really?" Louis says.

"Really. If you ask me to trust you on this, I will."

"Seriously?"

"OMG, Louis! I'm trying so hard to be nice. Why can't you just let it go?" I ask him. He's already made me wonder if I agreed with him too quickly.

"Okay. Thanks, Cassie. You don't even know how much easier you're making my life."

"You're welcome. It's getting late, Lou-Lou. I think it's time to say bye."

"You're absolutely right! It's almost eleven. Sorry I've kept you so late."

"I lost track of time myself. Hey, Louis, are you okay?"

"Yeah, it's not a big deal. Before I let you go, you have to promise me that you'll find the inner strength and talk to El."

"Louis, I can't promise that," I lie. I don't want to experience the same fiasco, so I hope my friends will tell me when it's the right time. Not directly, they'll imply. Maybe, this is that time?

"No, I don't know anything specific, but you have to try."

"Why? There is no point. As you just said, you don't know whether El even wants you around him. It's getting ridiculous."

"Because at least two of you deserve a happy ending," he says with tears in his eyes. *He's being so emotional. This is so weird. It feels as if he wants to pick a fight with me.* Finally, it hits me that Louis's crush isn't going anywhere, and that's the entire reason why he desperately wants to help me. I bet he thinks if El and I get back together, it'll be a good sign that he'll be with that guy Louis was talking about. That's so sweet, but Louis deserves better.

"Lou, how is it going with that guy from the art school?" I ask him, even though I've already figured out the correct answer. Louis hesitates to reply, and it makes me wonder whether he's thinking about lying. I don't blame him. Sometimes it's easier to lie. However, the more you do it, the harder it gets to keep up with volume.

It's a little bit unfair to think everyone is about to betray me. Maybe Louis' ashamed of his behavior towards Ally. It's just hard. I'm not judging him. I have no right to judge anybody, but I can totally relate to how Louis feels. It's painless to forget your own problems by fixing issues for everyone else, living your life through other people's. It could be fun at the beginning. Sometimes, you actually need a person, who stays in your corner no matter what, and I'm going to be there for my friend. I used to run away from these moments because I wanted to have my separation. Now I can't do the same thing. Now I won't be able to go to sleep until I make sure that Louis's doing alright.

Don't we all need a friend or a person who helps us through rough times? I wish I could be that type of friend for Ally. It's been challenging to move on from it, but the promise has been made. Nowadays, I take these seriously, so I'm trying to look on the bright side and learn to be there for people who care about me. I'm not going to lie that I'm not too ecstatic that one of my closest friends hides huge family changes in her life. However, if he needs me to let go, I will. I've had this feeling for a while. Lou-Lou has been closer to me since we've started school. It's time to give him the support he's looking for because he's done so much for me.

"He has a girlfriend," he blurts out. "I'm such an idiot."

"Oh! I'm so sorry. That's horrible. I can't imagine how much it must hurt," I immediately respond to his news. Honestly, I thought Lou-Lou's crush was totally into him, but probably it's not a good idea to mention it right now. I know how it feels when someone you love is unavailable. It feels like someone is ripping your heart out.

"It's okay. He doesn't know it yet," Louis says. "I'm just kidding. Ugh... I should stop joking like that because I swear one day it's going to get me in so much trouble."

"Seriously, Louis. Are you alright?"

"Yeah, I'm fine. At least, as fine as I can be. You know."

"I know. It'll get better."

"I feel like a fool."

"I've been there."

"I thought I had a real shot, that's the worst feeling when you think you have a chance, but in actuality, it's never meant to be. I'm such an idiot."

Louis looks so devastated, and I can see how miserable he's getting. I guess now I know why Ally hasn't mentioned her troubles to me. How can you? Even from glancing at him, my heart is melting, and I'm ready to say anything to smooth his pain.

"Louis, from the second I saw you two, I thought he was into you, too. Sorry," I say. I'm aware that it's not a good idea to tell him that, but he's always done the same for me. Was it the right choice to say to me that it'd be alright if I go out with both of the guys for a few dates before I had made a decision? No, but that was the answer I was looking for. The truth is I'd behave identically either way.

"Thanks, Cassie. I really appreciate it."

"Seriously, though. I thought you two were dating."

"I know. Thanks," Louis says. He looks a little bit happier, making me so happy. Then, he adds, "Okay. Goodnight, Cassie."

"Goodnight, Lou-Lou. See you tomorrow."

"See you tomorrow."

We both hang up, and I sit on the bed, staring in the distance. I think I've got a chance with El. That's the only thought on my mind. I'm not quite sure I'll be able to fall asleep that easily. Maybe, it's the excitement, or perhaps it's fear that I don't even remember our last kiss. Well, I can still recall the instances we kissed — especially the three amazing kisses. First, the kiss at camp — then there was the kiss right after he renamed himself "boyfriend" in my phone. And finally, the I-love-you kiss at the bleachers during Homecoming. However, I can't remember our last kiss because you never think it could be your last one. You don't wait for a moment to break up. Therefore, I haven't depicted our kiss. I don't even relive one in my head. I've forgotten how it feels to kiss El, and that's just sad.

It's impossible to get away from disappointment. I turn off the lamp and get cozy under the blanket. I stare at the night sky — the stars are incredibly bright tonight. It's pretty magical. My mind is racing back and forth, and I can't believe I've been close to giving up my hope. Maybe that's the reason why I'm not taking my eyes off the sky. I secretly wish to see a shooting star. It's merely the thing that could make my dream come true. However, before I even get a chance to spot the star, I fall asleep. It's probably a good thing.

Finally, I've got some positive news, giving me hope that El and I will be together again one day. Why can't I be happy about it? The next couple of days will be crucial. I've got to figure out whether nothing has changed between El and Emma during the break. If they're not madly in love by tomorrow, I'll talk to him as soon as possible. It's exciting. I finally feel I can do this.

I've been obsessing Louis's words — he isn't over Cassie. I think about that sentence over and over, just like a broken record, which is ready to give up. Am I prepared to give up?

Chapter 31
Friends

It's the first day back in school, and everything has stayed the same. I'm going to admit I've had expectations, and they haven't been met in reality. Three of us are standing right next to Ally's locker. There is no issue between my friends. I can guarantee they haven't even talked it through. They just continue behaving like nothing has happened. It'll never work for me, but apparently, it works for them. I'm keeping my nose away from their relationship. It's the best policy.

There is something positive that has happened. Ally has told me about her family situation the first thing in the morning. I can guarantee Lou-Lou's told her how it made me feel, but I'm not even mad because I needed to find out from Ally. It's hard to know what other people think all the time. I'd even argue that it's just impossible. That's why we all need a light nudge in the right direction, so if Lou-Lou was the one who gave her that push, I'd be totally okay with it. I can't believe I've been so upset about it. I couldn't quite understand what it means when mom says that sometimes it's better not to know.

Finally, I can fully comprehend the meaning when Ally mentions that her mom cheated on her father. She doesn't look at me while she's telling me about it. It makes me feel horrible. Her best friend has just done the same thing not too long ago — it's probably devastating. Maybe Ally doesn't judge me because not everything is about me, but it makes me look at myself. I don't see what I'd like to be there. I need to do better. The realization of the actual reason why my best friend hasn't told me anything until now has been hard on me. I wish I wouldn't perceive the specifics regarding Ally's family. I should have listened to her because she was right. I didn't need to learn about it.

My day hasn't started as smoothly as I've expected, but it's not important. I can't wait to spot El on campus. I think I'm ready to take another shot at apologizing. I've been going over how it'll happen a thousand times in my head, so it's time. However, the reality is much harsher because I'll totally freeze up if I notice El right at the beginning of the day. Nothing has changed. Watching how my ex-boyfriend walks down the hallway and says hi to everyone but you is overwhelming.

Three of us are chatting by Ally's locker when both of my best friends acknowledge my ex. They have to say hi. It's a part of being polite and friendly. I'm aware of it. All of them are still in touch, and I've been using the information they tell me. There are some benefits, so I shouldn't be so upset. Yet, it makes me feel like Elliot's stolen my friends, which is unfair. Maybe I'm exaggerating, but there is a code. It exists for a reason. Ally and Lou-Lou are my friends, and they have been my friends for a long time. It's happened way before El even considered transferring to our school. Therefore, when El broke up with me, he should have broken up with my friends, but he didn't do that. The most frustrating part is that I can't exclusively blame it on El. A break-up usually means your friends don't have relationships with your ex. Well, it hasn't happened yet, and it's time to let go of that dream. Everything got complicated when El and my friends became friends, then I betrayed all of them. So here I am, drowning in my bad decisions.

I don't recall what we've been discussing at the moment when I see Elliot. I can't concentrate on anything else but him. I'm staring at Elliot, waiting for my opening to catch his eye. I know it's a long shot. El usually ignores me, which isn't a surprise to me. I wish I could join them. If I do so, it'll be childish and naive. I'd even call it a cry for help.

El looks good, well-rested, and he's alone. Yeah, he never gives me anything to work with. At least, there is no Emma nearby. It's already a small win. Before the winter, he's been driving her to school every day. If they were dating, why would their new tradition suddenly change? Hopefully, they've drifted apart. I guess it's mean and desperate to think that way, and I know I should have let this go, but I still love El. I'm not over him.

"Are you okay?" Louis asks me, putting a hand on my shoulder. I want to hug him, but this is not the time to show my weaknesses to the entire school.

I've made a fool out of myself before, and I've decided not to repeat the same mistakes again.

"Yeah, let's go," I reply and start walking away from them. I don't want to wait. I just leave them behind. Maybe, it's a defining part of my old behavior, and I might be repeating the smoke circle. However, I need some air because everything gets fuzzy. If only I had time, I'd love to be away from everyone's eyes. I'd go to my spot right now and stare at the sky. Sometimes I dream about being a cloud. My life would be so much easier. Clouds always travel. They're alone, and they're always around other clouds. It sounds beautiful to me because all my thoughts are tangled among themselves. Nothing is clear, making it harder to shake off the feeling that El hates me, and he'll never forgive my behavior. It's been on my mind for the rest of the day. I've almost blacked out.

Since my tiny freakout after seeing Elliot, neither Ally nor Louis has mentioned or asked me any questions about it. I appreciate them because I have no answers. They're dying to know whether I'm alright. I'm not okay, and I have no energy to lie. I've hoped it'll be easier to approach him after knowing that El isn't over me. I was so wrong. It's not easy. There are no shortcuts I can take to fix this. I guess it's been the most devastating news. I've been looking for a magical unicorn, dreaming that Elliot will change his mind. However, unicorns don't exist. There's nothing I can do to make this better. I've been cheating on El since we've started dating. How can anyone make that better? I'm even more terrified than I was before the winter break. My fears haven't gone anywhere. Instead, my mental state has gone down the hill. I didn't expect I'd feel like that by now.

It's been two weeks since a new semester started. This time has flown by so quickly, faster than I'd like to. I should have fulfilled all my promises, but I've chickened out. To be fair, the winter break has gone by quickly too, and I barely had enough time to relax. I've built my expectations up too high, so when something didn't go my way, I couldn't deal with it. Even though nothing has technically changed, I feel even worse. El continues ignoring me just like he did before. My mom recommends I focus on the positive things, and I've been doing my best. However, as much as I'm attempting to concentrate on the idea that Elliot isn't over me, it makes me wonder what will happen when he is over me.

El would have already forgiven me if I had a chance to give him his Christmas gift. This year I've outdone myself because Ally and Louis love theirs. Ally and I have worn our matching bracelets since I gave them to her. I'm not even talking about my parents. Mom and dad loved their presents. I'm pretty sure I made mom cry when she saw the book. Of course, catching people's eyes is definitely the best part of gift-giving. I can't describe how much joy I feel when I see my parents' or friends' eyes light up like a Christmas tree when they open their gifts.

Every year I have to come with a perfect gift, which has become a personal challenge. I'm sure if El sees it, he'll immediately forget what I've done. It's vinyl. He's been looking for a few years. I know he'd love to have it. Yet, I'll never get a chance to give it to him. At this point, I consider sending it to him by mail. I want to do it, not quite, because I'm trying to wow him. Still, the real reason why I'm thinking about mailing it is that if somebody asked me the title of vinyl or its importance, I wouldn't be able to answer that. I don't even remember. If I had to guess, I'd say El's dad was the guitarist for the whole album. Withal, there is a big chance that I'm wrong.

The truth to be told, El talked my ears off about this vinyl. I'm ashamed that I didn't pay any attention. Even if I wanted to do so, I just couldn't. At that time in my life, I was trying to break up with Jake. Well, I should have done it earlier. However, the only reason I had the link opened on my phone is absolutely a miracle. I have a terrible habit of leaving every search opened until my phone starts discharging quicker. At least, that's what my dad says. I was about to clear all the tabs when I noticed the vinyl. I thought it was a sign that we'd make it work. We'd be together again. How did I even get there? When he receives it, I've hoped he'll realize how much I actually care about him, and the fact that I remember about the vinyl will melt his heart. Then we'll start dating. The whole premise is so nonsensical.

The plan by itself isn't that bad. Nevertheless, it seems so silly now because attempting to manipulate El's feelings after manipulating him for slightly over a month isn't such a good move in hindsight. It's not going to end as I hope because it's based on dishonesty. Yet, I immediately ordered the vinyl the second it'd become available. Apparently, it's a huge challenge to buy it since there are a few copies. I remember El has been struggling to get his hands on it, so it's a miracle I could get it. Even though I don't know its importance, I know it's important to him. He deserves to have it because I have no personal connection to it. It's only logical. Right? I'd like to think that it is. However, El made it very difficult for me to even come nearby. I feel like El has a restraining order against me.

It's killing me that having a conversation with Elliot has been the first thing on top of my to-do list after the winter break. Still, I'm not getting any closer to my goal. Although to be fair, I'm a little worried that El is considering transferring to his original high school. How have I come up with that? Well, for the past two weeks, I haven't wasted my time, I've been spying on El, and he's gone to the principal's office with his parents. There is no other explanation. Right? I recall how I used to dream about El transferring to a different school, but I've never thought I'd feel even worse about it.

Not seeing him at all has driven me crazy the whole winter break. I've started counting minutes until I go to school the next day, so I can take a look at Elliot. Every time I spot him by the principal's office after school, my heart drops. I think it's true he's about to switch schools. Why else does anyone go to see the principal with their parents? Maybe there could be other explanations, but they spend more than two hours every time. El is an excellent student with a bright future, so it makes sense our school officials don't want to let him go.

There are only two times I've waited until El and his parents came out because I couldn't wait over two hours. A few times, I've seen them walking out of the principal's office. They don't allow me to say whether they were happy or upset afterward. I've heard E's parents saying they'd be in touch, but it's not enough information. Therefore, I'm absolutely in the dark, leaving me with no chance to pinpoint the reason why they keep coming to our school. I can't even imagine my El-free life, and the entire idea puts me on edge. Ally and Louis have already tried to ask what's going with me, but we've agreed to leave it as it is because I'm not ready to have the talk. It's a little disheartening that they're absolutely right to be worried about me. I've been terrified that El's about to move on from me, and for a while, it has been the most terrifying thing until I realize there are the actual worst things, which can ruin my spirit. One of which is to lose the ability to see El at all, and it's my worst nightmare. I'm mentally not prepared for that to happen. At least, not yet. I can't share my fears with my friends that I've been barely asleep. I can't stop thinking about Elliot. If he isn't over me, he might be already moving on as I speak.

Depression is a silent mood killer. You never notice it until suddenly you can't even remember the last I know. I've started feeling depressed. It's happening partially because I can't see the end of it. There are millions of possibilities of how our relationship could wind up. Still, I'm not capable of finding the one, which doesn't lead to a complete transformation into a cat lady. I'm pretty sure El has no intentions to ever talk to me. Ally and Louis worry about me, and they're not happy that I'm. Yet, they will keep the boundaries.

Today is the twenty-ninth of January, and I'm redecorating my locker. I should have done it by now — I guess today is the day. I'm deep in my thoughts, thinking about my next step. However, I already know what it is. I just don't feel like doing it when Ally and Louis come up to me. I've decided a new semester starts with a new me. I haven't got a chance to re-decorate my locker. It's part of me, so it's a small part of what I have to do. Of course, doing it before the winter break is the right way to go, but it's a little too late. To be fair, I have a valid excuse — I've been depressed. Enough is enough, and here I am, clearing out the locker, making room for a new me.

Nobody knows how happy I am to be surrounded by my best friends right now because becoming a new person is surprisingly tricky. It's especially challenging when you're not ready to let go, and I'm not prepared to let go of El. I feel like I'm so close for something to change between us. It's like we're one step away from us, but we don't seem to be able to make the last push forward. The reality isn't getting easier because even though I have seen El around, I freeze up every time I notice him. I don't think I can just walk up to him as if nothing has happened.

El looks great. Actually, I'm pretty sure he's doing better than me. He's brand-new. I'd say he's better and happier. Every time it brings me back to the first time I met him. I'm not sure why, but maybe it's impossible for me not to overthink the reasons why he's so cheerful without me. There is some good news. To be fair, I haven't seen Emma around El. It's a small win, but I take it. I am that sad.

During the last couple of days before the winter break, Emma and El were always together. They were like siamese twins, and I wish it were a joke. Well, there was not a single moment I can recall when they had been away from each other. I used to blame Emma for my failure to talk to El. I used to believe it'd be just uncomfortable. I think it's partially like this because I know that Emma's aware of what I've done to El. Everyone does, so I shouldn't be taking it so personally. I guess I'm just scared to see in Emma's eyes what she thinks about me before I get a chance to apologize. At this point, I can guess how people could glare my way, and most of them mean you're a cheater and a bitch. I understand them, and I've become accustomed to other people judging me. It's shocking how quickly I've done that. However, I assume that anyone in my shoes would love to say I'm sorry to their ex-boyfriend before his new girlfriend gives you that dreadful pointed look. It's the type of gaze as if she's saying, "I can't believe he was in love with you."

Actually, I don't know what El used to see in me. If I had to be completely honest, I wouldn't believe that he could even like me that way. I'm not surprised I've screwed this up. El is out of my league — I understand. I just don't need anyone else to remind me of that. As upsetting as it has been for me, it's become clear to me that Emma isn't the one I should blame. I'm my own worst enemy, and the only person I should blame is myself. Of course, it's been convenient to believe in the opposite. After apologizing to everyone except El, I've realized how much I need to express the regret I'm experiencing. El deserves to know that I'm sorry. I bet he's aware that I crave that. Yet, El isn't making it easier for me to have an adult conversation with him.

It's challenging to see El on the school campus, and I get to see him a lot. Well, it happens more than I'd love to. We never run into each other, and it feels like we live in a parallel universe, where our ways will never cross no matter how hard I try to change that. I've noticed that Elliot's been spending a lot of time in the library. It's the only time when he's alone, which seems odd to me. El's parents have an amazing library in their house. I've seen it once, but our school library isn't even a comparison. I've started wondering if something happened to him. Something must have cropped up. Nothing else makes sense. I feel like I'm losing a person I love, and I don't want to lose El.

"Did you remember about that test?" Lou-Lou asks us. I shrug from the surprise. It feels like he's woken me up. "It was pretty difficult, right?"

"Yeah? Maybe, a little harder than I expected," I lie. *The test seemed very easy to me, but I don't want to make Lou-Lou feel bad. Plus, I can't let them know that I spend all my days staring at the textbooks because there is nothing else for me to do. They're my best friends, and I mostly spend my time with them. However, my friends have a life beyond our circle. I used to have El and Jake. I barely had any time to rest, and sometimes I didn't have enough time to crunch for every single test. I miss the times when I hardly had any time.*

"I totally forgot about it," Louis replies. "This is the beginning of the semester, and I'm already behind. I can't believe it. Nobody hates algebra more than me."

"Louis, get in line. I ran out of time yesterday, so I don't think I did well," Ally admits.

"I think it's crazy early for tests. I feel like I don't think our parents had such a huge workload at school. My parents always get defensive over this topic and pretty competitive, which makes me wonder…"

"Don't worry, I think it was a part of our final grade, and I'm pretty sure," I stop in the middle of the sentence because I notice El walking by, carrying a girl's bag. I forget about everything.

Well, it's not Emma, which is a relief by itself. Who is the girl? I don't know her. If I have to be completely honest, figuring out her name is just a waste of time. As Ally and Louis say, El is dating around, and this is what it means. It's hard to see your person is going out with different girls, but I shouldn't have hoped that El would forgive me. Love isn't quite real at our age, right? Is that what adults tell teens? However, if that's true, why can't I stop loving Elliot?

"Have you talked to him since?" Ally asks me, switching her look from El. I'm pretty sure she's already realized how upsetting this must be for me, so she quickly adds, "You've talked to us, and Jake."

"Well, I tried to have a conversation before the winter break," I cut Ally off, "and El was obvious that he wasn't interested in talking to me."

"Of course," Ally apologetically agrees, "I was wondering if you've tried again?"

"No, I haven't got a chance. The time is never right," I reveal how annoyed I'm getting. "It's not even my fault. El's just being weird, and there is nothing I can do about it."

I turn away, hoping that my friends won't notice how watery my eyes are. The trick usually works like a charm.

"What do you mean?" Louis wonders. I can hear the surprise in his tone.

"Maybe it's nothing, but you know the school has just started," I explain, "but he spends almost all his time at the library. That's kind of weird, right?"

"Actually, he's been working on his songs or something like that. El's dad is coming home after being away for a few weeks," Ally tells me, attempting to sound very casual. *It makes me so mad. To be completely honest, I'm jealous, and that's incredibly embarrassing. Yet, it's not Ally's fault that I feel this way. Even after everything that happened, Ally and Louis have stayed friends with Elliot. It's been hard on me to feel like one step away from him. We've made an agreement with my friends that they won't tell me anything about him unless it directly involves me or if I now ask about him.*

"Yeah, he's been working hard," Lou-Lou adds. "Pretty sure he wants to impress his dad."

Louis has always been very intuitive. He always picks up on my vibe and tries to make it better. However, nothing and no one can boost my spirit except me. Ugh, the most annoying part is that my friends know exactly how I feel right now — crappy.

"I see," I say, but I can even look at them right now. Yet, Louis knows me so well. He taps on my shoulder, attempting to catch my eye. But, even by furtively glancing at him, I immediately see that he won't let this go.

"You should talk to him, Cassie," Ally says out of nowhere.

"Yeah, why not? Maybe, I'll go and talk to him right now," I joke around.

"No, Cass, I'm serious! It's time."

"I don't think he wants to talk to me," I say and shake my head.

"No, girl, you have to talk to him. Otherwise, you'll never move on," Louis says as he tiptoes closer to me. Then, he whispers under his breath, "and a ghost of his disappointment will follow you... FOREVER."

I scream because I feel like something is crawling up through my shoulder to my neck. As I turn around, I quickly realize it's Louis. Both of them, Ally and Louis, are dying from laughing. Louis thinks he's so hysterical. I can't roll my eyes any harder — it's a cheap trick. Yet, it worked like a charm. Even Ally can't stop giggling, but at least she's been fighting the laughter.

"I'll kill you, Lou-Lou," I say. But, before Louis figures out my revenge plan, I start messing with his perfect hair. I can only imagine how much time he's spent on it this morning.

"Stop punishing me for telling you the truth. You needed to hear it, so I told you the truth," Louis proudly states, pushing me away. He hates when I mess with his hair, I don't do it very often. Only when extreme measures are required. It feels nice to make an acceptance sometimes.

"Louis, I already know the truth. Honestly, I just don't want to hear about it over and over. I know," I explain to my friends, "because nothing can be changed. I've given it a chance, but El's clear that he doesn't want anything to do with me."

"So what, Cassie? I have to agree with Louis since when do you give up after a first try?" Ally teases me.

"I guess I've changed. People change Ally," I reply.

"What do you mean you've changed? Don't be silly," Ally rolls her eyes at me, and yet she asks me, "but seriously, Cassie, aren't you going to try one more time?"

I shrug my shoulders because there is no point in torturing myself if El continues avoiding me. Ally and Lou-Lou are watching my every move, which means I have to make sure that they won't be able to read me like an open book. I hate it so much, why can't I be myself around my best friends all the time? Well, the answer to this question is simpler than I'd like it to be — I screwed up, and now Ally and Louis feel like they have to be there for me when I hit rock bottom. Well, my friends aren't aware that I've already gone through that. The most important thing I've learned is that everything is much easier with friends around. They've forgiven me, and I can survive through everything else.

"You've got to talk to El. It's time, Cass. It's going to be okay," Louis adds. I understand Louis wants to give me some hope and courage, but I really wish he wouldn't. It's just... more upsetting to believe it's going to be okay.

"Don't take me wrong. I also agree with you, guys. Yet, as you know, it's not that easy. I wish I could just march up to him and talk to him. Oh wait, I've done that already," I say, organizing books in my locker. I'm waiting for their comeback, but they don't say a word to me in response.

I look at Ally and Louis, and apparently, they have been staring at me the whole time. Yeah, there are no words to describe the judgmental look they're giving me, but I still pretend that I don't get what they're trying to tell me. Finally, I innocently ask them, "What?"

"Are you kidding me?!" both of them yell at me.

I shake my head. Of course, I know they're implying. They're right — I don't want to talk to El, I don't want to be ignored again. *I think I'm okay with living in my dreams. What is wrong with that? Reality has been harsh on me, so is it a massive crime to get stuck in a daydream once in a while?*

"Okay, I'll talk to him," I agree with them. I immediately realize that's precisely the answer they're looking for.

"When?" Louis asks.

"Soon," I reply. "I'm ready to go home. What about you, guys? Ready to roll?"

"Aren't you going to decorate your locker?" Ally wonders.

"Nah. I'll probably do it later."

"Are you sure, Cassie?" Louis asks.

"Yeah, let's go home."

They both nod as I close my locker. I've been a little concerned that Ally and Louis continue interrogating me about the timeline I'm thinking about, but they don't say a word. In a way, it would be easier if they did.

Chapter 32
It's Over, Isn't It?

Since Ally and Louis had an "El" intervention, I've constantly considered when I should approach Elliot again. My friends don't ask about it anymore, and I know that I should be happier. However, I haven't realized I want the opposite. I'd have a great excuse to avoid El, but it's not the case. There is no other choice — I've got to approach him when El's totally alone. On top of that, it's overdue. It's time.

I've been El's shadow for quite a while since the beginning of the semester. I know it's a little weird, but there has been no other choice. Even though he spends less time with Emma this semester, El's becoming more popular by the day. As a result, it's harder to find El by himself. The only place where I might get a chance to apologize is the library. Initially, I thought it was a phase, but he's been working really hard on something. He does some reading. El might be done with all books about music in our entire school library. So yeah, this is not my first lookout at the library. Or am I spying on El? Sometimes I even go to check the books he's been reading. I'd love to be closer to him, but I screwed everything up.

I walk to the middle of aisle J-35 because it has the best view of where El usually sits. Yeah, I know how it looks, but I promise I'm not a stalker. However, I do spy on Elliot every day. I only observe what he's doing, hiding behind the books. I'm watching him like a hawk. If El's there, that means I'll be at the library too. I guess that's become my ritual because I'm never brave enough to walk up to Elliot, which is pretty pathetic. But I'm fully aware of it.

I tell myself a thousand lies, so I won't have to do this and get rejected again. My go-to reason is I don't want to interrupt his work. To be fair, El's been working nonstop on something related to music. Ally and Lou-Lou probably know exactly what's going on, but I really don't want to ask. I can, but I can't. I don't know if it makes sense. It feels wrong to ask. They'd realize that I never paid any attention to El's explanations about his creative process. Having a routine is incredibly important, and being stuck at the library is a huge part of it.

Sometimes the reality is much simpler than you expect it to be, which isn't any different. Deep down in my soul, I'm terrified of the idea that he can be writing about me and how horrible I am. I genuinely hope it's not the case. However, today is the day I'm about to march up to El. Yeah, right? Sometimes you've got to do what you're going to do. The main issue is to make sure I won't change my mind at the very last minute, so I can't overthink this. I take a deep breath and start walking towards him. As hard as it is not to notice how everyone's staring at me, I'm doing well. Considerably. I can still feel burning glares flaring my way.

By the time I come up to El's table, he is the only one who hasn't noticed me. It's weird because I've expected anything and everything, but not this. I'm not sure what to do. I can't make a noise or run away because all eyes are on me, and nothing can be more embarrassing than a public retreat.

"Hey…" I mumble, hoping he hasn't heard me. However, it's not the case. El looks up at me and immediately closes a book. I quickly add, "El, I just want to talk to you."

"Really?" he asks, packing his stuff away. I nod.

"Are you kidding me?" he replies, not even hiding a smirk on his face, "I don't really want to talk to you, Cass. I thought I was pretty obvious about it."

"Yeah. You were, but can you just hear me out? Please," I beg El. "I promise I won't bother you again. Please. I understand if you can't talk right now. It's totally okay. But you should know I'll keep trying to have a real conversation until you change my mind. I'll wait as long as you need. And… I'm sorry."

"Stop. Fine, but not here."

El stands up. He's ready to go. Honestly, everything that's just happened. Why did he change his mind? I glance around and notice that all eyes are on us. It's clear to me that El just couldn't handle the social pressure. *What was I expecting? I'm basically throwing myself at him, and El is too nice to let me fall flat on my face in front of other people.*

"Let's go?" he asks. I nod and silently follow El. I'm not sure where exactly we're going, but he doesn't say a word the whole way. *He's never been so hostile around me. Even his presence is colder than the wind, which is blowing in my face. I hate the cold wind. Ugh, I would do anything to get his forgiveness. He doesn't look like he's in a good mood, but who would be? Especially when you're about to have a conversation you have been trying to avoid for months now. Maybe Ally and Lou-Lou are right, and there is no such thing as a perfect time. I just have to rip off the Band-Aid, which is the best way forward.*

We come up to El's car, and he stops in front of it. He won't even let me sit in his car. This is a bad sign — he must be very pissed at me. Still, I know anyone would be upset. I hadn't expected to behave as pissed as El was that night when he found out the truth.

"Okay, I'm listening," El says. His voice sounds so disinterested.

"First of all, I know you think everything I said and did was a lie," I start, "and honestly, I'd think exactly the same thing if I were in your shoes. However, I want you to know I really love you... loved you."

The entire time I've been able to look at him. *I've imagined this so many times, but I haven't expected this to be so hard. I can't believe I've just said that I love him. Why did I make everything harder for myself? Why can't I just be normal? Of course, it's not embarrassing enough that I have to give an uncomfortable apology. Still, I need to get rejected on top of that. Ugh...*

"I also thought I loved you," El says. "But it was before I found out I wasn't the only one who you were dating."

"I'm sorry about that. Really sorry. I've never been so sorry."

"And is that supposed to make me feel better?"

"No. Honestly, I don't understand how the whole situation got out of hand..."

"Yeah, I don't think the problem is that the situation got out of hand. Having this situation is the problem," he breaks it down for me.

"It's not what I meant."

"Hmm… So when you said let's do this, you didn't mean it that way too?" El asks me. Even though

"El," I attempt to explain, but El stops me.

"Or maybe when you said you'd be my girlfriend, it meant something else?"

I'm not going to lie that stings. This conversation is getting away from me very quickly.

"Umm. You know what, you're absolutely right. I meant, and I didn't keep my promise to you. I wish I could go back. It's so clear to me now. I don't know what I was thinking. I can't even explain this to myself, you know? However, I'd like you to know that I've tried to break up with Jake multiple times. Of course, it's not an excuse for my behavior. Lying is usually my go-to, but I've been working hard on telling people the truth. I've made a huge mistake. I'm truly sorry. If I could go back in time, I'd never do anything like that "

"I really don't understand you, Cassie," El reveals to me. It's not quite what I expected to hear, but he's talking to me. "It's like you're from a different planet. Why is it so hard for you to tell the truth?"

El doesn't understand me or my actions. Right now, I'm a mystery to him. If I tell him the truth, I'm about to become a huge disappointment. It's not going to be the first time I didn't hit the mark, so I just have to go ahead and shut down my go-to feeling. I must tell the truth.

"Heads up, it's stupid. I've warned you," I explain, "if nothing is real… If everything is a huge lie, then I won't get hurt. I can never be wrong or make any mistakes, but I didn't realize that I was lying to myself the most. That's the only way I can describe this. I feel like I was in a parallel universe. I didn't realize I was drowning in my lies until it was already too late. I hope one day you'll be able to forgive me. I didn't want you to get hurt. I screwed up. Sorry. Truly. I hurt and put you through everything."

El doesn't say anything. I don't know what I expected, but now I feel nauseated. *I should have rehearsed my speech. Well, I should have prepared it first. I felt like I've been thinking about what I want to say to El, and I forgot what I wanted to tell him. I can't screw up my apologies, but I'm pretty sure I just did. Why has he said anything? Of course, I freaked him out. Look at me now. I can't find the right words. Ugh, this is so annoying. I haven't said anything useful or new. I should have taken this more seriously. Come on, Cassie. You had one chance. One chance! I blew it. I could have done better. Please, just say something. El.*

"Thank you for telling this," El says out of nowhere. The fact that El's addressing me is throwing me off. Yet, I haven't felt so happy in a while. El continues, "I feel like I understand what you mean. Kind of. At least, I hope I do. You know I might still be in love with you, but I don't think I'm ready to forgive you."

"Ever?"

"I don't know, Cassie. But it's definitely a 'no' for now."

"What does this mean? Should I wait for you or..."

"I don't know. It's up to you."

"I understand. Thank you for listening to me," I say, barely keeping it together. However, there is no end to my disappointment. It's devastating — I want him to forgive me now. I want him to give me another chance now. I'd rather not wait and pick everything up where we left off, but it's not going to happen. I feel he knows that I'll never do that again, so why can't we just go back? It does make sense he doesn't entirely trust my words.

"Is Emma... Are you two dating?" I ask as my heart is trying to escape. Maybe I should have left Emma out of this, and I don't even know why it still bothers me so much. I guess I'm nosy.

"No, Cass. We're just friends for now."

"Oh. Well, I wanted to say that you'd look great together as a couple."

My words flabbergast El. He can't even hide it. *That's true, though. Emma and El look cute together, plus both of their names start with an "E." Is that a pure destiny? Yeah, I'm jealous.*

"Thanks? I guess."

"Of course."

We get quiet. I want to say something, but it feels like I've forgotten all the words.

"Well, I guess I'm gonna go," I say to El, but I just need to break this uncomfortable silence. "Thanks for hearing me out."

El nods. There is nothing else to say, but I don't feel like I'm any closer to getting the resolution I've been seeking.

"Bye, El," I say, hoping for El to stop me. *Obviously, he has no plans to do so. It's pretty embarrassing, but I really thought he'd do that. It feels like someone ripped my heart out, and I'll never be "me" again. I've lost my first love. Before this conversation, I tricked myself into believing that we've never been apart. However, I'm the only one who feels that way. El did say that he could still be in love with me, but... If he loved me, he'd find a way to forgive me.*

"Take care, Cassie," he replies. I nod and start walking away. Don't look back. Please. The further I go, the easier it gets. However, I can't stop thinking about the fact that we're broken up. Officially. El and I are two singles now. My soul is so empty. That feeling brings me right back to Homecoming. Of course, everything is different now — I don't have hope. I've got my answer. Sadly, it's not the one I hoped for. I guess this is a simple twist of fate. There is nothing I can do.

"Cassie!" I hear how El yells my name, and my heart drops. His voice brings me a chill. *What does it mean? Has he changed his mind?* I turn around and look at him, hoping for a miracle to happen.

"When you said you loved me, did you actually mean it?" El asks me.

"Yes, I did."

"See you around."

"Sounds good."

He nods and gets in the car. I wander away, trying not to think about El. *Is that it? He just wanted to ask me whether I actually loved him. OMG, does this mean he didn't believe when I told him that I still loved him? Ugh. I'm such an idiot. El can't forgive me because he can't trust me for a good reason. El will never forgive me. It's time to face the truth. I can't fixate on the last part of the conversation, but maybe...just maybe, it means that he might change his mind. Why on Earth would he tell me that he still loves me? Then, his reply makes total sense. He doesn't want to say to me that I should wait because it should be my choice. Well, Elliot, I will wait for you. I'll wait as long as you need. I won't disappoint you — I'll be right there, waiting for you. You'll see.*

Turn the Page for a Sneak Peak of
The Lies He Told Me

Chapter 1
A New "Friend"

Finally, everything went back to normal. Well, kind of. Even though most people continue to ignore me, I'm happy because I'm surrounded by true friends. The whole semester Jake has been busy with colleges, and he's got a lot of football scholarships. Apparently, he and Katie have decided to go to the same one, nobody thinks it's a good idea. However, they're happy, and I'm so glad for them. In a way, I feel a little bit jealous because I wish I could jump into something serious like that. I guess Jake has become more adventurous. By the way, we're about to take a summer break, and I've decided to take my chances and to be more courageous. I'm not sure how exactly, but it shouldn't be difficult to figure that out, right?

Elliot hasn't forgiven me, but I don't think he hates me anymore. We say hi, and we've even hung out a little at Ally's birthday party. However, nothing more. I texted him once after the party, but he hasn't replied. Obviously, it was a signal that nothing changed. On multiple occasions, Ally and Louis have told me to start moving on because it's time to love again. Yeah, it was Louis's point, but instead, I've decided that I don't need a boyfriend. "No boyfriend, no problem" is my new motto. Of course, my best friends know it's a procrastination tactic. Even if I try to date again, I'm going to fail. Therefore, it's time to find out who I am. I've been jumping into falling in love way too fast. I need to slow down so next time I meet the right person, I can be myself. I won't screw it up.

Doesn't that sound good? I hope so. Honestly, I've decided not to date anyone because I still want to be with El. Maybe, he'll change his mind if I stay single. Secretly, I still believe in us. I've attempted to forget about him, but El has a permanent residence in my head, and I can't get him evicted. I know how stupid it sounds. Love makes people stupid. I always thought that Jake was my first love, but I was so wrong. El is. I know he was my first love, and that's why I still want El by my side.

Today might be the day when El finally forgives me. At least, I hope. I have a good feeling about it. Not only is it the last day of school, but also I've been dreaming about this moment since the Homecoming Dance. The best part is that El wants to talk to me. When El texted me, I asked Ally and Louis to check if it wasn't a hallucination. It wasn't. Ally and Lou-Lou were as surprised I was, which is a good sign. El asked me to meet at the bleachers. The last time we were at the bleachers, I told him that I loved him. We were dating, and I've never been so happy. My excitement has no limits. Of course, I'm aware that it could be about anything, but I'm hopeful. I've been waiting for so long. To be completely honest, I've expected El to reach out to me during Valentine's day because he talked to me a few times right before. I thought we'd go to the dance together. However, nothing happened, and I stayed at home that night.

I even started doubting whether it happened. Maybe it was in my head, but it seemed like he was flirting with me. Well, I know it wasn't in my head. El was totally flirting with me. I have a witness — Lou-Lou. Unfortunately, he was an innocent bystander of our interaction. Even Louis agreed that El was sending a lot of signals my way. Therefore, it was only logical to expect a valentine, which would invite me to the dance. Looking back at the entire situation, I feel embarrassed that getting a valentine was even on my mind, which had never arrived. Honestly, I can't believe it took him so long to text me.

Don't take me wrong. I know it's a miracle that he reached out to me. By this point, I've already made several serious attempts to put the entire idea of getting back with El to rest. Yet, my heart can't accept the reality in which El and I will never be together. I can't take it. We always end up together when I think of us. I haven't lost hope even when I really should have had — El was dating other girls, which was the hardest thing I've ever done. It doesn't matter anymore because all my tears are about to pay off. After all, El will ask me to get back together. I've never been so sure about anything else, but I am this time. Why else are we meeting at the bleachers, right?

Even though I'm thrilled to start dating El again, I feel a little bit disappointed about the timing since it's already the end of the school year, and *my summer schedule is pretty busy. My parents have already decided that we'll see my grandparents in Oregon. Then I'm going to a Model UN summer camp. I don't think El will join me, and I can't change my plans. I've made a commitment. Even if he doesn't mind coming with me, I'm pretty sure there are no more spots left.*

Model UN will look good on my university application. My parents fell in love with the idea, but I can't stop thinking that I should have gone to the same summer camp I went to last year. It'd be weird to go to the same camp with my ex. Realistically, I didn't even expect El to text me. As much as we'd like to relive the moments of our past, but we can't. We can only move forward, but that's the reason why I've decided to be productive this summer, which means that El and I won't be able to spend a lot of time together.

I walk towards the empty bleachers and immediately spot El, staring at his cellphone. *So he's already there, crap. I should pick up the pace. Don't forget, Cassie, you need to be breezy. Breezy? Ugh... I sound like my mom.*

"Hey, El!" I yell, trying to get his attention. El looks up and smiles, which totally melts my heart. I just want to kiss him and forget about what we've gone through.

"Hey, Cassie," El says as I come closer. He gives me a light hug. *That's a good sign, right? Just be cool and chill.* I sit right next to him, attempting to keep my emotions under control.

The wind blows hair from my shoulders. I feel like my cheeks start blushing. I can't just hide how happy I am to be with El. It reminds me of Homecoming. Not the bad parts, good ones, and we have quite a few. In a way, it was the best day of this year because I told El that I loved him here. Everything else wasn't that great. However, it's all about to be behind us.

We've been quietly sitting for a while. I just want to move our conversation forward. *What is he waiting for? Isn't he ready? Because I'm ready, I've been prepared for a while.* This is when it hits me that I'm not sure that he wants to get back together. *Save it, Cassie. This is not the right time for a meltdown. Don't forget, you're not a victim here.*

"How are you?" I ask.

"Good, you?" El sounds a little relieved that I've started the conversation. Honestly, it's disappointing. Does he even have a plan?

"Good," I repeat after him.

This silence isn't a good sign. *The last time he was that uncomfortably quiet happened when he finally let me apologize and told me that he wasn't ready. OMG, he's going to tell me I shouldn't wait for him anymore.*

"Cassie," El says my name as I start freaking out, "I'm sure you know why I asked you to come here?"

"Ugh, yes," I lie, but his reaction shows me that El isn't entirely buying into this. I clear my throat and continue, "Of course, I know."

Honestly, I thought I had a pretty good idea why he asked me here, but I have a sneaking suspicion that I was a hundred percent wrong. I just hope to dance around this topic until I figure out what he actually means by that. Please, don't. Don't say that we're done for good. Please.

"I want you to know," he says, and my heart trembles. This is the moment I've been waiting for. El states, "I'm almost ready to forgive you."

"Ugh, I have a quick question before you continue," I say.

"Go ahead."

"You're almost ready."

"Yeah."

"Okay," I say. "I have two follow-up questions."

El gives an are-you-for-real look. I pretend that I completely don't understand. At this point, I need to get direct answers.

"Okay, go ahead."

"Almost? What does that mean exactly?"

"Well, maybe it means that I'm trying really hard here to forgive my girlfriend," he says and immediately goes quiet. *He called me his girlfriend, and I think it should have made me happy, but I'm not happy at all. El is ashamed of me. If only you could have seen his face, you'd know what I'm talking about. There is so much pain in his deep blue eyes. I've been waiting for this moment for so long, and it's not going as well as I would like it. I look away. I feel embarrassed because I am the worst.*

"Ex-girlfriend. Sorry, Cassie. It's not the point, and it's not what I wanted to say."

"No, it's okay. You're right."

I've never felt so far away from El while being so physically close to each other. That's how it was the same with Jake a few weeks before the truth came out. If Ally wasn't at that diner, we would be broken up. Maybe Elliot is done with me, but he doesn't know that yet.

"Sorry, I interrupted you. My questions don't matter. Would you mind telling me what you wanted to say?" I ask. El looks at me with a surprise in his eyes. I continue, "I really want to know."

"Oh. Well, I thought maybe we can reassess 'us' after the summer," El says. *Wow. What can I say in response? Yeah, this is not what I expected at all. I guess it's not a no, but I'm not going to lie — this is upsetting. Reassessment doesn't mean anything. It hurts to think that nothing has changed.* El glances at me, waiting for me to say something. Then he quickly adds, "However, now saying it out loud, it sounds not fair to you. I don't expect you to wait for me."

Thoughts are rushing through my head, but I can't say a word. I'm aware that El probably wants me to say something. I can't.

"No worries, El. I get it," I say even though I don't get it. *I've been single the whole time while he was dating around or whatever the heck that means. I think I deserve better, and the only reason I'm kind of okay with it is that I've cheated on him. However, it has to stop at some point. How long can he push me away before he forgives me?*

"Thanks, Cass," El replies. "Are you okay?"

"Yeah," I say. Then, to be more convincing, I nod.

"Are you sure?"

"Yeah."

"So, what do you think about it?"

"Um, I think I just need a little time to process the whole thing."

"Makes sense."

I nod and stand up. *I'm so ready to leave, I feel nauseated. This situation is very embarrassing. What do I think? Personally, I think it's a horrible idea.*

"See you in September, I guess. We'll figure everything out then. "

"Aren't you going to the summer camp this year?" El asks.

"No," I answer, hoping he'd realize that he is making a terrible mistake. *If he hopes that we'll relive last summer at the camp, it won't happen. He needs to act now.*

"Oh, I am. It's going to be kind of weird without you."

"Unfortunately, I'm definitely not going, but that's so wonderful that you are. You'll have a lot of fun."

"Yeah. Wait, how come you aren't coming? What are your plans for summer if you aren't going?" El asks with surprise in his voice.

"The plan is to visit my grandparents in Oregon, and then I'll be off to Model UN camp," I reveal to my El, who seems even more confused before my explanation. I add, "It's going to look really good on my university application."

"Oh. Well, that's great, Cassie. I guess I'll see you in the fall?"

"Yeah, I guess. Bye."

"Bye, Cass."

We awkwardly hug each other and slowly walk away. I *don't feel my knees, and all my thoughts are clouded. It's not what I expected to hear. Nothing is what I expected. This is incredibly disappointing. I was sure today was the day when we got back together. Well, El isn't willing to let me off the hook that easy. I guess I have no other choice but to wait for more. It's okay. Of course, it's not okay. Yet, I'm stuck in this reality, where Lou-Lou was right — I'm definitely on my way to becoming an old cat lady.*

There is nothing else to do at school. Most people have already left, but some people are clearing out the lockers. Others aren't mentally destroyed by the idea that they'll have to do the summer school classes. At this point, *I just want to go as far as I can from here. No, I need to go somewhere else.*

I rush down the hallway when my phone rings. I glance down and see that

Elliot is calling me. *He's changed his mind. He did! OMG... He changed his mind.* My hands are shaking, and I can't even swipe my phone to reply. For a second, my tunnel vision makes it hard to do anything. Then, it's a little too late to look up where I'm going because I'm running into someone as my phone falls down on the floor. Everything seems to be happening in slow-motion, including my unsuccessful attempt to catch it.

"I'm so sorry," I hear a male voice, but I have no idea who it is. El's already stopped calling, and he hasn't left a voice message. *No, not this. Ugh. I can't believe I missed his call.*

"Sorry, I wasn't watching where I was going," I say as I look up to see whom I've just bumped into. Surprisingly, I don't recognize the guy. I can't assume that I know everyone, though, but it's

"Hey, I think it's yours," the stranger says, passing me my phone.

"Thanks," I say, glancing at it. I quickly spot a text from El, which explains everything. *Apparently, it was a misdial, which is absolutely soul-crushing.*

"So sorry I ran into you," the stranger says. I look up at him with a smile. People say fake it until you make it, and every phony smile makes me a little closer to feeling normal.

The stranger smiles back at me. Nowadays, it's rare that anyone else smiles at me. Most people have been staying away from me. Maybe this blue-eyed stranger hasn't heard of me. *But what are the odds of that happening? Wait, who is this guy? Why is being nice to me?*

"I'm sorry again, and I'm Mike, by the way," the stranger finally introduces himself, and it hits he doesn't know me. *I guess he's the only person in the entire school who isn't aware of what I've done.*

"Cassie, nice to meet you, Mike," I introduce myself, and we shake hands. *I'm just polite, and this is not me, trying to forget about El.*

"Nice to meet you too."

We stand up and awkwardly look at each other. *Hmm, I'm pretty sure I've never met Mike before. Could this actually happen that I've never met Mike, and he wouldn't hear about my fiasco? Honestly, I was sure that I knew most people at school. Well, I thought I could recognize everyone who goes to our school. I was wrong, but to be fair, I know a lot of freshmen and seniors. Maybe, Mike is a junior. Maybe he was sick, and he didn't hear anything about me.*

"Again, I'm so sorry. I was also not paying attention, where I was going. I'm new here."

"Really?" I say.

"Yeah, my family has just moved here."

"So you're new here!" I say with a lot of excitement in my voice. I guess it's nice to chat with someone who doesn't know every single detail about me and my past. Sometimes I need a break from it. However, it's an impossible task when everyone around me knows my entire life story.

"Yeah."

"And already at the principal office, I see," I tease Mike immediately after I've noticed where we're standing.

"You're funny. I was planning to do a model UN summer camp at my old school. I just wanted to check," Mike explains, but he's never going to finish his sentence.

"OMG, are you serious? Our school is doing the UN program as well. I'm actually doing that program this summer."

"Oh really?"

"Yeah."

"That's so cool."

"Michael!" I hear a female voice from behind. "Let's go."

"Sorry, I've got to go," Mike says to me as he turns around and adds, "give me a second, mom!"

"Yeah, of course."

"Maybe see you at the camp."

"See you around."

Mike runs up to his mom as I've totally forgotten where I'm going. *He's cute. Not like that, but he's objectively attractive. Not like I'd date him because I'm waiting for El. Oh yeah! Now I remember what I was doing — running away from my past. It's nice not to think about El for a minute. I haven't got a chance to talk to anybody who doesn't know about my dating life. Don't judge me every second — I'm not just a cheater. Mike doesn't know me. He only has a first impression of me. It's exciting. Don't take me wrong, I'm still in love with El. There is no doubt. I'll wait longer for his forgiveness. I'll wait as long as he needs me to. However, I've realized one important thing. Obsessing over El or fantasizing about him isn't healthy for me. I can't control what he's going to do. Lou-Lou and Ally are right — I need to start living my life. Yes, I'll see El in September, and something might happen. Yet, it doesn't mean I can't enjoy this summer, and there are no guarantees that we'll be together...*

I wander back home with these thoughts when it strikes me that my first year at high school is over. *Wow, it was a rollercoaster with so many ups and downs. I'm so thankful that Ally and Louis are still part of my life. I think I've become a better person. At least, I hope so. I just need to stay positive. Just like my mom always says, everything will work itself out. Who knows what's going to happen this summer? Or Sophomore year?*

Made in the USA
Middletown, DE
15 June 2023

32686332R00170